THE EVOLUTION SER

HYBRID

Kathyrn

Thanks for all
the encouragement
you've given me

Vanessa
xx

THE EVOLUTION SERIES: BOOK ONE

HYBRID

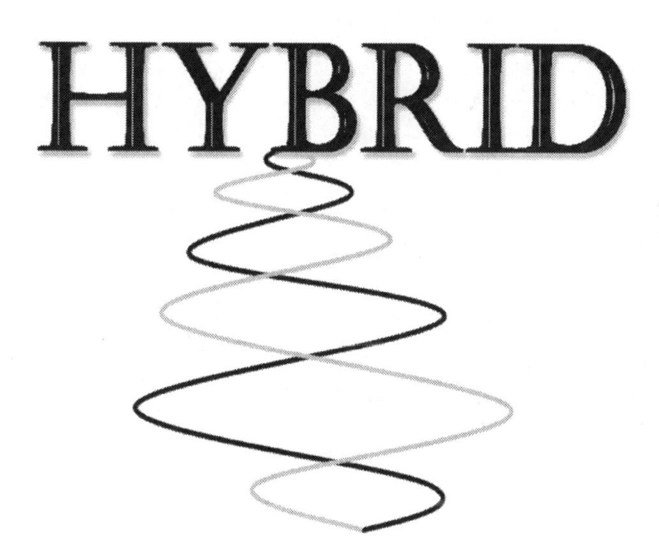

Vanessa Wester

Acknowledgements

Thank you Kay, Kathryn, Katie (all the K's!), my sister in law, Anja, and my parents in law, Heleen and Willem. Without your support, I would never have developed my writing. My style was so raw, yet, you gave me the encouragement I needed to persevere and believe in myself.

I would also like to promote Booksie and The Writers' Workshop – home of The Word Cloud, a free online community for aspiring and published writers. The advice I obtained has been invaluable. Although, it was through Booksie that I discovered the fun side of sharing your writing! I'd like to thank a few online friends. Barb – thank you for giving me the basic tools for a debut novel. Emma – thank you for your blogs. Tony – thank you for taking the time to edit some of my first chapters, you are a gem!

I would also like to thank my father, Malcolm, for taking the wonderful picture which I used to create my cover page.

And finally, to my husband, Robert – thank you for giving me the time to write.

To Michael, Elsa and Joanne

Table of Contents

Prologue

A New Life

It took a considerable amount of effort for Steven to blink. A simple thing he had taken for granted over the years. His eyes tried to focus on his surroundings. All he could see was a blur of green. The pace of motion seemed impossible – was he dreaming? Instinct made him want to move, to check he was actually awake, but something told him to wait. He needed to get a grip. As every second passed his senses started to snap open. He kept perfectly still as he took stock of the situation.

A frown set upon his face as he tried to recollect his last actions. Nothing could explain why he was slumped over someone's petite frame. A person or woman as he suspected, of this size should not be able to carry a man of his build so easily. Either way, if she was a woman, he should be able to hold his own. He was not a coward. Reticent, he clenched his hands into fists. He would have to regain control and find out what was going on. The moment he moved, motion stopped. A swift effortless action followed and he found himself on the ground. The cold, damp moss hit his body and caused an instant shiver, as his muffled groan escaped.

'Are you okay?' A female voice. Soft, full of compassion. It seemed out of place somehow.

He studied her face. The eyes. They were familiar. They were just like…his.

The memories started to surface and he flinched. Adrenaline surged through his body, and one by one, the visions engulfed his mind.

The family he had taken for granted.

The woman he loved.

The life he wanted.

All gone.

What had they done to him? Or more importantly, what had he

done? One memory lingered, persistent – Caitlin. In an ideal world, he would replace the face in front of him with hers. If everything he remembered was true, his life was not worth living. As bewilderment gave way to anger, he narrowed his eyes. Even though groggy, he mustered the strength to get up and face Emily – his mother. He would not give her the satisfaction of helping him further. She had done enough. Determined, he stood tall and raised his head, his eyes focused on hers. There was no way he would leave his *real* life behind. There had to be a way to get everything back.

'What did you make me do?' he snarled.

Chapter 1

A Chance Encounter

'I think we should go our separate ways.' Sally placed her hands on her hips with authority.

It amused Caitlin. Even though Sally was barely over five feet, her confidence by far outweighed her stature.

With one hand outstretched, Sally admired her immaculate manicured nails. In a superior and nasal tone, she added, 'We all have different interests, it makes sense.'

Georgina, a tall anorexic looking girl, glanced up waiting for their reaction. Her nails did not stand a chance. She was biting them a lot.

'That's probably a good idea,' the last girl said.

It did not surprise Caitlin that someone like Julia agreed. Caitlin could see she was more interested in what was going on around them. She had not stopped studying everything from the moment they had walked in. Julia's short cropped hair, streaked with red strands and the latest designer outfit, marked her out as a fashionista. Caitlin had a feeling what she was wearing did not meet the Julia standard.

'Shall we meet at the cafeteria, in say, an hour?' Julia suggested.

'Sounds like a plan,' Sally sang back. With a cheeky grin, she started to walk away. 'See you later on. Have fun, I know I will.'

Caitlin looked towards Georgina, who had paled at the thought of splitting up. On a hunch, Caitlin asked, 'would you like to come with me?'

Georgina fiddled with her glasses, her eyes transfixed on the floor. In a timid voice, she spoke, her voice barely above a whisper. 'Would you mind? I'm not really that bothered about where we go.'

'Of course I don't mind.'

Caitlin could not believe it – she was actually a student. It was a thrill to know she had a real student card. The fake one her older brother had made for her never fooled anyone. The shiny card, with her unfortunate picture, symbolised her newfound freedom. It was fantastic. The move into campus on the previous day had been hectic: arriving, unpacking, hasty introductions, and the thrill of sleeping away from home. It had all been exhausting. Even though the initial excitement of arriving at University was starting to ease, a new adventure began – Fresher's week.

The activity in the Southampton University students union was incredible. With stalls promoting a multitude of clubs and social activities sprawled everywhere. Seasoned representatives strategically positioned themselves with flyers at the ready, relishing the opportunity to lure new blood to their chosen pastime. Any student walking in with a campus map on display was an instant target.

Caitlin got the impression Sally was the ambitious type, so she was not surprised to see her head straight for the debate team stand. It took Sally just over a whole second to bat her eyelids at the handsome male student running the reconnaissance, before bursting into a flood of giggles. It was a pathetic display of womanhood – ambitious or not. In contrast, Julia marched towards the orienteering club, filofax tucked under her armpit.

With a smile, Caitlin remembered how in the first five minutes of meeting her, Julia had puffed up her chest and announced she held a Duke of Edinburgh Gold Award. For the next five minutes, she had rammed down her throat the importance of staying fit to maintain a healthy mind and body.

It had been fun to shut Julia up by letting her in on the fact that she had competed in numerous international swimming events, and had just missed out on the Olympics. It was not worth talking about the injury – Julia did not need to know.

Caitlin approached the University Swimming club stand, whilst Georgina hovered at a distance. Caitlin was sure that if Georgina tried harder to fade into the background, she would disappear completely. Proactive, she took a handout from the table. It listed the swimming sessions and schedules. As she attempted to read it her long, curly hair fell over her face. Flicking it out of the way, she ended up trying – and failing – to tuck it behind her ears.

The swimming club schedule was intense, as expected. And she had promised her parents that she would take it easy. Her swimming coaches also warned her enough times. It was just hard to let go of the sport she loved. A sign caught the corner of her eye and she glanced in its direction. As she turned to face it she raised her eyes and smiled. She had never considered joining a ladies' waterpolo club. Interest sparked, she made her way towards it. Perhaps, there was another way to swim and have fun.

'Have you played water polo before?' A girl, in a hooded sweatshirt emblazoned with the ladies water polo team logo, asked. There were a lot of white teeth on display.

'No,' she replied. 'But we did muck around with the ball in training sessions. Is it difficult to play?'

'No, if you're a reasonably good swimmer, it'll be no problem.'

'What are your training times like?'

'Usually Friday evenings, but we still don't know for sure,' she hesitated.

'No mornings then?'

'Nope, none at all, we don't do those! We do compete with other universities so we have some great outings. And we practice with the men's team – they're a good laugh,' she added, with a wink.

'Sounds interesting, I'll think about it then, thanks.'

'If you sign up, we'll send you an email or text when we have our first training session. Then you can decide whether to come along.'

'Oh, alright then, I'll do that.'

As she leaned in, Caitlin attempted to flatten her hair as she wrote her details on the paper. If she decided against competitive swimming there would be a bonus – no more early morning starts. Finally, a water sport with more civilised hours. The added benefit of playing in a team with boys was an unexpected perk.

The girl turned to another student with the same toothpaste ad smile, so Caitlin took her cue to leave. As she turned, she stuffed the leaflets into her bag, whilst trying to push her hair out of the way. She really hated her hair. As she started to think about chopping it all off one day, she bumped into the person behind her. A dull thud followed, as she dropped her hands and watched in horror. Out of control, her bag fell, its contents scattering on the floor like a wave. Frazzled, she leant down to pick everything up just as she heard a deep voice apologise. A pair of toned masculine hand's reached out to help.

When Caitlin looked up to see who it was, time seemed to stop. Transfixed on the spot, she gawped with a slightly open mouth. Conscious of the fact he had spoken, she snapped out of the trance and focused. She could feel the heat radiating off her cheeks.

'Hello,' he said his expression one of amusement.

'Erm, err, yeah, hello,' she stuttered. Mesmerised, she stared. His hair was thick, wavy and practically black in colour, and he towered above her by quite a few inches. But, it was the eyes that intrigued her the most. She had never seen amber coloured eyes with such exquisite detail. They looked like cats eyes, framed by dark, thick lashes and a perfect face.

'Are you a swimmer?' He asked, as he handed back the swimming club leaflet.

His received pronunciation gave away his upbringing. It was polished and refined, as expected of someone from a posh background. It would not surprise her if he had attended boarding school.

'I–I guess so, but I'm considering my options,' she said, holding up the water polo flyer. Instinctively, she looked to the right, unable to maintain eye contact.

'Interesting,' he commented, with a half smile. Taking a step forward, he moved towards the swimming stand. 'Well, I might see you around. Sorry to make your things fall like that.'

She could not believe he was apologizing.

Her jaw dropped as she saw him picking up the same leaflet she had only just been looking at. If he was a swimmer, hell would freeze over before anyone could stop her joining. Paranoid, he would notice her looking; she rejoined Georgina and casually glanced in his direction, before muttering. 'I didn't even say sorry for being such a klutz.'

'He looks nice,' Georgina whispered, she seemed to glance nervously in the direction of a few students chatting next to them.

'Too nice for me, that's for sure.' After her performance, Caitlin was convinced he must have labelled her as a complete idiot. Reluctantly, she walked away. But not before stealing a final glance.

***

Ingrid surveyed the room. It was like watching a hive of bees. Busy, busy, busy. She flicked her long, bleach blond hair and smiled at a boy leering in her direction. She was not interested in boys – they were so easy.

'What about that one?' Ingrid asked, her right hand firmly ensconced on her waist.

As far as she was concerned, it was time to choose.

'Don't make it too obvious you are looking,' her dad stressed. 'Even though here we don't stand out, we still have to be careful. You can attract them easily enough.'

'Sure, I'll be careful.' Ingrid scowled. She hated being told what to do all the time, especially by her dad. Why didn't he leave her alone? She would do anything for just a little taste of freedom.

'Can I go and look around?' Her brother asked, raising his pale blue eyes.

Ingrid could not believe Tomas had come along for the ride. He was too young, and definitely immature. There was no way he could be trusted.

'You can't allow him to go alone. If he goes, I go,' Ingrid pouted, crossing her arms over her chest.

'Neither of you can go alone. We are only here to observe. You have to learn how to choose.'

Ingrid tried to focus as she slowly surveyed the room.

Surrounded – no.

Boisterous – no.

Trendy – no.

'What about that one?' Ingrid hissed. She nodded in the direction of a tall emaciated girl, with wiry bland hair, and glasses. 'She looks weak; I doubt she has many friends.'

He shook his head. 'Look at the girl next to her – she doesn't look like a walkover. Another time – *alone*. Not with friends.'

Ingrid looked at the redhead next to the girl and shrugged in acknowledgement. He had a point.

'I'm getting hungry,' Tomas moaned, with his usual sulk.

'Then it's time to go,' her dad mused. 'We'll have to look somewhere else. Hardly any are alone. Give it a few weeks. Then we can come back.'

***

Sally threw herself onto the sofa, opposite Caitlin and Georgina, and exclaimed in a loud and overbearing voice. 'This place is fantastic isn't it? And there is so much talent. My eyes are popping out of their sockets. I just met the nicest second year Law student called James. He is to die for. A guy like that probably has a girlfriend though. There is no way he is available.'

As Sally rambled on, Caitlin stopped listening, lost in her own thoughts. That guy she had just met had blown her away in an irrational way. Normally, she did not allow herself to be swept away by someone's physical appearance – as far as she was concerned love at first sight was nonsensical. After a minute or so, she realised Sally was waiting for a reply.

'You look dazed. Are you feeling alright?' Sally asked, cocking her head to the side like a confused puppy.

'Sorry, I'm fine. What did you say?' Caitlin bluffed.

'Nothing much, anyway,' Sally continued, 'so how did you get on?'

'Great, I got lots of information. I've just got to think about it really.'

'What about you Georgina?' Sally asked, in what sounded like a bad attempt to include her in the conversation.

Georgina smiled. 'It was err…interesting.'

Sally frowned, then recovered and flashed a set of perfect teeth as she looked over her shoulder. Julia – with another trend setter. 'Hey, over here,' she shouted, her hands waved frantically.

Julia glared in their direction, gave what looked like an apologetic glance towards her new friends, and made her way over. 'Hello girls, I'm afraid we can't stay. We are going to meet up with some other people from our course. I'll catch up with you all in Halls.' With a fake, forced smile she sauntered off.

Sally watched her leave with a slightly open mouth. With a slight twitch of her lips and a few nervous hand motions, she shot up resembling a rabbit caught in headlights. 'I forgot I had to sign up for err, oh, debate club. I was so busy chatting to James – it slipped my mind. See you later.'

Caitlin knew a lame excuse when she heard one. Especially since the debate team stand was in the opposite direction. She had no doubt Sally was trying to catch up with Julia. 'And then, there were two,' she said, ominous.

Georgina glanced up. 'You can go too if you want. I know I'm not interesting.'

Caitlin could not believe how forlorn Georgina looked – it was hard for her to contain her own excitement. Either way, she did not have the heart to leave her alone. 'Got no other place to go,' she smirked. 'You know, you really shouldn't be so paranoid.'

'Sorry.'

'Don't apologise. Look, I need some hot chocolate. Shall we just head back and check out the halls of residence some more? I also need to grab some food supplies. What do you say?'

'If you are sure I'm not in your way.'

Caitlin smiled. 'Trust me, if you were in my way, I would have told you.'

Bags in tow, they got up and squeezed through the hoards of students ambling around the room. After arriving early, it was now packed to the rafters. It was probably the best time to make an exit. Casually, Caitlin looked around – it would have been nice to spot that guy again before she left.

Nothing.

Another time.

Chapter 2

Mingling

The girl Steven had crashed into came into view through the corner of his eye. It momentarily distracted him from his conversation. Something about the girl had grabbed his attention. Her thick, auburn hair was certainly prominent and hard to miss. But, there was something about her curious expression and slim build that made up for the scattering of freckles and white skin that screamed vitamin D deficiency.

'Hey, have you noticed how many hot chicks there are around? I think I'd like a piece of everything. Especially that blond hottie over there,' the voice drooled.

Adam, a total leach. Steven could tell after a few hours of being with him. Still, he followed Adam's glance, and saw three students walking past, two guys and a girl. The girl was striking – for sure. With long bleach blond hair, she reminded him of the girls' he had seen on a trip to Sweden. He suspected she was foreign from the way she carried herself. As he stared, she met his gaze and gave him a confident smile. For a split second, their eyes remained locked. Another day, he would have introduced himself. Today, he was distracted.

Raising his eyebrows, he faced Adam again. 'I doubt you'll have any difficulty finding someone. From what I hear, some girls tend to go crazy on fresher's week.'

'Yeah, finding someone is not usually the problem. But, all I want is to shag, nothing else. I bet you've had lots of girl's.'

Avoiding the question, Steven shrugged his shoulders. Something compelled him to go. 'I'll catch up with you later. Things to do. But hey, good luck with your shag fest.' Steven noticed Adam's startled expression, but he did not have time to worry about offending him.

Once through the congested hallway, he made his way out of the students union. Outside, he looked around. In the distance, he saw the redhead turn around the corner and disappear with her lanky looking friend. He could not understand the urgent desire to follow her. In the scheme of things, this was University, so he was likely to see her again. The thing was he did not want to wait for the moment to come up again. Something about their brief, and uneventful encounter, had intrigued him. They would get to know each other. He would make sure of it.

***

After unpacking an assortment of food supplies in her allocated cupboard, Caitlin found herself sitting in her bedroom, staring at bare walls. At home, she had posters covering every available space. Determined to rectify the situation, she took out the posters she had brought with her, opened the packet of blu tack and started sticking generous pieces on the back of her favourite – a massive A1 sized poster of a great white shark. Her mission was to transform the room, as soon as possible.

Whilst stretching on tiptoes on a chair, a faint knock on the door startled her, causing her to loose balance and fall off.

'Ouch,' she winced, as she rubbed her foot. 'Just a minute,'

When she opened the door, a blotchy faced Georgina stood in the hallway.

'Hi, am I interrupting you?'

'No, err…well actually I just fell. It was my own fault I could barely reach to put the poster up.'

'Sorry, I can come back later,' Georgina replied, taking a step back.

'No, it's alright. I've just added another bruise to my collection. You look upset; do you want to come in?'

Startled, Georgina replied. 'No, I'm fine. Can I help?'

Her tone was unconvincing but Caitlin let it drop – she probably didn't want to talk about it. 'You know, you are much taller than me, so you've come at the perfect time. Fancy helping me put these up?' Company was always welcome, especially if it served a purpose.

'I'd love to help,' Georgina replied. 'I have to get some myself, my room looks really sad at the moment.'

Caitlin could have sworn she had smiled. That was the most she had heard her say since they'd met. 'I'm sure I've got spares. You can have some of mine.'

'Really? That would be great.'

Caitlin picked up the slightly crumpled poster and ironed it out. 'Right then, this is it.'

'Where do you want it?' Georgina asked, holding it up.

'As high as you can get it,' Caitlin replied, with a hand gesture.

With relative ease, Georgina stretched her arms and stuck it on. The image of the deadly, yet graceful, shark dominated the room.

'You like sharks?' Georgina asked.

'As you see. I also love whales and dolphins – anything that lives in the sea really. What about you?'

'I prefer land animals. Tame ones, like rabbits. I had to leave Fluffy behind.'

Caitlin nearly laughed out loud, but she held it back. She did not know any teenager that still kept a rabbit at home as a pet. 'Fair enough, shall we get the rest of them up then?'

'Sure.'

After five minutes of concentration, they stood back to admire their handiwork.

'That's much better,' Caitlin exclaimed. 'Shall we go and do your room now?'

'Now?'

'Of course, I saved the landscapes for you, didn't think you'd want any shark ones.'

'Oh, I wouldn't mind. But, I don't know if I could sleep with a shark staring at me, so you're probably right. Thanks a lot,' Georgina replied, with a glint in her eye. It was the first time Caitlin had seen her even remotely excited.

Grabbing the remaining posters and blu tack, they hustled over to the opposite room to get started.

Georgina's room was really bare. It looked void of any personality. The room was immaculate, practically untouched.

'Where's all your stuff?' Caitlin queried.

'Oh, I, err…I like to keep a tidy room.'

'Have you unpacked yet?' Caitlin asked, suspicious.

Georgina froze.

'Do you want some help?' Caitlin asked. Silence confirmed her belief.

‘I did not want to unpack,’ Georgina admitted, her voice forced. ‘I have to be honest, I don’t know if University is for me.’

‘Hey, don’t get upset. It’s difficult to come to a new place. Especially if you are a bit shy. I’ll help you. Come on then, let’s get these posters up first to cheer up the room. Then we’ll grab a cup of tea and unpack your stuff.’ Caitlin held back from giving her a hug, she barely knew her.

‘Thanks,’ Georgina sniffed a reply. ‘I’ve never been outgoing. I come from a quiet village. This place is just overwhelming.’

‘I’ll look out for you,’ Caitlin smiled, as she placed a hand on her shoulder. It felt awkward, so she quickly removed it. At least, she made an effort.

The sound of talking alerted Caitlin to the return of Sally and Julia. They had company.

‘Shall we grab a cup of tea and see what they’ve been up to? They might not be that bad.’ Caitlin doubted it, but there was some hope left.

‘Tea sounds great.’

Caitlin wondered if Georgina ever said no to anything.

‘Oh, there you are!’ Sally exclaimed, as they entered. ‘Sorry, I missed you both earlier.’

She did not seem sorry to Caitlin.

‘So, here we are. Our second week away from home begins. Is anyone homesick yet?’ Sally asked ominously, bearing a cheeky grin.

Everyone shook their head, but Caitlin could see the signs of doubt in their eyes. Even the most confident could break, when some of their creature comforts were taken away.

‘I, for one, am looking forward to not having to deal with my baby sister. It’s blissfully quiet here,’ Caitlin added, as she turned to boil the kettle.

‘Quiet!’ Julia exploded. Her eyes wide. ‘Far from it, there is so much going on.’

‘Obviously, there’s a lot going on,’ said Caitlin. ‘But, trust me, its quiet. My baby sister never shuts up.’

‘Oh,’ Julia paused, with a frown. ‘I only have an older brother, and he usually leaves me alone.’

Breaking the silence, Sally jumped in. ‘Anna, Grace, this is Caitlin and Georgina.’

'Hi,' they both said simultaneously. Their little waves looked so fake.

'What are you both studying then?' Caitlin asked, in an attempt at casual conversation.

Georgina leaned against the door frame, at the entrance to the kitchen. She looked like she was trying to escape.

'I am reading Law,' Grace added, in a haughty tone.

'Oh, so I guess you'll be with Sally then?' Caitlin added. It always amused her when anyone said they were reading not studying – what was the difference anyway?

'Well, yes, of course,' she replied, glancing at Sally and raising her eyebrows. Sally seemed to shrug back apologetically.

If Caitlin had been confrontational, she would have told her to piss off. She had always resented those that thought they were better than everybody else. To stop herself from being rude, she looked towards Anna. 'So, what about you?'

'Same as Julia – Medicine.'

She could not believe it, lawyers and doctors, just what she needed. She was glad that her parents weren't there – they would have given her the look. The look that said; why didn't you choose a vocation?

'Good for you,' she faked enthusiasm. 'Well, I guess we'll leave you to chat about your stuff. We were just having fun. See you later.' Tea in hand, she carried both mugs to the doorway, handed one to Georgina and strolled out with her head held high.

As they entered Georgina's room, they heard a chorus of giggles erupting from the kitchen.

'Oh boy,' Caitlin sighed, putting her mug on the study table. 'I'm glad you're normal. Just, remind me though, you're not reading Law or Medicine right?'

'Nope, I'm doing Biochemistry.'

Caitlin nearly burst out laughing – a scientist. All she needed was a trainee teacher and a nurse and the circle would be complete.

'They don't seem that bad,' Georgina said. She lacked conviction.

'Trust me, they are the worst kind. I don't tend to judge, honest, I don't. But just by what they are reading, wearing and saying – I get the picture. We are not in their clique. But, hey, you never know, my mum is always reminding me not to judge a book by its cover.'

Georgina sipped her tea and nodded, as a short period of silence ensued.

Impulsively, Caitlin stood up and suggested. 'Shall we go and check out the bar? We might meet some other people down there.'

'I think I'll stay and read. I'm a bit tired.'

Caitlin was disappointed. She did not want to go alone to the student bar. Yet, she had to go out – she had not come to University to stay indoors, away from the action. 'Oh, okay then, you don't mind if I go right?'

'No, not at all. You go, have a good time.'

'Cool, I'm going to be brave.' Sipping the last dregs in the mug, she stood in front of the mirror and fluffed her hair. 'Well, there's nothing I can do to improve the face, so I'll have to go as I am.'

***

Steven held the cue like a true master and potted the last shot. The black slid into the pocket and sealed his victory. Pool was so much easier than snooker.

'Good game, I'll try my luck again later.' The student he'd been playing against shuffled off defeated.

Steven passed the cue to the students waiting to play, and headed off to get a drink from the bar. As he waited for his beer, he glanced towards the entrance and saw the redhead standing there, alone. She looked nervous. Without a second thought, he paid for his drink and walked in her direction. A few strides away, his opportunity was snatched away as a couple of girls bounded in front of her, all smiles. In a chorus of laughter, they headed off together.

Thwarted.

In an easy stroll, Steven sauntered back to where Adam was sitting. There were quite a lot of students acquainting themselves. A few had paired up and were getting close. He was not surprised a few were quick off the mark. After talking to Adam, he realised the only thing on some minds was how often they would get to make out or hopefully, when they would get to do more. He had already been inundated with female attention at boarding school, and experienced the freedom of living away from home – the novelty of having girls around had long gone.

He hadn't really given a lot of thought to getting involved. It was not the kind of thing he wasted time on. If someone came along and he liked them, then he'd give it a go, but he was never desperate. At least, not until this afternoon. He still failed to understand why he had been compelled to rush off to see where that girl was going. He had been weighing it up for a few hours, and come to a few conclusions. Her expressive blue eyes had caught his attention. Her accent did intrigue him. And the way she blushed was cute. The thing was it was completely superficial. He had never paid much attention to any of that stuff before. It was annoying. So much so that he knew he had to talk to her again. Just to check.

Chapter 3

Game, Set And Match

'Thanks for coming to say hello,' Caitlin laughed, relieved.

'It's okay, we saw you standing there looking, well, lost. There's nothing worse than being alone when you hardly know anyone, right. By the way, I'm Lisa,' she added, in a strong Brummie accent.

'I was totally scared when I got to my accommodation yesterday. It's so easy to panic. I was convinced no-one would talk to me. Then Lisa popped her head in my door and I relaxed,' the other girl added. 'Anyway, I'm Abbi.'

'Hi, I'm Caitlin,' she sang back, still nervous.

Looking around, Lisa started to introduce her. 'This is John, Dan and err, Megan was it?'

Caitlin gave a small, embarrassed nod in their direction. 'Hi.'

A few acknowledgements followed, before they resumed their conversations.

'We were just saying that this place is excellent. Have you settled in alright?' Abbi asked, taking a sip from her turquoise drink.

'Yeah, it's okay. Haven't been here long enough to tell,' Caitlin replied. 'What is that you are drinking?'

'Some alcoholic concoction. It was cheap, with a high amount of alcohol so I went for it.' Abbi chuckled. 'It's actually alright, fruity.'

'Let me see that,' Lisa sighed. Taking a sniff, she gasped. 'It smells lethal. I'm not carrying you back later.'

'I'm not planning to get plastered, just tipsy. I'm sure I can make my own way back.'

Lisa rolled her eyes. 'Guess I'd better join you and finish my drink then. Are you having a drink, Caitlin?'

'In a minute, I'm alright just now.' She was not in a hurry to embarrass herself in front of strangers. 'I'm not sure about my roommates. How have you settled in? I'm sharing with three girls.

One is really nice, just super quiet, and the other two are, well, to be polite, intimidating.'

'Really, in what way?' Dan asked, whilst he rubbed his stubble.

'Like just, oh I dunno, they seem really ambitious.'

'Aren't you? Isn't that what people come to University for?' He asked, all serious.

'Well, yes, but to be honest I don't have a clue what job I want to do eventually. They are doing Law and Medicine. Vocation sorted. Hard core, if you know what I mean.'

They laughed aloud, until a well spoken voice interrupted from behind.

'What are you saying about those studying Law then?'

No-one spoke, as Caitlin turned around. She recognised the voice, but was apprehensive about checking her suspicion. Suspicion confirmed, she could not stop her jaw from dropping.

It was him.

***

Steven tried to play it cool, yet his lips twitched as he smiled at her – he could not resist. Her expression and fidgeting hands gave her away. He *was* making her nervous. Conscious of the others sitting around the table, he turned to face them. 'Hello, I'm Steven and I'm reading Law. Am I welcome?'

'Of course, you're welcome,' a blonde haired girl slurred, all teeth. 'I'm Megan, nice to meet you. Here, sit next to me.' She shuffled up the bench, and patted the space.

'Thanks.' He took the seat which happened to be opposite the girl he was really interested in. Convenient. 'So, you were saying?' he queried, looking directly at her.

'Erm, well, just that anyone doing Law or Medicine knows what they want to do with their life.'

The brunette ran her hand through her thick brown hair and laughed aloud. 'Well, actually, Caitlin was saying anyone doing that was hard core. I'm Lisa, by the way. Have you met Caitlin already?'

He wondered whether it was that obvious.

He turned to Lisa and replied, 'Briefly.' Then he faced Caitlin. 'Caitlin is it? So, am I hard core?' Steven asked, he bit his lip.

'You bet,' Megan drooled, as she turned to face him, batting her long eyelashes. 'You can be my lawyer any day of the week.'

Steven ignored Megan – he was tired of girls that came across as desperate. Continuing to watch Caitlin, he waited. She looked unnerved. It was fun to see her squirm.

'I don't know you well enough,' Caitlin said. 'I'll let you know about that.'

'I look forward to it.' He noticed her pink cheeks were starting to revert to their normal colour. It was endearing she blushed so easily. Something told him it was the second time on that day he'd had the same effect upon her.

'Anyway, Steven is it? Do you play pool? I'm John, fancy a game? Anyone else up for it?' John looked around, a twinkle in his eye.

'Count me out, I'm rubbish,' Megan sighed and folded her arms.

'Another time,' Abbi excused herself. 'I'm going for a drink.'

Dan got up to follow her. 'I could do with one.' His eyes seemed to linger on Abbi's exposed long legs.

'I'm in for another drink,' Megan said. As she stood, she wobbled. She seemed oblivious of the fact that in the circumstances three was a crowd. For her sake, Steven hoped she was not planning to drink any more.

'So, I guess it's the four of us then. Will you partner me, Lisa?' John asked, giving her a decidedly flirtatious smile.

'Sure. You can play with Steven,' Lisa grinned, making eye contact with Caitlin.

'Are you alright with that?' Steven asked, as he eased alongside Caitlin.

'Of course, but you better be good. I'm used to playing against my brother, and I don't usually lose.'

Her quick and assertive response surprised him.

'The gauntlet is set,' he said, standing aside and holding his arm out. 'Ladies first.'

'Great, no-one is playing,' John said, as he took three pound coins out of his wallet and placed them on the table. 'Best of three?'

'If you insist, but you'll save a pound. I can personally guarantee it,' Steven said. 'Caitlin here is apparently a pro.'

'Really,' John smirked. 'Don't let me down Lisa, the stakes are high.'

'Good one, Caitlin,' Lisa grumbled.

John winked at Lisa and gave her a little nudge of encouragement. 'Don't worry,' he said, 'we'll annihilate them.'

On the flip of a coin, John beamed victorious as he held the cue and got ready to strike. Like a professional, he took aim and struck. The white ball pelted forward, smashing into the triangle, causing a stripe to pocket immediately.

'Yeah,' Lisa whooped for joy, punching the air. 'I guess we're stripes then?'

'We can choose,' John replied.

'I didn't know that,' she pouted, confused. 'Oh well, I like stripes.'

'Stripes it is,' John nodded, giving her a wry smile. Leaning into the table again, he took aim. Another stripe landed in another pocket.

'You know, you should give the rest of us a chance to play,' Caitlin said, pretending to yawn.

As John took aim for the third time he struck out. The white ball remained beside a stripe ball, within a shot of a spot.

'Our turn,' said Steven. With his cue, he walked around the table, planning his move. 'What do you think, partner?'

'Well, personally I'd bounce it off the side and pocket the red spot.'

'Okay then,' he passed her the cue. 'I'd like to see that.'

Even though her eyes widened at the challenge, she held out her hand for the cue and positioned herself. With a look of deep concentration, she held it like an expert, took aim, and did exactly what she claimed. The spot cruised in, as the white ball magically aligned itself for the next victim.

Caitlin raised her chin, and grinned. 'Do you want to take the next shot?'

Her expression made him smile.

'No, no, I don't want to rain on your parade,' he replied. 'You go ahead.'

After potting the next spot ball, she was left without an easy shot. So, she left the white hidden behind a group of spot balls instead, effectively snookering Lisa.

John huffed and shook his head. 'Dirty tactics,' he muttered.

'What goes around comes around. Can't give the game away,' Caitlin said, with a snigger.

Lisa looked towards John for help. 'Did I mention that I've never played before?'

'No, you didn't,' John replied, with a scowl. 'However,' he paused, as a smile eased across his face. 'I'm happy to instruct you.'

John took position behind Lisa, and showed her how to hold the cue. Steven watched the chemistry evolve, and wished it was him flirting with Caitlin. A minute later Lisa misjudged, barely hitting the white.

'Good effort,' John said.

Lisa shrugged her shoulders, and kept her eyes to the floor. 'Sorry I played.'

'Hey, it doesn't matter. I'm glad you're my partner. With a bit of practice, and my expert tuition, your playing would improve,' John added.

'This might not be a fair match,' Steven whispered in Caitlin's ear. He was sure he had detected a shiver when he got near. 'I'll play nice.'

Taking aim, he misdirected the white ball. It teetered into the pocket.

'Nice one, Steven,' John said. 'Now, move over and let the experts show you how it's done.'

Steven shrugged his shoulders apologetically, and made his way over to stand next to Caitlin again. 'Sorry, about the lousy shot.'

'You faked it,' Caitlin said, as she rolled her eyes.

'No, I didn't,' he retorted. He liked the way she tried to read him.

***

Even though it was obvious to Caitlin that Steven was not playing to the best of his ability, they still managed to beat John and Lisa.

'I think I'd like a drink after that,' John exclaimed, as he run his fingers through his spiky hair. 'Do you mind if we call it a day?'

'Not at all,' Steven replied, as he turned to face her. 'Would you like to play against me?'

Caitlin looked into his perfect face and nearly melted. Taking a deep breath, she mustered her confidence.

'Of course I'll play you, and you'll only need two pounds, trust me.'

He raised his eyebrows. 'You're on.'

After ten minutes of play, Caitlin was seething. It had only taken

two pounds. Unfortunately, he had won both games.
'Can I buy you a drink?' He asked. His voice low, tempting.
She refused to look at him, and mumbled. 'I think I'm going to head back now.' Lisa and John had not come back and she was tired. But, that was not the main reason she wanted to go. She was annoyed and confused. He had humiliated her by playing like a professional. Chivalry was dead.
'You did play really well, for a ....'
'Girl,' she snapped. She did not care if he was gorgeous and attractive. She wanted revenge. 'Don't worry, this girl can up her game. I will beat you.'
'I'm sure you will, and I promise that it won't be because I let you.'
'Ha,' she said, as an unattractive snort escaped. He really brought out the worst in her. Could he be more arrogant?
'Do you really have to go? Can't I get you a drink?' His voice sounded apologetic.
As her resolve started to crumble, she lifted her head to face him and was confronted with *that* look again. She was not going to let him think she was a walkover – she was not that easy. To add to it all, she was a very bad loser. 'It's nice of you, but I should go. See you.'

***

Tomas tapped his finger on the dashboard in a steady rhythm. With a grunt, he turned to Eilif. 'What do we do now?'
'We wait,' Eilif stressed. Even though Tomas was doing well for his first time away from home, he was far too impatient. Eilif hoped that given time his son would learn.
'This waiting around thing is not as much fun as I thought it would be,' Tomas continued, his lips pouting.
Even though Eilif had been through this before, it did not make it any easier. It was difficult to control his temper; Tomas was testing his patience to the limit. 'What did you think? That this would be a game. It is no game son, it's serious. You have to take it for what it is. We are not welcome here.'
'Well, only if they suspect what we are,' Ingrid blurted out, as she raised her eyes and shrugged her shoulders.
'Exactly.' He faced them both and narrowed his eyes. In a

steady voice, he stressed through gritted teeth. 'And no-one must ever find out about us – ever! Do you understand?'

'Yes dad,' they both sang back before staring out of the windows. Conversation over.

Eilif was frustrated. He remembered his first visit. The excitement and anxiety entwined in one. He did not blame his children. They were entitled to have their own views and ideas. Yet, he knew, deep down, they had to understand. This was just a visit, nothing more. It was a small concession. They paid a heavy price for what they were capable of.

Chapter 4

Banter

Caitlin stormed out of the student bar. Once the cold night air hit, she shivered. She hadn't thought to bring a coat. The sound of her footsteps clunking on the pavement distracted her, and she listened to the steady rhythm. She could hear a few students laughing here and there, mainly from indoors. To make matters worse, it started to drizzle. In a bid to get back quicker she started to jog. As she did she mulled the decision to go out. She was glad to have braved it alone. On the outcome, she was torn. It had been great to mingle with other people and meet Lisa and Abbi. Yet, if she was honest, the only person on her mind was Steven. She could not deny the attraction. He had got to her. This was unbelievable when you considered he was one of the most annoying men she had ever met.

Mr. Perfect.

The weird thing was, she actually got the impression he was interested in her. As much as she did not want to think it, she could not help wondering if he wanted to get to know her as more than just a friend. Her track record so far was pathetic. Loads of male friends, nothing more. What she could not understand was, if he was interested, then why had he thrashed her? He had played so leniently with the others. It was puzzling. He was puzzling. She just could not figure out why he was showing *her* attention? She knew she was nothing special. If he was interested it would be short of miraculous.

***

'Hey, wait up,' Steven called out. Caitlin's look of bemusement, as she turned to face him was priceless.

'You startled me,' she gasped. 'You know, anyone would think that you're stalking me?'

'Definitely, I am stalking you,' he said. He resisted the urge to smile again. 'But, I'm also starving. So, do you fancy going to get some fish and chips from the local?'

'In this rain?' she sighed, forlorn.

'We can go get an umbrella if you want?'

'Nah, it's just a drizzle.' She shrugged her shoulders.

'So, you're coming then?'

'Why not?'

He was sure she blushed again.

In silence, they walked up to the end of the road. Steven could not understand why he was apprehensive about saying the wrong thing. No girl had ever intimidated him before. The truth is he did not even know if she was actually intimidating him, it was hard to put the feeling into words. Annoyed at his stupidity, he braved it and asked the first lame question that popped into his mind.

'Are you catered or self catered?'

'Self catered, I like making my own food. What about you?'

'Catered.' He was relieved she had replied – and with a question of her own. It was promising.

'Lucky you, you don't have to cook.'

'I don't mind cooking. My dad recommended taking the easy option, just for the first year.'

'And you're still hungry, even though you already ate?'

'I'm always hungry.'

'Fair enough.'

He noticed she was keeping her eyes firmly on the ground, refusing to make eye contact. Of course, it could have been his imagination, and all she was doing was keeping the rain off her face.

'What are you reading?' He asked.

'Mathematics with Spanish.'

He could not resist. 'That's sounds intense – if a bit *hard core.*'

She flinched, and sighed. 'Sorry about that.'

'I'm just jesting with you. So, do you speak Spanish then?'

'I'm fluent.'

'Mucho gusto de conocerte,' he added, in his perfect Spanish.

In shock, she stopped in her tracks and stared. 'How do you know Spanish then?'

'My step mum is Spanish. But hey, it's not that difficult to say 'nice to meet you' right?'

***

Caitlin found Steven's voice melodic as he laughed in an easy going manner. A series of butterflies flit through her stomach and she winced at the unexpected reaction. Taking a deep breath, she added. 'Your Spanish sounds Andalucian.'

'You are correct.' He raised his eyebrows, and tilted his head to the side. 'I only know how to speak the basics, as I learnt what I know from my mum. It's the only way I know how to say the words. She came from Torremolinos originally.'

'I've been there on holiday loads of times. It's a small world isn't it?'

'Yes,' he mused.

'So why did you choose Law? I didn't mean to be rude earlier. I don't usually stereotype.'

'It's alright, but I don't intend to become one of the typical blood-sucking corporate types that are only in it to get as much as they can. I just like the idea of helping people.'

'Sounds very noble.' She could not believe it. He was too good to be true.

'Although,' he added, sheepish. 'I have a confession to make. I'm actually doing a degree in European Legal Studies. So, I am also planning to take the third year out overseas. We have something else in common, other than our language skills.'

'And swimming.' She paused, and then gritted her teeth. 'I mean, I think you were looking at the swimming stand.'

'I was. I'm impressed you noticed.'

She could not believe her ears. He was impressed *she* noticed him – it was laughable.

In an attempt to change the conversation, she added, 'I have no idea what I want to do in the future, other than to leave my family and start out on my own far, far away.'

'You don't like your family?

'Oh, they're okay, I guess. But, I just want a place of my own, away from my bratty sister and annoying older brother. And parents always telling me what to do,' she rambled. 'Sorry, you're probably not interested in this.'

'No, you carry on. I think I know what you mean, but I'm an only child, so I can only guess what it's like to have other siblings around. I always thought it was boring to be on my own, but I guess it was not such a bad thing after all.'

'Trust me, you are so lucky. Sharing sucks, big time.'

The sight of the chip shop made the conversation ebb. The smell of greasy chips beckoned.

***

Ingrid watched as the couple made their way into the fish and chip shop. It was such a British tradition. She did not see the charm in food that was deep fried and dripping in fat. The way he smiled at the girl left her in no doubt – he was interested in her. How much was difficult to tell. Either way, she knew that kind of attention. She had received it enough times. It was a shame she rarely reciprocated. All of the men back home were so boring.

With her head cocked to the side she focused on his features. He had raven black hair, an athletic build and a certain way of carrying himself. Confidence – she guessed? There was something about him. She was sure he was the boy she had stared at that morning. She vaguely remembered being intrigued by his eyes. Strangely, he had looked away. Usually, they all held her gaze. Her charms must be failing.

It was beginning to annoy her. She could not put her finger on it, but there was something about him – something familiar. She had no idea what it was. It was a niggling sensation, like when a deadline was coming up.

'Can we go now?' Tomas whined, as he slouched on the back seat.

Her younger brother was so annoying. If it was up to her, she would have sent him back home already.

'Fine,' Eilif conceded. 'We'll move on. Something else will turn up.'

As the car cruised past the couple, Ingrid glanced back at the male student again. She hoped to cross his path again. Maybe then she'd figure out what it was that bugged her.

***

'This portion is huge. We should have shared,' Caitlin said, unable to stop herself from tucking in. Chips made it onto her top five of guilty pleasures.

'Oh. I don't know. I can easily polish this off.

With a shrug of the shoulder, Caitlin replied. 'I'll give it a go.'

'It's good to see a girl with an appetite,' he added, apparently amused.

Caitlin stopped in her tracks. Placing her available hand on her hip, she pouted. 'Do you have a stereotype for what a girl can and can't do?'

'No,' he spluttered. 'Have I annoyed you again? I don't mean to. It's just a lot of girls back home never seemed to eat at all, especially when I was around.'

'Maybe you intimidated them, did you think about that?'

'So, does that mean I don't intimidate you?' He cocked his head to the side, with a curious expression.

She did not want to answer the question. 'Hey, the rain has stopped.'

'This is England. It comes and goes.'

'It sure does,' she mused. Steven was really annoying her now. Of course he intimidated her. There was just no way she was going to let him in on that. Besides, she had never had to think of cutting back on food, her weight had never been a problem.

'I don't mean to pry, but, where do you come from. Your accent sounds different, and you speak Spanish well, I take it?' Steven asked, as he popped another chip in his mouth.

'I'm fluent,' she said again. A cheeky grin spread across her face, as she continued, determined to have some fun of her own. 'I live in England now, but I used to live somewhere else. We moved when I was twelve. I currently live in Guildford. I bet you can't guess where I was born?' she challenged.

'You get more interesting by the minute.'

She felt her heart skip a beat – he thought she was interesting.

'Now you've got me. This is probably wrong but, South Africa?' he guessed, as he waved his finger in the air.

'Nope,' she smiled. This was a good game.

'Canada?'

'That is really cold, totally wrong,' she smirked.

'Ireland?'

'You are never going to get it, you know.'

'I am beginning to realise that,' he rubbed his fingers against his lips as he thought hard. 'Give me a clue, is it British?'

'Yes.'

'Is it a colony?'

'Yes.'

He chuckled aloud. 'Well, that's easy – Gibraltar.'

***

Caitlin's face was legendary. Steven was beginning to love watching the way her expressions altered with her emotions.

'How did you know? Most people have not even heard of the place.'

'Like I said, my mum comes from Torremolinos. Of course, I've heard of it. We've been on day trips loads of times. I've even gone to the top and seen the Barbary apes.'

'I am so glad you didn't call them monkeys, everyone does that,' she said. 'Where do you live then? You have a very pronounced accent. And I'm rubbish at guessing, so don't even go there.'

'I was brought up in Ilfracombe, but I went to boarding school for ten years, that's why I have a, what did you call it? A *pronounced accent.*'

'But, you're not a snob though, are you?'

Her directness was incredible.

'Snobs are much more pompous.'

She looked mortified. 'I didn't mean to offend you, again. I always say aloud what I'm thinking, bad habit. Your accent does give you away though. You must have gone to a really good school.'

'I did and I'm not ashamed of it. My parents sent me to boarding school at the age of eight, so I have to admit I'm a bit institutionalised.'

'Well, I won't hold it against you.'

'Good,' he said. Even if she did, it would not bother him.

To his dismay, he realised they were back at halls. 'Anyway, I guess I'll see you again some time. It's been nice to talk to you, Caitlin.'

'It has been nice to talk to you, Steven,' she replied. With a half-smile, she entered the pass code and disappeared through the door.

Steven turned around, and started to walk back. He definitely wanted to get to know her better now.

Chapter 5

The first day is the hardest

Georgina stared at the bleeping alarm clock and mustered the energy to get up. At the best of times, she had never been a morning person. Now, without her creature comforts or parents, the start to every day bordered on torturous. When she eventually got up, her head spun as though recovering from a hangover. What she was beginning to loath with a vengeance, was queuing for the shower. If there was something she wished she had asked for before arriving, it was to have an ensuite. That would make her Christmas wish list.

Getting into her pink polka dot dressing gown, she opened the door by a fraction to survey the corridor. The bathroom door was open and there was no-one in sight. Hastily, she rushed back in, got her shower gel and raced back outside. The door was now shut. Someone had beaten her to it for the third day in a row – words escaped her.

After sitting on the floor of the corridor for ten minutes, so as not to lose her place again, the bathroom door finally opened. Caitlin walked out with a beaming smile. In a songbird voice, she chimed out 'good morning' as she strolled past and got into her room. It seemed unfair – how could anyone look that perky in the morning? Over the past few days, an annoying thought teased and taunted her.

At University, there were a lot of intelligent people that were attractive, popular and extremely charismatic. They were not as nerdy and geeky as she suspected she was. At school, she had hoped that once at University she would meet other people like her.

The truth was she could not see that many, or if they were there, they certainly kept to themselves, which was not a huge surprise. It was a depressing thought to realise that even here, she still felt like a nerd – an outcast.

When Georgina finally got to the kitchen to have breakfast she found the rest of the girls were already chatting animatedly. Caitlin was blushing at something that Sally had said, and seemed reluctant to expand on the topic of conversation. Sensing gossip, Sally seemed to make matters worse by purposefully spilling the beans – it was like she relished making Caitlin uncomfortable.

'Caitlin's got a boyfriend,' Sally blurted out, a silly smirk on her face.

'He's not my boyfriend. We only just met,' Caitlin gave a deep sigh, as she glared at Sally with huge eyes. If she had been a dog, Georgina knew she would have growled.

'Well, there seemed to be more to your connection than conversation last night, if you catch my drift,' Sally insinuated, as she twiddled her index fingers together.

'It was nothing. I am allowed to have male friends.'

'A very good male friend by the sound of it,' Julia scoffed, scraping the last of the cereal out of the bowl. 'I heard that you were seen playing pool together. Very cosy! What about you Sally? Did you have any luck with that Adam bloke?'

'It looks promising,' she replied, as she rambled on again. She definitely liked the sound of her own voice.

Caitlin's shoulders seemed to drop as the tension eased. Georgina would not be surprised if Caitlin had a bust up with Sally and Julia, or both, in the near future. With her bowl, spoon and cereal, she sat down after helping herself to some milk.

Georgina was not an authority on boys, so there was no way she would join into their frivolous chat. Keeping her eyes on the bowl, she concentrated on eating.

One by one, the girls left the room. Eventually, she sat alone and finished her breakfast. Finally, she took her bowl to the sink to give it a rinse.

'Are you coming Georgina?' Caitlin asked.

Georgina turned round to face her and saw Caitlin's face poking through the doorway. 'No, I'm not ready yet, thanks for asking. '

'Oh, okay, sorry I have to go or I'll be late. I'll see you later.'

With that, she was gone and Georgina felt a surge of anguish rush through her. Hanging her head in her hands, she held back the tears desperately trying to escape. She wanted to cry. She wanted to scream. Deep down, she knew all she wanted was to go home. She did not want to be at University anymore.

***

Sally strode into the lecture hall in a steady swagger. She was brimming with confidence. The first lecture of the term was on Contract Law and since she had already covered most of the material on her A Level Law course, she was not daunted by the forthcoming lecture. Nevertheless, even for someone like her, it was amazing to walk into a room capable of filling over one hundred people. It felt far removed from the largest class she had ever attended of thirty five. Sally had attended a large state school in the outskirts of London. She had already dealt with plenty of adversities during her education. Regardless, even for her, the environment was intimidating.

The lecture room was large and imposing. It resembled an amphitheatre. All the seats inclined sharply, to give everyone a good view, and the room had a musty old smell of aging carpets and worn furniture. It was already half full, so she made her way to one of the middle aisles.

Efficiently, she removed the A4 size notepad and her favourite pen from the rucksack and waited for the start of the lecture. Whilst she waited, it occurred to her that now was as good a time as any, to review the opposition.

Glancing discretely, she surveyed the various students. At the front were a scattering of mature students, intermingled with other keen students seeking to please by taking front seats. Other students chatted, as though introducing themselves. She would have normally been one of them, but today she wanted to watch carefully, to get a feel for the lay of the land.

To her right, Adam caught her attention. He was sitting a few rows ahead. She could imagine running her fingers though his tousled brown hair. Next to him sat the dark mysterious guy she had seen Caitlin with the previous night. She did not understand the attraction, if there was any. She had never found that type remotely attractive. In her experience, they were usually either gay or taken.

Even though reasonably satisfied with her looks, she knew her limitations, accepting the fact that she would never look right next to someone like that. To compensate for her average features, she had taken to adopting a brash overconfident approach to get noticed. It always worked. With that thought in mind, Adam glanced back and saw her looking in his direction. Taking the opportunity, she gave him a subtle smile and a flirtatious wave. They held eye contact for a few seconds, before the lecturer walked in, prompting her to look towards the front. Knowing he was still looking at her, she smiled. Now, all she had to do was reel him in.

***

'I can't believe what I've let myself in for!' Caitlin exclaimed.

'It can't be that bad,' Lisa joked, flicking her long dark hair off her face.

'It's worse. I have no idea what they were talking about this morning. Most of it flew over my head.'

'You should join me in English instead,' Lisa suggested, as she took a sip from her tea.

'Or History,' Abbi threw in putting her cup down. 'I mean, no offence, but, the other night you seemed to think anyone studying Medicine or Law was weird. Well, Mathematics, erm, not exactly mainstream is it. I'll give you Spanish. It does sound exotic and exciting.'

'I like Math's,' Caitlin protested. 'At least, I did. Now, I'm not so sure. It's too hard for me.'

'Give it a chance – you've only done one day. Bet you are a brain box deep down?' Lisa encouraged, waggling her finger.

'Admit it,' Abbi said. She nudged her gently with her shoulder.

'Fair enough, I'll persevere, it's only been a day,' Caitlin admitted. She held her cup firmly within her hands and took a large gulp. As she was about to swallow, she caught sight of Steven walking past in the distance. Swallowing too fast, she started to choke.

'Slow down girl, what is it?' Lisa asked, following Caitlin's line of sight. 'Oh, now I get it. Was that Steven? Admit it; you have a thing for him?'

'The guy from last night, the lawyer? Really?' Abbi joined in, jumping up and down on her seat.

'Nothing happened. We just went to get chips.'

'YOU DID WHAT?' Lisa screamed.

'Shh,' Caitlin glowered and covered Lisa's mouth with her hand.

'Lisa!' Abbi exclaimed. 'Discretion please, it's obvious she has a crush.'

‘And that is when it’s time for me to go,’ Caitlin stated, getting her stuff ready to leave.

‘Don’t go,’ Abbi pleaded. ‘Serious, we won’t tease anymore. Will we Lisa?’

‘I’m not upset,’ Caitlin reassured, glad she had made them feel guilty for teasing her. ‘I really have to get back. I’ll catch up with you guys later, and don’t gossip behind my back.’

‘Promise,’ Lisa smiled, giving her a cheeky wink.

Making her way out of the cafeteria, she heard Sally’s pealing laughter from the distance – it sounded annoying and flirtatious. Caitlin smiled, wondering who Sally had set her sights on. As she got closer, she saw her standing next to a nice looking guy with mousey brown hair and a lanky build. Standing next to him was Steven. It was too late to turn back. Relief swept over her, as she noticed he was about to walk away. Unfortunately, Sally saw her and called out. The effect was instant as he glanced in her direction. She felt her heart skip a beat, as she saw him stop and wait.

‘Caitlin, let me introduce you. This is Adam,’ Sally blurted out. ‘And I believe you know Steven.’

‘We meet again,’ he added ominously.

‘It’s a small world,’ Caitlin remarked, hoping she would not start blushing again.

They stared in silence, until Adam spoke. ‘Are you in the same hall as Sally?’

‘Yes,’ Caitlin answered, relieved to look away from Steven.

‘Shall we go for that coffee now?’ Sally asked Adam, entwining her hand in his arm.

‘Sure,’ Adam replied. He glanced at Caitlin, then turned to face Steven and winked. ‘See you later. Have fun.’

The look Adam gave Steven was suspect. He looked like the cat that had got the cream. There was something about the way his eyes dissected Sally that she did not like. The thought did not linger as she became aware of the fact it was just the two of them again. She tensed and looked at the floor. If she looked at Steven again, she would definitely turn a deep shade of red.

‘The chips were nice last night,’ he said, as though tempting her to look in his direction.

‘Yes, they were.’ Cautiously, she glanced up. In daylight, she could not help admiring the way gold strands seemed to entwine in his irises.

'Anyway, I was just leaving,' Steven gestured with his hand.

'Oh. I guess I'll see you around then.' In a way she was relieved their encounter would be brief. Turning to face the main entrance, she realised he did the same thing. He was also going out. As they walked side by side, Steven broke the silence.

'I promise I was going this way anyway. I really am not stalking you.'

'Oh,' she replied. It was awkward but she had to see the funny side. She broke into laughter. Plucking up some courage, she added. 'I don't have any more lectures for the day so I'm heading back to Halls.'

'That's a coincidence.'

With a contented sigh, she smiled and stared into his eyes. A second later she blinked and looked away.

***

After forcing her way through a day of lectures and laboratory work, Georgina made her way back to her accommodation alone. She had actually enjoyed the first day of lectures since she did not mind the work. The course suited her perfectly. She just missed home. The sound of her lone footsteps against the pavement seemed to resonate loudly. It made her overly anxious. The fact that it was dark already, even though it was only four o'clock in the afternoon, did not help. She considered jogging back just to feel more secure. She had the uncanny suspicion she was being watched.

A set of running footsteps got louder behind her and she quickened her pace. They were getting closer. As her breathing started to sound forced, she heard a female voice call out her name and a wave of relief overcame her.

'Wait up, Georgina,' Caitlin called out, breathless.

'Sorry, I didn't know it was you,' she admitted, hanging her head down.

'We didn't mean to scare you, sorry,' Steven apologised.

'It's alright,' she said, as she noticed him behind Caitlin.

'Georgina, this is Steven.'

'You sure walk fast – I thought we'd catch up with you easily,' Steven joked.

She got the impression he was trying to put her at ease. He

seemed nice. Her first impression was usually correct. 'I like to walk fast.'

'Are you okay?' Caitlin asked.

'I'm fine,' Georgina sighed. Truthfully, she was far from fine – she was lonely and homesick.

'I've got to get back, so I'll let you catch up. See you around Caitlin,' Steven called out, as he rushed ahead.

'Looks like you made a friend. Don't worry. I won't tease you like Sally and Julia,' Georgina reassured.

'I appreciate it. He is great, but we barely know each other. So, there's nothing more to it.'

Georgina nodded.

'You sure you're okay. I'm here if you want to talk.'

'I just miss home, I guess,' Georgina admitted.

'That's understandable. I'd miss it more if it wasn't for the fact I'm enjoying being free of my baby sister's incessant moaning,' she joked, with a giggle.

In a sudden outburst, she came out with her true thoughts. 'I'd like to go home – I'm not enjoying this as much as I thought I would.'

'Oh,' Caitlin exclaimed, her lips curled down, worried. 'It's not long for Christmas, you'll be back soon.'

'I know.' She struggled against the choking sensation restricting her throat, as she held back tears.

'Hey, don't get upset, you'll be home soon. You could go back this weekend for a visit, if it's that bad.'

'I know.' A lone tear ran down her check, so she pushed her finger under her glasses and wiped it away quickly.

'What about a hot chocolate to cheer you up?' Caitlin suggested.

'Thanks – that sounds great.'

Chapter 6

Missing

The bed and table were littered with an assortment of lecture notes Caitlin was painstakingly trying to put into some order. She knew she would have to go and buy some folders soon, or she would lose track of the notes she had already taken. Seeking motivation, she stared at her favourite poster and remembered Georgina – she had not seen her recently. Even though she came across as a bit of a loner and had admitted to being homesick, it was difficult to know whether she actually wanted company. She had tried to get her to come out to socialise several times, but she constantly gave her the brush off.

Since it was only nine o'clock she put on her slippers, left her room and knocked on Georgina's door. Getting no reply, she tried again. There was no answer. Thinking it strange, she looked for her in the kitchen. There was no sign of her. As she walked in the empty bathroom, she struck out again. She was not there.

As she saw Julia coming out of her room, she headed in her direction. 'Julia, have you seen Georgina recently?'

'Now you mention it, no. I can't remember when I last saw her. But, she might be working late in the library. It does not shut until ten.'

'That's true. I was just trying to catch up with her. I'll ask Sally if she's seen her.'

'Good luck with that, we know where she is,' she guffawed, as she made her way towards the exit.

Julia was right of course, there was no reason to worry about Sally's whereabouts – they knew exactly where she was.

*

The following morning, Caitlin got up early and waited in the Kitchen to see if she could catch Georgina. Again there was no sign of her. As strange as the possibility seemed, it dawned on her from their previous conversation that she might have actually left the university. For the rest of the morning, she remained deep in thought as she wondered if she could have been a better friend to her.

In the cafeteria at lunchtime her phone bleeped and she saw it was a text from Steven. Giving a smile, she texted back to let him know where she was.

'Knew you'd be here before I'd even got your message,' he teased from behind. 'Can I join you?'

'Of course,' she replied, as she brushed her hair off her face and tucked it behind her ears.

Taking a seat opposite, he placed the palms of his hands together and twiddled his fingers in either direction before asking. 'So, you've been busy, I've barely seen you around lately, apart from your usual coffee break in the morning.'

'I have been very busy,' she confidently replied, as a huge grin spread over her face. 'In fact, there is something I have to do.'

'You always have something to do. You're like a busy bee.'

'Buzz, buzz, that's me,' she jibbed before looking straight faced. 'No, seriously, I'm worried about my flat mate. She's kind of, disappeared.'

'Really? Why do you think so?'

'She was really depressed last week, like just really homesick and stuff. And no-one has seen her.' She could not help but to pause, as she reflected on the fact that it was too easy to talk to Steven. Ignoring the thought, she added. 'I think she might have left.'

Scrunching up his face as he considered the problem. 'What are you planning to do? Do you want any help?'

'No, it's alright, but thanks. I'll go to the Biochemistry department after I finish lectures and see if anyone knows. She's probably just gone home.'

'If you're sure. I'd make an excellent chaperone.' The pleading stare nearly made her waver.

'Thank you for the offer,' she replied. With a half smile, she added, 'another time, maybe?'

'Say the word, I'll be waiting,' he said as he flashed another breathtaking smile. 'Anyway, I have some work to do, so I'm going to hit the library for my stimulating case study research.'

'Sounds like fun, all those musty books, so tempting.'

'Yes well,' he contemplated, eyebrows raised. 'Not as fun as sleuthing, but hey, keeps me out of trouble. Will I see you at training tomorrow?'

'Definitely,' she beamed.

'If your busy schedule allows, maybe you'd like to have a drink with me?'

Throwing in a light–hearted response, she added. 'I'll bring my filofax along.'

'You do that.'

As he walked away, she was sure that her heart rate had accelerated again. Something about him made her feel faint. Nevertheless, regardless of what her heart dictated, she had firmly taken control of the situation by refusing to act desperate. If there was any chance he actually liked her, then she would make him earn her affection. She had no intention of giving up her single, uncomplicated life, for a man she had only just met.

*

The afternoon dragged on, as she attended a Spanish history lecture which turned out to be extremely boring. Several students had actually fallen asleep, but the lecturer had failed to notice.

Keen to escape, she rushed off as soon as it finished. It was beginning to get dark outside and a fair wind had started to blow. It would be a nightmare if the weather turned into a torrential downpour since she had not thought to bring an umbrella. Conscience of time, she found her way to the reception area of Georgina's faculty. The hallway was deserted. She wandered aimlessly at first. It took another ten minutes of searching before she came across an open door with a small reception sign on top. She called out politely.

A woman in her thirties, that looked a bit too stressed for her liking, popped her head out from behind a computer and answered hastily. 'Yes dear, can I help you?'

'I hope so. I'm Caitlin, a first year student. I'm trying to find my roommate, Georgina May – she's also new. I have not seen her in our Halls of residence and I was worried.'

'Well, that's strange isn't it? It's not like first year students to stay somewhere else is it?' She remarked, raising her eyebrows in a suggestive manner.

'Maybe other students might choose to stay elsewhere. But trust me, Georgina is not the type. I'm sure she's missing. I just don't know whether she has left the university.'

The woman looked doubtful and sighed. 'Fair enough, I'll check to see if she has attended her tutorials this week.'

'Thank you,' Caitlin added.

After another ten minutes had passed, Caitlin was beginning to lose hope. Seated in the reception area, she gave a huge yawn, rubbed her eyes and blinked several times. It was getting late.

'Right, I'm sorry to tell you that you're right.' The woman sounded a little sheepish. 'Georgina has not attended her tutorials for the past few days. But, there's nothing to say that she had left the University. It is strange, so it's best to be cautious. I'll let the accommodation office know and I'm sure they'll send someone around shortly. You'd best run along. We'll look into it now,' she reassured, in a kinder voice.

Caitlin walked away with a sense of satisfaction at being proved correct. It was quickly overshadowed by concern. Where could Georgina have gone?

The campus was practically deserted as she walked out. The only small mercy was that it was not raining. Quickly, she zipped up her long coat and pulled the hood over her head. She walked in a steady pace. As she rounded the corner, a lone figure leaned against the light post.

'Need someone to walk with?' It was Adam.

She cringed at the way he seemed to dissect her with his eyes. But, she did not want be rude to Sally's boyfriend. 'I guess so, if you are going the same way.'

'Oh, yeah, I'm heading back too. I saw you from across the street so I thought I'd wait.'

In her head she heard herself say, 'why did you bother?' Yet, she could not do it, so she had a dig instead. 'Has Sally gone home already?'

Raising his eyebrows, he shrugged noncommittally. 'I don't know – we don't keep tabs on each other. We're not that serious.'

Perplexed, she frowned, wondering if Sally knew about their casual relationship.

'Oh, I just remembered that I have to buy something from the shop. So, I'll see you around. You don't need to wait,' she stressed firmly, as she hurried in through the door to the local shop without glancing back. Making her way to the end of the aisle, she hid behind the corner and then peaked out slowly.

She was relieved to see he had gone.

Breathing a sigh of relief, the sound of a voice behind her made her jump. Startled, she very nearly threw the neatly stacked tower of baked bean tins over.

'Calm down, it's just me,' Julia giggled. 'Who are you hiding from? You look so funny crouched behind the aisle.'

'Promise me that you will not tell Sally.'

'Okay, I will not tell Sally.' She moved closer to Caitlin and whispered. 'What will I not tell her?'

'It was Adam. I think he's creepy. He looks at me like I'm a piece of meat.'

'Maybe, he has a thing for redheads,' she laughed.

'Ha ha, you are so not funny. And don't call me a redhead, I hate that. Its strawberry blonde,' she pouted and folded her arms.

'So, are you planning to buy something or are you heading back?'

'I'm heading back. Are you coming?'

'Not yet. I just came in to get a few supplies. We've got an evening pub crawl planned. Do you fancy coming along?'

'Thanks for the offer, but you have fun. Tell me about it in the morning, if you don't have too bad a hangover that is,' she inferred, smirking.

Outside, Julia headed towards the main campus and Caitlin continued her walk back to Halls. At least there was no sign of Adam. Within twenty minutes, she arrived back. The corridor was quiet since no-one was around. On the off chance that Georgina had returned she knocked on the door, but still there was no answer. Key in hand she opened her door and dumped her bags on the floor. A minute later she headed out towards the kitchen to make some tea. As she did, she saw a woman coming in through the entrance.

***

Gladys had been working at the accommodation office in the university for ten years, and was extremely annoyed to be pulled away from her job to check on a first year student on the whim of another. She was convinced the girl in question would be fine and was probably temporarily residing in some boys' room, like they usually were these days. Once inside the corridor, she saw a sweet looking redhead staring at her. They always looked so innocent when they first arrived. She made her way towards her.

'Are you Caitlin? The girl that reported the missing student.'

'Yes.'

'Right then, well I'll have a look inside to check that nothing's wrong.' After knocking several times to check that the room was unoccupied, she put the key in the lock. Inside the room it was pitch black. Some blackout curtains had been placed over the window. A stale smell hang in the air, it made her gag involuntarily.

'Stand back dear,' Gladys warned. She had to keep Caitlin at bay. She turned the light on. She could not hold back the scream. Turning back briefly, she saw Caitlin staring in shock. 'Don't look!' In a bid to do something, she rushed over to the body to check for a pulse. It did not surprise her when she found none. She bowed her head in defeat.

The sound of Caitlin's scream forced her to get into action. Caitlin had started to hyperventilate, and had slid onto the floor of the corridor. The sound of her sobs echoed down the hall.

On the bedside table Gladys saw a note. All it said was 'sorry'. Without wanting to touch anything else, she backed out of the room and locked it with a shaky hand.

Then she put her hand on Caitlin's shoulder. 'Calm down dear. This is shocking, and very sad. I need to go and report this,' she paused and caught her breath. She fought the urge to panic; she had to stay in control. 'Don't mention what you've seen to anyone. It looks like she took her own life. We don't want her family to find out via gossip.'

'I–I won't s–say anything,' Caitlin stammered, through choking tears.

'I'll contact the police straight away. They'll probably want to talk to you. It's such a waste to bring a life short like that. It's probably best if you come with me, is that okay?'

'Yes, th–that's fine,' Caitlin faltered.

'You did the right thing.'

She put her arm under Caitlin's shoulder and helped her up. She glanced at the door she had just come through in horror and wondered why anyone would want to die so young.

Chapter 7

Rendezvous

Sally walked into the now familiar lecture Hall and kept her head low. A lot of students watched her as she sat down; they gave her weird glances she hoped would soon be a thing of the past. It was not her fault a girl had committed suicide in her corridor. Yet, everyone seemed to look at her accusingly, as though she'd actually had something to do with it. Although, she suspected it was more than that. They just wanted to know if she had any gory details to share – it was disgusting.

'Hey, gorgeous, how are you doing?' Adam said as he slid next to her and took a seat.

'You know me. Same as usual.'

'I think I can do something to help ease the tension. If you like we could slip out early, and forget the rest of the day.'

Needing the distraction, Sally leaned in and kissed him. The kiss soon got heated as his hand fumbled up her back, getting very close to her breasts.

A few voices muttered, and someone even shouted 'get a room.'

'Adam,' Sally sighed. She leaned back and pushed his hand away. 'Maybe later, I can't afford to flunk.'

'If you insist,' Adam pouted. The lost puppy look was getting old. 'I'll back down, for now. Anyway, you know it's my way of helping you to put the whole incident behind you.'

'Thanks for helping, but I'm fine. Caitlin's the one that's gone.'

'Why did she go again?' He asked, confused.

Sally grimaced, in a whisper she said, 'she saw her, you know, *dead.*' . Talking about it felt like talking about a contagious disease. 'University is supposed to be fun, now it's like, become dark – scary. It's hard enough to be away from home, let alone to have someone committing suicide.'

'I guess. At least they've put you in a new room. Which reminds me, we have not inaugurated it yet…maybe, tonight?'

'Is that all you think of?' Sally squealed, delighted and yet amazed by his needs.

'Only with you baby,' Adam teased, as he squeezed her hand.

'If it wasn't for the fact that I desperately need the distraction, I would class you as a nymphomaniac.'

'Like I said, only with you.'

Sally stared into his eyes, overcome by the desire he instilled in her. It was strange that she was always so attracted to guys that wanted action.

***

The sound of the song coming to a close, prompted Steven to grab his ipod and scroll through his selection to find a new track. As he did, he heard someone bang on his door. Even though hesitant, he opened it. Adam stood in the hallway, with one hand leaning on the door frame. He was wearing a pair of dark sunglasses, which he now pushed down his nose. 'How's it going? We're going to the bar for some drinks, fancy coming out to play?'

'I'm not in the mood for small talk right now,' Steven replied. He folded his arms across his chest and pursed his lips together.

'Look, I know it's depressing about that girl dying and all, but life goes on. Unless, you're just missing Caitlin,' Adam sneered.

'I'm not missing Caitlin,' he snapped.

'Sensitive, okay, whatever, will you come with or what?'

Reluctant, he shrugged his shoulders and grabbed his brown leather jacket. 'Sure, why not,'

The moment they walked into the bar, Steven noticed a few heads turn in their direction. It was something he was used to so he ignored the stares. Adam smiled broadly, oozing confidence, as he approached the group sat at the table.

'Hello there – we made it. Did you miss us?' Adam asked, looking directly at Sally whilst showing off his brilliant sparkly teeth. 'I had to force Steven out of his room.'

Steven did not bother to contradict him.

Julia looked directly at him, and smiled. Sadness lingered in her eyes – he had not noticed it before.

'We don't bite you know,' Grace blurted out, giving Steven a vixen like glare.

He noticed Grace wore an excessive amount of make up. It was beyond him, why some girls did that. It did not make her prettier. Purposefully, he diverted his eyes to the floor – refusing to succumb to her games. Ever since he had given her the cold shoulder by rejecting her advances, she had become the ice queen. He found it amusing that someone like her should get upset over the fact he didn't fancy her. He was sure any other bloke would be happy to receive her attentions – Adam included. He hoped he was wrong, but Adam did not strike him as the faithful type.

'I'm going for a drink. Anyone want one?' Steven asked, forcing himself to be polite.

After taking a few orders, he made his way to the bar, and waited staring into the distance. The truth was, he was worried about Caitlin – he just did not want to admit it. After being served he placed the drinks on a tray, and balanced them on one hand. With the other he took a sip from his beer. He braced himself for another laborious conversation. As he turned round, he accidentally crashed into someone, sending a few of the drinks flying up in the air. With no free hands, he watched as two glasses smashed on the floor.

'I am so sorry,' he started to say, mortified. The incident had a déjà vu feel to it.

'It's okay Steven, I shouldn't have been standing so close behind you,' the person replied. The voice was female, and she sounded confident. In a calm and composed manner, she brushed the liquid off her top, making it splatter on the floor. Steven tried to appear nonplussed, but it was difficult. He had no idea who she was, and therefore, could not understand why she had called him by name. The thought lingered as he turned to place the tray back on the bar and was handed a pan and brush to scoop the glass.

'You made it, you clear it,' the girl behind the bar shouted with a scowl.

'Sure, no problem,' he replied.

Before he bent down to clear the mess, he found himself staring at her features. Long straight blond hair hung over her chest. A pair of emerald coloured eyes twinkled cheekily at him. Her tight, knee length leggings, and the now wet, skimpy t–shirt clung to her frame leaving little to the imagination. Lowering his head, he stopped looking and got to the task at hand. After passing the pan and brush back over the counter, he turned to her again. She was still there, watching him.

'Sorry and you are?' He asked. He had not had the chance to ask.

'I'm Ingrid.'

A vague memory surfaced. He was sure he had seen her before. Unable to place the occasion, he asked. 'I don't mean to sound rude, especially after spilling the drinks on you, but how do you know me? I think I might have seen you a few weeks back, but I'm sure I never talked to you.'

'I don't know you,' she answered, her right hand on her hip.

'If you don't know me, then why did you just say my name?'

'I heard your friend out there mention it. Where I come from, we always use Christian names if we know them.'

'Right, that would explain it.' He remained unconvinced.

'Are you a first year student?' She asked. She took her hand off her hip and clasped her hands together. It was a girlie pose.

'I am.' He could not help being curious about who she was. She was not the usual type he saw around here. 'Are you?'

'No, I'm not a student at all. I'm just visiting a friend.'

That explained why he did not think she was a student.

'Right,' he paused. 'Sorry for getting you wet. I have to go and top up these drinks. I might see you around.'

'Sure, I'll look for you,' she replied. He was sure she batted her eyelids. He was used to girls flirting with him, yet the simple gesture, unsettled him.

After he had restocked, he turned carefully holding the tray with both hands. A casual glance, revealed Ingrid chatting to another bombshell at a table nearby. There was more than one.

'What took you so long Steven, did you get lost? Grace teased, as he placed the tray on the table.

'Mind your own business,' he snapped back. He resisted the urge to show her the finger. He was not in the mood for her antics.

'Someone a bit sensitive today? You know, its women that are supposed to suffer from P.M.T.,' she cackled.

Something about her, really reminded him of a wicked witch. Giving her a look of death, he sarcastically added. 'Thanks for the drink, Steven.' Then he took his drink and made his way over to the pool table. He did not have to be there.

As he leant against the wall watching other students play, a friendly face came up to him.

'Do you want some company?' Ingrid asked, her voice husky, tempting.

'Sure,' he answered. Her proximity unnerved him.

'So, seeing as you are not with your friends anymore, would you like to go for a walk with me?'

Even though he liked Caitlin, nothing had actually happened between them. He could think of no reason to refuse. 'Why not, I could use some air?'

As they were leaving the student bar, Steven caught Adam's eye. Adam grinned from ear to ear, giving him enthusiastic thumbs up.

'What's your hall's of residence like?' Ingrid asked. She was definitely batting her eyelashes.

'Would you like me to show you? I can even make you a cup of tea, if you like?'

'I'd love that,' she beamed.

'Okay.' He was sure all she wanted was to see where he was staying. Surely, nothing more.

After a few minutes, they walked in through the ground floor corridor and he led her to the kitchen. 'So what would you like, tea or coffee?'

'What's your room like?' She asked, as she twirled a strand of her hair between her fingers.

Stumped, he stalled. 'I can show you. Shall I make the drinks first?'

'We can come back for the drinks, show me your room,' she pleaded, giving a little pout. 'I'd like to see what a man's room is like.'

The fact that she'd called him a man was flattering. 'Okay, why not!' It was confusing. Surely, all she wanted was to see the room.

'Ladies first,' he said, opening the door to let her in.

Standing at the entrance, she placed her hands on her hips, and surveyed the surroundings. 'Basic, I like it. But, the walls are too bare. I like it when there are posters up. You need some,' she stated, as she went to look at the books on the table. Picking up a huge book on Contract Law, she smiled. 'This is heavy – do you use it for weight training?'

'It's not a bad idea,' he laughed, as he walked towards her. 'So, do you want that drink now?'

‘In a minute,’ she sighed, as she moved towards the door. Eyes fixed on his; she closed the door shut and walked slowly towards him. ‘I really like you.’

Before he got the chance to answer she thrust her lips onto his. Even though taken aback by her forwardness, he could do nothing to stop himself from responding. As she kissed him, she slowly made her way towards his throat. His nerve endings reacted, causing him to groan aloud.

Chapter 8

Confusion

The relentless sound of his alarm clock persisted. With a grunt, Steven pushed it off the bedside table. It crashed on the floor – still ringing. Annoyed, he moved to turn it off. Shaking his head, he rubbed his eyes hard and stared into space. The last thing he recalled was kissing Ingrid. He could not remember anything else. They were kissing and then – nothing. Glancing at his clock, he stared in disbelief, as he realised that it was already nine o'clock in the morning.

He was going to be late.

Throwing his legs over the side of the bed, he jerked up. His head spun and he collapsed back on to his bed. He was sure he'd only had one drink. Slowly, but surely, he made another attempt. Even though woozy, he could stand. Something told him, today was not destined to be a good day.

Half an hour later, he was rushing down the street to get to his lecture with a piece of hastily buttered toast in hand. He could have easily turned back and returned to the comfort of his bed, but he had to hand in his first assignment and he did not want to suffer a penalty for tardiness. Ten minutes late, he opened the door to the lecture hall and snuck in the back taking a seat next to Adam.

'Where have you been? Did you get lucky with the hot blonde last night?' Adam whispered in his ear.

'I don't know, I can't remember.'

'Wow, I've heard of being knackered, but that sounds amazing. An all-nighter!'

'I can't remember, so how could I have had an all-nighter, you idiot!' Steven grumbled.

'I just read it as I see it man, that's all.'

'Whatever,' he exclaimed, giving up on obtaining any chance of sympathy.

'Sensitive, if it's any consolation, you look like shit.'

'Thanks a lot, its good to know who my friends are. With friends like you, who needs enemies?'

'Give me your assignment, I'll hand it in for you. Then beat it, you need to go and recover from whatever you did last night. I say no more.'

'You're a pal after all.' Slipping his hand into his rucksack he took out the plastic wallet with the essay, and gave it to Adam. Then he snuck out again. He crouched down as low as he could to avoid being spotted.

At the end of University road he turned to the right to get back to his accommodation. Stopping dead in his tracks, he saw Ingrid standing completely still, like a statue. Breaking the illusion, she lifted her hand and waved. It looked like she was waiting for someone. She was only wearing a thin, long sleeved top and a pair of cut off jeans. It struck him as odd. The weather had turned. It was now even more bitter and cold.

'Steven, it's nice to see you,' Ingrid said. She gave him a beaming smile. It was a nice smile; he had to give her that. She had the most perfect teeth.

'Can I talk to you for a minute, or do you have to be somewhere?' He did not know if it was his imagination, but something about their meeting felt premeditated.

'Do you want to go and grab a drink?' She asked, her hand following the direction of the coffee shop.

'Why not,' he paused. 'Aren't you cold?'

'It's not that cold. I've experienced worse.'

How was he supposed to know what she was used to?

Inside, they headed straight for the counter. A dazed teenager looked up from behind the glass display. Transfixed by Ingrid, the boy looked up and gave a broad smile, revealing a set of braces. 'What can I get you?'

The question was directed at Ingrid, but Steven answered. 'I'll have the bacon bun, with a latte. What would you like?'

'I don't know,' she paused, twirling her hair around her index finger. She studied the menu on the board.

The boy continued to stare.

Making her mind up, she added. 'I'll have an orange juice.'

'No problem, coming right up.'

Handing over the money, Steven paid.

'Thanks,' Ingrid said, with a half smile.

'If you sit down, I'll bring it over,' the boy said. His cheeks blushed, as he turned away to get the order ready. It was obvious he could not keep his eyes off Ingrid.

Steven thought the boy's reaction was amusing. It was unfair to call him a boy; he was only a couple of years younger.

'So, are you from England?' She asked, as he sat down opposite her.

'Born and bred. You're not though, are you?'

'No, my accent gives me away. I'm from Sweden, but my family moved to England for my Dad's job.'

'That explains that.' From what he knew it was cold in Norway during the winter, so at least that explained her attire. Wracking his brain, he tried to figure out how to ask about the previous night.

Breaking the silence, the boy brought the order over and placed it on the table. 'Enjoy,' he remarked, glaring at Ingrid again. For a few seconds he stopped, before shaking his head in embarrassment and shuffling off.

Ingrid lifted her glass up to his and made a toast. 'Cheers!'

'Yes, cheers.'

She took a sip from her juice and surveyed him from the rim of her glass. 'How old are you?' Her intense green eyes seemed huge, dazzling.

'That's direct, how old are you?'

'I'm twenty,' she answered immediately.

'Fair enough, I'll be nineteen in September.'

Pausing for a split second, she took another sip from her drink. 'Are your parents from here?'

'My dad is, but my step-mum is Spanish.'

'Really, is your dad divorced then?'

Amazed by her interrogation, he paused and glared.

'I'm sorry, am I asking too many questions?' She apologised.

'It's okay. My dad never married my real mother. She left us when I was young.'

Ingrid's eyes seemed to come alight when he revealed that piece of information. 'But, you're okay about it now, right?'

'I didn't have a choice, did I?'

'I guess not.'

Finally, Steven plucked up some courage. 'What happened last night?'

Looking perplexed, she stared at him. 'What do you mean?'

'We were kissing and then I woke up. Did anything happen?'

'You must be hallucinating. You split your drink on me and then I did not see you again, until now,' she laughed.

'Really, that's weird. I'm sure you came back to my halls of residence,' he shook his head in confusion.

'But, if you'd like me to kiss you and come back to your room, I'd be happy to oblige,' she teased, interrupting his line of thought.

'Erm, it's okay. Thanks for offering.' For once, he wished he was not so damn polite – she was definitely lying. After putting a few squirts of ketchup on his bacon bun, he took a large bite. He was starving. Barely getting the first bite down, he took another larger mouthful.

'Don't let the dust settle,' she giggled.

'Yeah, I don't know what's up with me this morning. I feel weird.'

'It happens. You know when you start to make things up; it indicates the first signs of madness.'

'You have a sense of humour for a Norwegian,' he scoffed.

'I have to go, but I'll see you around,' Ingrid said. Downing her juice, she got up and made to go.

'Okay then, I'll see you.' As he watched her leave, he could not help admiring her form.

The boy came up to clear the table as Steven picked up a local newspaper left on the rack.

'Is she your girlfriend?' He asked in awe.

'No.'

The boy's face came alight and he whistled off carrying the dishes.

Steven appreciated the fact Ingrid was attractive. He just did not know why he could not trust her. It could have been a dream. The problem was it felt real.

Casually, he flicked through the pages. There was nothing much of interest, other than the usual advertisements and local stories. A sports article showed how the athletes had faired at their latest meet. Everyone looked so pleased with themselves in the picture. He remembered the countless swimming competitions he had taken part in. It had been a long time since he had taken to the water. There was nothing like swimming up and down a pool to drown out annoying ideas.

As he was about to put the paper down, an article on the front page jumped out at him. The heading read 'teen suicide was tragic and avoidable.' Usually, he did not read articles about death, especially not when the person that had died was close to his age. However, he was drawn to read it. The death of Georgina still lingered on his mind. The article revealed that the suicide victim was a boy, aged seventeen. He had been found lifeless in his room, after an apparent drug overdose. All he had left behind was a note saying 'sorry.' Pushing the newspaper aside, he stared at the floor annoyed. It was just a sad story of another wasted life.

*

Steven paced up and down his bedroom, in dire need of a distraction. Making his decision, he packed a small rucksack with a towel, swimsuit and goggles and jogged back to campus.

It was time to burn off some energy.

Luckily, the University had its own swimming pool in the Jubilee Sport Centre. The pool was not busy since it was approaching tea time. A total of five people graced it with their presence, two of which happened to be in the fast lane. From the way they were swimming, he had no doubt they would not be in that lane for long. He could easily overtake them. He walked up to the deep end and dived in gracefully before storming ahead. In no time at all, he managed to catch up with one of the swimmers. After five minutes he eased into his stroke and relaxed as his anxieties disappeared.

All he could think of was speed.

***

The lifeguard had been working at the leisure centre for a month. She was getting tired of watching the water for the looming accident and had been practicing a gaze that wouldn't make her look totally gormless. Looking out for talent was the only thing that kept her awake on most evenings. She was pleasantly surprised to see Steven striding out of the changing room and dive into the pool. Finally, something worth her while.

A scenario popped in her mind. He might ask her on a date.

Dreaming was free.

After watching him go up and down the lanes a lot of times she started to lose interest. Finally, he stopped and climbed up the side of the pool to leave. She stared in shock as she wondered what *that* was. As a matter of caution, she hopped off the seat and walked over.

'Hi, sorry to bother you, but I think you should get that checked out. I thought you were bleeding from the distance,' she explained, pointing at his neck.

Putting his hand to his neck, he turned his head to get a better look. There was no way he could see from that angle.

'Thanks, I'll check it out now,' he said, rushing in the direction of the men's changing room.

Resuming her position, at the side of the pool, she wondered what that strange mark was. She could have sworn it looked like some sort of love bite. She gave a sly smile as she wondered who the lucky girl had been.

***

Paranoid, Steven checked the changing room for occupancy before making his way over to the mirror. Words failed him. He had a red wound on his neck, just below his ear. Getting closer he noticed that the edge of the mark was purplish. It looked like a bruise. It reminded him of the effect left on his arm when he had donated blood months earlier. Moving closer, he noticed two tiny pinprick points. Shivers run down his spine as he recoiled in horror. It looked like a bite mark – the kind of bite mark normally associated with vampires.

Why would he think of vampires?

As far as he was concerned it was just a gory story, something made up to explain the macabre. Or, something to make children laugh – he always liked watching Scooby Doo. Yet, the marks – they looked remarkably familiar. Creative make up used to convey the perfect movie scene. Only, this was not a movie. The marks were real. And they were on his neck.

Chapter 9

Revelations

The street was practically deserted as he made his way back to Halls. The eerie silence did nothing to settle his mood. Ingrid had lied. She was the only person who had got close enough to give him a bite of any sort. Even though she claimed they had not been together, Steven was convinced she was holding something back. His dreams were never that vivid. He lifted his head to cross the road and saw her. He stopped dead in his tracks. Ingrid was coming out of the shop carrying a plastic bag full of what he assumed was groceries. She looked at him and smiled. After checking it was safe to cross, he made his way over. She watched and waited.

'Ingrid,' he said. He adopted a casual tone, he had to act normal.

'Steven, it's nice to see you. Have you been working out or something?' she asked, pointing at his wet hair and towel he had strategically placed around his neck.

'I've just been swimming to get my mind off things.' He paused, then added in a serious tone. 'We need to talk.'

'Again? I am popular today,' she scoffed.

'I think you left a few things out earlier,' he said, his right hand in a fist on the rucksack straps.

'Okay then,' she replied as she shrugged. He could not believe she looked surprised. 'I'll walk with you. I'm not in a hurry to get back.'

The words tumbled out of his mouth. 'Did you give me a love bite last night? If you want me to refresh your memory, look at this.' Pushing the towel aside, he revealed the mark. 'I just want to know what happened.'

Ingrid gave a hysterical laugh. 'Nothing happened with us. I didn't do that. Whatever it is, it looks like you got lucky with someone else.'

Steven felt his free hand go into a fist. Through clenched teeth he spat out the accusation. 'Don't lie to me. I remember us kissing. You went towards my neck before I blacked out. It was you.' He grabbed her hands and searched in her eyes. He could see her eyes flinch, he had caught her off guard.

'Let me go,' Ingrid said, her voice powerful and in command, if slightly irritated. She shook her wrists out of his grip and gave him a firm push.

Steven landed on his backside with a thud. It hurt. She was very strong – too strong.

'Who are you?' He asked. He looked up and tried to make eye contact. With the street lighting he could only make out her silhouette. Her profile was not attractive anymore. It was scary – even for him.

In a deep voice, she calmly replied. 'If I answer your question it will change your life. You should forget the mark, *for now*.'

The words sunk in gradually. He did not want to maintain the weaker ground, so he got up quickly. At least he was taller than her. It gave him *some* comfort. 'What exactly do you mean by for now? And do you mind letting me in on how you are so strong?'

For the first time he heard her waver. 'I can't explain anything logically to you.'

Just then he felt his energy levels drop as he lost his balance for a second. He straightened up. It could have been the swim. He was dehydrated and hungry. Or, perhaps it was the general frustration he felt. She was making no sense at all. 'Look, I don't know what you're talking about and I'm just too tired and hungry to try to figure it out. When you want to tell me the truth come and find me.'

Mustering every ounce of energy he had left, he broke into a run. After a few minutes, it became a steady jog. He had to get away from her. He had to get back to the comfort of his room. The cold evening air on his face brought some sanity back to his state of mind. He slowed down further and maintained a steady walking pace. The voice ahead of him made his hairs stand on end.

'Are you avoiding me now?' Ingrid stated, her tone assertive, threatening. She was leaning against the tree in front of him with her arms folded across her chest. The grocery bag was nowhere in sight.

'What would you say if I *was* responsible for the bite mark?' Her head was cocked to the side, a genuine smile on her face.

Steven stopped and watched her, unsure on what to say. He could not figure out how she was ahead of him. He had not heard her go past. ‘So, do you acknowledge it is a bite mark then? Are you are going to answer my questions honestly from now on?’

‘I can’t make any promises.’

Steven frowned. He was beginning to think that getting a straight answer out of Ingrid was like turning water into wine. ‘Did you do something to make me to pass out? Yes or no, it's a simple question.’

She stared into his eyes and nodded. It was a piercing look that made the hairs on the back of his neck stand up.

Reticent, he asked. ‘What exactly did you do?’

‘What do you think I did?’ She challenged.

Again, allusive. Just when he thought she was about to open up. ‘Stupid as it sounds, the mark would make me guess that…you were trying to drink my blood. But, that's just ridiculous, isn't it?’

‘Yes, ridiculous, isn’t it?’ Ingrid repeated, parrot fashion.

‘What is it that you’re not telling me?’ He sighed, he was losing patience again.

She looked away and glanced at the cars going by, lost in thought. A long minute later, she said. ‘I can not do anything to harm you. The mark must have been an accident.’

‘Wait a minute, does that mean that you would have done something to me, but you couldn’t? Can you cut to the chase and just tell me already?’

Irritated, she flicked her head back to face him. ‘I can’t tell you anything that I don’t understand myself.’

‘Fine,’ he muttered. He wondered where to go from here. His short time studying law had made him appreciate that if she was a key witness he’d have a hard time getting anything out of her. ‘Okay, time for a direct question. Did you bite me?’

She held out her hands. ‘Why does it matter? No harm was done.’

The suspense was killing. He raised his voice. ‘I’m just trying to find out who the hell you are. At the moment you’re making no sense at all.’

‘Let’s just say that I’m not like everyone else and keep it at that. I’m sorry that I’ve confused you. You really have to let this go,’ she reiterated, the Cheshire grin back on her blemish free face. Even though he imagined most men would faint at her feet, he was not under her spell. Her expression was completely insincere. She was doing nothing to win him over.

He lowered his tone and took a deep breath. 'Are you normal?'

'Me, normal, never,' she cackled.

He had no idea if she was joking. His shoulder slumped. 'Seriously, who are you?'

'You know that already, I'm just Ingrid.'

'Fine, you want to play it like that. Okay, so answer me this. Do you know me from somewhere? I can't help feeling like the reason I bumped into you was not an accident.'

'I have never met you before in my life,' she replied, a half smile on her face. An amused twinkle in her eye.

Just then it hit him. She might know something about him, something about his past. Why had he not seen it before? She had even known his name. 'But you know something about me don't you.'

'Not really, but something about you is familiar. I have to admit that. But honestly, I don't know why you are familiar to me.'

She sounded truthful. 'What is it? That makes me familiar.'

'Look, who cares if I tell you,' she said. 'You remind me of someone from where I come from. And the truth is we have something in common. Something that makes us different to other people.'

He was not sure if he wanted to know what she was talking about. For all he knew, she could be crazy. 'What is it?' His voice sceptical.

'I can't tell you,' she admitted, looking at the floor.

For that fleeting moment, she looked vulnerable. At last, her defenses were starting to crack.

'So let me ask something even more insane – are you, or *we* according to you, even human?'

Choking involuntarily, she laughed. 'Of course we're human.'

He relaxed his shoulders and then tensed again as she added, 'mainly.' The cheeky smile was back again. Ingrid was the most annoying person, or whatever she was, he had ever met.

'What does that mean?' He grunted, now pacing up and down.

'I know if I tell you that I did bite you that you'll think I'm something stupid like a vampire – who I'm not. Look, I give up. I never lie to our own. The truth is that I wanted human blood.'

'Be serious,' he gasped, as his jaw slackened. In a quiet voice he asked. 'So what are you then?'

They way she stood tall, remaining calm and collected, was starting to get on his nerves. The answer she gave did nothing to put him at ease. 'Look, a lot of stories have been written and it makes it hard to explain. The point is surely you don't believe in vampires do you?'

He laughed aloud, nervous. 'Not usually, but these circumstances make me use my imagination. Look, if it was human blood you were after, what was wrong with mine?'

'Your blood was no good for me.'

'Why?'

'You don't have normal human blood.'

'This gets more ridiculous by the minute. So what do I have, alien blood?'

'No, it's like mine.'

'What the…what does that mean?' He run his hand along his head and scratched his head, his pacing still frantic. Just then, he froze, and narrowed his eyes to face her again. 'Is that why you said that you never lie to our own, am I related to you?'

'I can't explain it now.'

'You are so infuriating. Tell me!' He shouted. As she remained still, refusing to retaliate, he added in a softer voice. 'And you say you are not a vampire?'

'No, I am not a creature of the night. And neither are you. Look, I can't tell you any more, just that we are different to other people and I don't know why you don't know anything about it.' She paused. Then she talked aloud, lost in her own thoughts. 'I have to try and find out. I'm sorry to have started you on a path that leads nowhere. If I can answer your questions, I'll come and find you. But, I can answer your last question. Of one thing I am certain, we are not related.'

In a split second, she got within breathing distance and kissed him on the lips with force. Too shocked to react he closed his eyes and remained still, fixed to the spot. When he opened them again she was gone.

'Ingrid,' he hollered. No-one replied.

His head pounded with questions that could not be answered logically. As much as he didn't want to know about his past, he realised that perhaps it was the only way to get some answers. Maybe, his biological mother left for a valid reason after all. Perhaps, he should try to find out about his real mother. His dad never talked about her, and he had no pictures or evidence to show she even existed. As far as he knew, she vanished. Ingrid had opened a can of worms. He just could not figure out if it was all in *her* imagination.

Of one thing he was certain, looking into the past had consequences. He did not want to hurt his dad, yet he did not want to remain in the dark. He was caught in a catch 22 situation. It was easier to believe Ingrid was insane. Unfortunately, his logical mind had picked up a few things that were not normal. Her strength, her speed, her beauty. She was not what he called run of the mill. And if she had said the truth, neither was he.

Chapter 10

Emily

It was hard for someone like Anna. All of her life she lived as a pair. Even though she had her own life, a husband she loved, her children – all of which her sister, Emily, had none – she never stopped being a twin. She hated being identical. Looks were nothing to go on. They had totally different personalities. Emily insisted on bending the rules – all the time. If what she had heard was true, this time her sister had gone too far. Yet, even though she knew her sister was going to be in a lot of trouble, it was inconsequential. She would be compelled to help her again.

She blamed herself.

In hindsight, it was obvious Emily had been hiding something. There was no other reason for her disappearance all those years ago. Still, she found it hard to believe her sister had actually hidden a son. A son conceived with a normal human being. It was a ludicrous notion. What had Emily been thinking? How could she be so irresponsible? Emily always managed to bypass rules, it was inbuilt. Either way, even for her this situation went too far. She had endangered them all by being so incredibly reckless.

Tucking her short black hair behind her ears, Anna braced herself. She approached the door and took a deep breath to calm down. Closing her hand into a fist, she knocked and waited.

'Anna, I'm so glad to see you,' Emily sighed, the picture of melodrama. She threw the door open and gave her sister an embrace.

'Emily, what have you done now? What's going on?' Anna asked, easing back and folding her arms over her chest.

Emily turned and walked away. It was a manoeuvre Anna recognised well. She always did that when she did not want Anna to see her expression. 'Has Ian been talking to you already?'

'You know he has.'

'So, what did he say?'

'I don't think so,' Anna shook her head. 'You first.'

Emily continued to study the wall. 'I guess he told you they found a boy like us in England.'

'Yes, to be accurate, a boy in his late teens.'

'Nineteen years in age.'

It was time to cut to the chase. 'Coincidence, or not?'

Emily turned around, her eyes glazed. 'Not, unfortunately not.'

Throwing her arms up in despair, Anna shrieked. 'For goodness sakes, Emily. What were you thinking? You conceived a son with a human.'

'I didn't do it on purpose,' Emily pouted. She always did that when she did something wrong.

'Some accident. Ian knows the boy is yours. Let's face it you're the only one that disappeared twenty years ago. Slight giveaway.'

'You have to help me,' Emily pleaded, rushing towards her and grabbing her hand. 'I don't want them to bring him here. Ingrid could have…she could have made a mistake. What if she changed her story?'

'Why would she do that?' Anna suspected she had something up her sleeve.

'She always listens to you.'

'Me, what does that have to…hang on a minute. You want me to lie for you? Is that your grand plan? Please tell me you can do better than that.' Anna gulped, backing away whilst slipping her hand out of Emily's grasp.

'No, no. You don't have to lie. I will do it.'

'Lying is one of your specialties,' Anna grunted as she rolled her eyes. She took a seat on the corner chair. The request for a favour was coming up. 'What do you have in mind?'

'I–I was thinking, if–if you cover for me, I can pretend to be you and go to talk to Ingrid,' Emily stammered, as she eased closer. Her eyes were wild, desperate. 'You have to do this for me. I know I should have told you more years ago. Truth is – I was scared. You know they won't let me leave again. Please you have to help me – you're my twin sister!'

Anna got up and paced up and down the room, mulling it over. 'This is dangerous and risky. You know I want to help you. If I do, you must promise me that you will return and not do anything stupid. If you don't come back, I will suffer the consequences,' she hissed, shaking her head. Emily had let her down before.

'You can cover for me. You know we can look identical. I just have to cut my hair to look like yours,' Emily squared up in front of Anna and put her hands on her shoulders. 'This is my problem. I have to fix it before it gets out of hand. He is my son after all. We have to put Ian off the scent,' she stressed, determined.

Anna noted the use of the word we. Now she was in on it. 'So, will you bring him back home?' Anna asked, eyes narrowed.

Emily walked away and took a seat. With a sigh, she added. 'I don't know if he will want to come here. I have no idea what he's like. I'll try, but I would not blame him if he said no. I would say no, if I'd had the chance.'

'If Ingrid could not kill him, the chances are that he is one of us, so he has no choice. He has to come. You know that don't you?'

'I know, I know.' Ruffling her hair with an exasperated look, Emily continued. 'Look, I don't want to take him away from his life yet, he still has some time left before the change. I'll figure out what to do.'

'It's not a question of figuring it out. The time has come, he needs to be prepared. He has to come here with us.'

'Okay, okay, I'll bring him back,' Emily surrendered, her hands raised. 'You're the best sister in the world you know that.'

'Yes, well. Someday, it might be reciprocated,' Anna said. It annoyed her. She was so weak. She would go to the moon and back to help Emily have a better life.

***

Emily sat in the Taxi on the M3 in high spirits. London Heathrow had been manic, now she had some time to reflect.

Today she would see her son again. The journey had been long. All she could do was hope it was not too late. The sound of a dance song belted out from the radio station. With a strong beat and pounding bass, the sound made her want to dance. It was liberating to be free again. Away from the restraints they imposed upon her. If circumstances were different, she would now be looking back on her past, surrounded by children, grandchildren and possibly even great grand children.

What a dream!

Then again, for all she knew, she would be dead by now, having lived a lonely and meaningless existence. She still found it hard to believe that in real time she was eighty nine years old – she did not look older than twenty. Emily was convinced her life was nothing but a sick joke. All she could do was to try and figure out the best way forward.

It was unfortunate Ingrid stumbled upon Steven. She never expected his father, Paul, to stay in Southampton. The last time she had checked they lived in a different place. Unless, Steven was the one who had returned by choosing to study in Southampton. That would be a strange coincidence. It was not that she had forgotten about Steven, but she had lost track of time. It was easier to ignore the fact that he was going to be twenty soon. Reaching that age would change everything.

A thought did cross her mind – if she failed to return, they would never find her. She could go anywhere in the world. She brushed the thought aside and focused. She had promised her sister she would return. The thought of letting her down again was not something she could contemplate. It was time to grow up.

As the car entered Southampton, via the A33, the Satellite navigation system tracked down the destination. A further twenty minutes followed through windy roads, surrounded by beautiful countryside. Finally, a majestic house perched securely on the steep hill came into view. The house looked old now, but it was a reasonable size, with a large driveway and a few acres of land. They had been careful to ensure no developments occurred close by.

'Stop here,' Emily shouted, at the car reached the bottom of the hill.

'I don't mind going up to the top,' the driver called back, in a cockney accent.

'Don't go to the top,' she insisted.

'Alright lady,' he huffed, pulling over to the side.

'Here is the fare,' she said as she handed over two fifty pound notes. 'Keep the change.'

'Great, thanks a lot,' he replied, his eyes wide, excited.

When she started to get out of the car, Emily hesitated for a moment. It would be so easy to give in to temptation. She needed some energy. She just could not afford to drop her guard here. With as much control as she could muster, she walked up the hill and did not look back as she heard the sound of the engine fade away. Reminding herself of Anna's traits and habits, she made her way up to the front door. Even though it had no bell to announce her, she knew they would already sense her presence.

As the door flew open, Ingrid held up her hands. A huge grin spread across her face. 'Anna, it's great to see you. You just could not keep away, could you?'

A wave of relief swept over Emily as she realised she had managed to fool Ingrid with her altered appearance. 'Ingrid, I hear your trip is proving eventful. You have to tell me all about it, but first, I'd love a cup of English tea,' she added, knowing Anna loved tea.

'Of course, come in, they'll all love to see you. I guess you heard about what happened?'

'Yes, let's talk about it inside.'

The house had a grand hallway, leading to a large winding staircase. A beautifully framed mirror hung in the corridor giving the illusion of depth and space. Next to the staircase, the hallway led to a series of rooms. Emily followed Ingrid to the heart of the house where the kitchen was housed. It had a massive Aga, surrounded by beautifully hand crafted oak worktops and matching cupboards. As the kettle boiled, Emily reflected on the last time she had stayed in the house. Back then, she had been so carefree and reckless. When she met Paul she did not hesitate at the chance to start a new life.

'Are you here to tell us about Steven?' Ingrid asked, pouring the hot water for the tea.

The sound of her son's name made her wince. Fighting hard to keep it together, she casually added. 'Kind of, do you have any sugar?'

'Of course, would you like one or two?'

Even though she hated sugar, she knew Anna had a sweet tooth. 'Two please, got to have a few vices in life.'

'Always the same Anna, have you attacked one of the bakeries yet and bought your favourite jam doughnuts?'

'Thank you for reminding me.' Emily cringed internally – the thought of eating anything that sugar coated made her feel sick.

Just then, a brunette with thick curly hair entered the kitchen and embraced Emily. 'Anna, I'm so glad you came.'

Emily hugged her back, knowing that Anna would have done the same. 'Good to see you too, Lana.' Anna was married to Lana's brother Juan, and they had always been close, so she had to keep up the façade.

'It's good to see you too, but, before the others come, I need to discuss something with you privately.' She was not used to having people like her, as they did Anna, so she was conscious of her need for an expeditious escape. If she was not careful, she would give herself away with uncharacteristic actions. It was prudent to just get down to business.

'Ingrid has fraternised with a human that is under my protection. I am sure she is aware he is like us. Otherwise, he would have died when she attacked him. I know this is a lot to ask, but,' she hesitated. 'This is going to sound terrible, but, I need you to tell Ian you made a mistake. If anyone finds out he exists, you will put his life in danger. I can't tell you more, but you need to trust me. If you want to talk about this, I must insist that you come and see me, and only me.'

She knew she was pushing it – she had no choice.

Ingrid and Lana glanced at each other.

'That's a lot to take in Anna. What exactly do you want us to do?' Lana asked.

'Steven needs to believe this is all a hoax. Ingrid you will tell him you were set up to scare him, say it was all a sick joke. He must believe you. Tell him whatever he needs to hear.'

'I think I can do that, but,' Ingrid protested. 'What if he does not listen?'

'Make sure he does,' she snapped, before changing the conversation briskly. 'When are you all due to go back home?'

Lana glanced at Ingrid for a fraction of a second. Emily started to panic. They did not like her tone. She would have to relax.

'We are planning to go back tomorrow,' Lana replied.

'Right, well. We better get a move on,' she smiled. 'Sorry, if I'm stressed out. This situation is, well, difficult.' Emily shrugged her shoulders, trying to act normal.

'That's a novel way to look at it,' Ingrid guffawed.

'Ingrid, you have to come with me. I need to grab some of those jam doughnuts,' Emily joked, attempting to sound at ease. 'I'll bring her back soon, so that we can all leave together.'

Before she could refuse, Ingrid's father, Eilif, walked in. 'Have you solved the mystery?'

Emily held back the urge to reply in anger. Instead, she adopted her most soothing voice, twirling a strand of her hair in her finger. 'There is no mystery. The boy means nothing. I've checked him out and Ingrid made a mistake. Something else must have gone wrong.'

'Ingrid, is this true?' He seemed surprised at the revelation.

Emily held her breath. She needed Ingrid and Lana to play ball.

'If Anna thinks so, then I must have made a mistake. Maybe, I–I just could not kill him for another strange reason,' she chuckled, uneasily.

Eilif laughed aloud and gave his daughter a hug. 'Don't be silly, I rarely ever kill any humans either. I'm glad to know I'm not the only one in the family that likes to stop.'

Emily shuddered internally – she had never been able to restrain herself from killing once she had started. Perhaps, she was the monster.

Chapter 11

The Cover Up

It had been one of those nights. A lot of tossing, turning, lying awake, going to the toilet, having a drink of water. Everything, but sleep. When Steven finally dozed off it was practically time to wake up. His head throbbed as he turned off the alarm. Woozy, he made his way to the small window and looked out. It was still dark, yet the street light gave sufficient light to make out the puddles. Rain – lots of it. It was tempting to get back into bed, but he did not intend to flunk. The clock read eight o'clock in the morning. He had to get a move on, his lecture started at nine. He could have skipped the first one, convinced no-one would even notice his absence. Unfortunately, boarding school had drummed routine into his core.

Shuffling over to his ensuite bathroom, he scratched his head and yawned. Raising his chin, he brushed his hand over his stubble – he would shave today. After applying the shaving foam and easing his razor across his neck, he rinsed the razor in the lukewarm water in the sink. As he lifted the razor to continue, he came face to face with the mark. It had faded to a dull purple colour, but it was still there. Shaking his head he finished the job and applied some after shave cream. Life moved on.

Wearing a black cap and his zipped up brown leather jacket he strode down the road leading to the University campus. Avoiding the puddles, his shoulders drooped. There was nothing he loathed more than rain. Forcing his way through the onslaught, he froze on the spot as Ingrid chimed next to him.

'Good morning, Steven.'

'Oh, it's you,' he groaned.

'I came to apologise.'

'What are you sorry for?' He snapped. 'Is it the fact that you kiss me and always leave, or that you tell fanciful stories?'

'Both,' she admitted, dropping her hands against her sides.

Even though it was raining hard, he had to stop to face her. 'What on earth are you talking about now?'

'I haven't been straight with you.' She curled a wet strand of hair in her hand. 'I honestly don't know how you made the wound on your neck. I was not trying to drink your blood. It was just a wind up. I thought it was funny when you started talking about vampires and stuff – as if, right? I'm heading back home now since our holiday is over, so you won't see me again. I'm sorry if I upset you,' she stated. She sounded like she meant it, even though alarm bells rang in his head.

Steven shook his head in disbelief. 'Great, your conscience is clear. So, it was all just a story,' he laughed aloud, as he folded his arms in a defensive position.

'Yes, it was all a story. Goodbye, and sorry again,' she muttered, as she turned to leave. The look on her face was sad and confused. Something made him want to call to her to comfort her, but he resisted the urge. She was sick in the head. What kind of weirdo would make up such a lie? He continued on his route. Not once did he turn round to check she was gone. Ingrid was history. It was over.

***

Ingrid made her way to the seat opposite Anna. She had done what had been asked of her. That did not mean she was happy about it. Something continued to niggle. She just could not put her finger on what it was.

'Coffee can have such an incredible taste. It's amazing how you can get it so wrong,' Emily gestured to her mug and shook her head in disgust. 'There are definitely some things that are not worth experiencing. And others that are – don't you think?'

'I guess,' Ingrid replied.

'If we could resist human blood it would be so much simpler. We could integrate if we could resist. It would still be difficult to hide the fact we don't age, but still.'

'Integration is not an option, is it?' Ingrid stared at Anna wondering where this was coming from. She had never talked to her about integration before.

'Of course not, I'm just chatting,' Emily smiled. 'So, what attracted you to Steven?'

'I was getting tempted to strike, when I came across Steven. Something drew me in. He looked lonely. I was planning to make it look like a freak accident, but as soon as I bit him and started to feed, I felt strange. The blood tasted wrong. He still fainted as they all do, but I could not kill him. I was not sure at first why, but,' she paused. 'Now, I guess you told us the answer.'

Emily leaned in and studied Ingrid. 'So what are your thoughts?'

'His blood repulsed me since we can not feed off our own – you did say that he is one of us. So, I reckon he doesn't know who he is.'

'He has no idea,' Emily nodded.

Ingrid pursed her lips. 'The thing I don't understand is why? Why would anyone let one of us live here? I have always been brought up to believe that all of our kind are accounted for and contained. Tell me why I should keep your secret? Isn't it too dangerous to let him live here – out in the open?'

Emily shook her head. After a long pause, she looked up at Ingrid, as though concentrating. 'Steven will have to join us eventually. His mother is one of us, but his father is human. We have been protecting him, because we had no way of knowing, if he would become one of us. That is, until you came across him.'

'A hybrid! How? Who is his mother? Can I know?'

'Not at the moment – I'd rather keep her out of the picture. You can understand the potential repercussions if our kind found out that it were possible to mate with humans.'

'But wouldn't that be a good thing. Think of the possibilities. Like you just said, we could integrate back into society,' Ingrid interjected.

'You would still have to kill humans to stay alive. There is no such thing as integration for us,' Emily replied, in a bitter tone.

'I would never choose to kill humans unnecessarily. Does anyone even know what a hybrid will be like?'

'No, he is an unknown. That is why you can't expose him. There are those that enjoy coming here for the kill – it's like a sport. Others simply view human life as expendable. If they realised that mating with humans was fair game, it could get ugly. I just don't believe that we can play God – it would get out of hand eventually.'

'I understand,' Ingrid looked at the floor studying the pattern, a tessellation of black and white identical alternating diamonds. She knew it was bound to be hard for Anna. Her twin sister, Emily, had caused a lot of problems for the Roberts family in the past. Out of the blue, the obvious dawned on her – the niggling sensation. The woman in front of her was Emily, not Anna. She had to be Emily – the coffee, talk of integration, change in character. And the most important thing, her eyes. Her eyes were just like Steven's. Of one thing she was sure, Anna had not had a child with a human.

With a poker face, she stared at her drink.

'We should go. Hopefully this can be put behind us for now. I hope I can trust you to keep this a secret,' Emily added, as she finished the dregs in her mug.

'Anything for Anna,' Ingrid replied as she looked up whilst maintaining a straight face. She owed nothing to Emily. She wanted Steven to come and live with them, the sooner the better. She would come up with a plan and she would make sure Emily was none the wiser.

***

The bed was covered with all of Caitlin's favourite cuddly toys, ranging from a tiny Nemo fish to a toddler sized fluffy teddy bear. Her wide array of different sized posters stared back at her, yet they offered no comfort. All she wanted to do was mull. She did not want to face up to what she had seen, even though she'd have to eventually.

A tiny knock at the door alerted her to company.

'Caitlin, can I come in?'

From the bed, she glanced at the door, before calling out, 'you can come in.'

'How are you doing?' Her mum walked in. It was obvious she had just come back from work. She wore the same haggard expression Caitlin had seen many times.

'Same.'

Taking a seat next to her, her mum held her hand out and placed it on Caitlin's. 'You know you can talk to me. You have to talk to someone.'

'I know. It's just, I-I don't get it mum, I just don't.'

With her other hand her mother wiped a tear from her eye. 'There, there, don't beat yourself up about it. You couldn't have known what she was planning to do.'

Sitting up, Caitlin snapped. 'But, I should have known. She was so depressed the last time I saw her. I should have made more of an effort to be her friend. I should have been there for her.'

'Caitlin, you can not live someone else's life for them. That's just the way it is sometimes. I know it hurts, and you wish you could have stopped her, but you can't. It's happened and now you have to move on. Just because she decided to end her life, does not mean that you have to lose track of yours. Does it?'

'I don't know,' Caitlin huffed, before leaning against the head board. Looking at her mother's reassuring smile, she faltered. It always amazed her, that her mum could be so compassionate on some levels and so annoying on others.

'You have to go back to University, sweetheart, you can't stay here. You know that daddy and I would come back with you if we could, but we need to go to work and we need to be here to look after Jeanie.'

Caitlin thought of her little sister Jeanie and sighed. In recent years, the focus of attention weighed heavily on Jeanie. Before she came along, her parents had more time.

'You will be alright. Time is a great healer.'

'I know mum, thanks for the chat,' she said, purposefully sarcastic.

'Caitlin, don't be like that. I can't do any more than I do already. You worked hard at school to get into University, and now that you're there, you can't let yourself lose track of your goals because someone else lost track of there's.'

'And there I was thinking that you were sympathetic,' she sneered.

Narrowing her eyes, her mum got off the bed and faced away.

After a few seconds had passed, she calmly turned around and began. 'You know, I don't know what's come over you recently. Of course I think it's awful that your flat mate took her life. I just don't see why you should allow yourself to wallow. I love you Caitlin, but you don't seem to understand sometimes that we are doing to best we can to make ends meet. We already pay for your brother to go to University, and now we are doing the same for you. You've been here for two weeks already when you should be studying.'

'So, it's just about the money is it?'

'No,' she practically screamed at her. 'It is not about the money.'

Taking a deep breath, she exhaled slowly. Lowering her voice, she continued. 'It is time for you to go back, whether you like it or not. You have to face your fears not hide from them. I'll let you think about it. I have to go and cook.'

'Fine,' Caitlin replied. She threw herself back down on her bed, grabbed the pillow and placed it firmly over her head. Her muffled sobs broke the silence.

Chapter 12

Reunion

Steven whistled to the tune of Star Wars as he cruised into his lecture. For the first time in a few days, he felt at ease. A huge weight had been taken off his shoulders. Even though the conversation he'd had with Ingrid a week ago had rocked him, it was already forgotten – she was a psycho. He'd probably been bitten by an insect or something else, nothing more.

'Hey, Mr. Happy – over here,' Adam hollered.

'No need for that,' Steven sneered.

'Well, it would be like you to stroll into lectures on a day as pitiful as this one with a smile on your face.'

'Is Caitlin back then?' Sally asked eagerly, as she poked her head out from behind Adam.

'I don't know,' Steven stated, surprised to hear Caitlin's name again.

'Oh, I thought that was the reason why you'd be happy. You've been miserable since she left,' she guffawed, nudging Adam in the ribs.

Taking a seat, Steven mulled over the suggestion.

It was true, he had been miserable since she'd gone. However, he had met Ingrid a few days after she'd left so that could have been a factor. Truthfully, ever since Caitlin had gone, University life had not had the same appeal. She was the first person he had really come across who he liked to spend time with and he had enjoyed their conversations. He hoped the friendship would lead to more, and they had got so close. But then, Georgina had died and everything changed.

'If you're interested,' Sally whispered, over Adam's shoulder. 'She's due back at the end of the week. I doubt you're interested, but I thought I'd let you know, just in case.' She giggled and snuggled into Adam's shoulder.

Steven mused over this information. Caitlin was due back. It gave him a warm glow.

***

Caitlin stared at her new room in silence. Even though she was lucky a student had dropped out and left a vacancy, it felt wrong. Regardless, she had no choice. It was three weeks after Georgina's death, it was time. The idea of resuming life as if nothing had happened made her cringe. Saying that, she knew she had to try. The best medicine to combat trauma was surely hard work, and a few weeks at home had reminded her of the reason why she had worked so hard to leave. She loved her independence. It was not going to be easy, but she was determined to make up for lost time and catch up on any deadlines missed.

Her new room was on the catered accommodation block. The last thing she wanted to do was eat alone. The selection of bags scantily arranged around the room, beckoned to be sorted and the walls looked bare and desolate, devoid of all character. She was not sure if she had the energy or enthusiasm to redecorate again. The memory of putting up her posters with Georgina remained. Sitting on the bed, she stared out of the small window and held back tears. Taking out her ipod, she put it on shuffle and placed it on the docking station. The sound filled the room as her chest heaved giving up all resistance.

A knock on the door, a few minutes later, startled her. Finding some tissue she wiped her eyes, took a few breaths and headed for the door. Even though she wanted to ignore everyone, hibernation had gone on for long enough – it was time to face up to her fears.

When she opened the door she did a double take – Steven was standing there giving her an incredibly smouldering look. Her stomach did a flip. All she wanted to do was launch into his arms and forget. She used all of her energy to hold back.

'Hello Caitlin, welcome back. I hope I'm not disturbing you. I just came to see if you needed help settling in?' He said, in his polite and refined way.

Caitlin reflected on the fact he always sounded so proper. To make matters worse, it looked like not a hair on his head was out of place. He was the image of perfection. Everything she was not.

'Steven, why are you here?' She asked, unable to suppress her astonishment.

'Well, strictly speaking I was here first. You moved in.'

'Oh, I did not realise. Are you staying here too?' She replied. She hoped she sounded normal.

'My room is in the hall below this one,' he explained. 'I'm not stalking you, I promise. I just happened to look out the window when you walked past half an hour ago.' Twiddling with the cord on his hooded top, he continued, as he held eye contact. 'I thought you might want some company.'

Speechless, she gawped. Even though she had thought about him a lot whilst she was away, she never dreamed he would have remembered her. She assumed he would have moved on to someone else. As she jolted back to reality she found herself saying, 'do you want to come in?'

'That would be nice, but,' he paused, as though surveying the mess inside the room. 'Maybe you want to come out to the bar for a drink or something. It's Sunday night after all, and I think they've got karaoke. It might cheer you up.'

'Karaoke?' She pulled a worried face.

'It's always entertaining,' he smiled, sending her stomach off on another flip.

Caitlin was having a silent discussion with herself. Half of her was screaming at the fact he was asking her out. The other side was saying – he's just being friendly. Either way, she wanted to go with him.

Her mood lifted and she replied. 'That would be great.' Self consciously, she trailed. 'I don't know if I'd be good company at the moment though.'

'I promise not to talk about it. I'm not the gossiping type,' he said, whilst he leaned in conspiratorially.

She felt herself blush, as she tried to suppress a smile.

*

The hall bar was heaving. A girl was killing a Madonna song slowly and painfully with a high pitched shriek. Steven turned to Caitlin and raised his eyebrows. 'Maybe this was not such a good idea after all?'

'It's just what I need at the moment,' she replied, giving him her best attempt at a reassuring smile.

'What would you like to drink?'

'I'll have a J^2O if that's alright, apple and mango if they've got it. Do you want some money?' She asked reaching for her bag.

'You can get the next one.'

She watched him head off to the bar and stared at the stage. From the side, she heard her name being called out so she turned in the direction. Sally rushed towards her and gave her a huge hug. In an intoxicated slur, she said, 'I've missed you. You alright?' Obviously, she'd had a few drinks. Nonetheless, the gesture was appreciated.

Caitlin did not want to answer, so she asked a question of her own. 'Where's Adam?'

'In the loo, I think,' she giggled. 'It's so good to see you again. We have to catch up. Are you alone?'

As Caitlin was about to answer, Steven handed her the drink.

Sally looked from Caitlin to Steven and winked, before laughing. 'I guess I'll see you later. You look busy.'

'You don't have to go,' Caitlin started to say, as Sally skipped off chuckling.

'Is she tipsy?' Steven asked with a half smile.

'Do you think?' She remarked, as her eyebrows rose. The sound of the song ended to her relief, and a new track began. It was no better than the last, as a rowdy group started singing along to Queen.

'Are you planning to sing?'

'Are you?' She retorted, horrified.

'Fair enough,' he guffawed. 'You never know, you might like singing.'

Hesitant, she admitted. 'I love singing actually, but I'm not sure this is the right time or place to show everyone what I've got.'

'Really,' he grinned, lowering his voice and whispering in her ear. 'Do you think this is below you? You can be honest, I won't tell anyone.'

The smell of his aftershave swept over her, as she leaned in and took a deep breath. It was an earthy smell, enveloped with cinnamon and exotic spices. Even though overcome, she forced a reply. 'No, I think I'm just too shy.'

'Hmmm,' he mused, as he moved back. 'I never took you for the shy type.'

'There's a lot about me you don't know.'

'So, will you let me find out?' he asked, his expression serious.

'Maybe,' she answered, lowering her eyes to her drink, before taking a sip.

After a short intense moment, she looked up and saw he was still staring at her. She could feel her heart pounding in her chest.

'It's really nice to see you again,' he added, with a grin that sent her emotions off on a rollercoaster ride.

Breaking eye contact, she turned to face the stage to see Sally attempting to sing an Enrique Iglesias song. Her endeavour to master some erotic dance moves was not going so well. Instead, she looked like a puppet being thrust around by a child.

'Oh no, look at Sally!' Caitlin exclaimed. 'I hope Adam's going to help her home. She looks out of it.'

Laughing aloud, Steven stopped staring at her and turned his attention to the extravagant display of exhibitionism. 'She certainly doesn't have a problem putting herself out there. I'm not surprised she wants to be a lawyer.'

'Yes, I'd be scared to come across her in court,' she giggled. 'It's my turn. Do you want another drink?'

'Yeah, that'd be great.'

'What would you like?'

'Just a beer, any will do.'

'Okay then,' she replied, as she headed towards the bar.

The bar was crowded with students that were either ordering or chatting casually amongst themselves. Huge proportions of the girls were dressed up for a night out and had gone to a certain degree of effort. The majority of guys were in casual jeans and t–shirts. Caitlin was not spruced up at all, so she felt plain next to the other girls. Even so, she could feel Steven watching her. The way he looked at her was so intense. No one she ever fancied had ever even glanced at her in that way before. She had no idea what he actually thought of her, but she had to admit that she liked talking to him. At the back of her mind, she was convinced he only saw her as a friend.

It was stupid to think of whether he liked her or not. She did not even want a boyfriend. She was convinced he did not think of her in that way. A thought did cross her mind – if he did see her in that way, could she refuse him? She knew the answer straight away. Probably not.

'Can I have a beer and a J²O please?' Caitlin asked the bartender.

'What type of J^2O would you like?' he shouted, across the counter.

'Apple and Mango,' she shouted back.

As he went to get it, Adam appeared next to her. In a slimy voice, he grinned. 'Is Steven into J^2O's then?'

'No, that's for me.'

'No alcohol,' he sighed. 'You know it helps loosen you up a bit, so you can have more fun.'

The way he said that made her shudder. She stared ahead, as she urged the pump to pour the beer faster. 'I don't need loosening up,' she snapped. It was at least an attempt to get him to leave her alone.

'Don't you, but you look so uptight,' he leered, running a finger along her shoulder.

'Don't touch me,' she warned. 'I'm here with Steven.'

'But, you're not together, are you? I know a way to make you relax,' Adam insinuated, with a lecherous glare.

'You are so full of yourself,' she grimaced in disgust. 'Does Sally know that you hit on other girls?'

Blankly, he shrugged his shoulders. 'Why does what Sally think matter?'

'I give up, I hope she ditches you soon,' she stressed, turning to leave.

As she got the drinks, he placed his hand on her arm and stopped her. 'Will you go out with me then?'

'No, piss off,' she spat in outrage. Was there no limit to his arrogance?

'I like a girl with vigour and I've never dated a redhead,' he appraised, folding his arms in triumph.

'Ugh.' Horrified at his unbelievable arrogance, she stomped back to where Steven was standing.

'Are you alright?' He asked, with a slight glance in Adam's direction.

'Fine,' she stated.

'What's he done? I know he can cross the line sometimes.'

'Nothing much, but I have no idea what Sally sees in him. It's not even worth talking about, just forget it.'

'If you're sure,' he sounded unconvinced.

Refusing to open up, she watched Sally finish her song and then race towards Adam. As if giving a theatrical display of affection, he lifted her up to kiss her passionately before smirking in Caitlin's direction. If Sally had heard him a few minutes earlier, she might not have proved to be so receptive to his affections.

'I think I'd like to head back now. You stay; I don't want you to miss out.'

'I'll walk you back, I insist.'

Confused, she blinked. 'If you're sure.' She could not understand how someone as nice as Steven seemed to be could be friends with an asshole like Adam.

Chapter 13

Absence Makes The Heart Grow Fonder

The cool night air made her shiver. The temperature had dropped significantly.

'Are you cold?' He asked, his voice a picture of concern.

'It's chilly tonight.'

'Here – have my jacket.' He took it off and handed it over before she had a chance to refuse.

She held the jacket in her hands. 'It's okay. It's only a few minutes away.'

'I insist.'

So as not to appear ungrateful she put it on. She resisted the urge to dig her nose into it, to bask in his smell.

Their arms brushed as they walked side by side in silence. You could have cut the atmosphere with a knife.

Making their way into the building, they got to the juncture where they would go their separate ways.

'You can have your jacket back now,' she said, as she slid out of it. 'It was very nice of you.'

'My pleasure,' he remarked, as he put it back on. 'Maybe, we could go out again sometime.'

Something about his manner gave her the impression he was nervous.

Cocking his head to the side, he half smiled. 'If you don't want to go out with me, then that's okay, you don't have to.'

'I would like to go out with you again,' she replied, lifting up her face.

'You would?' He staggered back.

'Yes, I would like to go out with you' she repeated.

Giving a slight bow, he added. 'I am honoured to be worthy of you.'

Scrunching her lips together, she bit her lower lip. 'Don't make it sound so formal.'

'It is serious. I really want to go out with you again.'

Unable to find words to counter with, she changed tack. 'Thanks for coming to get me. It was nice and you've cheered me up.'

'Nice, well I can work on nice,' he remarked obsequiously.

'Okay,' she laughed. 'It was more than nice.'

'Now that sounds better.'

She could not believe he was taking a step towards her. Their faces were inches apart. She stared up into his eyes and realised they were close enough to kiss.

Simultaneously, they leaned in.

'Sorry, I…' he apologised, as he pulled back.

Caitlin took the plunge, leant towards him, and kissed him with more force.

When they finally took a breath, he held her against him. 'I have wanted to do that since I met you.'

Surprised, Caitlin pulled away and blurted out. 'So what stopped you?'

'I didn't think you were interested. I still don't know if you are to be honest,' he joked.

'You make me sound much better than I am.' She was puzzled. 'Truthfully, am I that hard to read?'

'Actually, yes, you're extremely hard to read. Every single time I attempted to flirt with you, I seemed to fall flat on my face. Well, until now that is.'

Holding his hand in hers, she teased him playfully with words. 'Well, how was I supposed to know why you wanted to hang out with me? I just thought you were being friendly.'

'Do you have many other friendly guys that want to just hang around with you?'

'No, I guess not,' she laughed.

'It's great to hear you laugh. I promised not to say anything but I've been worried about you. I thought you'd never come back.'

'I'm glad you were waiting.'

'I've wanted to get to know you from the first moment I set eyes on you. It was my cunning plan to accidentally bump into you.'

'You did it on purpose?' She pulled back, in feigned outrage.

'Just kidding, fate brought us together,' he added, tapping his nose.

Relaxing her shoulders, she added. 'If we are being honest, I knew I liked you from the moment I saw you too.'

'Well that's promising then, isn't it?'

'Yes.'

Entwining their hands, she made herself comfortable against him. His heartbeat resonated in her ear.

A few minutes later she pulled back. 'I should go,' she admitted.

'Do you have to?'

'Yes, I do. But, I'm not going far.'

'Well, that's alright then,' he said, leaning in for a parting kiss. Holding back, he brushed her lightly on the lips with his, and she resisted the urge to kiss him again.

*

The next morning, Caitlin woke up with a huge grin spread across her face. A vivid dream, involving Steven, had awakened her. Putting her finger to her lips, she leant into her hand and gave a satisfied smile. There was no way the previous day had been a dream.

Her room had an ensuite bathroom so she got out of bed and made her way over to the bathroom. Turning the shower on to heat up, she brushed her teeth diligently. After removing her pyjamas, she got under the hot water and immediately felt its soothing presence.

As she wrapped herself in a towel, and got ready to get dressed she heard her phone bleeping – a text message. Curiously, she rushed across and threw herself on the bed to read it.

It was from Steven.

It read 'Good Morning, fancy having breakfast together? I'll be there in twenty minutes. If you're not awake yet, sorry if I woke you up! S xx.'

Eagerly she wrote back. 'I've been awake for ages, and have even showered. I'll meet you in the cafeteria. C xxx.'

Almost instantly, he replied. 'Good to know, S xxxxxx.'

Laughing aloud, she texted back. 'Too many kisses…xxx is enough.'

So he replied with. 'I can send as many as I like, Sxxxxxxxxxxxxxxxxxx.'

Raising her eyes to the sky in bewilderment, she created another text. 'That's far too many, now let me get dressed. C xxx.'

She could not resist looking at his reply. 'Anything you say, S xxx.'

The text had left her with a huge dilemma. What on earth was she going to wear? The next ten minutes proved turbulent. Clothes were put on, disregarded, put back on and disregarded again.

Finally, the right outfit was assembled.

Settling for her black fitted jeans, black t–shirt and a purple zip up hooded top she looked in the small mirror above the sink. Giving an audible sigh, she grimaced at her hair. Even though ironically her effort in selecting an outfit would be wasted by the fact that she'd have to wear a coat, there was nothing she could do to hide her hair. In the minutes that followed she tied it up, then pulled out the hair band and made it loose again and finally settled on a French plait.

The finishing touch involved the application of some subtle makeup since she had never been one to overdo it. After thirty minutes, she was ready to go out, and she prayed he would appreciate her efforts.

During the short walk to the cafeteria her stomach tensed. The anticipation of seeing him again was proving too much and she nearly turned back and bailed out.

*

The cafeteria bustled with bleary eyed students suffering from the effects of an overindulgent weekend. Monday morning thrust them back to the reality of having to attend lectures and take part in academic work. Some students failed to realise they actually attended University to further their education, not social life. Looking around discretely, Caitlin spotted Steven sat on a long table with a few other friends. A vacant spot next to him made her smile. He had reserved a seat.

As soon as he saw her, he got up and made his way over.

'Finally, I thought you'd drowned in the shower but then I remembered what a good swimmer you are.' He watched her without getting too close.

'I was getting ready, I like to take my time,' she pouted.

'So, shall we get breakfast then?'

'I thought you'd had yours. When I saw you with your friends,' she faltered.

'Nope, I waited, I told you I would.' Closing the distance he eased up to her and slipped his hand into hers. 'Do you mind?'

She squeezed her hand gently against his. 'Not at all.'

Hand in hand, they walked up to the food counter and then let go as they perused the range on offer. Heading straight for the cereal, Caitlin poured some muesli in a bowl and covered it in yoghurt, before helping herself to an orange juice.

'That's very healthy – unlike mine,' Steven noted, as he bit his lower lip and glanced at his plate of greasy bacon, sausages and fried egg.

'I'm not a huge breakfast eater, my appetite picks up as the day goes on.'

'Glad to hear it. Can I get you a tea or coffee?'

'Tea please.' She could not believe how civilised things had got.

'Coming right up,' he smirked, raising his eyebrows.

Taking their trays back to the table, they sat down to a few prying eyes.

'Hi there, I'm Charles. Are you settling into your new room okay?' Charles asked his tone mellow. He wore small rectangular glasses which he pushed up his nose with his finger. The perfect picture of an intellectual. His neatly combed hair only added to the effect.

Swallowing her mouthful, she replied. 'Yes, it's fine.'

'Good to hear it,' he added, before resuming a conversation with Steven. 'So, as I was saying earlier, how did you get on with your Contract Law essay? Do you know when we get the results?'

'It was fine, did most of it on my laptop in the library. I think we don't get it back until after Christmas.'

'Really, that long, I was hoping to tell my parents some of my results so far.'

'I'm not bothered, I'll just tell my parents that everything's going fine,' Steven shrugged, relaxed.

'Oh, they always want to know. It's a trifle annoying, but they mean well,' Charles raised his nose in the air in a superior manner to compliment his accent.

'I can imagine,' Steven added, with a hint of sarcasm.

'Anyway, I must go, I like to be punctual,' Charles stated. In what looked like a well practiced manoeuvre, he took his tray and marched off.

‘He’s a bit stiff,’ Caitlin giggled, whispering in Steven’s ear once Charles was out of earshot.

‘You can’t help your upbringing. He’s alright. Obsessed with doing well, but he’s okay.’

‘I bet you don’t think badly of anyone do you,’ she challenged.

‘Well,’ he mused, before breaking out into a laugh. ‘No, not usually.’

‘Is there anything about you that’s not to like?’

Swallowing his mouthful, he kinked his head to the side. ‘I’ll have to get back to you on that one, but I’m sure I’ve got lots and lots of faults. Just wait till you get to know me better.’

‘I look forward to it.’ As she stared, she became suspended in space – unable to look away from his eyes. Caught in his world of unique amber. Blinking, she forced herself to look away before she turned crimson again. She could stare at his eyes forever.

‘Do you have a lot of lectures today?’ He asked casually, as he popped a mouthful of sausage and bacon into his mouth.

‘Today is one of my busiest days, and I have loads of catching up to do, so I think it’s going to be a late one for me in the library.’

Swallowing the mouthful, he replied, as he wiped his mouth with a napkin. ‘Poor you, maybe I’ll hang around to check that you’re keeping sane.’

‘I think you would drive me to distraction, I need to concentrate.’

‘Awww, are you saying that I’m a bad influence?’

‘No, well, oh, you know what I mean.’ It annoyed her – surely, her face was now bright red.

As Steven took hold of her hand, she relaxed. ‘Just kidding, I’ll let you work. But, will I see you tonight? I don’t mind meeting you at the library later. We could go for a drink in the Union.’

‘That would be great. Shall I text you when I’m close to finishing?’

‘Sounds good to me. I guess we’d better get going or we’ll be late.’

Looking at her watch, she hastily got up and spilt her remaining juice on the table. ‘I am such a klutz,’ she huffed, fretting.

‘Don’t worry about it,’ he reassured, as he placed a few napkins on it. ‘Shall we go?’

Nodding wordlessly, she got her rucksack. After a few strides, he slipped his hand into hers, causing her to shiver involuntarily at the feel of his hand against hers.

Chapter 14

Dancing

Steven watched Caitlin from the distance. A part of him would have enjoyed staying there for a while, to observe. The way she moved her lips as she wrote, and fussed with her hair as it fell over her face. All of her little mannerisms. Completely engrossing. Addictive. He wanted more. This was the reason he had to get closer to her – watching was not enough. Taking her by surprise, he placed his hands over her eyes. 'Time's up.'

Jumping back on her seat as she went for his hands, she squealed. 'Steven, is that you?'

'Who else where you expecting?'

Conscious of the other people around, she lowered her eyes and gestured for him to sit down next to her. Once he had sat down, she whispered. 'I'm still working, you're early.'

'I'll read next to you until you finish,' he added, lifting up one of her books. Seeing it was a book on Algebra, he tossed it back on the table. 'Then again, maybe not this one.'

'Something wrong with algebra?' She quizzed.

'Nope, nothing at all. It's just I'm allergic to Math's.'

'Allergic?' She challenged, with the pout he was beginning to love.

'I come out in a rash, if anything number related gets close to me. Trust me; you don't want to see it. It's really disgusting.'

'Ummhmm,' she rolled her eyes. 'I'm not allergic,' she stressed, nudging her shoulder against his. 'In fact, it seems to take to me very well. Sooo let me get on with it.'

'Really. Are you still working? Come on, you know you want to take a break,' he pleaded, doing his best impression of a puppy dog face.

'I told you you'd be a bad influence,' she accused, with a wry grin.

'Not a bad influence, just ensuring your sanity.' He argued, using his most diplomatic voice.

'Tell you what, let me finish this up and I'll meet you downstairs in ten minutes.'

'Deal,' he cheered. Success.

Getting up, he glanced at her for a few seconds longer.

'Need to finish,' she hissed, without looking up.

'Okay, I'm going. Can't a guy look?' he complained, laughing as he walked away.

Resuming his original vantage point, he glanced back. Her lips were moving again. This time, however, she knew he was there. Glaring at him, she waved him away with her hands. Cocking his head to the side, he frowned apologetically and bit his lower lip again. A part of him enjoyed annoying her.

The library entrance was near enough deserted. It was Monday, there were no exams looming, and the weather was foul. Most students had, wisely, called it a day. Caitlin had some catching up to do, so she had no choice. The last thing Steven wanted was for her to fail and leave. He just wanted to be with her, it was that simple. Finding a seat at the entrance he waited, and picked up one of the student flyers. Another advert for a student social, or better said, piss up. He had attended quite a few of those, and he was already bored. He was not interested in the 'getting drunk or high to be cool' routine.

Perhaps, he was pretentious.

He just did not need alcohol or drugs to have a good time. He enjoyed a drink just as much as the next person. He just did not understand the point of dousing himself in it.

'Penny for your thoughts,' Caitlin chirped, coming alongside him.

'Hey there, done already?'

'Yeah, I needed a break. You were right. What's that then?' She asked pointing at the flyer.

'Nothing much, another social,' he replied, flinging it back on the table.

'I have not had the chance to go to many of those. Are they any good?'

'Depends.'

'On what?' She queried, with a half smile.

'Well, I don't know you well enough yet. This may be your

thing. I just don't drink a lot, so being in an environment where the challenge is to get as drunk as possible, is not my ideal scene. But, if it is your thing – fair enough.'

Giving a chuckle, Caitlin smiled. 'It's not my thing either. But, if I'm honest, I do like to dance. Nothing wrong with that.'

'What kind of dancing do you like to do?' He had actually learnt ballroom dancing at his school.

'Are you an expert on dance?' She jibbed, looking impressed yet amused.

Embarrassed, he replied too quickly. 'No, not at all. Just didn't know if you were like a professional dancer or something. You could do synchronised swimming for all I know.'

'Oh, okay. Well in that case, no I'm not a professional. I just like to dance socially, you know going to discos and concerts.'

'Right.' He could teach her in time.

'Do you like dancing? Or, is that below you?' She teased.

Touché. She remembered him teasing her about the singing on the previous night.

'Oh, I'm a pro. I can dance anything,' he replied, with a smirk. Relaxing his features, he mellowed as he decided to open up. 'I was forced to learn ballroom dancing at my old school. Don't tell anyone though, or I'll have to kill you.'

'With death as a threat, I'll keep it to myself,' she guffawed, rolling her eyes.

'Shall we go then?'

'Where to?' She asked, with a slight shoulder shrug and half smile.

She was not making things easy for him. Why did he feel the need to impress her? As much as he wanted to relax, he could not help being nervous. He did not want to disappoint her. For all he knew, she might have changed her mind and decided he was a dork. Even though she said she liked him, she could go off him. In the last five minutes, all he had managed to do was convince her he was a tea total, ballroom dancing public school boy. Impressive.

'Student's union. We can shoot some pool,' he asserted. Appearances, it was all about appearances. So long as she thought he was confident, nothing else mattered.

***

Everything about Steven impressed Caitlin. The more she got to know him, the more she liked. Even though, at first, she was convinced he was a super cool tough guy. Now she saw she had got him all wrong. There was a lot more going on behind the smouldering façade. Ball room dancing. That one definitely topped the lot. She could not wait to see that.

'Are you sure you want to play against me? I might make a comeback and thrash you instead. Or, I might have to kill you, if you don't let me get at least one ball in.'

'I'll play nice, I promise.'

'You better. Last time you annihilated me. It was so embarrassing,' she winced. She still had to get over her defeat.

'I'm sorry, was I terrible. Sometimes I can be a bit of a show off. I told you I had many faults,' he admitted.

A man admitting his shortcomings, now this was impressive. 'I'll let you off for the last time, just play nice today.'

'Anything you say.'

The way he said it sounded condescending. She found it so hard to read him. Was he being serious, or teasing again?

'Promise or I won't play,' she pouted. She folded her arms and stopped as they reached the entrance. She really was not up for being trumped tonight.

'Sorry, I did not mean to annoy you. I can be very sarcastic too. Another of my faults.'

'They are all coming out tonight,' she snapped, as she wished a huge hand would shut her up. He was getting a rise out of her, and she had no idea why. It was like his whole character excited and at the same time irritated her. Annoying.

'Let's go play, I don't want to expose myself any more,' he joked, taking her hand in his.

The feel of his hand made her relax. It seemed he really liked her. It was confusing – irrational. She still could not understand why he seemed to be interested in her – where was the catch?

*

The student union was not busy, but there were enough students around to make it comfortable. The pool table was busy, so Steven slid a few pound coins on the table to hold a place. After sitting down within eyeshot of the pool table, Caitlin started to wonder what she had let herself in for. She barely knew Steven; she had a lot of work to do to catch up, and Christmas time was just around the corner. Surely, now was not the time to get into a romantic attachment. The question was – could she resist him? No, the answer was no.

'So, how have you been anyway? I didn't know whether to ask, but I don't want you to think I haven't thought about what happened.' Steven asked, taking a sip from his beer.

'Thanks for asking. It's okay; I don't think I'm going to break down at the moment.'

He waited for her to continue.

'It's just, I don't know. Georgina was,' she paused, feeling the back of her throat constrict.

'You don't have to say anything,' he interrupted. 'I shouldn't have asked.'

'No, it's okay. I have to deal with what happened. I guess I don't understand it. She did seem depressed and homesick, but…oh, I don't know how to explain this. She was not the suicidal type. I just know she wasn't. I can't help feeling like something else happened. I just don't know what else could explain her death.'

'From what I read, it did not seem suspicious. I guess no-one knows why these things happen.'

'It's just,' she paused, unsure whether to continue. Making her mind up, she carried on. 'I heard she was missing a lot of blood.'

'Blood?' The colour seemed to drain from his face.

'I know, shocking right.'

Just then, the sound of glass smashing on the floor broke the subdued atmosphere. Turning to face it, Caitlin watched in horror as she saw a member of staff had dropped the glasses she was collecting, and a shard had accidentally embedded itself on her leg. Blood streamed down her ankle. She took a seat and someone applied pressure to the spot. It was not life threatening, but it looked and sounded painful.

'Ouch,' Caitlin grimaced, as she turned back to face Steven.

He was staring at the girl's legs with real intensity, it was almost scary.

'Steven?' Caitlin called out, trying to break his trance.

As though forcing himself to look away from the girl, he turned to face Caitlin again. 'I don't know what came over me. The smell, it's so strong isn't it?'

'Smell, what smell? Are you hallucinating? Are you telling me you can smell the blood from here?'

'No, no,' he shook his head and laughed it off. 'I can't smell it. Of course, I can't. Just a memory. When I was younger I cut my arm really badly when I fell off my bike, and I've never forgotten the smell up close.'

'Oh, right.' She was unconvinced, but he looked spooked, so she wasn't going to push it. He looked ill. 'Do you want to go back to Halls? We can play pool another time. You don't look so good.'

'You know, I think you're right. Another time.'

Draining the last of her drink, she saw Steven's drink was still practically full. 'Did you want to finish?'

'No, it's alright, like I said. I'm not a big drinker.'

Even though a moment ago, she was vulnerable as she relived the memory of Georgina, now she wanted to comfort him. Something had spooked him, and she had no idea what that was.

Chapter 15

Family Time

'What's up with you? Can I take some of that to give me energy to study?' Caitlin's Brother Mark rolled his eyes as he came down the staircase.

'Sorry, I can't bottle this,' she laughed, as she continued to twist some tinsel along the railing.

'So, are you in love?' He teased, grabbing a piece of tinsel and wrapping it around her neck. 'That's the only thing that makes girls act so silly.'

Caitlin pouted and pulled the tinsel off. 'You are just jealous. No-one seems to think you're much of a catch?'

'I have to swat them away like flies, they all want me,' he slurred, posing dramatically. With his bulging athletic muscles from his workout sessions at the gym, she knew he was not lying. Even though he was her brother, she had to admit that she could see why girls were attracted to him. He was funny for a start.

'As if,' she guffawed, in a bid to peg him down to size. 'Anyway, love is quite a strong word, which you would know nothing about.' She cupped her hands through the tinsel, enjoying the velvety touch.

'So, do I get to meet the guy to make sure he meets our standard or is he out of bounds?' Mark enquired, cocky as usual.

'Only if you come to see me, but I'm unlikely to invite you.'

'I knew there was a guy,' he beamed triumphant, as a smug look fell across his face.

'Fine, yes, there is someone,' she huffed.

'I'm always right,' he smirked, as he continued to the bottom of the steps. 'I'm happy for you sis, but can you cool it just a tad – some of us have finals to study for.'

'Hey, I have to work too, you know.'

'How scary – first year exams. Like they count for anything, all you have to do is pass. How difficult can that be?'

'Fine! Whatever! I'll try and keep my mood down for you, okay,' she screamed, placing her hands on her hips.

'Thanks, much appreciated.'

Shaking her head in frustration, she focused her energy on decorating the staircase as she hummed along to a tune.

***

Steven woke up on Christmas day and wondered what his parents had in store for him. His mum had already coerced him into helping to set up the decorations and Christmas nativity display. He had only avoided going to midnight mass on Christmas Eve by faking a stomach bug. It was the only thing that made his Spanish stepmother annoying – she was an avid Roman Catholic. Even though she would not force him to go to mass, he did not want to hurt her feelings by admitting that he was not into religion. It was still cringe worthy to remember his communion. The image of him dressed in white, looking angelic, would stay with him for life.

Dressing gown on, he made his way to the kitchen. The wheels were clearly in motion for the Christmas dinner preparations. The evidence was all around. Flour scattered across the table, an opened mincemeat jar and stacks of vegetables waiting at the side to be pealed. At the sink his stepmother, Clara, was washing her hands.

As he came in she turned and rushed up, giving him a huge kiss on the cheek and a hug which left the back of his dressing gown wet, from her yet to be dried hands.

With her dark brown hair, chocolate coloured eyes, rosy cheeks and Christmas themed apron over her rounded form, she resembled a cute and cuddly Christmas bear.

'Merry Christmas Steven!'

'Merry Christmas mum. Is dad busy doing your bidding already?'

'Yep, he's getting the vegetables ready. Are you planning to help?' She asked, her face lit up, hopeful.

'I think I'll go shower first.'

'Sounds good, but don't take too long,' she narrowed her eyes. 'You know your dad loathes peeling as much as you do.'

At his room he texted Caitlin to wish her a Merry Christmas. They had become near enough inseparable over the past few weeks. He hated being away from her now. Even though Caitlin had fussed over him, he was embarrassed to remember how weird he'd got over the blood incident. He still had no idea why he had become so strange. Maybe, the whole Ingrid business had affected him more than he thought. Even though his intention was to erase the memory, it stubbornly lurked its weary head every now and again.

***

Caitlin's heard her younger sister Jeanie before she felt the body crashing on top of her as she slept. Jeanie squealed, 'it's Christmas Day, Father Christmas has been, wake up, wake up.' Caitlin thrust the pillows firmly over her head; her worst nightmare had come true. If anyone else had woken her up, she could have handled it, but for some inexplicable reason, she loathed her little sister more than anything. It had probably been made worse by her incessant whining, huffs and mood swings over the past few days. They left much to be desired. What really got to her was the fact that Jeanie usually got her own way. Obviously, her parents had forgotten how to discipline by child number three.

With that thought in mind, the sound of her mum's voice hollered down the corridor. 'Jeanie, get out of Caitlin's room.'

Jeanie sighed, took her leave shrugging her shoulders, and blew a raspberry in Caitlin's direction. She had screamed at her the night before. Apparently, Caitlin was no fun anymore, and since she had left for university, she had become boring and adult like. Caitlin was a little sympathetic. Jeanie was the innocent eleven year old, who still believed in Father Christmas.

Caitlin twisted her head to face her clock and was shocked to see it was already nine in the morning. She groaned as she realised it was time to get up. In a way, she envied Jeanie for still getting exited. The whole Christmas experience had already become too manufactured and monotonous for her taste. She hated acting like happy families with the relatives when she could not stand most of them. Luckily, this year it was their turn to go to her Aunt's house, so at least she would not have to endure her mother's frantic preparations and sense of humour failure.

A bleeping noise alerted her to a text. She launched herself at the phone and hoped it was Steven. As she saw his number, she gave a whoop of joy.

Maybe, she would act nice today after all.

Only two weeks before they would see each other again. As the thought crossed her mind, she realised their reunion would coincide with her first set of University exams. All she wanted to say was 'Bah humbug' – she had always loved Mr. Scrooge.

***

Steven was busy sorting out parsnips. This year it was their turn to host Christmas dinner, so his Spanish Grandparents on his mother's side were coming. His other grandparents had opted to go on holiday in the Caribbean, not tempted to experience the English climate. His Spanish Uncle, on his mother's side, and his family were also coming along.

Luckily, they were renting a cottage nearby otherwise the house would be bursting at the seams.

Busy peeling, he sat with his Dad, Paul. They did not need to talk; it was the usual ritual as they listened to the news on the radio. At the end, the Christmas songs returned with a vengeance. When the band aid song started playing again and prompted his dad to sing out of tune again, he started to lose the will to live.

'Shall I take these into the kitchen?' He needed an escape plan – fast.

His dad lifted his head and nodded sagely. With his greying hair and developing bald patch, he looked a lot older than he really was.

Balancing the pot full of potatoes and the one with carrots, Steven made his way into the kitchen. He was desperate for some fresh air. Ultimately, all he wanted was an excuse to check his phone for a text from Caitlin. Leaving the pots next to the hob, he snuck back to his bedroom, ecstatic to see the flashing light on the phone.

The message read. 'I'm in hell at the moment! I just got woken up by my bratty sister jumping on my bed – joy! But anyway, Merry Christmas or Feliz Navidad! Hope your day is going better than mine. I can't wait to see you, missing you loads, Caitlin.'

Laughing aloud, as he read the message, he impulsively dialled her mobile number. When she picked up, he pinched his nose to speak. 'This is the Samaritans. We have been led to believe that you are in need of some emotional support at the moment.'

'Steven, ha ha, you are hilarious,' she squealed, in her high pitched shriek.

'Aw, was it that obvious,' he protested.

'Only by the fact that I can see your number on my mobile.'

'Oh yeah, annoying phones. It must have been so much easier to take someone by surprise when you could not see who was calling beforehand.'

'I guess,' she replied.

'So, is it really that terrible,' he asked earnestly.

'It's worse. My family is unbearable.'

'Hey, I'll have to concentrate all day, since there is going to be a lot of Spanish flying around.'

'Can I come?'

'Just hop on in.'

'If only,' she gave an audible sigh.

'My mum wants to meet you,' he added, distracting her.

'What have you told her?' she enquired.

'Nothing much, but she's shocked that anyone manages to get me to talk for longer than a few seconds. She thinks you've bewitched me.'

'Hey, I have not.'

'Haven't you?'

'You tell me?'

'I'm pretty hooked, that's all I'll admit to.'

'Ditto.'

There was a brief pause, as he wondered whether he should reveal his inner thoughts. 'I miss you,' he admitted, before tagging on quickly. 'And I hope you have a good day. Just remember those of us that will be totally confused.'

'I'll try, call me soon okay. I miss you too. I much prefer to hear your voice, than to see your words on a computer or mobile.'

'Ditto, I'll try to call you later. To check if you survived.'

'Okay, bye then,' she paused. 'Steven, are you still there? Come on, you hang up first.'

'Nope, you do it.'

'This is your phone line.'

'My parents are paying, it doesn't bother me.'

'Not fair. Are you really not hanging up?'

'No.'

'Okay then, I love you.' With that she hung up.

He stared at the phone in bewilderment. That was the first time she had said those three significant words aloud. She had slotted it in, when he was totally unsuspecting. With a big fat grin, he lay back on his bed. He resembled a cat that got the cream.

***

When Caitlin got to the bottom of the stairs, she heard laughter coming from the dining room. As she walked in she saw Mark standing next to another boy, who she vaguely remembered.

'Is this your sister, Caitlin?' The boy asked her mum, with a cheeky wink. His tan leather jacket made him look way too suave. In response, her mum placed her arm on his forearm and giggled – it was pathetic. After all, he was just Mark's age. How could she react to his compliments?

'No, *I'm* his sister,' Caitlin snapped.

'Are you coming to play with me now, Daniel?' Jeanie asked, bounding into the room like a puppy dog.

'Sure, I'll play,' he replied, as he followed her out.

'Who's that?' Caitlin asked, trying to act disinterested.

'Don't you remember him?' Mark asked in astonishment. 'I've only been his best friend for like, years.'

'Is that the Daniel, as in your best friend for like forever?' She asked in shock, as the penny dropped.

'He's changed a bit, hasn't he,' her mum added. She raised her eyebrows as she wondered out. At the door, she turned around and winked at her. 'Not just a kid anymore.'

Caitlin felt sheepish as she grabbed the newspaper and pretended to read it. It was lucky she did not have to worry about what anyone else thought. She had Steven now.

Chapter 16

Taking The Next Step

After the New Year was upon them again, it was time to make new resolutions and return to the normality of lectures and student living. Caitlin was just a tad guilty about being excited to go back, especially as Jeanie had burst into tears as she was about to walk out of the door. In that moment, she had actually felt for her but not enough to want to stay. Her little sister had done her outmost to irritate her throughout the holiday, to the point where Caitlin had ashamedly wished her parents had thought to use contraception. Even though she did not really mean it, it certainly made her aware of the consequences of spontaneous actions. A mistake like that was not worth it at this time in her life. Even if she spent a stupid amount of time dreaming of a dimpled, cute baby with Steven's features!

After giving her mum a hug and a kiss, she was seated on the train and independent again, with nothing for company but music, a book and her mobile phone. As the train pulled out, she took out the phone and texted Steven to let him know she was on her way. Almost immediately, she got the reply to say that he was already seated and on his journey. She could not help but to withhold a laugh at the thought of where he was. Whilst she was sat comfortably on a fast train service, he was going on a scenic tour of the countryside – courtesy of the National Express bus service. His parents had booked him the seat, convinced it was the cheapest and easiest way for him to get back to Southampton. Since they funded his University life, he'd had no choice but to accept it.

She smiled as she recalled their conversation.

Steven actually admitted that he understood his parent's reasoning. Even though his parents could afford to pay for his train fare, they insisted that he travel via the cheaper coach option. His parents arguably had a point – it had less transfers. Ultimately,

Steven knew they wanted to instill an appreciation of money. In the scheme of things, he was lucky – not every student avoided the burden of student debt, when taking into account the rising cost of higher education. Steven's parents paid for everything. He would be debt free at the end of his studies. Whereas Caitlin was convinced she'd have to work for years before she would cover the cost. The joys of Government grants.

The fact he understood and justified his parents actions made Caitlin respect Steven even more. It was these qualities, along with many others that she loved. She was not blasé enough to ignore the fact that Steven was gorgeous by anyone's standard. Yet, the fact remained – there was more to him than looks. She eagerly anticipated peeling back the layers that kept Steven Thorn together, one at a time. The best bit was, she was not in a hurry to do this – she had all the time in the world.

***

It was freezing outside. To top it all, the rain was coming down in bucket loads. A gusty wind made anything lightweight fly overhead. The street resembled a dump site. It was this scene that greeted Steven as he clambered down the bus steps to retrieve his luggage. After a minute of being subjected to the diabolical onslaught, he was wet through. Luckily, his cap and waterproof jacket took the worst of it. His jeans were not so lucky. They felt sticky and uncomfortable, firmly pasted to his legs. As he trailed up to the bus stop, dragging his feet, he was tempted to spend some of his money on a taxi cab.

He stared longingly at the taxi stand and then made his way to the bus stop.

Arms folded, a sulk pasted on his face, he waited under the bus shelter for the right number. It was not the best way to start a new academic term. All he wanted to do was crawl into bed with a hot drink. One thought kept him motivated to return – Caitlin. After being separated for three weeks over the Christmas break, he could not wait to be with her. The fact they talked every day was neither here nor there.

*

After an arduous bus journey, the hall building came into view as he rounded the corner. The grounds on campus were pretty deserted. It was obvious most students had decided against hanging around. As he walked, he texted Caitlin to let her know he was nearly there. Once in the comfort of his room, he dumped his things on the floor and started to take off his soaking jacket. He was just debating whether to just go and have a shower, when he heard seven rhythmical knocks on the door.

As he opened it, Caitlin lunged, giving him a huge hug.

'You're very wet,' she remarked. With a seductive smile, she teased. 'Maybe I can help you to get rid of your clothes, so that you can get more comfortable?'

'You think?' Her forwardness caught him by surprise. 'You could, but….'

Without giving him a chance to finish, she kissed him hungrily and he responded with vigour. They laughed unanimously as Caitlin helped Steven to peal off his soaking jeans.

***

The tiny single bed was a squeeze for two. Somehow, they made it work. Caitlin nuzzled into Steven's chest. It was not as embarrassing as she expected it to be, when you took into account the fact they were naked together – for the first time.

'Did you miss me?' She asked, as she twirled her finger around his chest hairs. He did not have that many but it was enough to make him manly.

'Do birds have wings?'

'I missed you too,' she admitted. She nestled against him. As the realization of what they had done hit her, she sat up and kept the covers firmly over her chest. 'I can't believe we just did that. I've been thinking about it during Christmas, but I never imagined it would be anything like that.'

'Sorry to disappoint you,' he sighed, pulling the covers over his face.

'Awww, you know what I meant,' she said, pulling them off.

'I know.' He paused. The feel of his hand on her hair made her lean to the side towards it. His hand trailed down her face before it dropped onto her hand, his eyes searching. 'Are you glad? It felt right to me.'

'Of course. It was a bit funny that you were so well prepared,' she teased, with a light nudge of her elbow.

'Well…,' he started, as he bit his lip.

She decided to let him off the hook. 'It's okay. I have some in my room too. You never know when you might need them, right?'

'Yes,' he recovered. 'Well you are very sensible. But, who were you planning to use them with?' Lying back on to the pillow, he folded his arms under his head and winked at her.

'Well, err…you know.' The heat was instantly on her face.

'I'm only teasing,' he sat up again, grabbed her firmly within his arms and pulled her down.

Face to face, Caitlin could not stop herself from bursting into a fit of giggles. Once recovered, she became serious. 'You know, as much as I would love to stay here with you, we should actually think of making a move.'

'Do we have to?' He kissed her lips.

Caitlin pulled back. 'Yes, you've had your wicked way. We can't stay in bed all afternoon. We have to eat.'

'If we must, but you didn't seem to complain a few minutes ago.'

'That's because my body was lusting after yours,' she admitted. 'But, we women are practical. Our bodies have other needs too.'

'What are you saying about men then?' He pulled a face that feigned offence.

'Well, if you must know,' she said, with a half smile. 'After thinking about sex pretty much all the time, its limited really.'

Picking up the pillow, Steven wafted it on top of her head, before pinning her down on the bed again. 'Well if you weren't so gorgeous, maybe, I would stop to think about other stuff like our upcoming exams.'

She was helpless to his charms as she succumbed to his kiss.

Before things got out of hand, she broke off and added. 'Okay, we really have to go to get some food – I'm starving.'

'Okay, okay, you are harsh,' he said. In a swift action, he got off and went in search of his underpants. He grabbed his wet jeans and put them over the radiator. Then dug in his bag and pulled out another pair.

Caitlin watched him for a moment, before easing off the bed to get her own clothes. He really was something else to look at. She had never felt so attracted to anyone, let alone lusted after them. It was like her hormones were on overdrive. The need to be with him was addictive, and yet, completely natural. At the back of her mind, there was a reluctant part of her that wondered whether things were developing too fast.

*

The Gully restaurant was buzzing. It seemed like everyone was catching up on their Christmas adventures, or lack of. The mood was buoyant and full of energy. Holding hands, Caitlin leaned against Steven, as they approached the food counter. After they had sat down with their food trays and started to eat, she noticed Sally and Adam approaching. She did not mind Sally, but she loathed Adam.

'Can we join you?' Sally asked, as brazen as ever.

Sally was such an interesting character. Under all of the bravado and longing to fit in, she was a nice person who was definitely being taken advantage of by the likes of Adam. When she got the chance, Caitlin intended to ask Steven why Adam was his friend. She never got that.

'Sure, how are you?' Caitlin asked politely, whilst averting her eyes from Adam's direction.

'Great, did you have a good Christmas?'

'It was bearable, just you know, same as always.'

'Missing Steven?' Sally added, winking. 'Don't worry, I missed Adam like crazy,' she said, as she tightened her grip on his arm and looked up towards him.

Adam pulled a neutral face, which made Caitlin wonder whether he was beginning to reciprocate less than Sally would hope. Perhaps, he was finally showing his true colours.

'Do you fancy shooting some pool?' Steven asked Adam.

She was sure he noted the tension.

Enthusiastically, Adam replied without giving Sally a second glance. 'Great idea.'

Leaning over to kiss Caitlin, Steven whispered in her ear. 'Shall I annihilate him?'

'Definitely,' she giggled, stealing a quick kiss. She could not help but to admire his pert backside.

'He's totally besotted with you. You are so lucky Caitlin,' Sally added, her expression forlorn.

'Adam is still going out with you, isn't he?' Caitlin asked. She did not want to know, but she realised Sally might need a friend. Sally was not as tough as she seemed.

'I'm not sure anymore. We were totally into each other last term. But over the holidays he barely rang me, and since we've got back together today he seems distant. Maybe he's had a change of heart and he's just not into me anymore,' she sighed, deflated.

'If he's not, it's his loss right? Better that you know and move on, there's plenty more fish in the sea,' Caitlin reminded, trying to keep the conversation light. Sally could definitely do better than Adam.

'I know, you're right, it's just that every time I think I've met the guy, he ends up disappointing me. I should have held out and not done it with him. That would have kept him keen.'

'You don't know that,' Caitlin added, picking her finger nails.

'Trust me – once a guy has his way, he loses interest. That's my experience anyway.'

Caitlin swallowed and frowned, prompting a quick response from Sally. 'But, if you have done it with Steven, I wouldn't worry – not all of them are the same. You might have found a keeper. It's all a lottery really.'

'I hope you're right. I could do without a broken heart right now,' Caitlin said. She knew Adam was nothing like Steven. She played with the spoon and pursed her lips. After a brief, pause, she added. 'Shall we go find them?'

'I guess so, I've got to prepare myself for another potential break up,' Sally sighed, as she dropped her shoulders.

As they made their way to the student bar, Caitlin remained deep in thought. Sally had made her uneasy. As much she wanted to believe that she had found the love of her life, she could not help but wonder – would Steven be a keeper?

Chapter 17

Disturbance

Caitlin was convinced she was going to be sick. The knots in her stomach twisted tighter with every breath she took. On the menu for the day, two Mathematics exams that comprised a core part of her syllabus. In her head, she had already failed. She always reacted in the same way to an examination of any kind. For her driving test, she had simulated appendicitis! Luckily, her parents had ignored her charade and made her take the test, with positive results. Now, alone, she knew if she turned and fled, no-one would come after her. The weather outside did nothing to appease her. It was gloomy and overcast. It gave her a sense of impending doom.

After what felt like years, and a million twists of hair, they finally let her into the vast examination room. She decided to take a seat close to the entrance – just in case she needed a quick exit. Slowly and meticulously, she removed her pencil, pen and math's equipment from her pencil case and laid them out neatly in front of her. As she listened intently to the instructions, she tried to stop herself from hyperventilating and thought of Steven. It actually had a calming effect. She was eternally grateful to have such an amazing boyfriend.

At last they were allowed to begin.

Turning the page, she looked at the first question and momentarily froze. A second later, she attacked it with vengeance. Adrenaline kicked in, as her nerves started to subside.

***

Steven finished his exam paper and reread his answers to make sure he had not missed anything. He was sitting a Contract Law exam, which happened to be his favourite topic. Even so, he was amazed that he still had thirty minutes to go, and yet, as far as he could see, there was nothing more he could do. Internally, he debated whether it would be too arrogant to leave, when it was obvious that many of his counterparts were still furiously scribbling. A lot of them looked a bit too stressed for his liking.

After waiting for a few more minutes, he decided he had better places to be. A cold lecture hall, where he was confined to a tiny desk and remained paranoid of being accused of cheating, was not his idea of fun. Putting his hand firmly up into the air, he looked towards the invigilator. The shoes clicked on the floor, as the man made his way over.

'Can I help you?' The invigilator whispered, leaning in conspiratorially.

'I've finished,' he replied, handing out the paper.

The invigilator narrowed his eyes, pursed his lips, and asked, 'are you sure?'

As Steven held out the paper, the invigilator shrugged his shoulders and gave him what looked like a pitiful look as he took it. Confidently, Steven got up, took his things and cruised out of the room looking forward to freedom.

***

Caitlin waited for the final call as she rechecked her paper for the hundredth time. She mulled over the answers, unconvinced, but unable to improve on what she had written. After handing over the paper she breathed a sigh of relief. As much as she dreaded the outcome, at least it was over. She had tried her best. Taking her time, she got her things together and eased out after the other students. Out in the open, she saw Lisa and waved. Lisa's bright red jacket brightened the dull winter day.

'So, how did you get on?' Lisa asked curious, yet wary.

'No idea,' Caitlin sighed.

'It wasn't totally bad though, was it?'

'No, not totally bad, hopefully, I'll have done enough to pass it.' Caitlin attempted to sound enthusiastic.

'Look whose waiting!' Lisa exclaimed, rolling her eyes. 'Will I get an invite to the wedding?'

Caitlin followed her line of sight and saw Steven leaning against the entrance door, looking sublime, as usual. 'Shh, he might hear you.'

'You live in each other's pockets; I don't think he'd mind.'

'Marriage is not high up in my priorities at the moment. He's my boyfriend. I'm not looking to elope.'

'Either way, I am so in awe. We have so got to go out together. Maybe, you can help me get one,' Lisa pleaded.

'If you actually showed John the right signs you would have one. I'm sure he's still keen on you?'

'John and I are just friends.'

'Whatever you say,' Caitlin said, as she rolled her eyes.

Steven cruised towards them and ended the conversation. 'Lisa, it's been a while. Did you have a good Christmas break?'

Caitlin loved the way he was always so polite.

'Yes, it was great. Anyway, I've got to go and paint my nails or something. I guess I'll see you around then.' Looking at Caitlin, she gave a cheeky grin, before breaking out into a chuckle.

***

Steven only had eyes for Caitlin. He was totally infatuated. Before Caitlin, he had never even come close to having feelings for another girl. If he did not know any better, he would have said he was in love – if infatuation was love. He wanted to tell her how he felt. The words were hard to say. Instead, he kissed her on the lips and wrapped his arms around her. As the kiss came to a natural end, he eased back. 'So, how was it?'

'Terrible, as usual,' she sighed, his favourite pout in full view.

'But, you're a genius. I bet you'll have done just fine.'

'You sound like my mum.'

'I'm not sure that's a compliment.'

Laughing aloud, she tightened her grip on his hand. 'It is and it's not. I guess. How about you, how did you get on?'

'It was alright,' he shrugged. He had never been the type to analyze an exam after the event.

'At least, it's over now. It's time to party. Shall we go to the students union bar tonight? They are having a huge event.'

'Party it is,' she agreed.

He held her against him for a moment and relished the body contact. Maybe later, there would be time for more. A weird sensation came over him as the thought vanished. He was overcome by a sense of unease as a shiver crept down his spine. In that moment, he was convinced something was going to happen – something bad.

'You alright?' Caitlin asked.

'Sure, why do you ask?' He was sure she could *not* read his mind.

'I felt you tense up.'

'I'm fine.'

He did not want to lie to Caitlin, but it was stupid. What was he going to say? I have a feeling we are in danger. It was probably just the weather. The weather was a good thing to blame. In truth, he was surprised at how time had flown since he'd arrived at University. Life seemed to speed up. In a few months time, on the fourth of September, he would be twenty years old. His teenage years would come to an end. It was weird to acknowledge any notion of becoming a responsible adult. At least, if things with Caitlin went to plan, his future had a rosy horizon. A smile remained as he shook off whatever it had been.

***

Caitlin had been called up for a silver service waitressing job at a nearby Hotel. Since she had registered with a local temping agency she had obtained a steady stream of work, and it paid well. The event was for one hundred and fifty people which made the service nerve–wracking. It was hard to remember which side to serve the guests from, and ensure she held the spoons properly. The last time she had accidentally dropped a piece of broccoli on an elderly man's lap and received a severe scolding. It was only funny as an afterthought.

At the end of the evening, one of the girls agreed to give her a lift home. It was better than the bus.

'Do you mind if I drop you off here? I'm late getting home as it is,' her friend asked.

'I'll be fine,' Caitlin replied. She opened the door, got out and waved goodbye. Once around the corner she'd be back within the safety of Halls. The sound of her footsteps echoed in the night air, as she crossed the bridge. It was dark. She wished she had thought to ask Steven to meet her. There was no-one around. It really freaked her out. Just as she approached the entrance of the accommodation blocks, she heard a car roaring down the road. Instinctively, she turned to see how fast it was travelling. She stared in shock as it screeched to a stop next to her. Before she had time to react, a man leapt out of the car, grabbed her and threw her into the back of the car.

She was too stunned to scream.

As the shock subsided, the tears flowed. Between sobs, she tried to pay attention. Two men sat in the front, talking a dialect she could not understand. They had tied her up with rope around her wrists and covered her mouth with duck tape. As far as she was concerned, it seemed inevitable. Her life would shortly be coming to a close. After what seemed like hours, they stopped close to a wooded area. She was sure it was within the New Forest. One of them lifted her up and removed the duck tape. Her lips stung.

Caitlin sat still, wide eyed. Silent.

'We are sorry to have to put you through this,' the man in the drivers seat said, in a strange accent. 'We need to get to Steven and you seem like very good bait. We do not intend to harm you.' He glanced over at the man in the other seat.

Even though, she was partially relieved by the information, she was nevertheless apprehensive about the reason for her abduction. 'What do you want with Steven?'

They both laughed, before the man on the passenger side said in an innocent, yet unbelievable, voice. 'We want to help him, that's all.'

What they were saying was totally confusing. In anger, she spat. 'How can helping someone mean scaring his girlfriend to death?'

The man on the driver's seat shook his head. 'Unavoidable really, we need both of you to understand that everything we tell Steven has to be kept quiet. Otherwise, there will be consequences.'

The man on the passenger side grew impatient. 'Enough – we need to call your boyfriend and convince him to meet you here. Do not tell him anything about your situation. We don't need anyone to get hurt now do we? Trust us when we tell you that we can easily cause anyone you love harm.'

The man opened up her phone and dialled Steven's number. He put the handset to her ear. She did not want Steven to get into danger, but she had a feeling that if she did not help them, they would find another way to get to him. After a few rings, he picked up.

'Steven, it's Caitlin,' she said working hard to control the tone of her voice.

'What's going on Caitlin? It's nearly midnight.'

'I know. I just got held up, that's all. I need you to do something for me without asking any questions?'

'Sounds ominous – I'm game,' he replied, in his usual jokey manner.

'Can you meet me in the New Forest?'

'Now?' He paused. 'You sound upset. Are you sure you're okay?'

'I will be, if you help me. I need you to come on your own. Get a taxi to drop you off in our favourite spot,' she pleaded, trying to keep it together.

'Caitlin, what's going on? You're scaring me.'

'Steven, if I could tell you more I would. Tell the taxi driver to drop you off and wait for me. It's our only hope,' she sniffed, now fighting to hold back the tears. 'I love you.'

With that, the phone was snatched from her hands and the call ended.

'That was not so hard,' one of the men sneered.

Caitlin could have sworn he had licked his lips. She had never been so scared in her life.

***

Steven ran out of his room and dialled the number for the taxi firm he used after a night out. A taxi agreed to meet him in five minutes. As luck had it one was in the area. As he waited outside, he wondered what Caitlin could be doing in the middle of the New Forest at this time of night. If her friend's car had broken down, she would have mentioned it. There was no reason for them to drive in that direction.

Her words rung in his ear – *if I could tell you more I would.*

With his options limited, there was no choice but to go blind. It was not as if he could call the police – he had no crime to report. Even so, there was no point denying the fact he was worried. Something was not right. It was that sixth sense all over again.

After a short drive, the taxi arrived at the deserted location. Wary, the taxi driver turned to face Steven and asked, 'is this where you need to be?'

'Yes, this is fine. Thanks.' Steven got out of the car, paid for the trip and started to walk. Once in the spot, he waited.

Barely a few minutes had gone when he heard the distinctive sound of crunching leaves. He turned around and was stunned to see Caitlin flanked by two men. A sense of déjà vu overcame him. He wondered whether he had met one of them before.

'I'm so sorry,' Caitlin cried in hysterics, as she run towards him and cowered in his arms.

Confused, he looked up at the men. They were both in casual clothing and did not look threatening at all. One of them had bleach blonde hair and a lithe build. The other looked ordinary – just a typical man of average height, weight and build with brownish hair.

The ordinary man studied him – it was unnerving. 'Finally, we get to meet you. With the right incentive, a lot can happen. Don't you think?'

Steven was on alert. For someone so ordinary, looks could be deceiving. 'Who are you, what do you want?'

The man ignored Steven, and carried on talking. 'I have to admit that even if I did not suspect it, I would have immediately recognised you as my sister's son.'

'You know my mother?'

'There is no question about it. You are Emily's son.'

'Who is …?' Steven trailed off, lost in thought. His Dad had never mentioned her name. It sounded normal enough.

'Emily,' the man finished his sentence. He smiled and nodded towards the man standing next to him.

'Let start from the beginning,' the other man added. 'My name is Eilif. I am Ingrid's dad.'

The penny dropped, as a flashback run through his head and he recalled Ingrid. He looked so much like her. 'Surely, you meant to say brother. You could not be Ingrid's dad, unless you conceived her when you were born,' Steven chuckled, uncomfortable. Things were getting weirder by the minute.

Eilif pursed his lips, without giving a reply.

The ordinary guy spoke instead. 'I'm Ian, your uncle. I'm disappointed to see you know nothing of your past. It's time we put you in the loop.'

Chapter 18

Non–existent

Steven woke up with a thumping headache. Dazed and disorientated, he sat up and looked around. He was in bed; pyjama's on, just like he always was – how? In theory, it was plausible it had all been a dream. Had he really gone to the New Forest to meet Caitlin, and talked to those men, Ian and Eilif? It all sounded like a dream. In need of reassurance, he scrambled off the bed and retrieved his wallet. The twenty pound note he used to pay the taxi fare had gone. Logically, he must have gone out. It did not make sense. Unable to come up with an explanation, he got in the shower. Once under the hot water, he tried to relax. After ten minutes he remained tense – something was not right.

He pulled the towel off the rail, wrapped it around his waist and glanced it the mirror. His reflection revealed red puffy eyes. He swallowed two paracetamol down with water. His medical supplies were scanty. He stared at the empty paracetamol packet in his hand. It dawned on him that he had been having a lot of headaches recently. He had put being lightheaded and nauseated down to stress. Stress. That was a new concept for him. He was never stressed. He never buckled under pressure. The throb continued. If it was possible, it was more intense than the others. He hoped it would go away – soon.

It was frustrating to know Caitlin would have left already. She always had an early start at the beginning of the week. He could have texted or called, but he felt stupid. It must have been a dream. There was no point to calling her. He'd see what she said later on.

***

Caitlin sat through her Spanish history lecture in a trance. She was trying hard to concentrate. No matter how much she tried, nothing went in. It was all incomprehensible. Rubbing her eyes, she forced her eyes to stay open. She was so tired. It had been hard work at the hotel the night before. She did not even remember putting on her pyjamas or getting to her room. It was weird. She felt as though she had forgotten something important. Whatever it was, she could not stop a tear running down her cheek, as an unexpected sadness descended.

It was ridiculous to be tearful. If she did not know any better, she would have sworn her heart ached. As though she'd gone through a major break up. It was like being ditched by Danny Young at fifteen all over again. It was laughable. She had nothing to be heartbroken about. It was her time of the month. She could confidently put it down to hormones.

***

Steven waited in the Student union cafeteria for Caitlin, and started to wonder why she had still not turned up. In his confused state, he had left his phone behind that morning so he could not even text her. He would have to go back for it. Looking up, he saw Adam walk past, so he called out after him. 'Adam, how's it going?'

Adam walked up to him in his usual, relaxed manner and pulled a quizzical expression. 'Sorry, do I know you?'

'Of course you know me. Are you feeling alright?'

'I'm sorry, I don't know who you are, but hey, I'll see you around.' With that, he turned and walked away.

Weird. It had been the same all morning. He kept getting strange looks from people he'd sat next to for months.

Aware Caitlin wasn't going to show, he went to pay and showed his student I.D. card at the till to get a discount.

'I'm sorry, this card is not valid. You have to pay the full price,' the lady said, a snooty voice.

'Oh, that's just perfect.' Everything had turned topsy-turvy.

*

At the entrance to the halls of residence, he was thrown further into further confusion – his key did not fit the lock. He cursed inwardly. Someone had it in for him today. He waited, until a girl came along who he vaguely recalled having met.

'I've left my keys behind, can you let me in?'

The girl nodded, showing no recollection of having met him before.

Picking up the pace, he made his way up to the second floor and buzzed for Caitlin's Hall. A foreign girl, of what looked like Malaysian descent, peaked from behind the door. 'Can I help?'

'Can I come in? I've come to see Caitlin.'

'Oh, okay.' She opened the door, but eyes him suspiciously.

She had seen him before. This was getting ridiculous. He made his way to Caitlin's room door and knocked.

When it opened, Caitlin stared at him with a blank expression. 'Hello?'

'Stop kidding around – it's me,' he paused. 'I've had a hell of a day already so please, have mercy on me.'

Caitlin pursed her lips, as she normally did when annoyed, and started to close the door. 'I'm sorry; I have never met you before in my life.'

He held out his hand and stopped the door from closing. 'Please let me in, I need to talk to you.'

'I don't know who you are, but if you don't let go of the door, I will scream.'

She sounded like she actually meant it.

'Caitlin, it's me Steven. You have to know me,' he continued. His voice took on a desperate edge.

She paused, for a split second. Her eyes faltered, even though her face showed outrage. 'I'm sorry for you, I really am. I don't know you and I can't let you into my room. Please leave.'

Overcome, he let go of the door. It slammed shut in his face. He had been banished. A sense of hopelessness came over him as he snapped out of his trance and wondered down the hall. He looked back and checked her door did not open again. She had a warped sense of humour sometimes.

The door did not open. It was not a joke. Even for Caitlin, this kind of humour was a stretch too far. Something strange was going on, and he needed to find out what it was – fast.

Aimlessly, he wondered back towards his room. Things could not get a lot worse. Yet, they did – his key did not fit the lock.

'What the hell?' He screamed.

It was too much.

In a rage, he slammed his body against the door and it gave way. He could not believe he had forced the door open. It did not even hurt. Inside, he fell to his knees, his arms limp at his sides. The room was bare – nothing remained. It was nothing but an empty shell. A shiny metallic object remained on the desk. His mobile phone. He used all of his remaining energy to get up. His hand hovered above it, almost scared to touch it. Before he could change his mind, he snatched it up and looked at the face. He scrolled through the relevant keys and looked for his address book entries. All of the entries he knew had gone.

In frustration, he threw the phone on the floor and thumped the table. The wood split. The crack made him wake up. Whatever was going on was all wrong. Determined to find out the truth, he picked up the phone again and manually typed his home number.

After a few rings, it went straight to the answer phone where a short message ensued. It was his mum's voice. Hi, Paul and Clara are not here. Please leave a message after the beep – Adios.

Again, wrong.

What happened to Paul, Clara *and Steven*?

Was he still in the dream?

Flustered, he scrolled through the remaining entries in his phone. Two new entries had been added. The names of the entries were Ian and Eilif.

'No, please. Just wake up now. Wake up,' he shouted.

'Cool it dude,' Adam yelled, as he walked into the room with his hands raised. He was staring at the broken door. 'Oh, it's you from earlier. Are you moving in or something?'

'No, I am not moving in. This is my room. For crying out loud the joke is over. You win. Adam, you know me. Don't you?' He trailed as he realised Adam had taken a few steps back.

'Sorry dude, I told you earlier. I have no idea who you are. If this isn't your room, I think maybe you should go,' Adam replied, as he folded his arms across his chest. A challenge.

Not now.

'I'll go. Whatever.' Steven brushed past Adam.

It was not dream.

Something had happened, and whatever it was had led to his being ostracised from everyone he ever knew. If Ian and Eilif were behind this, he intended to find out.

***

Eilif placed his hand on the arm rest of the sofa as his index finger tapped in a continuous motion. It gave him scant consolation, yet strangely, the monotonous noise was comforting. He stared at his finger going up and down and closed his eyes. The waiting game was not something he was good at, even though it was a certainty that Steven would call.

The events of the last few weeks whirled in his head.

He found it hard to understand why Anna had lied. Why did she say Steven was not one of them? If only Lana and Ingrid had confided in him sooner. Either way, the past could not be changed – it was the future that mattered. Ingrid had spilled the beans. He could always rely on his eldest daughter. It still annoyed him that Ingrid had spoken to Carmen, Ian's wife, before telling him the truth. He could not help feeling like she had some ulterior motive – what exactly that was he did not know for sure. Lana suspected she wanted Steven to be hers. Eilif did not like the idea. Either way, it was not up to him. No-one could tell Ingrid what to do or feel, especially not if love was involved.

'He's definitely Emily's son,' Ian stated, as he walked towards him, grinning from ear to ear like a Cheshire cat.

'Without a doubt,' Eilif replied. 'You know something's bothering me. Why did Anna tell Ingrid and Lana to back off?'

'I've thought about that a lot. I have a suspicion, but I won't know for sure until we get back.'

'What's that then?'

'I don't think Anna came back. I think Emily snuck out. Didn't you notice how she'd cut her hair recently. Sure, she ties it up to disguise it, but she did it all the same.'

'But, she's not allowed to leave. How?'

'Anna must have helped her. The sisterly bond overcame rational thought. They always did have a strange connection. At least Emily came back this time, let's be thankful for that.'

'I guess, but why leave Steven here? Emily should have known better.'

'She should. Then again, when has my sister ever shown common sense?' Ian laughed aloud, mocking. 'It's alright now – we'll clear up the mess, as usual.'

After a pause, Eilif added. 'Do you think Steven will accept his fate?'

'If you've done everything right, he has no other choice. His life here is over.'

'True.' Eilif had reason to feel guilty. He had been responsible for alienating Steven from his current life.

Just then, Ian's phone rang. The wait was over.

Chapter 19

Revelations

It was eight o'clock in the evening. Steven sat outside The Cowherds, a local pub on the edge of the Southampton Common. His eyes remained fixed on the distant trees. A million thoughts raced through his mind which he attempted to drown out with beer and a beef, mushroom & Guinness pie. He wondered whether this would be the last time he ate here? Since it was obvious he was not in a dream, the things Ian had said were starting to filter in. Emily. His mother's name was Emily. Ian was his uncle. Eilif was Ingrid's dad, even though he was her age. It was a lot to take in. They had some serious explaining to do.

Steven needed answers, fast. Otherwise, things could get tricky. He was down to his last pound. At least he had chosen the perfect location – they would blend in easily. It was important to remain level headed. By surrounding himself with normal people, he stood a better chance of not losing his cool – trusting Ian and Eilif was going to be a challenge, to say the least.

'Steven, that looks nice,' Ian's voice said. It sounded sincere. It did not make any difference to Steven what he sounded like.

'It's the most normal thing I've done all day,' he contemplated, as he took a deep breath. He had to keep calm. He turned around to face him.

Steven watched Ian make his way round the table to sit down. Eilif watched Steven for a few seconds, and then he gave a slight nod, as though apologetic and took a seat next to Ian. They each held a pint of beer.

'We got some nuts,' Ian said. He threw a few packets of salted and roasted nuts on the table. It could have been his idea of a peace offering.

The beer and nuts made them look normal. Yet, Steven suspected appearances were deceiving. He stared at his unfinished plate of food. It was unsurprising he had lost his appetite.

'So, here we are,' Ian stated, holding his hands up with a smile. 'Are you ready to start your new life then?'

Steven looked at them with a sense of foreboding gloom. He did not want a new life, he wanted his old life. It was not that easy to just erase everyone he had ever loved from his thoughts.

'No, I'm not ready to start a new life. I want my old one back,' he snapped. He was trying to keep it together. It was going to prove difficult. 'What did you do? Why?'

'How much do you want to know? It could take a long time. It might be best to leave it for the journey,' Ian replied. He took a long sip from his beer, and then wiped his mouth with the back of his hand.

'Journey?'

Eilif spoke. 'We could call it an adventure.'

'Hah,' Steven scoffed. 'Has all of this got something to do with what Ingrid said?' He paused.

They looked on without saying a word, waiting for him to carry on.

'Is it true? Am I different?'

Ian popped a few peanuts into his mouth and started to chew. 'You could say that. You are different.'

'What am I?' Steven did not want to ask, but he had to know.

'Now, that's a long story. Hmmm, to cut it short, let's just say – you are a member of a more advanced version of humanity. Although, to be honest, you are the first of your kind. You are the only one ever born part human.'

'What the hell does that mean?' He hissed again under his breath, his fists now clenched in a ball.

'Well, my sister Emily, or should I say your mother, seems to have had a liaison with your father. Obviously, you're the outcome. You're a hybrid. You are unique. Consider yourself lucky – the first.'

'Lucky!' Steven concentrated on the table. Without lifting his head, he whispered 'So, what are you?'

'Again, that will take some explaining,' Ian said. He looked like he was discussing the weather.

'It's not a bad thing,' Eilif interjected.

Steven looked up and narrowed his eyes. 'Try me.'

'I don't know if you're ready,' Ian speculated.

'Why didn't you wipe my memory? Wouldn't that have been a bit more humane?' Steven grimaced.

Eilif turned to Ian, and then replied. 'The hypnotism I perform and manifest upon others only works on humans. For some reason we are not affected. That includes you since you have inherited your mother's immunity. We have spent years studying our extra gifts…to be honest; we are still a long way from knowing their limitations and full advantages. Relatively speaking, we have not been in existence long enough to know what we are capable of.'

'How long have *we* been in existence for?'

'Since 1942. I was born in 1932,' Ian replied, as he took a sip.

It felt like he was having a friendly drink at the local pub. It was anything but. What they were saying changed everything.

'Really?'

'Yes, really,' Ian took a deep breath, and began. 'The year was 1942 and my father, Jeff, was a member of the exclusive team of scientists secretly conducting nuclear tests in Los Alamos, New Mexico – that's in America.'

'I know where New Mexico is,' Steven snapped.

'Good, glad they still teach Geography. Anyway, the fate of the Second World War hang in the balance, and his team was designing the ultimate weapon.'

'The atom bomb,' Steven interrupted again.

'Correct again, do you want to tell the story?' Ian grinned.

'No, you carry on,' Steven replied.

'As I was saying…the atom bomb. The most powerful weapon ever made by man. As history showed, it did indeed change things a lot. A deadly weapon with lasting consequences.'

Steven nodded.

'This is going to sound crazy, but trust me – it wasn't. I have never been so scared in my life. I was only ten years old after all,' Ian paused.

Steven did not care if he had still been a baby. 'Get to the point.'

'I told you this was not the right time to tell you,' Ian said, the faint trace of irritation in his reply.

'I'm just not interested in your melodrama. You were ten years old, so what? It doesn't look like it bothered you in the slightest.'

'You're right – it didn't. I never once questioned what happened.

I accepted it – in a way, my young age was a blessing.'

'I was born in 1948, so this is also a history lesson for me,' Eilif admitted, head on his hand.

'Are you going to be patient?' Ian asked, with a serious expression.

'I'm listening,' Steven replied. He took a long slug out of his pint of beer. For once, getting drunk didn't sound like such a bad idea.

'Okay, so we were attacked by radioactive vampire bats,' Ian added, his face lit up, overly dramatic.

Steven was not impressed, but he kept a straight face and nodded. The story was beginning to sound like a horror movie.

'All the bats died, but their bite infected many – fourteen people in total. My family, the Roberts family, made six: your grandparents, Jeff and Judith; my oldest sister, Catherine; the twins, your mum Emily and Anna; and me. The Santos Family, who were Spanish in origin made five: Franco; Elena; and their children Hortensia, who is now my mother in law; Lana and Juan. There was also a married couple from Sweden called Morten and Arla Clausen. And finally, there was a single man called Isaac Abel, a German Jew who escaped Germany in the early 1930s.'

'Quite a mix,' Steven remarked.

'Indeed, the key thing is – all of us eventually changed. Anyway, that's enough for today. I don't want to inundate you. The point is the accident led to a further step in the evolution of mankind. All you have to know for now is that you are due a change. When you do, you will still retain your individuality. We breathe, eat, sleep, think and do all the things we used to. But, you will have other needs…'

'Needs that make you kill for blood,' Steven added. It was classic. Leave the best bit to the end.

'Sometimes. Death is not always necessary. It's complicated, I know,' Ian mused.

'It's not a bad thing to be one of us,' Eilif added. 'As you can see we don't age after the change. Think of that perk!'

'Perk! And watch everyone else die around you,' Steven spat, disgust, thick and heavy, in his voice.

'That's the point. None of us will die. Don't you see that we have made it easier for you? We have cut loose the ties that bound you to a normal human life.' Eilif continued, in a blatant attempt to justify their actions.

For a brief pause, no-one spoke, as Steven contemplated their undeniable logic.

'Can I just ask you one more thing?'

'Sure,' Ian replied drinking the remains of his beer.

'Why was the charade with Caitlin necessary? Why didn't you just come to talk to me, and then make me disappear?'

'Steven, you have to understand that there was no other way in which you would have taken us seriously. She can not be in your life anymore. This is the best way forward. You realise you could have killed her, in a few months time.'

'Will she ever remember me?' Steven asked, looking towards Eilif.

'Truthfully, I don't know. Maybe in a few years time the memory will come back. Probably, she'll think it was a dream.'

'Will my parents ever remember me?'

'Again doubtful. In time, like I've just said, they might remember something deep in their subconscious. The conscious mind will never convince them it was a reality.'

'Can I ask one more question?'

'Go for it,' Ian conceded.

'Why do you have to kill occasionally?'

'Ah, now that is more difficult to answer. In a few months you will understand that one better. The truth is you will need human blood to change. After that all mammal blood tastes good, but if you like, human blood is our chocolate. Not for overindulgence.'

'I need human blood to change?' Steven winced.

'Yes, you do,' Ian replied.

'Is it impossible to live amongst normal humans after the change?'

'That is our firm belief. If we started to allow that it would be like opening a can of worms. Who knows what the consequences would be? We are respectful of human life.'

'So, I won't become a bloodlust, insatiable vampire?'

Eilif laughed.

'Not from our experience. But you are the first of our kind to be born half human – half vampire.' Ian tweaked his fingers to form speech marks at the word vampire. 'So I can't give you a foolproof guarantee of what you'll become. Which is why you should be with us now,' Ian finished with conviction.

After another pause, Steven looked up. Even though he did not want to go, he did not see that he had any choice in the matter. 'When do we leave?'

'Now is as good a time as any.' Ian downed the rest of his drink and stuffed the unopened packets of nuts in his pocket. 'Ready?'

'Not really, but I'm as ready as I'll ever be. Don't expect me to be overjoyed.'

'We are realistic. We didn't expect you to be jumping through hoops. You have a great future ahead of you. This is not the end, it's the beginning,' Eilif said. His voice and expression were full of optimism.

Steven did not share their enthusiasm. If this was the beginning, he'd skip and read the end.

Chapter 20

Journey to the unknown

A baby continued to wail, as the parents frantically rummaged in a huge rucksack. The moment was tense. They were obviously flustered, too slow to appease the demanding babe. Finally, the bottle of milk was thrust in the baby's mouth, followed by blissful silence. At the same time, a group of boisterous teenagers started to have an argument, whilst their unfortunate parents grimaced in the background. A lone businessman frowned, appalled at being sandwiched between the crazy baby and mutinous siblings.

Amongst it all, in the queue for the passport checkpoint, Steven mulled his predicament. He wished his life was like theirs – normal. But, he had no alternative – where else could he go? Strangely, this stage of his life brought about a farcical element of excitement. Saying this, he was still in denial. There was no way his existence had been erased. Tomorrow, he would wake up to find it had all been an extravagant dream.

In truth, he was disappointed. All of his childish notions had been quashed when he realised they were travelling on a normal flight. He hadn't really considered any other options, but a plane seemed way too ordinary. To add to it, he was still travelling under his real identity with his valid passport. Even though, to all intents and purposes, he did not exist, his passport was still the legal document that would allow him to leave. He was determined to look disinterested, and had worn a scowl ever since they had set off from Southampton. He was curious. Just not in the mood to have a friendly chat with his new guardians.

As he walked through the metal detector he willed it to beep. As they waved him through, he resigned himself to his fate. Finally, it was time to head to the gate. The flight was going to Sau Paulo.

'So, do you know where Sau Paulo is?' Eilif asked.

'No,' Steven huffed, intent on keeping up appearances.

'Do you want to know?' Ian asked, a smirk stretched across his face.

'Not really bothered,' Steven added. He dug his heals in.

Eilif pulled a face and glanced at Ian, who then raised his eyebrows in disbelief.

'Drop the act, we know you're curious. The sooner you cheer up the better. It's not our fault you got left behind in the first place.'

Choosing not to respond, he kept his head down and closed his eyes. Whatever his personal views, he was not going to give them the satisfaction of thinking he was impressed by any of it.

'It's in Brazil,' Eilif stated.

Steven opened his eyes and saw Eilif heading off towards the bookstore. It would have been his usual haunt.

Waiting around at the departure lounge was excruciating. Several times, Steven held back the urge to run up to one of the guards and explain that he was being kidnapped. It felt like it anyway. Even though he had no way to prove it. It was unbelievable to think his destination was Brazil. He had never been to South America. Their final destination was Manaus, going via Sau Paulo. His knowledge of geography was scanty at best, but he had a feeling it was in the heart of the Amazon. It made sense to hide a new species of man in a place teaming with dangerous and unique wildlife.

*

The flight from London to Sao Paulo took nearly twelve hours. Steven managed to watch two films and sleep for a proportion of the time.

The flight was nearly full, since it was summer and there were a lot of tourists heading towards South America. A few children screamed throughout. It prompted a rise in the volume. He could not understand why parents thought travelling with young children, on a long haul flight, was a good idea. The food was decent, as far as airplane food went, and it kept hunger pains at bay.

Steven noticed how Eilif and Ian blended in. He could see how they kept up the façade. There was no way anyone would ever suspect they were anything other than normal. It was still difficult for him to accept that he was going to need blood to survive. It was inconceivable. He could not fathom how he was going to develop the need to kill any of the people around him. They claimed they were not vampires. He could see why. The species he apparently belonged to was different. In the same way human beings are natural omnivores, he would have to survive on a combination of food and blood. He was sure the concept of evolution had never been so complicated.

The wait at the transfer lounge took a few more hours. At last, they boarded the flight to Manaus. Finally, after nearly a whole day of travelling, they landed with a jolt. As soon as the doors of the plane opened, Steven suppressed the urge to run out for freedom. In a sheep like manner, he followed his companions to passport control and onto the arrivals lounge to retrieve the luggage. The luggage seemed to have multiplied. They had enough bags for six, not three. Having been unable to take his clothes with him, Steven was travelling light. It was doubtful his English wardrobe would have been suitable for a tropical climate.

Outside of the airport, they headed for the car park and loaded up a four wheel drive. The climate was scorching, even though humid. A light drizzle of rain provided the only relief. Steven climbed into the back seat in the car and looked out of the window, studying his surroundings.

Ian turned to face him. 'We still have a way to go. Try to be patient and enjoy the ride.'

Steven nodded. He didn't exactly have any other choice.

After five minutes, Steven decided to ask the question. 'So, why did you all move to Brazil?'

'I'll let you do the talking now, Eilif. You know this as well as I do,' Ian grunted.

'Fair enough,' Eilif replied. 'The original fourteen left Los Alamos using the excuse they had to go back to Europe to help with the War effort. It was easy for them to fake their deaths – everyone seemed to be dying in the war.'

Steven hoped that was not an attempt at humour.

'They moved to Mexico City. The ones that had already changed indulged their newfound needs and desires, before cementing their ideas for the future. After exhausting all the available possibilities, it was agreed they did not want to remain in civilization as hunters. Their vision was to recreate a new civilization – somewhere they would be protected from the outside world. Eventually, the community was born within the tropical undergrowth of the Amazon

Jungle in Brazil. Their enthusiasm and vision allowed them to utilise their new found abilities and scientific expertise to create a safe haven that would allow them to remain invisible. When Morten and Arla discovered they had retained their reproductive ability, everyone rejoiced. The first child born within the community – me. Those first few years are considered to have been amazing. As far as everyone was concerned – they had created a utopia.'

'It certainly was that,' Ian guffawed.

Eilif grinned. 'They led normal lives, fed off other mammals in the Amazon, and realised that they did not need to hunt humans, if none where available. The complication arrived when Juan was a month away from his twentieth Birthday.

Over night, he developed a fever and became sick – they all thought he was going to die. Jeff was the one who recognised the symptoms. He had seen Emily and Anna succumb to the same conditions in Los Alamos. It had also happened on the advent of their twentieth birthday. He knew the only thing that would save Juan was human blood – and he was right. From then on, it became obvious all adolescents would have to return for human blood to complete the evolutionary process. Otherwise, they would die.'

Ian beeped the car horn three times. Someone had left their car in the middle of the road, doors open. The driver sauntered back, nonplussed. He glared in defiance at Ian, as he got back in to drive away.

Ian pulled a face and was about to hurl some abuse in the man's direction when he reconsidered. 'I don't need a confrontation now,' he huffed.

After ten more minutes of stop start driving, the car pulled in to a space.

In a bid for fresh air, Steven opened the car door and got out to see where they were. It was obviously a main port, since all around them people were going about their frantic business. A series of fishing boats were scattered around the area and some makeshifts shacks seemed to be selling the fresh catch of the day.

Ian had made his way towards a small vessel.

Eilif grabbed one of the large suitcases and handed it to Steven. 'Make yourself useful and take this over, will you?'

At the waters edge, he took a minute to inspect the transportation. It looked like a very old and outdated version of a river cruise ship, about ninety feet in length. If he did not know any better, he could have sworn it was the ship used on an old Agatha Christie film adaptation of Death on the Nile years earlier. In the scheme of things it looked reasonably safe. Its size made him wary. He had no idea how much longer the trip would take.

Using all of his strength, he lugged the heavy and cumbersome suitcase up the narrow ramp. As he was about to hoist it onto the floor, a hand reached out and grabbed it. Nimbly, she picked it up and threw it over her back as if it was a feather.

'Is it a bit heavy for you?' She sounded condescending.

Open mouthed, he looked up and gawped.

What shocked him at first was the fact she was so unbelievably strong. After he had got over that all he could feel was resentment. The last time he had seen her he expected it to be the last. Now, it dawned on him he would be living alongside her. To make matters worse, if what they were saying was true – it could be forever.

Mouth closed, he pursed his lips together before he spoke through gritted teeth. 'Ingrid, we meet again.'

'Did you miss me?' She teased, cocking her head to the side, in a coquettish manner.

'Hardly,' he murmured. He stared away from her and pretended to study the floor.

To his surprise, another woman came out from behind Ingrid and held out her hand. She had short black hair, chocolate brown eyes and a tanned complexion. Totally different to Ingrid. 'It's a pleasure to meet you Steven. I'm Ingrid's mum, Lana. I've heard a lot about you.'

The fact her name was Lana made him stop and think. It was a name more commonly used in Spanish speaking communities. Obviously, her roots were Spanish. 'Right, I hope some of it was good,' he said. As he looked from one to the other he rolled his eyes. 'I guess I'll get used to the age thing eventually.'

'I'm sure you will,' Ingrid added.

'I've got work to do. I'll see you later.' Lana gave a curt nod, glanced at Ingrid for a split second, as though wary, and walked away. He got the impression she had only come up to see what he looked like. He wondered what Ingrid had told her about him.

'I'm not usually one to bear grudges, but I think you've got a heck of explaining to do,' he stressed, head cocked to the side, arms folded.

'We've got the trip. I'll answer as much as I can.' She seemed to stare at him, in a strange, glossy eyed, kind of way.

'So, what happens now?' He asked, as he shoved his hands into his trouser pockets.

'We'll be heading off soon. Your new home waits. It really is nice to see you again.'

'So are you ready?' Ian called out, as he pulled another box on to the vessel. He sounded at ease.

'As ready as I'll ever be,' Steven replied. There was no point acting childish.

Ian laughed out loud and walked off, still busy with the preparations.

A lot of bags and extra supplies continued to amass on to the ship. Steven was not the sort to mope, so he figured he might as well pitch in. After loading the car onto the ship with a jib crane, the ramp was raised they were ready to go.

The spluttering sound of the motor started, and Ian called out. 'At least the motor's still working.'

Finally, they cruised down river, the journey seemed never-ending. Steven was convinced they were travelling to the end of the earth.

Chapter 21

Ingrid

A group of river dolphins swam next to the boat. It was plain they did not have a care in the world. The way they frolicked in the waves and swooped in and out of the surf made Steven jealous. He yearned to have that sense of freedom again. He leant overboard and was splashed in the face as a dolphin leapt up out of the water. With the back of his arm he brushed the water off his face and could not help chuckling. He lost track of time as he searched the dense undergrowth ahead and saw civilization disappear from their point of origin. He wondered when he would be with *normal* humans again.

After about twenty minutes, something weird started to happen to the river water. The dark colour of the river they were coming from met with a light green coloured water from ahead. They eased alongside each other, stubborn in their quest to remain independent. It was a metaphor for his life – two sides, different and in cohesive. He heard someone come up behind him, yet he pretended he did not know they were there and continued to study the water.

'The Rio Negro literally translates into...'

'Black river,' he interrupted, eyes fixed downwards. 'I can translate some Spanish.'

'Right,' Ingrid remarked. She said it in a bemused tone, obviously impressed. 'As the black river meets the Solimões River the two waters run side by side without mixing for about eight kilometres.'

'Why don't they mix?' His curiosity was sparked, he decided to play along.

'Well, the Rio Negro is a darker, slower and heavier body of water. If you dip your hand in to either side you'll notice the difference in temperature.'

He frowned, impressed. It really was an interesting display. The fact unknown perils, such as piranhas, lurked under the water made him unlikely to test the theory.

'The waters will merge soon. Welcome to the Amazon River.'

Steven stared in awe at his surroundings. The environment was exotic, alluring, and practically prehistoric. The picture of land before time.

'I'm sure you must be tired, would you like a place to rest?' Ingrid asked her smile genuine. He would have to try to cut her some slack.

'Yeah, thanks.' He was tired and fed up. A place to crash sounded great.

***

Once she had left Steven in one of the cabins, Ingrid made her way back to the deck. A pair of macaws squawked as they flew across the river. They were such amazing birds, so colourful and intelligent.

'You okay?' Lana asked, as she came up alongside her and placed her arm over Ingrid's shoulder. 'Looks to me like Steven bears a grudge against you.'

'He'll get over it. I did what I had to. It's not me he should blame.'

'True, but it might take some time. You might want to give him some space,' Lana said.

Ingrid knew her mum was perceptive, it made her wary. 'Sure. I–I just… forget it. I'll give him some space,' she faltered. She could not admit the illogical attraction. Changing the subject, she added. 'Isn't it ironic? Some species of Macaw are facing extinction because of the constant deforestation of the perimeter by human beings. It's not exactly us that are the monsters.'

'I know, but humanity has a way of excusing itself.'

'Do you think they'll find us someday?' Ingrid asked. She was scared of what humans would do to people like them.

'Maybe, but if they ever get close we'll be ready or we'll move on. Somewhere new. There are many places to hide in the world.'

'Do we always have to hide?' Ingrid asked her tone slightly exasperated.

'You know what could happen. Humans are cruel towards anything they see as a threat to their existence,' Lana explained, adopting a familiar teacher stance.

'Yet, they are lenient against those that create havoc within society in so many other ways. The endless list of crimes committed in the quest for peace is depressing,' Ingrid sighed, as she started to twist a strand of hair in her fingers.

'Are you okay? What's this about?' Lana asked. She put both of her hands on Ingrid's shoulders and stared in her eyes.

Ingrid looked away and shrugged Lana's hands off. 'I just wish things could have been different for Steven. If we'd brought him back sooner, it would have been easier. He might not hate me.'

'I'm sorry about that. You shouldn't worry about what he thinks? You are my daughter, and I love you. You did nothing wrong. You know we had to give Anna the chance to fix it.'

'But, she didn't and now he doesn't trust us – and so close to his change.'

'Look, I should have done something too. I tried to talk to Anna, but she told me it was under control. What you did was not right, you should have talked to me before you went to see Carmen, but it will be better for Steven in the long run. Emily needs to explain things to him. We all know he is her son – just look at the resemblance. There is no way Anna had him twenty years ago – it's impossible. But, Emily was and still is unstable at times, so leaving him couldn't have been easy.'

'I get that. I just hope Steven adapts to our way of life. He has not had the proper preparation, and we still don't know how his change will go. He's not like the rest of us.'

'Maybe, but then Emily was human too, before the accident. She wasn't prepared for what happened either. I'm sure she'll know what to do.'

'I guess. I don't trust her. I think… forget it.' Ingrid suspected Emily was responsible for the cover up in England, but she did not want to jump to conclusions.

'You feel very protective of him don't you?' Lana asked, her head cocked to the side. Concerned, in a motherly kind of way.

Ingrid bit her lower lip. It felt stupid to say she was in love with Steven – she barely knew him. 'Well, I feel like I got him into this mess.'

'But, just imagine, if you had not found him? He would have gone through the change alone. Think of the repercussions.'

'Emily would have checked on him first.'

'You know she can't leave without permission. No-one knows what she was planning to do,' Lana said, with a slight shake of the head. 'The point is. He is going to be ready now, and it's all thanks to you.' Lana wrapped both arms around Ingrid and gave her a huge hug.

Ingrid leaned her head against her mother's shoulder. It was difficult to know what she was really feeling. After making the change a few years earlier, she had fully accepted what she had become. She never doubted whether taking human life was right or wrong – it was necessary. Since the attack on Steven, she had become confused. Remorse was not a sentiment she experienced often. Now, she felt more drawn to him than ever. Seeing him again had made her remember why she had chosen him in the first place. It was illogical.

***

Steven woke up disorientated, for the second time in two days. The motion of the water caused the surroundings to sway gently, in a constant reminder – they were not on dry land. His body was drenched in sweat and his clothes clung to his body, totally saturated. Sitting up, he noticed a new set of clothes folded neatly on the chair. It looked like a t-shirt and shorts. He would have given anything for a shower. Somehow, he doubted there would be anything to resemble his ensuite where they were heading.

A loud rumbling sound caught him unawares. He was hungry – starving in fact.

After he left the sanctuary of the cabin, he made his way down the narrow corridor in the direction of what he hoped to be the kitchen. A mouth watering aroma infiltrated the air, making him salivate at the thought of a proper meal. An open door revealed the small kitchenette facilities. Ingrid stood in front of the hobs, stirring an enormous pot.

'Hi,' she said, as she turned around to greet him.

He could be courteous. 'Something smells good, what is it?'

'One of our specialties, Piranha soup.'

'You're kidding. I thought they'd want to eat me?'

'Actually, they don't attack that often. In fact, Piranha attacks are rare. Usually, an attack on a person has only taken place when someone is injured and showing signs of distress.' She seemed to waffle, he sensed nerves. 'We regularly bathe with them swimming around.'

'I'll take your word for it. I'm too hungry to be squeamish. Is it ready?'

She stopped stirring and smirked. 'A bit direct all of a sudden, aren't you?'

'I've lost all my inhibitions recently. Politeness is for the faint hearted.'

'Fair enough, we'll have to work on your manners then. But for now, it is actually ready.' A little bell positioned in the hallway started to ring as she pressed a button by the stove. In a matter of seconds, you could hear lots of movement. Everyone seemed to come out of the woodwork at once.

Ian walked up to Steven and grinned. 'So, are you feeling better now? You looked pretty worn out when we arrived.'

'Yeah, all that travelling took it out of me.'

'I think you know everyone, but as a recap, let me introduce you,' Ian said, turning to face the rest of the ship occupants. 'Ingrid and Eilif you know. This is Lana, Ingrid's mother, and Inna and Tomas, Ingrid's older sister and younger brother. Not that age matters – we tend to look the same age,' he joked.

No-one else laughed.

'I'll take you to meet my wife, Carmen, later on. Someone has to steer the ship whilst we eat,' he finished, as he settled in a seat, ready for food.

Steven froze as he saw Lana. He still found it hard to believe she was Ingrid's mother. It was impossible. Vaguely, he remembered seeing Tomas. He could not remember where. They all looked so alike.

For a few minutes, it was silent, as the stew was passed round and everyone tucked in. The soft fish melted in his mouth, like butter. Steven was completely convinced – piranhas were totally edible.

'Have you been tired recently?' Ian asked, scooping some stew into his mouth.

'Yeah, but then, it's been a hell of a journey,' Steven replied.

'It's not the travelling that's making you tired,' Eilif chipped in. His tone was ominous.

'What is it then?' Steven asked, as he lowered his spoon.

'Your body is starting to need more than what you give it. It is preparing for the change,' Lana answered, her voice soft yet full of authority.

'Is it like this for everyone?'

Ian replied. 'Everyone who has gone through the change from an adolescent to adult form has had the same experience. At first you are energised and almost invincible. Your focus sharpens and your ability to concentrate is unparalleled.'

'So that's why all my grades were fantastic.'

They all smiled, as though acknowledging his experience.

Ian continued. 'As you start to approach your twentieth Birthday your body starts to deteriorate and you start to get sick. There is only one thing that can heal you and stop you from dying.'

Steven blurted it out. 'Human blood.'

'Exactly,' Ian nodded.

'So how do you find a victim? Does someone always have to die?'

'As far as we know,' Eilif interjected. 'A few times we have been able to keep a human alive and make it look like an accident. I can easily erase any memory they have and make them forget the truth.'

'Could we do that for me? I don't want to kill anyone.'

'For a change it is impossible,' Ian snapped. 'We are unlikely to be able to make you stop in time. It's not something you can control.'

'Where there is a will, there is a way,' Steven stated, with what he knew could be misplaced confidence.

'Doubtful, but I like your conviction,' Ian remarked.

Chapter 22

The Killer Within

Steven was not about to let it go. He wanted to have some answers. 'So? What about my first question? How do you find a victim?'

'That's not difficult. We never attack anyone in this area. We usually go somewhere overpopulated or remote where no-one would question the real cause of death.'

'So why were you in Southampton? It's not exactly inconspicuous.'

'We were visiting the Robert's family home. Your grandfather and grandmother's original house,' Eilif answered.

'My grandparents lived in Southampton. When?'

'Before the war. They kept the house. They had means by which to prevent it from falling into other hands.'

'That's where my dad met Emily. He used to live in Southampton.'

'Exactly,' Ian grinned.

'So what happens then? How do you decide what human to attack?' Steven continued, he was not going to be sidetracked.

Lana tentatively answered. 'Usually, we look for someone vulnerable. Someone not surrounded – a loner.' She paused, taking a breath, and then added apologetically. 'This is going to sound terrible, but we make it look like a suicide.'

'A suicide!' The puzzle pieces aligned to reveal the picture. 'The student suicide, Caitlin's flat mate – surely that was not your doing?'

Ingrid looked up with a guilty expression. 'That was us.'

'That's sick. How can you live with yourselves?'

'We have no other choice,' Lana defended, staring at him with wide eyes.

'I guess I have a lot to learn,' Steven shrugged. He toyed with the rest of his food for a minute, but it was too late. He had lost his appetite. 'I need to go get some air.

***

Lana could see Ingrid was not happy. Steven had got to her. Of all the men available, she had to get hooked on a mere boy, a hybrid. Worse than that – Emily's boy. It was tragic, yet there was nothing she could really do. Just as she predicted, Ingrid got up to follow Steven.

'I'll go talk to him,' Ingrid said, eyes on the door.

'Just remember, don't tell him what he does not need to know,' Ian stressed.

With a curt nod, she walked out.

'I'm worried she's going to get hurt,' Lana sighed, as she nuzzled into Eilif's shoulder.

'I don't think there is anything we can do,' Eilif said.

Lana lifted her head off Eilif's shoulder. Then she added, exasperated. 'It's the first time she's fallen for someone. Why did it have to be him?'

'You think Ingrid is in love with Steven?' Ian asked, as an amused huff escaped.

'You don't choose who to love, it just happens. Isn't that right Ian? You and Carmen fell for each other when neither of you expected it. It does happen – you of all people know that,' Lana pouted and clasped her hands together.

'You never know, it might work between them,' Ian added, waving his finger in the air as he laughed again. 'Maybe, he'll fit in then.'

'Glad to hear you sounding so optimistic,' Eilif said, his voice laced in sarcasm.

Lana narrowed her eyes in Ian's direction. She'd look out for Ingrid – she always did.

***

The moonlight shining on the river caused the ripples to glisten like silver. The beautiful scene did nothing to comfort Steven as a million thoughts raced through his mind. Everything around him was unfamiliar and disconcerting. He longed for the sight of something normal and man made. Everything they said disgusted him. It had to be a lie. He had no intention of killing anyone.

'Can we talk?'

Ingrid again. Would she ever learn to leave him alone?

Steven gave her a cursory glance. 'Why not, doesn't look like anything I think or say makes any difference anyway.'

As she leaned against the railing, she said in a casual tone. 'Do you realise you are already a killer?'

With a grunt, he turned sharply to face her. 'How do you figure that?'

'Well, you are not a vegetarian are you? You eat meat – animals die as a consequence.'

'Oh, yeah well, it's not the same thing but, I guess.'

'Did you realise that it was only a few centuries ago that different tribes performed human sacrifices and cannibalism in this area?'

'So, what's your point? Aren't we supposed to be civilised now?'

'Animals still die in your world – you kill them. Let's face it – men and women die every day in the name of war. Is that justified?'

'I have never personally killed anything or anyone?' He stated, as he leaned away from the railing and folded his arms across his chest.

'Really, you've never killed a fly or stepped on an ant?'

'Oh, come on, give me a break,' he huffed, indignant.

'Killing is killing. Doesn't matter what it is. Humanity has a way of excusing itself when it's convenient.'

Amused, he gave a half smile. 'You got me – I'm already a killer.'

'So now,' she spoke slowly, as she stepped closer to him. 'Try to imagine how you are going to feel when you have to kill a stranger for your survival. A natural instinct takes over. You have no control.'

'I see.' He stared ahead, getting closer to the railing. He was determined to keep his distance.

'I hope you do. I know what happened last year did not make sense. But, I can't regret having found you. The chances are that Emily, I mean your mother…'

'Emily,' he snapped. 'Just because she is my biological mother, does not make her my mother.'

'Fine, Emily would have come to get you. But, we could not wait any longer. You need to know who you really are.'

He noticed she was close enough to touch him. Taking a step away, he shook his head. 'I wish you had told me the truth when we met.'

'I did start to, if you remember, but then...,' she paused. 'It was a mistake. Everything will be alright now.' She moved closer and held out her hand to touch his face.

Fury surfaced and he took a step back. 'Everything is not alright. I am in love with someone special, who I am not looking to replace. So, don't go getting any ideas – I'm not available. And even if I was, I would not want to be with *you.*'

It was a slap in the face – outright rejection. The shock in her face was instant.

'I'll give you some space then. If you want to talk, as a friend, I'll be around.'

In a series of rapid movements she disappeared. Perhaps, he had been too harsh.

***

Ingrid ran back to her cabin, shut the door and collapsed in a heap on the floor. Tears started to build up in her eyes. She did not want him to get the better of her. Unfortunately, he had managed to weaken her defences. Taking an enormous gulp, the constriction hurting her throat erupted. She had never cried so hard. The tears streamed down her face. It sounded like a tantrum. Slamming her hands onto the floor, she groaned, recognising the need for some time away from him. It was Steven that had made her re-evaluate her existence from the moment she had bitten him. He had forced her to reconsider their need to kill.

The resulting obsession with Steven was impossible to contain. Something about him drew her in – no-one had ever had the same effect before. The hours she had waited, the months of hope. To find that now, after all of her efforts, she was too late. He had fallen in love with someone else. She wanted to scream. It was not fair. She forced herself to calm down and took a few deep breaths. Her eyes fixed on the loose nail on the floor. She clenched her fist and rammed it down as she bit her lip.

She would have him. Even if it was the last thing she ever did.

***

Ingrid disturbed Steven. He could not understand why she was still trying it on. Sure, there had been some attraction when he first met her. But, then…well, it wasn't worth reliving what had happened. There was no way he was going to be with someone like her. Perhaps, she felt responsible – she did find him after all. Either way, it was not her fault he was one of them. If she had fallen for him, he felt sorry for her. It was not the first time he'd failed to reciprocate someone else's affections. The truth was he didn't feel bad rejecting her. She looked tough enough to cope.

There was no denying her beauty. It was just a shame she was so cold-hearted. For Ingrid, human beings were takeaway, dispensable. In a way, he knew he could not take on too many airs. She was right; humans did kill all the time. Nevertheless, he could not see how she could view human death so naturally. He had so many unanswered questions. The sound of steps made him turn to face them. If it was Ingrid, maybe he would apologise. There turned out to be no need for sympathy. It was only Eilif.

'Steven, I was hoping to catch up with you. Do you mind if we talk?'

'No, just don't ramble on about how great my future is going to be, okay,' Steven replied.

Eilif chuckled. 'Fair enough. All I wanted was to let you know how sorry I am for how things turned out. It must be tough right now. I won't go on about your great future, seeing as you've told me not to,' he paused, with a smile.

'Thanks for saying sorry, but I don't think I can forgive you. I'm sure you understand,' Steven snapped, a half frown remained.

'Sure. In time, maybe,' Eilif said, with a slight shrug of his shoulders.

Steven kept silent. He doubted he'd ever forgive him.

'Do you know about the Spanish explorer, Hernando Cortez?' Eilif asked, as he leaned against the railing and looked out at the water.

'Not really.'

'He led the Spanish to conquer Mexico, and in turn destroyed the Aztec civilization. Some say he thought it was the humane thing to do – the Aztecs performed human sacrifice. Yet, the Aztecs firmly believed that if they did not perform these sacrifices, they would have been punished by the Gods.'

Steven listened, wondering what his point was.

'Humanity has always been faced with the question of choice –

someone's death can always be justified in the name of God, War or Survival. In our case, we need to kill to survive. It's Darwin's theory of evolution – the survival of the fittest. In order to survive, a species finds a way to evolve to sustain its population.'

'I understand the theory of evolution,' Steven said, unimpressed.

'You realise, we might now be the fittest race in the history of mankind? Think about it. Anyway, I'll leave you to it. Just please, try and think of us as your family not foe,' Eilif pleaded, before he turned and walked away.

It was a lot to take in.

Steven closed his eyes and turned his thoughts to Caitlin. He was desperate to talk to her. She always knew the right thing to say, had the best way for him to deal with any situation. He missed her puzzling over whimsical issues. Now, his problem was huge. If only it was something simple. He envisaged her confused face, just before she had slammed the door in his face. It hurt to have been treated like a stranger. He let out a groan and shook his head. His legs started to move, seeking a refuge. At the back of the ship, he focused on the bubbles left in its wake. There was no way he would put his past behind him and forget everyone he ever loved and everything he stood for. They did not know him at all.

Chapter 23

Memories

The silver bracelet glistened in the moonlight, as Emily twisted her hand from one direction to the other. Its intricate links were oval in shape and it had a single heart shaped charm attached to it. Simple, yet irreplaceable. It had been given to Emily by Steven's father Paul, a week after they first met. She had then vowed to cherish it forever and had kept the promise. It remained on her wrist – a cruel memory.

The resemblance between Steven and Paul was uncanny. Even though Steven had her eyes and dark hair, the rest was all Paul. Paul's height, build, expressions – all Paul. Steven had reminded her of the life she missed. A life with love. There was nothing she wanted more than to live out her life as a wife, a mother, a normal human being. Determined to torment herself further, she played back the last conversation with Paul in her mind.

*

'I've been hiding something from you. I don't know how to tell you the truth,' Emily confessed, as she fidgeted with her bracelet. It was a bad habit she could not resist.

'There is nothing you can't tell me. You know I love you no matter what,' Paul replied. The warm, irresistible smile he gave her nearly melted her resolve.

'Do you want to know where I go at night?' Her hands started to shake. 'I don't want to tell you, but…'

'What's going on?' Paul whispered, as he sat next to her and gently placed his hands on hers. His grip tightened, as though he was trying to help them keep still.

Keeping her head low, she barely got out the words. 'I don't think I can stay here anymore.'

'I don't understand.' Paul froze, as his hands automatically let hers go.

'I can't live here anymore. I don't belong here.'
'Of course you belong here, what are you saying?'
Eyes to the floor, she continued, adamant. 'I don't love you and I can't look after Steven. Motherhood is not what I thought it would be.'
His hands let go of hers and fell limply at his sides. She did not dare look at him but she could tell he was shocked. His frame had gone rigid. He sat like a stone. 'Are you serious? Please don't say things to break us.'
Fighting hard to keep her emotions under check, Emily got up and left Paul to mull over what she had said. She needed to see her baby again. She did not have a lot of time. Once in her son's room, she edged over to the side of his cot. Steven breathed loudly, deep in sleep. Even though she was biased, she knew he was gorgeous. A perfect baby boy. There was nothing she would not do to protect him.
As she tiptoed out quietly, she turned to face Paul. He still sat on the bed, his hands now over his head. Without a hint of emotion, she coolly said, 'I'm leaving now. I have a taxi waiting. Please look after him for me and tell him I was just protecting him.'
Paul looked up; his eyes glazed, and opened his mouth. But, he didn't or couldn't say anything. His head slumped back into his hands. She had broken him.
'I'm sorry,' Emily whispered.

*

When she opened the door and left, her life ended. The only two people she cared about were gone. Emily recalled the journey home. A million times, she had nearly turned back. It was the most excruciating trip of her life.
Back then, her decision was clear. It was for the best to leave them both to lead a normal life without complications. She had no doubt that Steven would be well looked after by Paul – she knew he would be a great father. All she needed was for Steven to remain normal. That was her bad luck. He wasn't. It had all been for nothing. With the benefit of hindsight it was easy to see – she should have taken her son with her. Now, her worst nightmare had come true – Steven was destined to become one of them. Even though she looked forward to meeting him, she was no fool. She

knew it would come at a price.

***

Anna walked at a brisk pace down the dimly lit corridor. Confronting Emily was not something she enjoyed doing, but she had been left with no choice. If Emily did not take the time to talk to her, then she had to go and find her. She had to find out what Emily was planning to do. She had helped her to cover up for Steven, but she had not dealt with the problem. She had left Steven behind. It was crazy. Steven could not stay behind. Emily had to go to get him, the question was, how? Anna suspected she would have to help Emily again. It was not something she looked forward to.

Anna clenched her hand in a fist and held it in the air for a second, before she knocked on the door. Emily was one of the few to insist on a real door. Even though it was not locked, she would give her sister the courtesy to answer. After waiting for a minute, she tried again without getting a reply. She knew Emily was there. She could sense her presence. Left with no choice, she took the handle and pushed it down to open the door. Her patience had run out.

'Emily, I know you're here, I need to speak to you.' Almost immediately, she felt deep sorrow ease through her. 'Emily, stop that and come out to talk.' Anna hated the fact she could feel Emily's emotions. Since they had evolved, a psychic link kept each of them in tune with the other.

It was annoying.

Anna only felt pain and sadness when Emily was hurting. It went against her grain, Anna being a natural optimist. As luck would have it her twin sister, Emily, was the opposite. The eternal pessimist.

Anna saw Emily peek out from behind the curtain, a vacant expression on her face. She glanced briefly at Anna, then turned away again and faced the opening on the wall, her window to the outside world.

'I don't know exactly what you are thinking, but you need to talk about it,' Anna said. She needed to engage her in conversation. 'You are making me feel lousy – can you snap out of it please? What's going on?'

Emily walked towards the chair and sat down. Hands limp on her lap, she looked up. 'Look, what do you want me to say? I'm sorry, I can't help it.'

'Have you decided what to do about Steven?' Anna asked. She did not want to beat about the bush.

With a huge sigh, Emily replied. 'No, I haven't decided what to do about Steven. I know I have to explain what we are. I'm just scared. Lying to him or even helping him to become one of us is not something I want to do.'

'I know you don't want to, but you have to,' Anna said, exasperated. 'If you don't tell him, he won't understand the change when it happens. What if his instinct kicks in and he kills someone. You know that would be a disaster. He wouldn't know how to cover it up.'

Emily ran her hands through her hair. Her expression wild. 'You're right, I know, but how do we tell him? It's not that easy to explain is it? Hey, Steven, you'll never guess what. I'm your mother. Yeah, that's right, your mother, I know I'm a bit young, but…oh, by the way, you're going to become a killer soon. How? Oh, don't worry about it you just need some blood. I'm sorry, yes, that's human blood.'

Anna scowled at her. 'You are so annoying sometimes. There's no need to be sarcastic. I'm just trying to help you. That's all I ever seem to do.'

'No-one asked you to be my guardian. I can look after myself.'

'Really? Is that why you managed to get pregnant with a human?' Anna sulked, her right hand on her hip.

'Oh come on, Anna, give up the act. I made a mistake. Not everyone is designed to accept our way of living. I was never destined to lead this life. I wanted freedom, a normal life.'

Anna could not believe Emily was crying. She could not remember the last time she had seen Emily cry. Maybe, she could ease up a bit. Anna made her way over and gave Emily a hug. In a repentant voice, she cooed. 'I'm sorry, I never realised for all those years how trapped you felt. If I'd known before you left, I might have been able to help you. Look, let's just forget mistakes made in the past. We'll figure something out, okay, calm down.'

Emily stopped crying, her sobs now more of a simper. 'I just couldn't resist them Anna, I was too weak. I know I have to stay here where I can't do any harm. I'm evil. I would never have made a good mother.'

'You are not evil. We are led by instinct, that's all. Anyway, that doesn't solve the problem now. Why didn't you tell Steven the truth when you had the chance?' Anna asked, still maintaining a soothing tone.

'I couldn't face him. I didn't want to take him away from his life. I couldn't…. How do you prepare someone for this way of life? We only created this place so that we could live normal lives, without becoming fugitives. I wish there was another way.'

'No-one has thought of a better way. There are only so many suicides we can make up, before they begin to look suspicious.'

'True, but don't you feel like sometimes,' Emily sniffled. 'We don't actually have control anymore. Don't you sense the unease? There is a growing restlessness amongst our kind. Don't you realise that there are others like me that do not want to hide? The new generation do not understand the human world – they think they can just go there and take what they need. They think…they think, they can integrate.'

'I know what you're saying. We can't teach them about persecution. But, we have to remain strong. If our resolve crumbles, then this place will fall regardless of how tight we keep security. You never know, Steven could be the missing link. He might be the one that reinforces the need to lead separate lives. Maybe, it was destiny that had a hand in his birth. He understands the human world more than the ones born here. Surely, he would realise that living out there would be futile for us.'

'Maybe, but you know as well as I do that sooner or later, we will need to find another place to live. We can't all carry on living together – there's no room for a start! The time will come when someone will have to lead and take up a new location.'

'That's for the council to decide. You should bring it up again.'

'You know they don't listen to me. No-one trusts me.'

'There's a reason for that, but what you did happened a long time ago. What you have to say will be heard when everything blows over. Now, we have to come up with a plan. Let me think about it. We'll get Steven home, here is where he belongs. Maybe, Ian could help?'

Emily grimaced. 'The last person I need rubbing my nose in my mistakes is my snotty younger brother.'

Anna laughed, it felt good to relax. 'He's not that bad you know. I've got to go. Do me a favour? Please do something to keep busy.' Anna smiled as she took her leave. She would have to find a solution to Emily's problem – again.

Chapter 24

The Past

Emily struggled to get to sleep. The conversation with Anna had ripped open old wounds and made the all too real nightmare return. As she tossed and turned in bed, she relived the past and remembered the day her life changed.

'I hate you. LEAVE ME ALONE.' Emily ran at full pelt, she intended to get as far away from Anna as possible. Anna did not understand her, she never did. Just because they were twins, everyone expected them to be the same, but they were like chalk and cheese – total opposites. Once alone, Emily mulled over her limited options. As soon as the war was over, she would move away from her annoying family to start a new life of her own. She would stay in America by herself; after all it was the land of dreams. Now that talkies were all the rage she was sure there would be plenty of work in Hollywood. Not that she wanted to be an actress. Her ambition was to write film scripts and work alongside the likes of Cary Grant, Humphrey Bogart and Clark Cable. What a dream that would be! She was sure she would be able to do the job just as well as any man – *if* she was allowed!

All that running had made her even hotter than usual. She flopped on the ground and flapped her dress up and down, to create a cool breeze. It was always so hot in Los Alamos. Dry, scorching – unbearable. All she longed for was the sea breeze on her face – she missed her hometown of Southampton.

As she threw stones into the stream, she lost track of time and only realised it was getting late when she looked up at the sky. The sun had gone. Another day wasted. A faint sound made her flinch. As it grew louder and more urgent she got up and looked around. She was sure she could hear her mother calling her name.

Being a typical laid back teenager, she dragged her feet as she made her way back. The sound coming from the distance should have warned her, but she was too preoccupied with thoughts of a better life. At the approach, she could ignore the cacophony no longer. It was only then that she noticed black swooping animals flying over her head in a densely packed cloud formation. They snapped at the air, erratic, out of control. Their distinctive wing span gave them away. Bats – lots of them.

'Emily, hurry,' her mother shrieked.

Emily ran towards her mother, as panic set in. Just when she was within reaching distance a few bats swooped towards her and caused her to trip up. She felt herself faint, as something bit into her wrist. When she started to rouse, she could hear her mother calling her name, over and over.

'I'm alright mum,' Emily said, even though she did not mean it. She titled her head to look at her wrists and saw they were wrapped in some material. The material looked uncannily like her dress material. She hoped they had not ruined her dress. It was then she noticed Anna next to her. She turned and gave her an embrace. 'I'm sorry Anna. I didn't mean to fight with you. Are you okay?'

'I'm fine. I've just got a few scratches like everyone else.'

'Why did they bite us like that? They were crazy.'

Anna bowed her head. 'I don't know.'

'At least they're dead now. It's over now,' her mother, Judith, said.

Emily looked around and saw the bodies of dead vampire bats scattered around the floor. The sight did nothing to appease her.

*

A few days later, Emily watched her parents whispering secretively to one another for the third consecutive day. As Morton Clausen, the Norwegian scientist, joined them, they pulled a sullen expression. Whatever he had said had not made them happy. It had been the same every day since the attack. Lots of chatter and speculation. No real explanation. The only thing they came up with was that the bats had become radioactive. Whenever Emily asked what they were talking about; her parents fobbed her off with the usual remarks. It was frustrating. She knew something else was going on. It scared her.

It was on that afternoon when she heard a story that chilled her to the bone. The cooks were talking about a local animal attack which had resulted in the death of a teenage boy. It appeared the boy had lost a lot of blood and had marks on his neck and wrist. Desperate to know more, Emily went to see her older sister, Catherine. She hoped Catherine would tell her the truth.

'Why do you think there is anything wrong Emily?' Catherine sighed, a tone of exasperation evident.

Emily bit her lip. Even Catherine was edgy. 'Since the bat attack, everyone has been acting weird, especially the adults.'

'No they haven't, I'm the same right?' Catherine added.

She hadn't thought about it that way, but Catherine was old enough to be classed as an adult. 'Really?'

'You always worry, don't you? Whatever you think is going on will sort itself out. I'm sure of it.'

*

As her twentieth birthday approached, Emily set her doubts aside and focused on the Birthday preparations. It was not every day she stopped being a teenager. Sat in front of her table mirror, she brushed her hair and studied her reflection. She wondered how much older she would actually look when she turned twenty. With her face but a few inches from the glass, she studied her reflection and searched for signs of wrinkles. As she did, she saw red veins creeping along her eyes. A minute later they were bloodshot. Startled, she leant back and could not control her hands as they started to shake.

*

The sound of an early bird roused Emily from her sleep. The night before was a blur. She hoped she had not missed her Birthday.

'Emily, you're awake.' It was her father's voice.

When she sat up, she saw Anna in the bed next to her. Had Anna also fallen ill? 'What happened daddy?'

'Don't worry about that now. You both got sick in the night. We have to leave so that you get better. Everything will become clear when we are gone,' Jeff said, she had never seen him look so anxious. The last time he had ever been so serious was when he had told them they had to leave England.

'I feel different, why is that?' Anna asked.

'It must have been something you ate. Nothing to worry about girls,' Judith reassured, as she stood an arms length away. It was strange for mother to keep her distance. She looked worried, almost frightened. Something about her eyes made Emily doubt her words. As Anna started to laugh at a face Ian was pulling from behind Judith's skirt, Emily's suspicious thoughts were replaced with joy. Then just as it had happened the happiness disappeared and left her in a void. The switch had flicked as soon as Anna stopped laughing. It was so strange. She could have sworn that Anna's happiness was her own.

*

After what Emily considered to be very hasty packing, they left the next day. She could not understand the hurry. It was when they stopped at a café that she noticed something about her *had* changed.

'I keep having visions of drinking blood,' Emily said, her tone light-hearted yet serious.

Around her, you could have heard a pin drop.

'So do I,' Anna added, in a quiet voice.

'Must be a weird twin thing,' her ten year old brother Ian, guffawed.

Their parents, Jeff and Judith, and older sister Catherine laughed – the laugh did not sound genuine.

*

That night Emily woke up parched. When she saw Anna was also awake she got out of bed and stood next to her. 'I'm so thirsty.'

Anna nodded. 'So am I.'

Emily looked at the corner of the room. Ian slept soundly. Her parents bed and Catherine's bed was empty. They tiptoed out, so as not to disturb their brother. Once outside, Emily was surprised at how clear her vision appeared even though it was dark, the moon barely visible through the clouds. Her throat complained again as a sweet scent filled the night air. 'What is that smell?' Emily asked.

Anna shrugged her shoulders and pursued it, as though in a trance.

As instinct took over, they found the scent. Five minutes later, they were surprised to see a couple, walking hand in hand along the street. They edged closer, unable to stop.

Anna made the first move.

Emily followed.

The couple did not scream. They watched in awed silence, as if hypnotised. Before they could react to the attack, they were subdued and shortly after, they were dead.

Emily sat on the ground in shock as she let go of the woman's arm. She stared at the dead bodies and it hit her – the scent was blood. They had killed them for their blood.

'Now you know what you need,' Jeff's voice announced, from behind.

As Emily turned around to face her father's voice, she found herself running into her mother's arms.

'What are we?' Emily asked, big eyed.

'We don't know,' Judith said, in a sad voice. 'But we can't stay here anymore.'

*

Emily woke up and sat up in her bed. With the back of her hand she wiped the sweat from her brow. Restless, she got up and threw herself on her favourite chair. She could not help the tears from streaming down her face again.

Even after the change, she had never stopped thinking about her home town of Southampton. She had long abandoned any ambitions of moving to America. All she dreamt of was home. It was with this thought in mind that she had come up with a cunning plan. Since it was clear all adolescents needed blood to change, she suggested they return from time to time. She figured they would need to stay in touch with any developments that happened in the outside world. It seemed like a totally logical and plausible idea.

When it was agreed, she had punched the air. Recreational visits would be allowed every ten years. Since no-one seemed to age, everyone assumed they had developed a form of immortality. She remembered the feeling of euphoria – all of them were so happy to be a member of a new species. Emily was the only one that was not over the moon. She missed her normal life.

It had taken over forty five years for Emily to be allowed to make the trip back to her home town in Southampton. Even though the experience had been magical, exciting even, it changed her life. The day before she was due to return, she met Paul. No-one saw her again until she returned two years later.

Falling in love with Paul had been so unexpected. When she found out she was having a baby, it was easier to remain in denial. It was only when she stared into her sons eyes for the first time that her maternal instinct kicked in – she had to defend and protect her baby. The only way she could think of doing this at the time was by leaving. The honeymoon was over. Since Steven was a hybrid, there was no way to know whether he would go through the change. So, she left them. The pain remained wedged in her heart for all eternity.

Every last shred of hope she maintained had vanished when Ingrid found him. Only then, did her worst fear become a reality. His change was inevitable and time was running out to explain who he really was and what awaited him. The question now was – how was she going to approach the problem?

She snapped her head up and wiped her face. Something was very wrong. She could feel Anna. She had never felt Anna in so much pain. Before she got to the door, Anna burst in.

'What is it?' Emily asked.

'I don't know how to tell you this so you don't get upset.'

'Tell me, what's going on?'

With pursed lips Anna stared in her eyes. 'It's Ian. He's gone to find Steven.'

Emily's jaw dropped, she was speechless.

Chapter 25

The Community

The ship started to slow down as it got into position to dock next to a jetty set up by the river. Lana made her way over to the deck and saw Ian, Eilif and Tomas securing the ropes to the supports positioned strategically on the jetty. It was time to unload. She heard Ingrid and Inna chatting behind her. Practically everyone was ready.

'Where is he?' Ian asked, he looked to Ingrid for an answer.

'Haven't seen him since earlier,' Ingrid replied, before adding quietly. 'Do you want me to go and find him?' The offer sounded reluctant.

Lana smiled at Ingrid and held her hand up. 'I'll go. You can stay here to help.'

Lana noted the look of relief on her daughters face, and wondered what was going on between them. As much as she did not want Ingrid to get hurt, a part of her was glad to see Ingrid finally smitten with someone. She never seemed to be able to find the right partner. If there was anything she could do to help, it would be worth a try.

In front of Steven's cabin door, she knocked. When it opened, she asked. 'Are you ready to get off this ship?'

'Definitely.' He looked relieved, if concerned, as he gave a half smile and scrunched his eyes.

On the way down the corridor, Lana spoke quietly. 'My daughter does not mean you any harm. She cares about you.'

'I didn't ask her to care about me,' he snapped.

'Do you have to ask people? It just happens,' she said, her tone serious. 'None of us mean you any harm, and it would be good if you started trusting us. Ingrid is not a bad person, she is my daughter, and I am very proud of her. I am asking you to think about it before she ends up getting hurt. I would not be happy if she got hurt.'

'That's sounded like a threat,' he retorted.

'Not a threat, a warning. We look out for each other. You would be wise to make an effort to fit in.'

'Fine.'

As she sped ahead, she sensed he followed closely behind. Even if he did not take heed, at least she had tried.

***

As they reached the deck, Steven heard Ian call out. 'We have company.' All he needed now was another confrontation. Even though, his little chat with Lana was unlikely to make him change his view on Ingrid, he knew to be cautious. He did not want to make enemies so soon. From the deck, he could tell Ian was talking to someone standing on the shore. He could just make out the words.

'Anna, it's so nice to see you.'

'Ian, where have you been?' Anna asked, a tone of exasperation evident.

'On a reconnaissance mission – seems we have a new member of the community no-one knew anything about, until recently. So where is our sister then?'

'She can't leave the community without permission, you know that. So, who exactly have you found?'

'You know who he is.'

'Do I?'

'Apparently, that's what you told Ingrid and Lana. That he was under your protection.'

'I never said that.'

'That's right, you didn't,' Ian paused, triumphant. 'Emily did. I knew you hadn't gone to England,' he accused, as he jabbed a finger in her direction.

'It was me,' Anna answered, lacking conviction.

'How could you let her leave the community? What if she'd disappeared again?' Ian ranted.

Defiant, Anna continued. 'She didn't though, did she?' After a pause, she added. 'What gave her away?'

'Coffee,' Ingrid said, aloud. 'You hate coffee and she was drinking it happily at the café with me.'

Anna sighed in defeat.

'So, back to the original question, who is he Anna?'

Before Anna had the chance to reply, Steven walked out to face them. As Anna gazed at him, she gave an audible gasp. She stared, speechless.

'Who are you?' Steven asked. Everyone remained silent.

A second later she replied, 'I'm your Aunt, Anna. My twin sister, Emily, is your mother.'

Ian broke the moment by returning to the job at hand. 'Right then, well glad that's out in the open. We've got a lot of stuff to move, so let's get on with it.'

As everyone got busy, Steven watched in two minds. Anna stood still, waiting. Steven decided to leave the unloading to the others. He walked down the narrow ramp and stood an arms length away from her.

'Can I show you where we live?' Anna asked, obviously apprehensive.

'I've come this far, I might as well find out what hell I'm destined to live in,' he sneered.

Anna nodded, as she bit her lower lip. 'Follow me.'

His feet crunched against the loose bark and bracken on the floor.

'This way,' she said, turning to face the massive Amazonian trees. After a few minutes of walking, Anna spoke. 'So, how was your journey?'

'Long,' he answered, in a flat and disinterested voice. He did not enjoy acting aloof, but one word answers were all he could handle.

'I hope it was bearable, you have a lot to discover here.'

Lifting his head up, he considered saying something but then changed his mind. Shrugging his shoulders, he looked ahead. Unable to find anything else to talk about, they walked on in silence.

Steven was actually in awe of the environment. He did have a lot of questions, but he put them aside, unsure of where to begin. The fact that nature was all around disconcerted him. Just as he started to appreciate it, he jolted back to reality, as the sound of a car broke the peace. To the left hand side, there was a clearing that seemed to run from the river in the direction they were heading, acting like a makeshift road. It was obvious they had chosen the area because of the tall Amazonian trees, but he wondered where the ship was kept, to remain out of sight.

After walking for a further ten minutes, they started to approach a huge mountainous rock formation that was surrounded by trees. The only thing that could have made the incredible sight was an inactive volcano. The scene was breathtaking.

Anna pointed towards an area at the base of the rock. It looked like a cave entrance. 'We have to go in here.'

Steven nodded and followed.

Inside the entrance was a carved out tunnel with electric lighting fitted onto the ceiling. The cables were neatly tucked away in an electrical conduit made from a flexible plastic piping system that obviously gave the wires protection and routed them around the area. Somehow, this was not the image he had expected when he entered the cave entrance. It would have been more appropriate to have fire lit torches, like those in adventure films. They walked for a few minutes longer before they arrived at a huge steel door with no keyhole. A keypad took its place.

Steven was surprised. It was starting to feel like Fort Knox.

Anna entered the password and a voice registered who she was by saying 'welcome back Mrs. Santos.' As the door slid open, it revealed another corridor. This time it was made of steel walls. It looked like an underground scientific research centre.

'Is this what you expected?' Anna asked, as she paused to face him.

He shook his head and laughed. 'I don't know what I expected to find in a dormant volcano in the middle of the Amazon Rainforest – but, it certainly wasn't this.'

'I hope I can surprise you some more.' She gave a simple half smile and carried on.

As they turned around the corner, they were face to face with another barrier. This time it was a lift, with another password protected keypad. Anna dialled a number swiftly and the doors opened. She pressed the L button. There were five settings: 2, 1, U, L, and G. It looked like they were on the U level. Steven assumed they represented Upper Level, Lower Level and Ground Floor. The button for the upper level was controlled by a key. Escaping was not going to be an easy option. As the doors opened to the L Floor, Steven remained glued to the entrance as he watched in awe.

'Come on, you have to get out of the lift,' she encouraged.

He must have looked dumbfounded.

The scene before them was surprisingly familiar. It looked like a typical English shopping complex. There were people walking around in groups, little stalls selling a variety of goods, and small shops on the sides that looked incredibly *normal*. Robotically, he got out of the lift and started looking around.

The shop fronts had subtle differences. A clothes shop had no mannequins dolled up to impress customers. All you could see were simple railings with a range of clothing.

A greengrocer's display was filled with colourful fruit and vegetables of different shapes and sizes, unlike any you would see in supermarkets. The main and glaring difference was the lack of prices. No buy one, get one free signs to tempt the wary consumer or general sale or discount signs. The goods were just there.

'Anna,' Steven called out, unable to hold back his questions any more.

'Yes.'

'Is it me or is something missing?'

'What's missing?' She smiled.

'Where are all the prices? How do people know what to pay?'

'I wondered how long it would take you to notice,' she smiled. 'We don't use money. Everyone has a job to do and you just take what you need from each other. It's based on the barter system, without anyone taking account. We all trust each other; no-one takes more than they need. We all work hard and help to sustain one another.'

His mouth opened wide in amazement. 'Does no-one want more? Isn't it human nature to succumb to greed and jealousy?'

'Are you like that?'

'No!'

'Well there you go. Greed is like a sickness. If you feed it, it will grow. We do not promote selfish or singular behaviour. We work together. We have always had to; otherwise our days would have been numbered from the start.'

'But you obviously have resources to provide electricity and other luxuries.'

'Well you don't expect to put together a group of nuclear physicists and not have electricity do you?' she said, as she chuckled.

'Nuclear physicists? Why are there…?' he trailed, confused.

'I didn't know how much you have been told. We'll get to that soon.'

'How do you generate electricity here?' he asked.

'We currently have access to solar, hydro electric, fossil fuel, and wind generated electricity. We are in the process of investigating a geothermal method.' She paused for what felt like effect, then added. 'We are quite an intellectual bunch. We like a challenge. In effect, the community diversified naturally. Some preferred to take on the role of providing food, others preferred focusing on the living arrangements, and others preferred looking after the younger members of the community. In time, you will find your calling.'

'You know as much as I am impressed by what I see, I'm still not totally convinced that I would like to choose my calling and stay here. No offence intended.'

'Steven, only time will tell what your future holds, but try to keep open minded.'

Her comment pushed him too far. 'Look, you lot have just made me leave the girl I love, my family and my life. I don't know if I want to be more open minded,' he shouted, in frustration.

'Keep your voice down,' she warned.

'I wanted to be a lawyer someday, but somehow I don't think you'll have much need for one here,' he ranted on, as several people started to stare at him.

'Let's move on,' Anna said, her eyes narrowed, nostrils flared.

'Fine,' he huffed, suddenly self conscious, as he noticed everyone staring.

Anna smiled at those watching, and a few of them raised their eyebrows curiously.

After walking through the shops in silence, Anna stopped and turned to face him. 'I'm sorry about what happened to you. Are you hungry?'

'Yes,' he admitted. Even though he was angry, it only made him hungrier.

Chapter 26

Exposure

The gigantic entrance carved into the rock, gave way to a huge area. Stone tables and wooden benches provided the base for the hive of activity, as a range of people chomped into their meal. For the first time, Steven took the time to observe. He had never seen such a distinguishable group of people. Some had olive skin and nearly black hair – he assumed these had to be people of Spanish descent. Others had bleach blonde hair and blue eyes – just like Ingrid and her family. A few wore, what looked like Jewish caps, or kipput – as Steven had learnt during his religious studies course. They had to be descended from the Jew they had mentioned – Isaac Abel. The rest were a real mixture. At a guess, Steven conjectured they were offspring of all the different permutations obtained after couples of different descent had paired off. The array of people was mind boggling.

One thing was clear – no-one in the room looked over the age of twenty.

A lot of children scampered around the room. Some sat down, eating. Most ran around chasing and playing with what looked like older siblings or friends. A few mothers's nursed their babies, showing no sign of embarrassment. The scene reminded him of something out of a bible story. That was until he spotted an area similar to a canteen serving station – a modern one.

Steven was aware that a few heads had turned in his direction. He was sure some of them had been there when he lost it with Anna. By now, they must have realised he was a stranger.

Anna laughed out loud, as she feigned amusement. Whispering in his ear, she sharply added. 'Don't say anything. Your accent alone will give you away. Let's just get some food.'

At the serving station, Anna introduced Steven. 'This is Mike, Annika and their daughter Sian. Everyone this is Steven.'

The three of them stared, transfixed.

'Steven,' Annika glared, quizzing her husband with a casual glance, before holding out a hand.

'He will be formally introduced soon, but for now, can we have some food please? He just got here,' Anna reiterated.

Everyone in the room, barring the children, stopped talking.

Mike nudged Sian. Coming out of her trance, Sian poured a helping of food into a wooden bowl and handed it to him – she was not smiling.

The steaming food made Steven's mouth water, as his stomach rumbled.

Anna spoke to Mike in a different dialect; he shook his head in response. 'Let's sit down,' she said.

It was not a request.

Anna steered him towards an empty table and seemingly ignored the puzzled expressions she passed.

Once sat down, Steven picked up the spoon. Ravenous, he tucked in before stopping to examine the contents. 'What am I eating today?'

'It looks like Caiman stew. We do grow our own vegetables so it does actually have things you would recognise, like potatoes.'

'Hang on a minute. Caiman, as in, crocodile stew?' He spluttered.

'Of course,' Anna smiled; she looked amused at his reaction.

'I've got nothing to lose.' He put some more in his mouth and relished the taste – it was a cross between chicken and fish. Again, a pleasant surprise – he ate with vigour.

'Glad to see you have an appetite.'

The sound of new arrivals made him glance at the entrance – it was Ingrid and Lana. As they walked, the older children ran up to them, pestering, asking the same thing over and over.

'What do they want?' Steven enquired, as he noticed Ingrid was smiling, happy.

'Whether they have brought any treats? There are many things we can't get or make here.'

The reply puzzled him – he was surprised by the humanity of the situation. He hadn't known what to expect. In honesty, the environment simulated a lost and ancient civilization, not a recently formed one.

'What is the language you talk?'

'It's the language we developed,' she replied.

With a full stomach, he could not stop his eyelids from drooping, as tiredness set in.

'You need some rest,' she observed.

'I could fall asleep on the spot,' he admitted.

'I'll find you somewhere to sleep. Let's make a move.'

As they stood up to go, the sound of shouting made him look at the entrance again. A woman, who looked remarkably similar to Anna, was pointing her finger at Ian. The words became clearer as everyone was silenced.

'You bastard, how could you go behind my back. How dare you. Tell me where he is – tell me now,' she screamed, fuming.

Ian looked around the room, his signature grin on full display. Extending his arm, he pointed towards Steven, giving an unapologetic shrug.

The woman stared at Steven and froze. Aware of her impromptu audience, she turned and fled.

Reticent, Steven asked, 'is that my mother?'

Anna looked embarrassed, as she gave a slight nod. 'This is a lot for her to take in. She needs as much time as you do.'

'I doubt that,' Steven retorted.

'Your mum has not had it easy – I'll leave it at that. Finish your bowl and let's get out of here,' Anna said. Now, she looked annoyed.

Everyone was looking now.

*

As they followed a smaller exit, on the other side of the room, a series of stone steps revealed their exit – he was sure Emily had just taken the same route. The steps led towards a maze of corridors, with rooms dotted in between. On the whole, the room entrances were covered by curtains, not doors. It was obvious safety was not an issue, which caused him to wonder if anyone valued their privacy as much as he did. Once at the end of the hall, they came across one of the few wooden doors. There was no lock since Anna opened it without using a key. It struck him that once inside, safety relaxed – he wondered whether the high level of security was to stop anyone or thing from coming in or whether the aim was to keep them in.

Inside, a small lounge area led to a balcony. On the right, a curved, door height, entrance was covered by a curtain.

'You can sleep in there,' she indicated, pointing to the curtain. 'I'll let you be. You rest, I'll come back later.' In a sympathetic voice, she said. 'It's nice to have you home.'

Steven nodded, not having the energy to argue and headed towards the room. A huge bed, made from intricately carved wood, greeted him. The welcoming mattress was covered in a purple sheet and matching pillow. As he collapsed on the bed, he closed his eyes and switched off.

***

Ian was annoyed – Emily was out of line. The only reason he hang around was to eat, but he refused to answer any questions.

As soon as he was done, he left in a hurry – there was no way he was going to be exposed to a Spanish inquisition for longer than necessary. A swim was what he needed. With a fresh set of clothes, he headed towards the underground lagoon. The soothing sound of water, whooshing down and bubbling as it met the surface, echoed in the underground cavern. The sight of the waterfall never ceased to amaze him. Leaving his clothes strewn on the floor, he dived into the pool and swam under the waterfall. Instantly, he started to feel at ease.

If there was one thing he loved about what he was, it was his constant energy. It was great to look and feel his twenty year old self. He had been the same for over fifty years, and he had definitely come to terms with his eternal youth. Ageing was not for him. The sound of someone approaching made him look up just in time to see Eilif throwing himself into the pool in the same manner he had just done. The dive was graceful and he disappeared under the surface of the water for a while.

Finally, he surfaced giving a shriek of joy. 'It's great to be back.'

'Definitely,' Ian agreed.

As Eilif approached, Ian voiced his thoughts. 'People look so withered out there, don't you think? Here everyone is so youthful. Well, apart from my mum and Dad,' he guffawed.

'At least they show the ones that have never left what people look like when they age. Even if they always look the same,' Eilif observed, as he performed a perfect eggbeater kick in the deep water.

'They do look older, but they are relatively young compared to those aged seventy and above.'

'Do you think they mind? You know, having been frozen in time, at the age of fifty and forty six – forever,' Eilif asked, his hands sculling back and forth.

'I don't think they are bothered. It is what it is. Their change did not give them the ability to reverse, just to freeze the aging process.'

'It's so dirty in the outside world, isn't it? I mean I like going to visit, its part of our heritage. But to quote Dorothy from The Wizard of Oz – there's no place like home.'

'The sad thing is I remember watching that film when it was released. I must have been only eight years old at the time. It was before we went to live in Los Alamos. What a different time. No-one knew then how the War would change and destroy countless lives in the name of creating a better race. It always gets to me that Hitler genuinely thought he was on a noble quest to create better human beings.'

'It was on that basis you all decided to vanish and create this utopia wasn't it?'

'Well, you know all this from your teaching, but yes. My parents and the others realised that they had become in some ways, superior or stronger than normal human beings. They did not want to conquer or take life unnecessarily. The War was doing that already. So, it felt like a natural solution to disappear from society and develop a place that was hidden from the rest of the world. The thing is – we still have so much to learn about ourselves. We've barely scratched the surface. But, at least we have full control of our destiny. We are not subject to the laws imposed by man.'

'Do you not think though,' Eilif paused, uneasy. 'It will only be a matter of time before we can not sustain ourselves here? The population is growing and there is a restlessness developing.'

Ian sighed, before saying, 'I know.'

Changing the subject, Eilif added. 'Do you think Steven will adapt?'

'I hope so. He can't go anywhere else.'

'From my observations, it is obvious that humanity does not usually like being caged up. Even though we are not strictly speaking, normal human beings, our emotions are the same. The level of protection we have installed is just looking for someone to try to find its weakness.'

'There is no flaw in our security,' Ian snapped, his stare resolute.

'Look I know you change the security codes and have a high level of surveillance equipment installed. All I'm just saying is I'm not the first person to think it. Steven is new to this. I'm not convinced he'll just accept.'

'He has no choice. He'll *have* to do as we say.'

Eilif shrugged, dived under and disappeared.

Before he had a chance to resurface, Ian swam to the waters edge, got out and hastily put his clothes back on. The conversation was not going anywhere productive. Even though reluctant, Ian had to admit that Eilif did have a point. Steven did not seem like the type to lie low, yet, he did not get the impression he was radical enough to try to escape. Either way, even if Steven tried to find a way out, his security was impenetrable.

No-one would get out unless he authorised it. They never had and never would. The only blip in all the time he had been in the community was Emily, and she was allowed to leave. He would not make the same mistake again.

Chapter 27

Meeting Mum

Emily knew she was not exactly role model material, yet, there she was pretending to be the picture of responsibility. She was the teacher. It was funny to an extent. She would never dare say aloud what she was thinking. The facts spoke for themselves. So far, she had: managed to get infected by a bat and become an abnormal human being; become dependant on blood for survival to the extent that she had killed human beings; lived within the confines of a surreal environment; given birth to a forbidden half human child; abandoned the said child; and attempted to get on with her life, albeit a disgruntled and unsatisfied one. Someone had to see the irony of her situation. It dawned on her – she could walk away. Refuse to take the lesson. Her trauma warranted a sickie day. Then again, what was the point? She had to *try* to carry on as normal. She had to rise above it.

'As all of you know I'm Emily, one of the originals.' She hated that word – originals. She did not feel superior to anyone else because she was bitten by the psycho bats. 'I'm here to develop your new abilities, and to enable you to enhance them. Anyone got anything to start us off with? Can you do something new, that you couldn't do before?'

An eager girl at the front raised her hand in the air. She flapped her hand higher, as though she might explode unless she was allowed to reply.

'Please tell us,' Emily obliged.

'I can see perfectly at night,' she beamed, using a lot of hand gestures to continue with her explanation. Her frizzy, brown hair bounced as she talked. 'On the hunt we attended the other night my vision was so clear, I couldn't believe it. It was amazing. The veins and arteries pumping blood around the animal seemed magnified. I knew exactly what to do.'

Emily kept a smile pasted on her face. It was important to act like a teacher, even though in a lot of ways, she considered herself to be a pupil. She had seen the girl grow up, and knew her parents were both two of the finest hunters she had ever met. 'That's excellent,' she praised.

'Anyone else?' Emily asked, scanning the room. It was hard to keep track of all the new additions. Since the only two members of the community that could not reproduce were her parents, the reproductive ability of the rest of the community appeared endless. The community reminded her of a rabbit warren – forever expanding, with no control mechanism or natural predator. The young were the most vulnerable until they changed, but they had designed their home well. Only a few had died since they had arrived. That had been at the beginning, before they had been prepared. Now, there was a very limited chance of them being attacked by a Jungle predator. Even diseases had been wiped out by the development of vaccines – they had thought of everything. They had defied the odds and prospered.

As Henrik started to explain how he was able to perform complex calculations in the blink of an eye she felt her thoughts drift away. She wondered what Steven was doing right now. Henrik stared at her, waiting for a reply, and she focused. 'Just like your great grandfather, Morten, good for you.' What he said was fascinating, just not new.

True to form, her nephew grumbled at the back. Ian's son was showing signs of her rebellious streak.

'Speak up, Antonio,' Emily demanded. 'What's on your mind?'

'The only special skill I want to have is the knowledge to get out of here,' he said, then guffawed and smirked.

Emily sighed. It always came up. 'That part of your training will be covered another day. We are not capable of living out in the open – it's too dangerous.'

'Not for me, it's not,' Antonio continued. 'Let them try to take me on.'

'Like I said, you'll discuss that further in another class.'

It was frustrating for Emily to have to lie. She knew exactly what he meant. Yet, his father was responsible for bringing someone else to this confinement – her son, Steven. It vexed her. Taking out the necessary equipment, she focused back on the lesson, and split the six pupils into two groups. Then she left them with their assignment and stared into the distance. Immortality, it had seemed like such a dream when they first discovered they were not ageing. For her it was her living nightmare. She did not want to live forever. The thought of living indefinitely had lost all of its appeal. It was her dream to live a normal life, where she would grow old. She could not help being annoyed. She was responsible for teaching the new ones the beauty of what they had become. Someone was having a joke at her expense. She was nothing more than a hypocrite.

***

The sight from the balcony was impressive. It looked directly upon the heart of the rainforest. Anna knew she was lucky. Since she was one of the first to arrive, she had one of the few rooms located on the periphery of the volcano. As the numbers in the community had increased, the rooms had been created where there was space, so outside light was not always guaranteed. Sitting on her favourite rocking chair, Anna looked out and waited. It was a matter of time before she would turn up. As the door opened, she turned around and smiled. 'You took your time.'

'I had to teach – and calm down.'

'You certainly lost it with Ian. You always let him get to you.'

'Younger bratty brother.'

'You two never got along.'

Emily made her way over to the chair next to Anna and sat down. 'I miss the room I used to have – it was just like this. Now, I'm in the dungeons.'

'Your room is not that bad, and hey, you only have yourself to blame.'

'I guess,' Emily frowned, as she fiddled with her fingernails. 'So, what's he like? Is he okay about being here?'

'I have to be honest. He's barely talked to me. Truth is he doesn't seem happy to be here.'

'Great,' Emily sighed.

'Do you want me to leave, so that you can talk to him when he wakes up?'

'I don't know.' She paused, and then bit her lower lip. 'Do you mind staying?'

'Not at all,' Anna replied. She turned to face Emily and half smiled. It was the first time Emily had ever admitted that she needed her – in a round about kind of way.

***

The sound of two women talking woke Steven up and he realised it sounded like Anna – only twice. Sitting up, he stretched his arms in protest. He wanted some time alone. Unable to stall the inevitable confrontation, he made his way through the curtain. Anna got up from her chair to greet him.

'You're awake.'

'Just about,' he replied. Through the corner of his eye he saw Emily frozen on the spot, her hands on her knees.

'Steven, you need to talk to your mother. Will you speak to her, please?'

Steven could not answer.

'Steven. Please talk to her.' Anna sounded insistent. Was his mother such a coward? He was not going to be scared. With pursed lips, he gave a nod.

'I'll wait here,' Anna said, as she moved out of the way and indicated he go to the balcony.

Steven wondered over and stared out into the Amazon. He did not look at her. She had to speak first. After a few minutes had passed, Emily finally broke the silence.

'This is quite a view, don't you think?'

Steven hummed in agreement, before he asked. 'How long was I out for?'

'You've been asleep for a long time, but I only just got here. I suspect you must have slept for over twelve hours.'

'Really? I don't usually sleep longer than eight hours.'

'Your body is preparing for the …' she stopped and hesitated.

'Change,' he said. He was sure he knew more than she expected.

'So, they told you about it.' She shook her head, pain etched in her face.

'Yes, they told me.'

'It should have been me, I'm sorry,' she apologised. 'I–I should have found a way to prepare you for … wh–what will happen.'

'Yes, you should.' Her pathetic composure made him feel a bit sorry for her. He wanted to be angry. 'Why didn't you come to get me? If you are so sorry, you should have done the job yourself –

instead if sending your brother.'

'I didn't send him – he went without my consent. It's no excuse though. I should have told you – I am a coward. If only Ingrid had given me more time.'

'What did Ingrid have to do with it?'

'She told Ian's wife, Carmen, about you. She is the reason Ian knew you existed. But, it's not her fault – I should have told you when she found you.'

'You knew she found me, and you did nothing. Why didn't you just tell me the truth? It would have been different *then*. Now, my life is ruined. I was happy.'

'What do you mean?' She asked, agitated. Emily turned to look at him for the first time. 'Didn't you choose to come here? What did they do?'

'Well, where do I start?' Steven was angry now, in fact, he was livid. 'They kidnapped my girlfriend, erased my existence, left me homeless and penniless and then told me I was going to become a killer. What else was I supposed to do?'

With a face of utter horror, she spat. 'They did what?'

Emily got up and started to pace up and down. She mumbled to herself and fidgeted, as she clasped her hands together. Steven watched and felt bewildered, as his anger subsided. She looked crazy, erratic. Something about the way she acted made him realise there was something not quite right about his mum.

'I'm so sorry,' she said, as she stopped and looked at him again.

He could not look at her, so he stared at the floor. 'Sorry doesn't help me now, does it?'

'No, I guess not.' In a voice stricken with pain, she continued. 'I know I am not your idea of a good mother. Just, if you can, try to understand that I left you because I loved you. I never wanted you to have this life. I hoped you would not be like me.'

'You really are my mother? It's so hard to believe.'

'Again, I'm sorry. Yes, I am your mother.'

'And, I'm really your Aunt,' Anna said smiling, as she eased back into the balcony. 'Let's talk about something else. What do you say?'

'Sure.' Steven agreed, glad to end the conversation.

'How about something to eat and then a swim?' Anna asked, with a cheeky expression.

'Both sound good,' Steven replied. If he could swim away from here, he'd be glad to go.

Anna put her arm through Emily's and led her into the room. They looked so alike and yet were so different. Emily looked, well, broken. Anna was her rock that was obvious.

*

The sound of a waterfall took Steven aback. Nothing was normal here. Anna had led him to the entrance of the bathing area, and left him with a set of clean clothes. Through the rock formation, he was face to face with the most breathtaking sight he had ever seen. It was so amazing; it made his hairs at the back of his neck stand on end.

'Incredible,' he whistled, in admiration.

The waterfall cascaded from the top left hand corner of the cave into a pool of water that bubbled and frothed in response. To the side of the pool, was a huge lake that stretched out for about one hundred metres. It beckoned Steven to swim it. The only problem remained – he had no swim suit. Apparently, they didn't use swim suits. That would take some getting used to. Confident, no-one would join him, he started to undress – it was supposed to be empty at this time of day. After reassuring himself he was alone, he stripped and jumped into the pool like a lightning bolt. The relief as the water hit his body was immediate.

Just as he was beginning to get comfortable, he heard a splash behind him and was caught unaware. It was too late to make a quick exit. He braced himself, kept calm and considered his next move. If he swam for the lake he would expose his bare bottom to whoever had joined him. Even though this did not bother him, it made him falter momentarily. If he had gone for that swim, he would not have heard the voice behind him.

'Hey, are you enjoying the water?' A female voice asked.

Ingrid. He wondered if she would ever get the message.

Chapter 28

A Pool Like No Other

The sound of Ingrid's voice made him tense up. At least, the visibility underwater was poor – he was camouflaged. 'I was told no-one swam at this time of day. The last person I expected to see was you,' he remarked, his tone bitter and disappointed.

'It's nice to see you looking more alert,' she said, as she swam in his direction.

He kept his eyes in the direction of the waterfall, only too aware of the fact she was getting too close for comfort. As she continued to approach, he burst out. 'Is it normal for everyone to swim naked in the same pool?'

'Yes,' she said, as she continued to glide towards him in a graceful breaststroke. 'But I had a feeling you'd be here when I saw Anna walking in the other direction, so I thought I'd say hello.'

'You thought it was a good idea to get into the water at the same time as me, knowing I would be naked?' He turned to face her. If she was not embarrassed he had no reason to be either. Her tenacity had to be admired.

'I have been bathing naked with other women all my life. On the odd occasion, I have been in here when men were around. But no-one is bothered. Does it make you uncomfortable?' She asked, unable to hold back a snigger.

Her expression was flirtatious. Something told him she was not going to give up easily. Her breasts remained hidden under the surface, but his imagination was starting to wonder.

It had been a while.

Taking a slight gulp, he continued. 'Well, if I'm being frank – yes it does. I have never been swimming naked with women, or men for that matter.'

'Interesting, Adam and Eve have a lot to account for don't they?' She joked, as she nose dived under water.

He had no idea what she was up to now, but he did see her behind. It was firm. He looked from side to side trying to figure out where she was. A minute later, she surfaced behind him. 'Quit playing Ingrid, what do you want?' Steven snapped, annoyed with her game.

'You,' she replied, with a straight face. 'I'll wait as long as it takes. Have a good swim.'

Steven felt his jaw go slack. He watched her dive again, this time he could not help studying her form. She was very attractive. He could not help reacting. He swam to the side and held on to the rock, before he saw the water break at the entrance. That was one hell of a swim. He swam over, as fast as he could and saw Ingrid was already out. She was wearing a long red dress, soaked from her wet body. It clung to her form, making him take another unwanted gulp.

'See you around, Steven. I'll be waiting, until you change.' She waved and gave him a breathtaking smile, a twinkle set in her eyes.

In frustration, he sprinted towards the pool, before stopping slightly out of breath at the other end. Shaking his head, he groaned out loud. It was only Ingrid after all – the one responsible for his misery.

He hated being sexually frustrated.

***

Emily paced up and down, anxious to speak to Steven. After Steven had told her what they had done, she had resisted the urge to go and punch Ian's lights out. Her younger brother took too many liberties. What he had done was unforgivable. His arrogance defied belief.

Some day, she would get her revenge. Footsteps brought her back to reality. Bracing herself, she smiled, as Steven walked in through the door.

'How was your swim?'

'Interesting,' Steven paused. 'Although, I have to say, I didn't realise this place was so liberal.'

'Liberal? It is many things, liberal is not what I'd call it,' she scoffed.

'Ingrid came in to the water to join me. She was naked. I'm sure she knew I was there before she got in. Where I come from, swimming naked with people you barely know is liberal.'

'Did she?' Emily gave a wry smile. The thought had crossed her mind already – was Ingrid after Steven? Did Ingrid want Steven to be her compliment? Was that why Ingrid had defied her and told Carmen – so that Steven would return? Regardless, it did not matter to Emily what her reason was – she would never forgive her. 'Nothing happened did it? You don't have to tell me if you don't want to.'

'Now, you sound like a mother – no, nothing happened.'

'Don't trust Ingrid.' She warned.

With a loud guffaw, he sneered. 'You don't need to tell me that. She wanted to kill me. Talking of trust, no-one has told me what happened between my dad and you.'

Avoiding the obvious, she exclaimed. 'We had you.'

'That part I knew,' he sighed. 'Seriously, why am I here now? You could have brought me with you, when you left my dad, and saved me the aggravation.'

A stab at her open wounds. 'I hoped you would be normal. I didn't want you to be like us. I never wanted you to live in this circus.'

'Don't you like it here? Everyone else seems to think this is the best place in the world,' he remarked, his voice laced in sarcasm.

'Its fine,' she lied. Walking over to the large wooden chair, draped in a thick animal fur, she sat down and covered her face in her hands, considering her options. She did not know if she could keep up the charade.

A few minutes of silence passed. He waited.

Through a raspy throat, she admitted. 'I was not destined to live here. I was looking forward to an independent life before the attack happened – they did tell you about the bats right?'

'Yes.'

'I just wanted to be free from everyone telling me what to do. I wanted a life of my own, away from my parents, away from the War. My dad was like a mad scientist, I did not want to be a part of that. All I wanted was a new start. When the attack happened everything went wrong. Now, I was the mad scientist. I was like Dr Jekyll and Mr. Hyde. I had no say anymore. I was trapped in a body I did not want.' Taking a deep breath, she paused. 'When I eventually managed to make my way back home…'

'To Southampton,' he interrupted.

'Yes,' she snapped. Her calm composure melted. 'I did not want to leave. I fell in love with your dad so I just decided – what the heck – I'm staying. I was due some happiness, I deserved some.' She stopped and stared at the wall. Her voice mellowed again.

'Then I came along and ruined the dream,' Steven added, as he dug his hands in his pockets.

'No, it wasn't you,' she gasped. 'You are the best thing I ever did,' she admitted. She had to fight to keep tears at bay.

'So what then? Why leave so soon? You could have stayed for a few years.'

'I couldn't stay any more. I would have been discovered. I could not resist,' she sighed, embarrassed by her admission.

'Resist, oh,' he paused. 'You were killing people – is that it?'

'Yes. When I had you, I thought my heart was going to burst – I was so happy. But, it was short lived. I knew as soon as I saw you that I had to protect you. The only way I knew how, was b–by leaving. I–I thought I'd done the right thing,' she stammered, her resolve crumbling.

'What about me? Why didn't you bring me here?'

The look he gave nearly crippled her composure. 'Like I said, I hoped you would be normal.'

Seeing his face harden, she braced herself.

'Look, I'm not here to mull over the past. We can't change it. Can you just explain to me what is going to happen and why it's better that I'm here. That's what I can't get my head around. I got over not having my real mother around years ago.'

The comment stung more than she expected.

Faking enthusiasm, she smiled. 'You have to go to school.'

'School! What do you teach – How to become a vampire?' His features had softened again as he let out a small, but significant, laugh. It made her hope – perhaps, he did not hate her after all.

'We are not vampires, but anyway,' she grinned. 'You need to know more about our history and what to expect. Call it your preparation. For whatever its worth, you need to know what you are, even if you don't think it's important.'

'Great – I can't wait,' his shoulders slumped, as his face pulled into a pout.

Even though, she wanted to talk more, she knew the conversation was over. Another day, she would try again. 'Do you want me to get you some accommodation with the others? I doubt you'll want to stay with me.'

'No offence, but, yeah, that would be great.'

The fact he said no offence pleased her – at least he was polite. 'I'll take care of it.'

*

Steven frowned at his new accommodation – a tiny room with no natural light, split into four even smaller areas. A single bed, with a pale blue cover, beckoned him in the corner. There was no side light, bedside table or bookcase – just a bed. To make matters worse, the three other beds meant company. His face turned to a scowl, as his entire body deflated. The prospect of having a place of his own – vanished. Earlier, he'd had the pleasure of meeting the grumpy male warden. He failed to remember his name, he exuded no charisma. He didn't even respond when Emily told him Steven was her son – the introduction of another student, regardless of who they were, held no added thrill. In a dry monotone voice, he reeled off the rules to Steven, listing his duties and responsibilities. It had been difficult to pay attention.

Before long, the warden had dumped him here – the cell, at least it felt like a prison cell. And left. A real welcoming. His head spun from information overload. In a nutshell, it appeared all adolescents approaching the change were kept together in the final months. All of them were expected to pitch in. A sense of impending doom swept over him – he never had a set of jobs to do at home. At University, he got by. Housekeeping was not his forte. What a wake up call. He doubted in a small community like this, there would be any room for slackers. The job he dreaded was the communal area checks – it could only mean one thing. Toilets! Ugh! Even in this community, he doubted it would be any different from any other.

'You must be Steven,' a male voice asked.

He turned round to find himself face to face with a blond and Nordic looking man of around his age. 'Are you related to Ingrid, by any chance?'

Giving a crooked smile, the man replied. 'I guess we all look alike, don't we?'

'You do have very distinct features – that's for sure.'

'I've been sent by Emily to show you around. I'm Jensen,' he held out his hand formally. 'She thought you could do with a friend.'

Instinctively, Steven held out his hand and gave a firm handshake. If there was one thing boarding school had taught him, it was the importance of a firm handshake – it spoke in volumes. 'Is that what you are – a friend?'

Dropping his hand, Jensen shrugged. 'Only if you want one – I'm not going to impose myself on you. I'm just showing you around as a favour. But, we are sharing this room. So, it's not a bad idea to try to get along. I know this is all new to you, but it's not really my problem. You might as well get used to it.'

'Fair enough, I don't need your sympathy.'

With a smirk, Jensen turned away from him. 'Let's go.'

Steven trudged behind. He was beginning to get tired of being told what to do all the time. It was like being back in boarding school.

Chapter 29

A Warm Welcome

Steven tried to focus on what Jensen was saying. He was listening; it was just a lot to take in.

'To your left and right are the accommodation blocks. The senior members of our community are entitled to the bigger rooms. Obviously, we get the smallest. The teaching rooms are on the second floor, that's where we are headed.' He grinned, as if he was hiding a secret.

'Teaching room's?' Steven groaned. He was sure none of their teaching would interest him.

'I'm sure you had them back where you come from. In our case, it's where we prepare for the change. School is school after all, no matter where you are.'

Steven was sure he was having a dig. His lips twitched as he suppressed a smile. It amused him to think anyone actually had a sense of humour here.

'We learn about a range of subjects. I can't really explain them all to you now – you'll just have to learn as you go. Other than this, we lead normal lives as you would outside, I mean, in your world.' He paused and cocked his head to the side as if undecided. With a casual look around, Jensen leaned in and whispered. 'By the way, what's it like in your world?'

The question made Steven stop short and frown. As if they were in on a conspiracy, he whispered back. 'Totally different to here in a lot of ways. In a lot of ways, I'd say it's more complicated by the look of things. Things here are a lot more…simple.'

'More complicated, jeez I don't know if I can handle that. Hang on a minute, are you calling us simple?' Jensen's voice got louder. He did not sound aggressive, just diverted.

'No, not simple. That's a bad choice of word. It's hard to explain – I don't know.' Steven ruffled his hair with his hand for a moment and then looked up to continue. 'It's like here you don't have to follow the normal rules of society. You make your own – like for example not having to use money. It blows my mind.'

In an ominous voice, Jensen added. 'You forgot the part about having restricted movements, being contained to this site and having to apply for vacation time. Not forgetting the fact that you are only eligible for a vacation, with a chaperon, five year's after you change.'

Steven felt his last shred of hope disappear. Five years. That was too long. Way too long. 'Does that mean that you have never left this place?'

'Yes,' Jensen replied, as he shrugged his shoulders. He did not seem bothered about it. Perhaps, he had a reason to like being within the community. Steven bet he had a girl. A girl made all the difference.

'So, effectively, this is almost like a civilised jail?'

Jensen laughed aloud. 'You got it in one. I think we'll be friends all right – you're sharp that's for sure. I can do with someone like you to teach me the ropes. Someday, I'll brave it outside. There's no hurry, right?'

'Maybe not for you. I wouldn't mind going back home.'

'It's not my call. Can't help you there.'

'Fair enough.' Steven half smiled, and felt himself relax. Jensen seemed like the good sort. 'Seriously though, what's it like living here?'

'It's great – don't get me wrong. I have to admit that sometimes I can't help being curious about what's out there. But, I get it; our kind can't integrate into normal society. After the change, I think we should get an even better idea of what our true nature is like.'

Steven stiffened, defensive. 'I don't understand how it could change who I am.'

'None of us do, that's why we need to prepare.'

The conversation came to an end as they approached the second floor. It appeared deserted. There were rooms to either side, carved into the rock. It was difficult to see inside as they walked past, but Steven sensed a series of eyes watching as he passed. At the end of the curved hallway, an arched opening greeted them with the words *we are here to help* etched on the stone. As they eased through, an imposing hand made wooden table dominated the room. A stunning brunette sat behind it.

'Jensen, what can I do for you today?' She asked, a twinkle in her eye. Her long, black hair swished to the side as she flicked her head. 'You are not skiving again, are you?'

'Not at all, I am acting as a tour guide. We have someone new joining us today. This is ….'

The lady held up her hand to silence him and gasped. With a broad smile, she got up and walked towards Steven. An arms length away, she exclaimed. 'Is this Emily's son? Are you Steven?'

'Nothing gets past you does it?' Jensen joked, pursing his lips.

'Well, it's not everyday that I meet a cousin I knew nothing about – an outsider. Someone who lived in the human world, who is actually one of us.' Extending her arms, she took him by surprise by giving him an embrace and kissing both of his cheeks.

Under her watchful glare, Steven was both stunned and speechless. He knew she had to have a Spanish side, only his step mum's family ever kissed him like that.

She gave him a dazzling smile. 'It's amazing how much you look like Emily. It's a pleasure to meet you. My name is Sofia. I am Ian's daughter. My mother is Carmen Santos. So I am half Spanish.'

The statement made him nod as a half smile eased across his face – it was good to be right.

'It's going to be important for you to remember where we all came from. It will be a big part of your teaching,' Sofia continued, with one hand on her hip. '¿Hablas Español?'

'Un poco,' he replied. He hoped she was not expecting him to have a whole conversation in Spanish, but he could hold his own for a little bit.

'¿Hablas Español?' She said, repeating the words, impressed. She folded her arms and studied him.

Steven was sure he was not that interesting.

'What are you two talking about?' Jensen asked, perplexed. 'Are you talking Spanish?'

'Our friend here talks Spanish like my family.' Sofia stated. 'That's very useful.'

'Don't you speak Spanish?' Steven asked, as he turned to look at Jensen.

'No, I learnt a bit, but we developed our own language,' Jensen replied. 'You will have to learn it too. It's a cross between English, Spanish, Swedish, German, and Hebrew. It was developed to keep outsiders from understanding what we were saying in the outside world. English is the common tongue and we do need it for most things. We do actually have access to the internet, as backwards as we are.' Jensen raised his eyebrows.

Steven was beginning to regret referring to them as simple.

Sofia sat down again, folded her right leg on her left knee and crossed her hands together, deep in thought. 'So, I guess we need to register you for classes immediately. No time to lose,' she laughed, at a joke he did not understand. 'Steven when are you due to change?'

He thought about the question and looked perplexed.

'Your birthday,' she clarified.

'Oh, right. Fourth of September.'

'Right well, since Jensen is due to change on the 11th August you will be in the same classes. This is your schedule.' Sofia handed Steven a piece of paper, after the sound of a printer reeled it out from under the desk.

It was weird for Steven to see such a normal thing happening in such an abnormal setting.

'Just follow Jensen until you find your feet. Have fun,' she beamed.

'Okay,' Steven looked at the sheet. He felt totally inadequate. He gave a quizzical glance in Jensen's direction.

'You ready?' Jensen asked, as he turned towards the exit.

'Sure.' Steven shrugged. He might as well follow and pretend he knew what he was supposed to do. He had no idea what the rest of the day had in store for him.

'Look, it's nearly lunchtime, so I suggest we skip the end of this lesson and go through the rest of the day over some food. You must be hungry.'

'Starving. Sounds like a plan.'

'I like that saying – sounds like a plan. I'll keep it in mind. If it's any consolation, I'm hungry all the time too,' Jensen said, before he rolled his eyes. 'Let's eat.'

After leaving the administration room, they turned into one of the smaller archways. The corridor widened as another arched doorway revealed another room. Above the doorway, the words *we all need fuel* were carved into the stone. The most amazing aroma wafted into Steven's nose. His mouth watered immediately. The sight of the goodies made his eyes widen. At the far end was a table filled with exotic fruits. Next to them were huge clear jars filled with a range of coloured juices. All around the room an array of wooden tables and logs moulded into chairs created a homely appeal. It looked like a version of a school cafeteria – just a much more sophisticated one. No plastic chairs and wonky tables to greet him here.

Like in the larger room he'd seem the previous day, a serving station in the corner housed the food. It was split into two sections – hot and cold. The hot food was piled into heated covered containers. The cold options comprised a variety of bread rolls, delicatessen and salads.

Steven was awed over the selection. 'Where do you start?'

Jensen gave him an encouraging shove. 'Anywhere you want. Indulge.'

Just as Steven took a plate from the neatly stacked section, he heard muffled sounds behind him. It sounded like a herd of elephants approaching. He turned around and saw the hungry herd approaching – students.

'You better hurry, they are a hungry bunch,' Jensen smirked.

The mixture of people coming through the opening was amazing. They all looked of school age, but the difference in skin colour made him distinguish some of their origins. You could easily spot the Hispanic colourings of the Santos family and the bleach blond look of the Swedish Clausen Family. All at once he was surrounded. Everyone grabbed a plate and headed straight for the food. What struck Steven was the fact that none of them had stopped to stare.

They ignored him.

Had they been told to do this? It seemed too obvious. Normally, some would glare at the new kid.

'Well, come on then, you better get some, before it's gone – we're not going to hold back for you,' Jensen remarked, his plate already full to the brim.

Steven had a déjà vu moment – he was back at his cousins wedding the previous summer. It was always awkward when you had to blend into a situation you had no control over. Since no-one seemed to pry, he kept his eyes focused on the food and concentrated hard on choosing things he recognised.

The first thing he took was a bread roll. It looked like any other normal white bread roll he could have bought at the supermarket. Then he got some slices of what looked and smelled like ham. He wondered whether they bred pigs. He'd have to ask Jensen later about their livestock. Then he helped himself to a banana and a mango. He gave a quick glance at his colourful and healthy plate and nodded, impressed. His step mum, Clara, would have been proud. With a glass of, what he was sure was tropical juice; he headed off to find a seat. Selection over, it was time to taste.

Even though no-one was watching him he felt self conscious all the same. Most the tables were already taken. He moved towards the back to find a seat. Out of the corner of his eye he saw someone waving. It was Jensen and it looked like he had saved him a seat. He could see others sat at the same table. This was going to be interesting. At least Jensen seemed to accept him for what he was. Jensen was beginning to make Steven feel, well almost, normal.

Chapter 30

The School Cafeteria

Jensen nodded as Steven approached. 'Hey, you didn't think I'd bail on you already, did you?'

Steven took the seat, and then replied. 'I thought you might have had enough of me.'

'Nah, not yet. Anyway, did the food selection meet your expectations?'

'Pretty good. It's like a glamorous version of a hall cafeteria.'

'What's a cafeteria?' A girl to the left of Jensen asked as she looked Steven straight in the eye.

'Erm…its catering provided for students that live on the university campus.'

'What's a university?' The same girl asked, her curiosity sparked. She took a bite of her roll and chewed as she waited for his reply.

Steven gave a half smile. She sounded harmless. 'I guess there's a lot you don't know about life out there.'

'Obviously,' another girl sitting opposite him said, her tone huffy.

'Well I'll answer your question first. Then, I'll do the best I can to answer any other questions. I do have a request of my own.' Steven looked around the table, then continued, 'you have to answer mine.'

'That's a deal,' Jensen said out loud. Everyone else nodded, keen to be in on the arrangement. 'But where are my manners, I have not even told you who everyone is.'

Steven smiled and glanced at the table, self conscious all of a sudden. They all knew who he was – that was obvious.

'Well, you know who I am, but maybe you should introduce yourself first,' Jensen said.

Steven flinched. Jensen had just thrown the ball firmly in his court. Perhaps, he had underestimated him. He hated being put on the spot. Steven thought for a few seconds about what he could say.

Finally, he gave a half smile and began. 'For the past nineteen years, I have led a normal life with ordinary humans.'

A few of them raised their eyebrows.

He took a deep breath and continued. 'Ingrid tried to kill me. She was, let's say, taken by surprise. I turned out to be like you.

'Well, not exactly like us,' Jensen said, with a smirk.

Steven rolled his eyes. 'Smart Alec. Anyway, my former existence has been erased. I was more or less kidnapped or coerced into coming here. Since, I am half human, like Jensen just inferred, I have no idea what the change will do to me. Frankly, I would prefer to go back to the way things were. No offence to any of you, but this is all a bit too weird – I mean, let's face it, vampires are supposed to be a myth. It's ridiculous.' He burst into nervous laughter. Everyone around the table stared, dumbfounded. None of them laughed now. It dawned on him that sometimes less is more. It surprised him when everyone started to sit up straight. All of a sudden, he got the feeling someone else was listening.

A deep voice reverberated behind him. 'And yet here you are, and here we are.'

Steven turned, freaked out. Standing behind him was a man in his late forties, possibly even fifties – he was too old to be one of them. It did not make sense. He had a small gray moustache and beard – it made him look like Robinson Crusoe. He held out his hand to shake Steven's.

'My name is Jeff, or grandfather, if you prefer it. I am Emily's father and I was born in 1892. I should be over a hundred years old by now, and yet, do I look like it to you? Ridiculous is a pretty strong word to describe something that is true. You are right about something though, vampires are a myth. We are not like the creatures written about by Bram Stoker in his Dracula. We are as you can see for yourself very much alive. The question is what are we then – what do we call ourselves?' He gave Steven an intense stare and waited in silence, almost challenging him to speak.

Steven waited, perplexed.

The girls at the table broke out into a series of giggles, amused at his apparent ineptitude.

'I guess the cat got your tongue. Be careful to air you views so willingly. You have a lot to learn. We'll catch up some other time I'm sure. It was nice to finally meet the grandson I didn't know existed.' With that Jeff took his leave and walked out of the room.

Jensen gave a whistle of admiration. 'He never ever comes in here anymore. You must have made him think it worthwhile.'

'Yeah, but I didn't exactly impress him, did I?' Steven mumbled, embarrassed. Even though he didn't know Jeff, something about his grandfather exuded importance.

'Nah, if anyone had asked him before he was bitten, he would have said the same thing. We know enough to realise that the reason we live like we do is because we are different and unusual. I wouldn't call myself ridiculous though.' The girl that had first spoken to him smiled.' Anyway, my turn. I'm Susanna Abel. My parents are Benjamin Abel & Lina Santos. My grandmother, Catherine, is your aunt so we are second cousins. I have never left the community, and am happy to be oblivious about the outside world. I like living here.'

Susanna gave Jensen a sideways glance, and blushed. It gave Steven the impression Susanna and Jensen were an item. If his suspicions were right, Susanna was the girl that made Jensen want to stay.

'I'm Kayla Clausen,' the other girl started. 'I am Susanna's first cousin, but I am not related to you at all. It gets quite complicated here when you look at the web that the families have created. My mother is called Beatrice Santos and my Dad is called Jan Clausen. Jensen's father, Doctor Johannes Clausen, is my uncle. So, are you keeping up yet?'

'No, I'm totally lost,' Steven admitted, apologetic.

'I'll have to draw you a map of who's who then so that you can keep up. But I have to admit, it's hard for the rest of us at times,' Kayla laughed. She flicked her hair to the side and gave him a flirtatious smile. 'The thing is – we are a bit overprotective on avoiding cross breeding.'

'What do you mean cross breeding?' Steven asked, now completely baffled. Genetics was never his strong suit.

'Well,' the younger boy sitting quietly opposite, spoke for the first time. 'It's a bit like this. No-one wants parents, siblings, or first cousins getting together in your world right?'

'I guess – it's not acceptable practice.'

'So the same applies here. It's important that we know what our parentage is and that anyone we consider dating has no family connection whatsoever. At first, it was easier to maintain. Recently, it's becoming a problem.' He paused, bit his lip and checked around for anyone listening. Once satisfied no-one else was listening, he whispered. 'It's hard to keep all the lines clear which is why *you* have made a lot of people think about things differently.'

'Me? What have I done?' Steven was at a loss.

'Think about it,' Jensen said, as leaned in.

Steven stared, waiting for enlightenment.

An uncomfortable expression came upon all of the faces around him. None of them wanted to say aloud what they were thinking. Something about him in particular was taboo, something was unknown. When it hit him, he felt like a fool. In a loud voice, he exclaimed, 'of course, anyone here can mate with a human!'

'Shush…,' Kayla said, she looked all around her, then leant in closer. In a voice barely above a whisper, she continued. 'We're not supposed to even contemplate it as a possibility. What Emily did broke all the rules they implemented in setting up this place. You should not exist, let alone live here with us.'

'We're all a bit nervous about what you are,' Susanna added, she kept her eyes down and focused on her long fingernails.

Steven sat back and folded his arms. 'Great, so is that why no-one around us is daring to acknowledge I exist.'

'Exactly, you're an anomaly. You have all of us on tenterhooks,' the boy added, with a superior expression. 'Anyway, I have not introduced myself. I am Susanna's brother Gideon. I guess it's too late to ignore you now.'

'I guess so,' Steven looked around the table. It struck him they were just as clueless as he was. They had no idea what was to become of them either. The conversation had got far too serious, too soon. 'So, where do we have to go now?'

Jensen, Susanna and Kayla looked smug, then they all simultaneously said, 'Mathematics.'

Gideon laughed and got up. 'I have a different class, so have fun! Steven, this might be a bit above you. Don't let it get to you, okay.' He winked and laughed as he walked away.

Whatever was going on, it was not funny. Steven hated mathematics.

***

Catherine Abel could not believe it – after forty years of teaching she had developed nerves. Under normal circumstances, she would not be fazed over a lesson, especially not to adolescents. Of course, today was not like any other lesson. Today, she was going to meet her nephew. A student like no other. She had discussed the problem at length with her husband, Isaac, and they had come to the same conclusion – there was no question on whether to accept Steven. She would treat him like anyone else. It was not in their nature to reject anyone, especially when taking into account Isaac's background. It would be two-faced to turn their backs on someone different, because of whom they were – Isaac had seen enough discrimination in his youth. He would never reject anyone for being different. And neither would she.

Nevertheless, Steven was potentially a dangerous hybrid, an unknown, a threat to their existence. Then again, he could be a new possibility. There was so much to consider. It was hard to come to terms with the fact her sister, Emily, had conceived a son with a human – she had kept her secret well. The problem remained. No-one in the council wanted the community to even consider living amongst humans as a viable option. It just couldn't be. Everyone was unanimous. The only one who had ever objected had been Emily. However, since Emily had stopped attending council meetings after her disappearance, the issue had not raised its weary head in years. Now, it was back with a vengeance. These were not good times. Steven's presence opened a can of worms.

Catherine had never had any issue with taking human life for survival. Taking human life for pleasure was another matter – it was unacceptable. This was the keystone of their beliefs. The only exception being during reconnaissance, or vacation. The compromise was necessary to ensure they kept up to date with new developments. It also gave a renewed vigour to those that left.

That was the only occasion where the rule was broken. Emily had gone against everything they had worked towards when she conceived Steven.

In retrospect, it should have been so easy to spot. No-one was ever good enough for Emily. She was always the rebel – always after what was forbidden. With that last thought in mind, she heard the pupils entering her class. As she looked up and smiled a barely audible gasp escaped, as she stared into her sister's eyes. She would have known he was Emily's son anywhere. Keeping her emotions in check, she wondered how Emily could have left her child for the sake of the community. The sacrifice must have been great. It was time for Catherine to set things right. She would accept Steven and cast her doubts aside. Maybe then, Emily would learn to trust her again.

Chapter 31

Gifted

Steven was taken aback by the woman standing authoritatively in the middle of the room. She was about his height, wore a serious expression and had blazing red hair – it was even brighter than Caitlin's. There was something familiar about her stance, but he could not put his finger on what it was.

As he got closer, she welcomed him, hand outstretched. 'Steven, I am your Aunt Catherine. Your mother, Emily, is my sister. Welcome home.'

'Thanks,' he muttered, surprised at the formal introduction. At least it explained the familiarity.

'Please, sit anywhere you find a space,' she said, as she walked back to the centre of the room.

Steven sat on the closest seat. It was one of several wooden benches, arranged in a circular fashion around the central teacher's round table. There was nowhere to write, which he thought unconventional. He liked the idea of no writing being involved. In total, there were six pupils in the room, including Steven. They all looked similar in age. He wondered when the others would be undergoing the change.

'For the sake of our latest addition, can you all introduce yourselves, please?' Catherine added, holding out her arms in an open gesture.

Jensen, Kayla and Susanna went first, having been already acquainted.

A girl of similar complexion to Susanna stood up. 'I'm Lisbeth Santos.' Then she sat down again.

'Lisbeth is a very gifted Mathematician, I'm sure you'll get to know her more in time,' Catherine added. She was trying to break the moment. It was obvious to Steven that Lisbeth was *not* too keen to be acquainted with him.

The last student stood up. 'I'm Tobias Abel; I'm your second cousin. I don't need another cousin though, I have enough cousins already.' He sat down and folded his arms.

Steven had to suppress a smile. Another relative, unwanted at that. Overnight, he had gone from being an only child with limited family, to having an enormous family. He was not sure how he felt about that. Catherine looked uncomfortable, yet she did not reprimand Tobias for being rude. Steven thought she should have done. Manners were always welcome where he came from.

Catherine gave him a beaming smile. 'Introductions aside, let us begin. Steven, this lesson will help you stretch your mental agility. You have probably never thought to test your mind in this way, but, it is something we realised we could all do after the change. Therefore, we try and prepare you to use this ability, before the change. You have to be aware of the different facets you will be able to explore. Jensen, Susanna, can you stand up please and give our guest a demonstration.'

Steven rolled his eyes, *now* he was a guest.

Jensen and Susanna stood up and faced each other, then grinned, as if they were sharing an intimate joke.

'Jensen you start,' Catherine instructed.

'Okay then, one thousand, three hundred and fifty six times four hundred and sixty seven. That should not be too complicated,' Jensen asked, his expression smug.

Almost immediately, Susanna smiled, 'Six hundred and thirty three thousand, two hundred and fifty two. My turn! One million, seven hundred and twenty two thousand divided by fifty six.'

'Thirty thousand, seven hundred and fifty back at you. And I started out playing nice,' Jensen remarked, wiping his fingers casually on his shirt.

They made it look so easy.

'Okay, thank you for the demonstration,' Catherine said, as she motioned them to sit down. 'Steven, it's your turn.'

'Sorry I can't do that,' Steven said. He shook his head and remained frozen on the spot. This was not funny.

'Yes, you can. It's inbuilt. Let your instinct take over. Go on stand up and give it a go.'

Steven did not want to get up but he did not think he had a lot of choice in the matter. Reticent, he stood up and slouched.

'Don't think about the answer, just know it.'

That was funny. She had no idea how bad at math Steven actually was. With a huge sigh, he looked at her and pouted. 'How do I do that?'

'Don't think.'

Steven shrugged his shoulders. 'Fine, whatever.'

'Lisbeth, can you give him an easy one please?' Catherine encouraged.

Lisbeth stood up, and raised her chin. Steven doubted she would give him an easy one. Lisbeth avoided eye contact and said, 'one hundred and sixty two times twelve.'

Steven felt his palms get sweaty. He had no idea what the answer was. All he could think of was that everyone was waiting and watching. He had never felt so inadequate. The more he thought the worse it got, until eventually his mind went blank.

After an eternity of silence, Catherine interrupted. 'You are trying to work out the answer with your head. You are not allowing your instinct to take over. Close your eyes this time – pretend none of us are here.'

As much as he tried, Steven could not see the answer. He felt stupid. In desperation, his mind scrambled through the numbers, trying to come up with the solution, but it failed to materialise. Silence ensued. It seemed like the harder he thought, the more allusive the answer got. Finally, he opened his eyes and shrugged his shoulders. 'I don't know.'

Catherine could not hide her disappointment. She tried to cover it up with an encouraging shrug. 'That's fine you can observe for today, practice with the others and try again next time.'

For the next hour, Steven watched, perplexed, as they all tested themselves on a variety of mathematical questions that were not restricted to number. Most of it went over his head. He had never been good at mathematics, just average. He had passed his G.C.S.E. and been glad to see the back of it. What they were expecting of him, was impossible. After an hour of mental calculations Steven needed caffeine. He had never felt so lost or confused by anything academic in his life. This took things on to a different level.

'That's enough for today, see you all tomorrow.' Catherine said, as she turned to her desk and sat down. She looked up as he was leaving. 'Don't be down hearted. You'll get there in the end.'

Steven gave a half smile. In his head he felt like screaming at her 'are you out of your mind.' As he followed Jensen out of the room, he remained deep in thought. He could not help but consider what other skills they had been hiding. The issue was would he be able to do what they could? He had definitely flunked that class.

'That was intense,' Steven admitted, once he was sure he was out of Catherine's earshot.

'That was quite a mild one actually,' Jensen added.

'That was mild?' Steven grimaced.

'Afraid so,' Kayla sighed.

'I don't stand a chance,' he pouted.

'We've all been there. It takes a long time to learn to trust your instincts. We've been preparing for this a long time. It's only recently that we understood what they had been saying. The change is drawing near and our instincts are sharpening. But, it's a two way process – nothing happens unless you let it,' Susanna explained, in a teacher like manner.

'I'll take your word for it,' he scoffed.

Steven wondered what was next. Lisbeth and Tobias had scarpered at the end of the lesson, not hanging around to get acquainted. Even though he had been selective about his friends over the years, he had never had people actively avoid him. The whole situation would take some getting used to. For now, it seemed most people within the community saw him as an alien – a different entity. Maybe when the change happened, he would be accepted. It annoyed him to think it mattered whether he was accepted. He had never wanted to be one of a crowd. Even so, he could not deny the pull of the family bond. Like it or not, the fact they were all in this together made him want to belong. For the first time ever, he knew there was something about him that linked him to everyone else here. It was unnerving, but enticing. He had a family now, whether he wanted one or not.

*

After a lesson on Amazonian animals that had nearly sent him to sleep, Steven relished the thought of the last lesson. According to Jensen, this was the best one. It involved a trip to an underground cave.

Once inside the gigantic cavern, another older man waited.

'He is one of the originals,' Jensen commented.

'What do you mean originals?' Steven asked.

'One of the first to be bitten – first generation.'

'Right,' Steven nodded. He considered the point. It made his mum an original and him second generation.

He noticed Kayla easing up alongside him, before she leaned in and whispered. 'That's Franco, my grandfather.'

This time Steven was not singled out as a new arrival. He kept to the background, hoping to go unnoticed. There was a mixture of ages in the group. He guessed they ranged from about fifteen years to his age.

'So, do we have a volunteer to step forward,' Franco asked.

Gideon stepped forward and nodded.

'Good, right go to the far end of the room. You know how this works. No-one will be able to see you, but you should be able to see us. Do not move or make a sound. Silencio.'

Steven was confused. He stayed at the back and watched as a girl went first.

She looked towards the direction Gideon had gone and walked in his direction.

'Close your eyes, let your senses take over,' Franco commanded.

The girl started to walk in the direction Gideon had gone and disappeared.

After a few minutes, they heard a thump. 'Ouch,' the girl cried out.'

Coming back into the light, she rubbed her nose.

'I bumped into the wall, it was pitch black,' she admitted, her face crimson.

'Good try,' Franco added. He searched the crowd for another victim. 'You at the back,' he motioned, then pointed right in Steven's direction.

Steven rolled his eyes, so much for not being singled out. 'Me,' Steven asked. He felt like a small child intimidated by a burly school teacher.

'Yes, show us what you can do. Remember just follow your instincts.'

Steven walked to the front and faced the direction Gideon had walked. He thought what the hell? He might as well give it a go. He had nothing to lose. He decided to go the whole hog, closed his eyes and made his way forward. The darkness of the cave enveloped him as he eased forward. He was slow to start. Gradually, he gained confidence and increased his pace. Instinctively, he whispered Gideon's name and listened. An echo seemed to lead him ahead. He focused on a miniscule sound in front of him. On a mission, he walked on and held out his hand in anticipation. When it landed on Gideon's shoulder he could not suppress a smirk. He had done it.

'You're a natural, that's amazing,' Gideon said, his voice gushed with admiration.

Steven could not help but to wonder how he had done it. It was mystifying. Back in the open, Steven received his first rapturous applause.

'That's how it's done,' Franco beamed, as he approached. 'Tell me, since when have you been able to locate things from a distance so easily?'

'It's been coming for a while, but, in the past year or so I seemed to be able to hit targets in games easily,' Steven replied, just as bewildered.

'Your skills were naturally homing in on the targets.' Turning to face the rest of the group, Franco announced. 'Everyone, we have a natural example of human echolocation. Some of you will develop the skill quickly, others will have to practice. As most of you know, this is a skill that has been passed on to us by bats. They have used it to track down their prey for millions of years and now we are lucky enough to have inherited the same trait. Right, enough show, time for you all to partner up and practice.'

Steven was completely taken aback. Who would have thought that he'd be naturally talented at something like echolocation? It wasn't like he hadn't heard of the term before, but it was incredible to think that it was something he could use. He noticed a few impressed glances. Perhaps now, some of them would see him in a new light – the new boy might actually belong after all. It was certainly a turn in the books.

Chapter 32

Food For Thought

Steven found himself in a group of mixed ages. There was a girl of about sixteen, a boy that looked like he had barely reached puberty, and Kayla.

'I'll go first,' said Kayla. She winked at Steven as she murmured. 'See if you can find me, Steven.'

The other two shrugged their shoulders and took and step back. With no alternative, Steven made his move. He closed his eyes as before and let his senses take over. Once he was enveloped by the darkness, he called out her name softly and waited. Almost immediately, he knew where she was. Once he had reached touching distance, he opened his eyes and held out his hand. When he felt her shoulder, she turned towards him and reached out with her hand for his face. He froze as she traced his face with her fingertips and run her index finger over his lips. A second later, she leaned in and kissed him. The kiss was soft, yet longing. When she run her tongue along his, he could not help reacting. Then, as quickly as it had begun it was over.

She eased back and whispered in his ear. 'Hmm, nice. I just had to know what that would be like, hope you didn't mind.'

Steven stood motionless, as she walked back into the light. Inadvertently, he let out a stunned laugh. The day before, he had been bathing naked with Ingrid, and now he got kissed in the dark by a girl he barely met. This place was more interesting than he expected. A guilty pang hit his conscience – Caitlin. Even though he had been forced to leave her, a part of him felt as though he was contemplating cheating on her. It did not feel right. It was not her fault he'd been erased from her memory.

***

Jensen became pensive on the way back to the food hall. Since he had witnessed Steven's dismal failure with mathematics and natural talent at echolocation, he was intrigued. In his case, mathematics was child's play. It came naturally. However, his homing skills still left much to be desired. He could not understand why they all seemed so different. He was also troubled by the conversation they'd had earlier on. Kayla seemed interest in Steven and Jensen suspected many other girls would soon follow. The quest to keep their species diversified had got more interesting the day Steven arrived.

His heart was already well and truly taken. For as long as he could remember there was only Susanna. He had been patient and soon their time would come. Luckily, he knew she felt the same way. All they had to do was wait for their change, then they would be together. It had been ingrained upon them to avoid getting involved until they had fully matured. Somehow, it did not seem worth the risk, even though at times it was hard to suppress his desire.

As curiosity got the better of him, Jensen turned to Steven, who was also quiet, deep in his own thoughts. 'Kayla is nice, isn't she?'

Steven flinched, as though Jensen had intruded into his private space. Perhaps, it was too soon to expect Steven to open up to him. 'Sorry, I didn't mean to pry.'

Steven shook his head and looked ahead. 'Kayla, hmm…she is certainly forthcoming. Can I trust you to keep a secret?'

Jensen did not hesitate. 'Of course.'

'She kissed me.'

Jenson could not help laughing. 'Really?' He could not believe her nerve. So much for waiting. 'You realise you are going to be popular with a lot of girls and women now right.'

'Why? I thought everyone wanted to keep away from me.' Steven stopped walking and frowned.

Jensen cocked his head to the side and explained. 'Anyone who has no link to the Roberts family will see you as a great prospect. The fact that you are an anomaly will only make them want you more. It's only natural to be attracted to something unique and potentially bad for you. Lucky for me, Susanna is related to you. But, you must understand – any attraction you feel must be suppressed until after the change. You don't know what you are going to be like until then.'

'Will I change that much? Does everyone wait to get involved until after the change?'

Jensen shrugged his shoulder and started to walk again. 'For everyone it's different. But in your case it's a complete unknown. And yes, we all wait. At least, as far as I know. It's not like we have that many chances anyway,' Jensen sighed.

Steven kept up the same pace. 'Well, I was not attracted to Kayla, anyway.'

Jensen was not sure if Steven was being completely truthful, he sensed a little hesitation. 'At least that's a start.'

'But, she's not the first to come on to me,' Steven added.

Jensen's jaw dropped as he stopped again. 'You've only just arrived. Who else can there have been?'

'Ingrid.'

'Ingrid, of course.' Jensen raised his eyebrows.

Of all the people available, Ingrid had decided to go for Steven – it was so typical of her. 'She's my cousin and for as long as I've known she's always been impulsive. I feel sorry for you if she has set her sights on you – she usually gets what she wants,' he paused, unable to hold back a chuckle.

'She's not getting me,' Steven snapped.

'She's not that bad.'

'How come she's not found someone else then?'

'Touché. Don't know, she has always been a bit fussy. Although, I guess she can't be that fussy if she's interested in you, right?' He kept the conversation light-hearted as he gave Steven a nudge with his shoulder.

'Very funny.'

Jensen went all serious, he had no reason to keep anything from Steven. 'Look, as far as I know, she has had plenty of suitors but it never worked out. What makes you think she likes you in that way?'

'I don't know for sure, but where I come from, women don't tend to swim naked with you unless they are interested.'

Jensen did a double take. 'She did what?!'

Now it was Steven's turn to look smug.

'I went to bathe the day I arrived and she followed me. Nothing happened but it was intense.'

'I'll bet. I can't imagine what I'd do if Susanna did that with me. Not that I haven't been in the bathing area with women before – it's just that it's different when you are attracted to one and you're alone.' Jensen leaned in. 'Did you want something to happen?'

'I don't know. My natural urge was to react. I just couldn't get over the situation. Even though I have been with a lot of girls, you can trust me when I say no-one has ever come on to me like that before. It's surreal, first Ingrid gets naked in the water with me and now Kayla kisses me. I've had girls fancy me, but I'm not used to them being so forward.'

'Well, you can't think it's a bad thing.'

'Jury's out. I do have some pride.'

'Hey, that's not all I have on my mind either, but sometimes the mind is allowed to wonder.'

Steven started to walk so Jensen followed.

'I just don't want to see women as sexual objects. I was in love not that long ago. Now, I don't know what I feel.'

Jensen swallowed. He could not imagine having to let go of Susanna. 'I'm sorry if you had to let go of a girl.'

'Not as sorry as me.'

The cafeteria was a sight for sore eyes. 'Anyway, we have other things to worry about now, like food and sleep – lots of both. We need to stock up like bears.'

'Now you mention it – food sounds great!'

***

The food hall bustled with activity, as students queued for food whilst others sat down and socialised as they ate. Steven followed Jensen in and tensed. This time he could have sworn everyone was watching him from the corner of their eyes. It did not look like they were ignoring him anymore.

'Jensen, how's babysitting duties going?' A beefy boy hollered, from a crowded table, before bursting into laughter. His friends joined in the joke.

'Better than being a member of the jerk brigade,' Jensen replied, a scowl on his face.

The boy made to stand, but a girl next to him grabbed his arm and gave him a look. He shrugged and sat down.

'They look friendly,' Steven remarked.

'Keep away from that lot, they're bad news.'

'I can see that,' Steven said, as he saw them sticking their feet out to trip up a girl of about fifteen years of age. Before anyone could warn her, she jumped over the legs balancing her plate with precision – it looked like a well practiced manoeuvre. Steven took in his surroundings. Apart from the fact the hall was carved out of rock, it looked like a school cafeteria. Everyone around Steven was of school age. In fact, he could not see anyone that looked pre-pubescent. The younger children had to be taught elsewhere.

As he came upon the hot section, Steven recognised a dish – it looked like toad in the hole. There were even mashed potatoes, carrots and peas. Nostalgia overcame him. He drifted in its direction, eager to taste familiar flavours. When it was his turn, he grabbed a huge helping and drizzled on the gravy, mentally adding a quick prayer of thanks. Turning to find a seat, he saw Jensen and the others at the same table they had sat on earlier. He rolled his eyes, amazed – even here, people were territorial about seating places. As he sat down, the others smirked. They were obviously amused about something.

'Are you hungry today, by any chance?' Susanna teased, as she explained the joke.

'A bit,' he admitted. 'This was my favourite meal back home.'

'Well, it won't disappoint you, for sure. We have some brilliant cooks here,' Jensen added, as he tucked into his portion.

Steven tentatively stuck his fork in the sausage and cut it, adding a small helping of the Yorkshire pudding. Then he placed it in his mouth. Almost immediately, he felt his taste buds explode. This was the taste of home. The gravy was rich and thick and the sausages burst with flavour, reminiscent of his favourite – Cumberland sausage. He was in sausage heaven. It dawned on him that with such a strong Spanish contingent there had to be some Spanish cooks around too. Then, his taste buds would be completely satisfied.

'Is it as you'd expect it to be?' Kayla asked her smile sweet yet deadly.

'Better,' Steven admitted, as he devoured another huge mouthful.

Silence fell upon the table as they ate. It made Steven ponder over the simple things in life. Food was definitely a satisfying part of being human. At least, he would never lose that.

'I wonder if our taste buds will be different after we change,' Gideon mused, with a full mouth.

'I sure hope not,' Steven spluttered, covering his mouth with his hand as he talked.

'I'm sure our pallets will be satisfied in other ways.' Kayla battered her eyelids, flirtatious again.

Steven finished his mouthful and glared back. 'My pallet is perfectly satisfied at the moment. I hope nothing about me changes.'

Kayla pouted, and then carried on picking her salad.

'Jensen, are we done for the day?' Steven asked. Surely, he had done enough.

'Afraid not, we have chores. Farming area next.'

'Kayla and I are making new clothes today. I've been checking out the internet for the latest look – should be fun,' Susanna added, with a cheeky and very girlie shrug.

'And I have to go and feed the animals,' Gideon groaned.

'What livestock do you keep here?' Steven asked.

'We keep chickens, goats, guinea pigs, and armadillos,' Gideon reeled off, naming them as he pointed to his fingers.

'Armadillo's?'

'Yes, did you like the sausages?'

'Why?'

'Tasty Armadillo's don't you think?'

Steven's mouth gaped open – he had just eaten Armadillo sausages.

'And of course we can catch a variety of fish, as well as growing an array of vegetables. Fruit is so plentiful here; we can just pick it off as we need it.'

Kayla and Susanna laughed out loud. Obviously, amused by Steven's facial expression.

'Enough Gideon, remember this is all new to Steven. Give him a break,' Jensen interrupted.

'Sorry,' Gideon remarked, uncomfortable.

'It's okay,' Steven reassured. 'I'll get used to it. Like I said – best sausages I ever tasted.'

Chapter 33

Hunter Gatherer

The descent into the unknown filled Steven with a sense of curiosity and confusion. The grey walled nondescript lift reminded him of the one at the Law faculty, back at Southampton University. He had to remind himself he was not there, even though he wished he was. It was only when the lift doors opened that Steven knew for certain. Nothing was normal. The smell alone was overwhelming. It was a fusion of the scents you would associate with a florist, a garden centre, and a refuse disposal site. He followed Jensen and paid attention.

'On the left hand side are the natural fruit trees and berry plants. Ahead, we have cultivated the ground for a multitude of vegetables. Of course we also have chillies and more exotic plants. To the right, we have the livestock. As you can see it's surrounded by secure fencing. We have to protect them from the predators out there.'

'Like what?'

'Mainly the big cats, such as the jaguar and leopard. It's rare for them to find a way in, but sometimes it happens. Anyway, we have to go to help to dig up vegetables. So, muscle up. I'll introduce you to Lucy Santos. She is in charge of production. You'll be happy to know you're not related, but don't worry she's been around for a long time so I don't think she'll be jumping on you any time soon,' Jensen said, a cheeky grin pasted on his face.

'Funny,' Steven huffed.

A maze of plants and soiled terrain dotted the path. Geographically speaking, it looked like they were in the mouth of the old volcanic site. Steven took a deep breath and relished the fresh air, it was a welcome change. Steven had not realised how stuffy it was inside until now. He arched his back and examined the height of the volcano. It was way too high to climb. Ahead, through the vegetation, Steven could see what looked like a large greenhouse. It was constructed out of wood, metal and glass. It looked like it had seen better days.

Jensen knocked on the wooden door. 'Lucy, are you here?'

A voice called from the corner. 'Jensen, is that you?'

Steven followed the voice and saw a woman lift her head up. As they got closer he was surprised at her attire. She wore dark green overalls, covered in splodges of dirt, her hands practically encrusted in soil. Something about her face intrigued Steven. It could have been the shape. He was taken aback by the fact she looked the same age as him, not a single wrinkle blemished her smooth heart shaped face.

'Hey, who's this you bring me today? I have not had a chance to check who was helping. I've had people coming in dribs and drabs and they're out there working the land. But, you know me, always busy. We have a lot of people to feed.' She held out her hand, after wiping it on her trouser leg. 'Hi, I'm Lucy. You know, I can't remember having seen you before? But then,' she laughed, 'I lose track of everyone all the time. I can't keep up.'

'I'm Steven.'

'Steven, hmm...who are your parents again?'

Jensen sniggered. Steven could not believe someone remained in the dark. 'Emily is my biological mother; my Dad is a normal human.'

'Lucy, have you not heard yet?' Jensen asked, his expression perplexed.

Lucy mumbled to herself, her eyes fixed on the ground. 'Oh, that's what they were talking about. I wasn't paying attention. Sorry, well, err...welcome. Unexpected.' Silence ensued for a few seconds, before she recovered and looked up. 'I'm sure if Jensen is looking out for you, you must be the right sort. A pair of helping hands is all I'm after.'

'Where do you want us to go?' Jensen asked.

'Oh,' she continued to stare at Steven.

Steven noticed that her eyes were deep blue, just like the ocean. It was obvious her mind was elsewhere. She was not really looking at him, more like looking through him. It was weird. In a brisk movement, she got to her feet and retrieved a list from the table. She did not look at Steven as she spoke. 'Can you go and pull out these vegetables for tomorrow? Here's the list. Then take it to the prep area as usual, okay.' She handed the piece of paper to Jensen and turned away.

As far as Steven was concerned, she was definitely weird. Yet, she was the first person he had felt any sort of connection with, in the strangest possible way. The way she muttered as she went left Steven convinced that something had shaken her too.

'Eccentric?' Steven asked, as they left the greenhouse.

'Yes,' Jensen glanced back. 'The story goes that she was good friends with Emily many years ago. Apparently, she was in love with your uncle Ian. As you know, he married Carmen in the end. Some suspected that she kept up the friendship with Emily just to see him. When Emily disappeared for a few years, she had no excuse to be around Ian, so she withdrew and ensconced herself in her work. She has never met her complement, and even when your mother returned, the friendship was never the same. It's sad – she's a beautiful woman.'

'Hiding in a giant allotment,' Steven joked.

'What's an allotment?' Jensen queried.

'Oh, it's just a place where you grow things.'

Steven knew Jensen had a point. No-one with eyes that beautiful should be hidden away.

***

The years of isolation should have made Lucy immune to feelings of a romantic nature. Love was painful and best avoided. Nevertheless, she had been caught unawares – Steven had shaken her up. As she walked towards the back room, she stared out into the distance. They would be hard at work now.

An easy explanation, for her irrational response, was the family resemblance between Steven and Ian – it couldn't be more. It was bizarre. The last time she had ever sensed unease like that was when she pined for Ian. It had taken her so long to get over unrequited love. She did not want to recall those foolish days when she had watched Ian and Carmen. She had acted like a moth heading for a bright light, closing in on death. Every time they held hands and laughed together, the knife had gone deeper into her heart. Life had been tortuous – it forced her to go into hiding. Ian had been nothing more than a big brother at the beginning. Then, as she neared maturity, she started to see him in a different light. Emily was the

way in – she was her friend.
Then Emily disappeared. Emily had deserted her, in her hour of need. Little had she known Emily was fighting even bigger demons – she had bred with a human and had Steven. If only Emily had not gone. Then Emily would have helped Ian fall in love with her, not Carmen. In fairness, Lucy had ignored Ian's friendship with Carmen. Carmen was so much younger – she forgot the age difference would be insignificant eventually. Everyone, but her, suspected there was something going on between them.
All she had now was the body of a twenty year old with no-one to love. Yet, the old sensations she was convinced were long gone, appeared to have been dormant. Just waiting for the right time to reawaken. Perhaps, she was foolish to give up on love so easily. She could still find a complement. With a slight smile, she shook her head and frowned. She doubted she could ever be with someone like Steven. A thought did cross her mind, as she stroked the leaf of her baby fern. Steven for Ian – it seemed fair.

***

Steven had never laboured so hard in his life. A couple of hours had gone by and all they had to show for their efforts where two wheelbarrows full of produce. He never realised how hard the job was. He was not sure he wanted to get to know more. His back was already in agony. It was like he had aged a couple of years.
Jensen wiped his brow and took a swig out of an army style water bottle. Then, he handed it over to Steven.
'Thanks, are we done yet?'
'Yeah, I think we can call it a day.'
Steven followed Jensen with his wheelbarrow. At the end of the narrow path they came upon a prep area. A lot of other people waited with their efforts. Eventually, they handed over the produce to some other men. There was not a single smile in sight. They nodded at Jensen, ignored Steven.
As they walked away, Jensen said, 'thanks for helping out.'
'I guess it's what everyone is expected to do here.'
'Well yes, but it's still nice to be grateful,' Jensen reiterated.
'I appreciate it. I still sense, from the lack of conversation from the men back there, I'm not really welcome.'
'Give it time,' Jensen called out, as he started to run. 'Let's go –

it's time for a bath, you've earned it!'

'Is this mixed bathing again?' Steven howled, as he sped up.

'You'll get used to that too. But, the women here tend to bathe when the men are at work. They are usually involved with the prep and cooking, whilst we have our turn.'

'So that's why it was deserted when I went the other day – everyone was eating.'

'Exactly. Last one there's a loser.'

The sounds of splashing and chatter stopped, as they approached the bathing area. There were several men in the water and some drying themselves outside. At least, there were no women in sight which was one consolation. Jensen stripped down and run up to the water's edge to dive in. Steven felt a brief moment of self consciousness as he mulled over the fact that a shower back at home *for one* seemed so much more private. Here he was exposed. He put it to the back of his mind and started to undress. He had to.

Jensen popped his head out of the water momentarily, and called out. 'Get a move on.'

Steven slipped out of his shorts and t-shirt and kept his underpants on. With a shrug, he made a run for it and dived in. The lukewarm water provided him with instant relief for the second time. It had to be the best bath in the world, even if it was not exclusive. He swam across to the waterfall and let the water splash on his head – it felt like getting head massage. Caitlin was very good at those.

After a few minutes, he made his way towards the lake on the other side, and started racing in a perfect front crawl. It felt good to swim again. When he stopped, he heard a distant voice coming after him.

'Hey, don't thrash too loud or you'll rally up the Piranha's,' Jensen hollered.

'Piranha's here?' Steven exclaimed, swimming towards the waters edge.

'Joke man, just a joke. We keep them out. The look on your face was priceless though.'

'Funny.' Jensen was turning out to be a bit of a joker.

'We better get going. It's time to fill up with fuel again.'

'Absolutely, race you back.'

Steven swam back in a powerful stroke, he passed Jensen with ease. He was out of the water and dressed, before Jensen had made it out.

When Jensen came up alongside, he nodded in approval. 'Nifty swimming, that's a useful skill.'

'What for – to out swim the Piranha's and Caiman?'

'You guessed it. No, seriously, we need good swimmers to go and help with fishing duties. I'll put a mention in, so that you get reassigned. It might be more up your street.'

'I didn't mind digging veg.'

'Sure, but it's good to try out new things.'

'Since when are you my guardian?'

Jensen frowned, confused. 'You tell me.'

'Thanks for looking out for me. I'm just jesting with you, English humour. Fishing, I might just give it a go,' he laughed aloud. He was definitely intrigued by the idea of going out into the Amazon River.

Chapter 34

Jensen

The main catering hall was always full at mealtimes, a constant hive of activity. It was the social hub; the focus of all gossip, flirtation and melodrama. Emily sipped her coffee and contemplated the mood. Everything seemed as it was. Nothing had actually changed since Steven arrived. It appeared on the surface that life had moved on. She was not sure it was truly the case. She suspected many were biding their time. Waiting for when Steven changed, to see what would happen. The truth was Steven had adapted to his new lifestyle. Remarkably, he fit in. He got on with it. He had earned a lot of people's respect by working hard on all the tasks they threw at him.

This meant a lot to Emily. It was nice to know her son was not a lazy, arrogant man, like many of the human men she had met. In truth, it had not surprised her at all – Paul was always the perfect gentleman. The only one who had not got her act together was her. She had failed to get to know her son. She had tried but it was awkward. Today, she would try again. She watched the entrance and waited. If she was lucky she would get the chance to talk to him. She had not given up yet.

In answer to her thoughts she saw Steven walk through the doors. Jensen was at his side again, they were obviously close. She wondered if she would ever develop the same friendship with her son. Steven looked at ease as he bantered with Jensen. She had chosen the right tour guide.

Out of interest, she turned towards Ingrid, to see if she was also following Steven. Ingrid was staring right at him. Emily wondered how many other girls lay in the wings, waiting for his change. He was open season for anyone not linked to the Roberts family. Honestly, she felt sorry for him. A woman's obsession could be deadly.

As much as she wanted to talk to him, she was apprehensive. She already fell short of ideal mother material. Regardless, it was important for her to show everyone he was a part of her life now. She downed the rest of her coffee and made her way towards them. It could have looked like she was on her way out.

'Jensen, nice to see you,' she said, her tone polite. 'Steven, it's good to see you settled in?'

Steven seemed disinterested, he shrugged and glanced over her shoulder as he spoke. 'Its fine, *Jensen* has been helping me out.'

It was just what she needed. She knew she had not done much to help his integration. It was hard to get a reminder. In a futile attempt at conversation, she continued. 'I hear you're helping to teach echolocation now, since you are so advanced. Good for you, it's also one of my strengths.'

Another shrug, before the reply. 'I guess so.'

He really did not want to talk to her.

In order to salvage her integrity she made her move. 'Enjoy your meal. Come and see me sometime. We still have a lot to talk about.' She gave a half smile and walked away. She tried to keep her head high. Even though she felt like a complete failure, she would not drop her guard.

***

Steven could not believe Emily was his mother. She looked more like a sister. He had no idea what she would want to talk about – as far as he was concerned there was nothing else to be said. He had started to come to terms with his new surroundings – he had no other choice.

He still believed a lot of people remained wary of him. The way they kept an eye on him was very subtle. No-one ignored him, or treated him differently; they just did not seem too forthcoming. Then again, neither was he. Perhaps, he was paranoid. They probably didn't care he existed.

After eating another great meal, he got up to go, not in the mood to hang around.

'You want some company?' Kayla asked, about as innocently as a shark in the middle of a feeding frenzy. She was still trying to convince him they were meant to be, even though he had made it clear from his actions, he was not interested.

‘No thank you,’ he said in his politest voice. No point offending her.

A quick glance at Jensen confirmed his suspicion. Jensen looked even more worn out than he was. They must have worked harder than usual today. As he approached the stairway leading to the accommodation, he heard footsteps behind him. He turned around to see Ingrid trying to catch up. He shoulders dropped. He hoped some day she would also give up.

‘Are you okay?’ She asked, running her hand through her hair.

‘Fine, just tired – I’m calling it a night.’

She bit her lip, before she added with a look of concern. ‘Make sure you tell someone, if you start to feel sick.’

‘I’m not sick just tired – I’m sure I’ll know the difference. Can I go now?’ He wondered why she was still following him. Everywhere he went, she always seemed to be lurking in the wings. It was almost as though she was waiting, always waiting. He could not figure out what, exactly, she was waiting for. He hoped it was not him. She would be disappointed if she was.

‘Okay then, let me know if you need,’ she paused, ‘a friend.’

‘Thanks for the thought. I’m not sure I’d turn to you though – you nearly killed me, remember,’ he said, as he shook his head.

Ingrid pursed her lips, her eyebrows furrowed. ‘Can we put the past behind us, please?’

‘I don’t think that’s possible,’ he replied. ‘Sorry.’

The expression on her face looked sad and forlorn. She looked to the floor, then she stared at him again and blurted out. ‘I thought you also kissed me back that first time, we shared a connection from the beginning.’

‘That was a long time ago. If my memory serves me right you entranced me, remember? Do yourself a favour and stop dreaming of something you can’t have. Find someone else.’ With a pitiful sigh, he turned and carried on walking. He had no doubt in his mind that some things needed to be said – better to be cruel, than to be kind. His intent was not to hurt her, but he couldn’t take the words back. She was the one that had started his nightmare. Even though things here were not as bad as he’d thought, he was not prepared to forgive and forget.

*

Steven woke up, disturbed by a series of deep snores and the sound of tossing and turning. He listened intently and realised it was coming from Jensen's bed. It sounded like he was thrashing around a lot more than usual. Even thought the other two were practically shaking the room with their thunderous sounds, Jensen held his own, making a series of disjointed sounds.

Fumbling around for the tiny torch, Steven turned it on and looked around. He was desperate for the loo. Making his way out, he headed for the toilet and instantly felt better. As he made his way out he heard the sound of beating, like a heartbeat. He decided to investigate.

At the end of the tunnel the area widened out. He pointed the flashlight up towards the high cave ceiling. A multitude of bats scampered around. He had seen them before, but it was still an impressive sight. They looked so innocent hanging upside down, minding their own business.

He jumped back in surprise as a bat landed on his head and hopped onto his shoulder. It looked him in the eye for a fleeting moment before it flew away again. Steven could not help but to wonder if they were just as curious about him as he was about them. With an amused huff he retraced his steps and started to make his way back. The sound of footsteps made him turn around.

'What are you doing up. It's the middle of the night,' a grumpy voice mumbled.

He turned, to find he was face to face with the warden. 'Sorry, I had to go and then I got lost.'

'You had to go where?'

'You know to go.'

'You had to pee,' Jan said the word, as if it was a swear word.

'Yeah.'

'Get back to bed,' he grunted.

The warden had to be the strangest person Steven had met.

Just as he was getting comfortable in bed and had closed his eyes to drop off, he heard Jensen moaning – he sounded in physical pain. He flashed the torch in his direction and was shocked to see the sight of him. In the dim light, he could make out a lot of perspiration on his forehead. He was convulsing, his eyes upturned. Quickly, Steven jumped out of bed and gave him a little shake, to try to wake him up. Jenson's mouth started to foam, he looked like he was having a seizure. He had no idea what he should do. He held him up and shouted out for help. The other two woke up. Rod, who was the friendlier of the two, got into gear straight away and raced out with his flashlight on. Steven was glad someone knew what to do.

After a few minutes passed, several people rushed in, including the warden, with a stretcher in tow.

'We'll take over from here.' The warden said.

He let Jensen go and watched as they put him on the stretcher and took him away.

'Go back to sleep, there's nothing more to be done.' The friendly warden again.

The other two got back into bed and started snoring again a few minutes later, as if nothing had happened. Steven stared into the black abyss unable to sleep. The main friend he had grown to depend on, had just been carried away. It was obvious that Jensen was sick – it had to be the change. He was stupid. He had not noticed the time go by. He could not help thinking if he would end up the same way. The only thing he asked himself was – would Jensen still be his friend when they next met?

***

Emily watched her son from her table. He sat amongst the others, but he was miles away. Jensen's absence had hit him hard. It was obvious. She had heard that since Jensen had gone the week earlier Steven become withdrawn. He appeared to have no inclination to be with anyone or talk to them much for that matter. It annoyed her that he had inherited her lack of social awareness. She had never been that good at integrating either. Now, it was easy for her to see why she never found her complement within the community. She knew people called her proud, even conceited, but that was just an image. She did care about others – she just did not know how to show it.

Anna had inherited all of the social tact. It was always Anna that was in the middle of things. Anna was always the sociable one. It was always embarrassing when someone mistook her for Anna and then shuffled off quickly when they realised it was only her.

It was the main reason she had been swept off her feet by Paul. He just took her at face value. His chat up line had been so corny, and yet, completely irresistible. Her mind drifted again, it seemed to do this so much more recently. The past was a happier place.

*

She had been getting a drink at the bar, when she heard someone cough next to her. As she turned, she found herself staring at a handsome man with the cutest smile she had ever seen.

He simply said. 'Would the most gorgeous girl that I have ever seen in my life, please have a drink with me?'

No-one had ever called her gorgeous or asked her to have a drink with them before. She had been blown over. That first night, they had talked endlessly – the attraction was instant. She knew then she would never cause him any harm. Of course, this only turned out to be only physical harm. She had hurt him. Emily had no way of knowing how badly. It was so stupid; she had fallen in love with a human. She did not care. There was no way she was going to apologise for how she felt. For the first time since she had changed, she felt normal – alive. It had been such an impulsive decision when she agreed to elope a few days later and left without telling anyone where she had gone. So foolish and yet so right. If she had never taken that chance, she doubted that she would have ever experienced true love.

This was why it scared her. Steven looked so vulnerable. He reminded her of her own inadequacies. She would have to try to help him – there was no other way.

Chapter 35

Lost

Anna watched her sister make her way over to where Steven was sitting. She felt sorry for Emily. She knew the inner turmoil tormenting her – she felt every bit of her pain. It was excruciating. Anna wanted to help Emily, but her husband Juan was watching. He did not approve of Steven, and he thought even less of Emily. The only reason he tolerated Emily, was because she was her sister – but that was as far as his tolerance leant. His family was not happy about the situation. Lana and Beatrice, in particular, were annoyed. Steven could be a potential suitor for their daughters, Ingrid and Kayla.

Even thought they knew the option was potentially a good one, they were all extremely concerned about Steven's suitability. Until he changed, he could not be trusted. Anna had given up arguing with Juan – there was nothing she could do to change his views. She could help Emily another way. She put her head in her hands and made sure she could not be seen. Then she closed her eyes and channelled her energy towards Emily. She thought of happy days, filled with laughter and peace. She thought of her children and the love she held for her husband. She concentrated on the trust she endowed on all of her friends and family.

Once she was full of compassion, she looked up and sent all those thoughts towards Emily.

A small gesture, but it might help.

***

The walk towards Steven made Emily feel like she was trawling through thick, sticky mud. Even though Steven now sat alone, she was apprehensive. She was sure he hated her. As she was about an arm's length away, pure joy surged through her. Adrenaline, like a drug. Hyperactive, her voice squeaked as she asked, 'can I join you?'

'Sure,' Steven replied, without raising his head.

'Just checking if you were doing okay, you seem, withdrawn,' she rattled on. She knew she was talking too quickly but she could not help it. Suspicious, she glanced at Anna. When she saw her watching, she shook her head. She could tell Anna had been amping up her emotions. Only Anna could influence her mood in the same irrational way.

'I'm ticking along,' he stated, noncommittal.

'I see.' Emily looked at the table and tapped her finger. Anna's enthusiasm was starting to diminish. She felt verbally incapacitated.

After a pregnant pause, Steven looked up and sighed. 'You don't have to try to help me fit in. If it's any consolation, I've always had trouble fitting in to other people's ideals of social etiquette.'

Emily stared at Steven and bit her lip as a sadness overwhelmed her. It was her fault – it was her inadequacy. 'I'm sorry about that.'

'It's not your fault.'

'Actually,' she stopped, trying to use the right words. 'There is a very strong chance that it is one hundred per cent my fault. I am your mother after all, and I am useless at fitting in. But, and don't tell Anna I admitted this, I always had a sister to steer me along. If it had been up to me, I would have ended up as a recluse in a convent.'

Steven looked up, his eyes alight. 'Are you religious then?'

Laughing, she replied. 'No, I'm just different. Not that I'm not tolerant. Obviously, we have different faiths represented in our community, so I do respect other people's beliefs.'

'I was raised as a Roman Catholic by my mother.'

Even though Emily found it hard to hear him call someone else his mother, she broke into a smile. 'You'd better keep that quiet around the Santos family – you'll be even more popular around their unmarried girls. They are all avid Catholics. Eilif and Jan had to convert to Catholicism before they could get married.'

'So, people get married here?'

'Of course.'

'Well, I have never really followed religion out of choice.'

'Trust me. I don't think that Ingrid or Kayla would be too bothered either. But, that's why the Santos Clan is naturally suspicious of change. It's either a gift from God or an omen from the devil. They are still unsure about you and that's my fault too. I brought you into this situation. I'm sorry.' She stared into space again. Even though they were talking, she could not help feeling remorse. She had made him what he was.

***

Steven watched his mother as she bowed her head and stared at the table. She looked totally vulnerable. Even though he could not really feel affection towards her, he was sympathetic. He was not heartless. He just had no idea what he was supposed to say or do. She had brought him into a cursed existence. He could not see anything good about being gifted with eternal youth when you were not allowed to use its full potential.

'I'll be okay. Thanks for your concern.'

'If it's any consolation, I hated leaving you both.'

'It's good to know.' Hearing it aloud brought some comfort. 'I know it must have hurt to let us go. I understand that.' He stared into her eyes, still confounded by the similarity to his own.

Emily looked up, and gave a weary smile. 'I'll always be here for you – please try and remember that.'

'Thanks for the gesture,' Steven said. 'I've got to go. There's always something to do.'

Steven reflected on the fact that it had been the longest conversation they had had to date. In time, he might give her a break.

***

The next few weeks proved uneventful. Steven got into a routine, attended classes and helped with either farming or fishing duties. The highlight of his week was always the fishing expeditions. It was refreshing to be outdoors, amongst the Amazon River.

Jensen remained in isolation. He had tried to see him, but so far, all attempts had been futile. The policy was strict – no visitors. It annoyed him, why all the secrecy? Without Jensen, he became withdrawn. It was easy to keep all conversation to a minimum. He had plenty of female admirers. He just had no interest in getting to know any of them better. Of late, his thoughts always drifted back to Caitlin.

As he pulled on the ropes he was amazed at the sight of the fish they'd caught. 'These fish are huge,' he gasped, as he hauled the last one on to the boat.

'They are called Pacu,' Ian yelled. 'Not as deadly as the Piranha, but watch out for their teeth. They can cause some damage.'

Steven looked at the fish thrashing on the floor. It was about a metre in length, with a rounded form. Its teeth looked big – almost human.

The afternoon stretched out, as they prepared the fish for easy delivery. It would be a novelty, to actually sit down and do nothing for a change. He was so tired.

Ian came up alongside him. 'You alright.'

'Fine, just fine,' Steven replied. He wasn't, but he wasn't going to tell Ian just yet.

***

Ten minutes away from home, Ian noticed Steven retching over the side of the ship. The signals were loud and clear. Motion sickness had nothing to do with his problem.

'Is he sick?' Tomas asked. His overalls soaked, after hauling the fish into the enclosure. His bleach blonde hair, slicked back into a pony tail completed the wet look.

'Not *sick*, if you know what I mean.' Ian rolled his eyes.

'So, it's actually happening then… wow,' Tomas paused, rubbing his chin. 'Does he need to go into isolation?'

'We're keeping an eye on him – but it's not going to be long.'

'Where will he be taken?'

'I don't know. It's not my call.'

Tomas studied his face. 'Who's in charge then? I though you always did it.'

Ian smiled. 'Well, my twin sisters Anna and Emily are going to go it alone, apparently,' he scoffed. 'Anna always has a soft spot for helping Emily, even when it defies logic.'

'Well, hell, I know she wants to help her sister, but…,' he gasped, exasperated. 'What does Juan have to say about that?'

'I'm not getting involved. Last I checked he was furious.'

'Emily's never gone out to help with the change before, as far as I know of anyway.' Tomas shrugged. 'Can anyone else go?'

'I don't know, but Ingrid would be up for it – she's taken a shine to the new boy.'

'Girls only – sounds like a disaster. Shall I offer to go with them? Ingrid is my sister after all.'

‘If Ingrid goes along for the ride, then I agree you should go with them. Why don’t you convince Anna to take your uncle Juan along too?’ Ian suggested.

‘If you’re not getting involved, I’m not going there either. Juan is not happy Steven exists – I don’t think he’d want to help him become like us.’

‘Good point, well just see if anyone sympathises. The last thing we need right now is for something to go wrong. Things are bad enough. This overcrowding problem is getting worse.’

Tomas leaned his head to the side, and bit his fingernail. He was choosing his words carefully. ‘Some of us think we would be able to defend ourselves, if any human tried to take us on.’

‘Do they?’ Ian looked at the defiant expression on Tomas’s face. Perhaps, he was not the right person to go for Steven’s change after all. ‘Do you share those views? Do you want to chance it out in the open?’

‘I’ve never really known a life out of the confines of our community. I left for the change, and went with my family to England last year. The first I barely remember. The second was cut short for obvious reasons. Saying that, I could not help but notice,’ he paused. ‘How fragile humans are – compared to us. We could dominate them easily. And the fact that we can mate with them, makes integration viable in the long run.’

Ian fumed. Uncharacteristically, he shouted. ‘And how would you explain your eternal youth? How could you justify killing innocent humans? You want to kill them, is that it? You are talking nonsense. Don’t talk about something you don’t fully understand.’ Ian knew Tomas was still young, his views immature.

‘Maybe,’ Tomas muttered. ‘But, there are many humans I could kill that are not so innocent. I’d be doing society a favour really.’

‘You’re not God. None of us are.’

‘I don’t think God exists anyway. We are the superior race on this planet – we deserve to live outside of our self enforced borders.’

‘Have you told anyone else what you think, or are you just venting?’ Ian asked, subdued. Curiosity told him to calm down.

‘Just venting, you don’t need to think the worst of me.’ Tomas replied, with a pout. With a wary smile, he added. ‘I still want to help. Don’t worry, I wouldn’t do a runner.’

‘If you ever did, I would find you,’ Ian chuckled. An underlying menace in his tone.

'Understood.' Tomas nodded.

'Now, stop having too many ideas – they are dangerous after all. Get back to work,' Ian ordered.

Tomas huffed before he turned and walked away.

Ian glanced at Steven and wondered about his chances. If he survived, the floodgates would be open for integration. The conversation with Tomas had left him cold. He knew Tomas was not the only one who believed he could live out in the open. Thoughts of integration had begun to spread like a virus, and it had started the day Steven arrived.

He had failed to anticipate the problem.

They would have to step up security. No-one would ever be allowed to escape. A fine line now divided his role as protector, from that of a potential prison warden. This was not something he was proud of. How could he make people understand that a life outside their walls held no added benefits? A childhood saying popped in his mind and he cursed. It was human nature after all – *the grass is always greener on the other side.*

Chapter 36

It's Time

It should not have been possible for Steven to throw up any more, yet the bile kept on coming, relentless. As he spat another mouthful out, his throat reacted and throbbed, irritated by the acrid acid. With a loud and guttural cough the sickness subsided and he leant his head on the side railing. A few minutes later he attempted to lift his head, but he couldn't, every movement an act of torture.

'You alright there, Steven?'

Steven glanced over his shoulder, disoriented. It was just Ian. In a raspy voice, he managed to reply. 'I think so. I don't know what's come over me. I'm not usually seasick.'

Ian seemed to hesitate before he spoke. 'I hate to break it to you, but...I have good news. It's not motion sickness.'

'It's not?' Steven stared, bemused, just before the realization set in. 'It's the change isn't it? How much time do I have left?'

'I'm not sure, it's different for everyone.'

'So, soon I'll become a killer,' Steven sighed.

'No-one thinks Piranha's are killers – it's their nature. They were born carnivorous. You know, it's ironic. Even though the human species is constantly dominating the world, by killing animals for food and using up any available natural resources, they consider themselves civilised. Why is that?'

Steven groaned internally. He did not think he could cope with another lecture. 'I guess I don't know the answer to that. It just feels wrong to have to kill another human being.'

'Some tribes considered cannibalism normal in the past,' Ian added, smug.

'Sure,' Steven replied. He was too tired to argue.

'Look, forget this, just go and get a drink and freshen up. We'll be back soon.'

Steven dragged his feet. He could not believe the change was nearly upon him. A part of him was relieved the suspense would soon be over – finally, he would find out what his future had in store for him. On the other hand, any premature relief was short lived. Soon, he would have to kill another human being. The main question was would he develop blood lust, or was it true that he was not destined to become an insatiable, immortal vampire? It did not matter to him if they never used the term vampire, the facts spoke for themselves. If he was going to drink human blood to survive – he was going to become a vampire.

With a sigh, Steven shuffled inside and made his way towards the kitchen. Once at the fridge he gave the door a tug. Even the small effort of opening a fridge door seemed too much. Eventually, it eased open to reveal exactly what he needed – a bottle of homemade lemonade. In no time at all, he had downed it in one.

'Thirsty?' Tomas asked.

Steven had not heard him come in. 'Just a bit,' he admitted.

'You'll get thirsty for more soon,' Tomas scoffed.

'I know.' Steven looked into the distance. He understood the pun.

'Don't worry,' Tomas continued, as he took out another bottle of lemonade. 'You'll feel right as rain in no time.' He walked away and gave a low, throaty chuckle.

Steven remained transfixed on a spider scuttling across the floor. After a few minutes, he came out of his trancelike state as he felt the ship shudder to a halt. They had arrived.

Out in the open, Ian faced him again. 'Just go Steven, you've helped enough. You need your rest today.'

Steven nodded, then concentrated on following the path. Once inside the entrance, he made his way back along the usual route, not really paying much attention. His legs felt heavy and his head throbbed. He had no idea how long it took him the get back to his room, but as soon as he got there, he threw himself on the bed and passed out.

***

'You're back,' Emily scowled. 'Finally. Where's Steven?'

'He's gone already. He needed to rest,' Ian snapped.

'I told you not to let him go out anymore, but you did not listen,' she rambled.

'Emily, stop lecturing me on best practice, you're not exactly an authority,' Ian smirked.

With a deep pout, Emily narrowed her eyes. She would not give him the satisfaction of replying. She was too worried about Steven to react to her brother. As she swept her hair off her face, she turned to leave.

'Emily, stop, I need to ask you something,' Ian called out; there was some urgency in his tone.

Even though annoyed, she stopped. 'What do you want?' she spat.

Ian stared at her, and asked in a calm voice. 'I know you want to go with Anna. Can you please reconsider? Whatever you think of me, you know I can help you.'

'You've done enough already,' she snapped. 'I'll go with Anna.'

'Is Ingrid going too?' Ian asked, a bitter tone seeping through.

'Of course not, who mentioned her?' Emily asked, her eyebrows furrowed.

'She did. You know that she's taken with Steven.'

'Is she? Well, I think he's got a few admirers, so she can just join the queue. It's just going to be Anna and me. We will cope. I know you men seem to think that woman are incapable of doing things without you, but trust me, we'll be just fine.' Emily stormed off with her nose held high. She loathed her younger brother.

As she approached the corridor where Steven was staying, she saw the commotion up ahead. Someone was being carried away in a stretcher. She rushed up to intercept them, fearing the worst. As she neared the stretcher, she saw Steven writhing uncontrollably in a comatose state. He was foaming at the mouth. It was time.

'I'm coming with you,' she shouted, as she stared into Steven's expressionless eyes.

She hated the change.

Once they had arrived at the preparation chamber and placed Steven on a bed, Emily took hold of his hand. He had stopped convulsing, but his face was covered in sweat, his jet black hair matted down against his scalp. His body quivered and his breathing sounded irregular and forced. With her other hand, she reached out and stroked his face. She could still see a flicker of the little boy she had left behind. A tear crept down her check and she wiped it away, annoyed at her reaction. This was no place for weakness.

'Is it time?' Anna asked, as she placed her hand on her sister's shoulder.

'Yes, we have to leave,' Emily replied.

Anna walked around her sister, and crouched down to face her. 'Emily you don't have to pretend that you don't care. I can feel you drained of all energy. You have to let go. Embrace the fact that you are scared and worried about him. He is your only child.'

Emily looked up, tears streaming down her cheek. 'What have I done? Why did I…?' She could not finish the sentence, as she found herself gulping for air. A hysterical sob overcame her usually calm composure.

***

Anna embraced her sister and smiled. Finally, the ice had melted. Crying would help ease Emily's tension. She could feel her own mood start to lift as the tears took away some of the pain. Emily continued to shake for a few more minutes until she started to calm down and breathe normally, through a stifled sob.

'Better now?' Anna asked, smiling.

'Definitely,' Emily admitted, with a childish giggle.

'You know, you have nothing to be ashamed about. For too long, you've kept your distance. It's not weak to show emotion. You are human too, even though you think you are a monster. Now let's sort ourselves out and make your son better.'

'Yes mum,' Emily teased. 'You always were better than me at knowing what to do in a bad situation.'

'Maybe, but I don't know if I would have been selfless enough to leave my son for his own good,' Anna admitted.

'You would have done the same thing if you thought there was the slightest chance he would be able to lead a normal human life.'

'Maybe… you know, what I don't understand is – how did you keep your emotions to yourself for all this time?'

Emily faltered, and then answered. 'Self preservation. I did not only lose a son – I lost a husband too.'

Anna gave her a final hug, and winked. She would go and get the bags and equipment ready for the journey.

Anna had a heavy heart, as she watched Emily carry her son like a baby. Now, she looked like a mother. Even though Anna was used to seeing grown men or woman being carried like feathers by her kind, it still looked strange to see her petite sister carrying her nearly twenty year old son. The truck waited at the ready, loaded with the bags and supplies. Emily placed Steven carefully in the back seat and covered him with a blanket. He was still shaking and running a fever.

As Emily took her place next to Anna, the engine roared to life.

'It's time,' Anna said, giving the best reassuring smile she could muster.

'Let's do this,' Emily asserted.

It was an adventure, not a rescue mission.

The truck whirred into action as they drove up to the external gate. Anna entered the security code into the keypad. As the gates opened to give them access, they drove out of the confines of their protective home, and made their way out into the Amazon Rainforest.

After driving for a while, Anna asked the question she suspected Emily was dreading. 'Who should we choose for him?'

Without hesitation, Emily answered. 'It should be someone old. Steven wanted us to respect his need to preserve life. At least, if the person is old he will know he did not take away someone's entire life.'

'Sounds reasonable, it should also prevent any suspicion of foul play.'

'Correct.'

'So you are sure you want to go over the border, into Colombia?'

'Yes, the Cahuinari national park. There are still a small number of indigenous people living there, who will not be missed by the general population. No-one really knows how many really live out there anyway. We have to look for the weak in the community.'

'I don't think we've gone to Columbia in over ten years. It should be a safe option.' Anna contemplated, confident about their arrangements.

'Just keep your eye out for those big cats. They will sense an easy target in Steven – we have to protect him at all costs.'

'The cats might sense his weakness, but they will also sense our strength. We have nothing to fear – have faith.'

*

Eight hours later, Anna needed a break. It was Emily's turn to drive. They had no intention of stopping until they reached their destination. After changing shifts twice and watching the steady decline in Steven's disposition, they finally arrived at the dug out caves constructed many years earlier. Using their unique strength, they worked together and pulled back the huge boulder that concealed the accommodation. It revealed a simple room kitted out with a basic table and chairs made from tree bark remnants. There were a few bowls and cups in the corner but everything was covered in cobwebs and dust. No-one had been here in a long time.

A few hammocks had been constructed using some material stretched between huge wooden sticks. Anna tested one out and was relieved to see it hold. She gave Emily a nod. When she did Emily went to get Steven. Once back, she placed Steven on the hammock and stood back. Anna took the opportunity to leave to get the supplies. Anna placed the bags on the floor and noticed Emily sat on the floor next to Steven, head in hands. Emily did not have the luxury of time.

Anna knelt down beside her. 'I'm going to go to see if I can find a local village where we can find a suitable candidate.'

Emily gave a small nod, without making eye contact.

Anna decided to make a move. She could not help either of them by staying. Before she left, she glanced back at Emily. She had not moved. Head bowed, Anna made her way out, determined. It was up to her to ensure everything turned out as it should.

Chapter 37

The Change

Emily knew her emotions teetered on the edge as a million thoughts raced through her head. She had to stay in control. She had to keep strong. For Steven. She lifted her head to see if Anna was still there. Her shoulders drooped as she saw an empty space. Anna had put everything on the line to help her. She closed her eyes as she contemplated how much she owed Anna. There was no way anyone would have let her leave the community without Anna. Emily had to rise above everything that had happened in her life. For the first time ever, she would be the kind of mother Steven would be proud of. She would not let either of them down.

Perhaps, it was the journey. It had taken them two days to get to the location after all. She was probably just tired and hungry. She would quash the thirst when Anna returned. She could not risk leaving Steven alone; he only had a few days to go.

The sound of Steven rambling again made her rush to his side. In a faint, whispery voice he mumbled. 'I'm so sorry Caitlin – I love you.'

Caitlin had to be the girl – the girl he still loved. Emily slammed the ground with her fist and cursed. She could not believe it. Another vicious cycle. If he could not let go of his feelings for the human girl, he would not integrate into their way of life. She would not allow him to repeat her mistake. A solitary journey in life was not a worthwhile prospect. When his change was complete, Emily resolved to make it her personal vendetta to find him an appropriate mate. He could not return to his previous way of life – it was impossible.

She knew he needed to eat so she made her way over to the supplies and mixed some water with crushed fruit. With considerable care, she spooned some into Steven's mouth. He gargled and swallowed, before coughing and spluttering half of the contents on to the floor. His eyes sunken, his face pale. He had lost too much weight. She hoped Anna would return soon. Reluctant, she took a piece of stale bread and soaked it in the juice and water to make it more palatable. Every mouthful was forced. Even though she knew she had to eat, she did not have the appetite.

She rinsed the cloth on his head with some water and placed it over his feverish brow. His temperature was soaring out of control. She could not understand why she felt so broken, her emotions a mixture of concern, anxiety, frustration, self pity and regret. The overpowering sensation was fear. Not fear for herself, fear for her son. She had no idea what would become of him. Or if she would actually help him in the end.

*

Finally, after nearly a day of waiting, Anna returned to relieve the lonely vigil. The sun had just started to rise, giving way to daylight and you could hear the rainforest coming back to life. It was raining hard, the sky overcast and gloomy. It gave the atmosphere a feeling of impending doom. Anna found Emily slumped over Steven, sleeping soundly. She did not want to disturb her, but time was precious. She walked up to Emily, and shook her shoulder gently. 'Emily, I'm back.'

Emily woke up, startled and panicked. 'What is it? Did I fall asleep?'

'It's alright, nothing has happened. Some sleep will do you good,' she said. The fact was, Emily had red crazed eyes and looked terrible, but Anna was not going to break the news to her sister.

Emily placed her head in her hands, as if she was forcing herself to think. 'Did you find someone?'

'Yes, it's about four hours from here. There is an old lady who is on her death bed – a perfect candidate.'

'Good, that's good,' Emily repeated.

Anna could see Emily's hands were shaking.

'You need to feed – let me keep an eye on him so that you can go.'

'Is there any human scent in the air?'

'No. You might get lucky and run into a Puma. I managed to sink my teeth into a juicy Tapir, out for its nightly hunt. *It* didn't have a successful hunting trip.'

Emily smiled at her sister. 'It's the circle of life. By the way, thanks for everything. I know I'm not the easiest sister in the world, but I'm grateful for what you're doing. I know Juan disapproves.'

'I'm not doing it to be a martyr. You'd do the same for me, right?'

'Right,' Emily replied.

***

It was easy for Emily to reassure Anna. Anna never needed help. As she walked out to the entrance, she glanced back one last time – Steven looked depleted, haggard. There was no more time to waste. She made her move. Outside, Emily took a deep breath and focused. A jaguar had been through here. Following the scent, she stalked the jaguar and picked up speed – she was silent, but deadly. She knew she was getting close so she leapt up on the tree and scrambled up the bark.

In the distance, she saw the jaguar lying down on the mossy floor, its tail flicking up through the air, relaxed and unsuspecting. In her well practiced stealth mode, she circled the location to surprise the animal from the rear. With an enormous leap, she landed behind the cat and snapped its head. Big cats had large claws – she did not want to risk it fighting back.

As her teeth extended, she sank them into the jaguar's neck and took her fill. Energised, her maternal instinct kicked in – now she was up for anything.

Back through the door, panic ensued. He was worse. His skin was shrivelled, and his face gaunt. His breathing was even weaker than before. Emily zoomed up to her son and lifted him up carefully. Turning to Anna, she stated, determined. 'Lead me to the village.'

Anna nodded, and pushed the boulder aside to give Emily access. Then she looked at Emily, winked and started to run.

At a pace no human could match, they raced to save Steven's life.

Emily prayed everything would work out – it had to.

***

'There it is,' Anna whispered, relieved.

The village was quaint, lit with a series of fires scattered around. A few of the locals remained, as they made preparations for the next day. The air reeked with human scent. It made her mouth salivate.

Glancing at Emily, she saw the familiar longing in Emily's eyes. She did not want to think the worst of her sister but at least she appeared focused. If she didn't have a full stomach, there would be no way to resist. The sun had just about set, leaving darkness in its wake. This was good. The cover of night gave them protection – the last thing they needed was to be seen.

With a nod of the head, she signalled to Emily. Anna walked towards the back of one of the huts. With the use of sign language, she motioned her sister to wait, and made a quick reconnaissance. Finally, she nodded to encourage Emily into position. Moving over to the clearing alongside the accommodation, Emily placed Steven on the ground.

Anna returned to the hut in the far side of the village, and peered in through the makeshift window.

In the middle of the room, lay the old woman. A young woman slept close by. Anna slipped in, covered the old woman's mouth and carried her out. The old woman blinked in momentary confusion, but as soon as she looked into Anna's eyes, she accepted her fate – resistance was futile.

***

When the old lady was placed next to Steven, Emily looked into her aged eyes, and spoke softly. 'I take your life for my son to live. You have lived your life. Now, you will enable his life to begin. It is an honourable way to depart from this world. Please think of that as your final thought. Thank you.'

The old woman closed her eyes in submission.

Carefully, Emily moved Steven towards the woman's neck. The woman's artery pulsed right next to his mouth. Using her sharp fingernail, she dug into the artery causing some blood to spurt onto his lips. As the blood entered his mouth, the reaction was instant. Instinctively, Emily licked her lips. Like a baby, taking a hold on its mother's breast for the first time, Steven formed a suction cap with his mouth over the area and drank the woman's life out of her. Once finished, Anna cleaned up the woman's neck and covered up the area with the natural concealer they used. There would be no visible sign of the assault.

Emily cradled Steven in her arms; she could see the life returning to his face. Through the corner of her eye, she was aware that Anna was lifting the limp lifeless body.

All they could do now was wait.

***

It took a considerable amount of effort for Steven to blink. A simple thing he had taken for granted over the years. His eyes tried to focus on his surroundings. All he could see was a blur of green. The pace of motion seemed impossible – was he dreaming?

Even though instinctively he wanted to move, to check he was actually awake, something told him to wait. He needed to get a grip. He could definitely feel his strength coming back. As every second passed, his senses started to snap open. He kept perfectly still as he took stock of the situation.

A frown set upon his face as he tried to recollect his last actions. Nothing could explain why he was slumped over someone's petite frame. A person, or woman as he suspected, of this size should not be able to carry a man of his build so easily. Either way, if she was a woman, he should be able to hold his own. He was not a coward. Reticent, he clenched his hands into fists. He would have to regain control and find out what was going on. The moment he moved, motion stopped.

A swift effortless action followed and he found himself on the ground. The cold, damp moss hit his body and caused an instant shiver, as his muffled groan escaped.

'Are you okay?' A female voice. Soft, full of compassion. It seemed out of place somehow.

He studied her face. The eyes. They were familiar. They were just like…his.

The memories started to surface and he flinched. Adrenaline surged through his body, and one by one, the visions engulfed his mind.

The family he had taken for granted.

The woman he loved.

The life he wanted.

All gone.

What had they done to him? Or more importantly, what had he done? One memory lingered, persistent – Caitlin. In an ideal world, he would replace the face in front of him with hers. If everything he remembered was true, his life was not worth living. As bewilderment gave way to anger, he narrowed his eyes.

Even though groggy, he mustered the strength to get up and face Emily – his mother. He would not give her the satisfaction of helping him further. She had done enough. Determined, he stood tall and raised his head, his eyes focused on hers. There was no way he would leave his *real* life behind. There had to be a way to get everything back.

'What did you make me do?' he snarled.

A mirror image crept up alongside. Twin sisters stared at him. They wore beaming smiles, they were proud of themselves. It figured.

'How can you smile like that?' he asked, as he shook his head in disbelief.

Emily and Anna looked at each other, before they burst into laughter and embraced. Then Emily stretched out her hand to touch his shoulder. In a knee jerk reaction, Steven stepped back.

'You've changed, Steven,' Anna announced.

'Well done, Sherlock. I figured that one out all ready. You let me kill someone, didn't you?' he accused, he looked at Emily.

'You fed off an old lady, she was practically dead,' Anna replied. 'Her death was graceful – she accepted having a part in saving your life.'

'She said that to you?' He asked, his tone unbelieving.

'Well, she did not need to say it out loud. It was in her eyes.'

'I bet,' he laughed aloud. With a strong hint of sarcasm, he added. 'I doubt she had any choice.'

'Well no,' interrupted Anna. 'But, it was not a painful way to go and she was near death anyway. We hoped that would give you some comfort.'

'It gives me sooo much comfort. *Thank you.* Are you insane? I killed her! No matter what,' he glared. 'I still have a conscience.'

Anna smiled. 'And for that we are glad – otherwise you would be on the road to becoming a killer. The fact that you feel regret and compassion is a good sign. We should all respect any life we kill for our survival,' Anna said, she gave Emily a sideways glance.

'So? What now?' he asked, as he looked from one identical face to the other.

'We thought you'd never ask,' Anna remarked. Her tone playful.

It worried him.

Chapter 38

Anger

If Steven had been asked a year earlier to describe his first year at University, he would never have expected it to involve the Amazon jungle. And yet, here he was. Everything he had taken for granted was gone. Everything he thought he knew was wrong. His survival instinct had overcome any thoughts of compassion. He was a killer. He had killed someone to survive. A life to spare his was the price of avoiding death. How it had happened was a complete mystery. He was confused, disorientated, lost. And yet, he could not help noticing the change in his physique. A surge of energy pulsed through his body, as his muscles arose from their dormancy with a vengeance. He felt as if he had just won a swimming race – it was exhilarating. He was not tired anymore. He was strong – invincible. Just, disorientated.

'Ok, let's try something,' Anna said, as she clapped her hands together. 'Focus on the trees. Listen carefully, and then say anything you want and wait.'

Steven was dubious, but he was game. He had practiced this many times before the change. A rustling sound up in the trees made him look up. Forming a cup with his hands, he whistled. Almost instantly, a magnified sound returned. It happened so fast. In a split second, he calculated the distance.

At the adjacent tree, he started to climb whilst holding on to the branches. It amazed him. He was quick and nimble, as he scaled the tree in seconds. In the exact spot he anticipated, an unsuspecting monkey sat cleaning itself. A laugh escaped, as he jumped off the tree without thinking. He landed perfectly on his feet. He shrugged his shoulders and gave a half smile. He should have broken a leg.

He cocked his head to the side. 'Obviously, I have fine tuned senses and reflexes – human echolocation, right? I also have stronger bones by the look of it. Am I indestructible?'

'No. You can be injured and killed like any human,' Anna replied. 'But, even on the point of death, if you drink human blood you will be rejuvenated. Human blood is our healer.'

He thought about this for a few seconds. 'I don't need to drink it all the time?'

'No, you eat, drink and sleep as normal. The only catch being, every week you will need to supplement your diet with a mammal's blood to survive. Human blood is the only blood that can heal. We believe animal blood keeps us fit and healthy.'

'I feel stronger,' Steven stated, as he picking up a stone. 'Can I crush this?'

'Try,' Anna challenged, with a smug look.

Squeezing the stone with one hand, he barely managed a visible dent. 'I guess not. So much for superhuman strength,' he shrugged, as he bit his lip.

'The gift of eternal youth is not something to scoff at young man.' Anna adopted a preachy tone.

Anger surged through him. 'So what can this gift do for me then? Why would I want to live forever?'

'It's not an issue of what you want – it's the way it is,' Emily blurted out, her eyes crazed.

'Well, I'm not sure I accept that. I don't want to live like a recluse, in a small community where my movements are monitored and controlled. I may not want to live like you at all. What would you do to stop me, if I decided to leave right now?' he challenged.

'I wouldn't do that if I were you,' Anna warned.

'Anna, don't,' Emily said. She held her hands up to her face, as though she could not watch. 'Steven there is nothing out there for you. We are your family. Think of your friends. Jensen is keen to see you again.'

Steven started to back away.

'Stop moving back, Steven, I'm warning you,' Anna repeated.

'Steven, please, I'm begging you. Don't try to escape – there is nowhere to go,' Emily pleaded.

He had no idea what Anna would do – it was probably an empty threat. Mind made up, he turned and ran. The pinprick sensation at the back of his head was the last thing he remembered.

***

Anna lowered the pipe that had inflicted the sedative coated dart. 'I'm sorry Emily, but it was my job to make sure he did not escape.'

'I–I know,' Emily stammered, as she made her way over to Steven. Taking a seat next to him, she studied his now calm and innocent expression. 'I'm glad you did it. I would never be able to contain him against his will. He's going to hate us.'

Anna made her way over, and folded her arms in front of her chest. 'They all forgive in the end.'

'I'm not as sure as you are about that,' Emily sighed.

'No-one likes being confined. All new changelings always feel unbeatable. He'll get over it.'

'Maybe,' Emily remarked, deep in thought. 'I just hate the way it's done.'

'It's for his own good.'

'Really, for his own good,' Emily snapped, coming out of the trance. 'Not for the good of the community. I hate my life here. Everything I am, I hate. I can't lie to my own son. I can't tell him it's all wonderful. I don't want to be here, why should he? We should have let him run; we should have let him decide his fate. Perhaps death is a better option than this existence.'

Anna's eyes widened. In a quiet voice, she asked. 'Do you really think that? Has your life been that terrible?'

Emily studied the ground for a moment. Then she lifted her head, her eyes narrowed, hands in fists. 'No, it's been worse. You have no idea, no-one ever understood. I did not want this,' she spat, her hands flared.

'I feel sorry for you. You are what you are, and so is Steven. Maybe for him, you should make an effort to fit in. Maybe, you should try to accept some of the advances you get – I know you have rejected many admirers. Move on with your life – help Steven make the best of his.'

'Maybe,' Emily replied, deflated.

Anna did not get her. 'Let's get on with it, and get him home. The last thing we want is to have to sedate him again.'

Emily nodded and waited in silence.

With great care, Anna lifted Steven off the floor and cradled him in her arms. Emily did not look like she could carry him in her current state and it was definitely time to go.

***

Steven opened his eyes and looked around, confused again. He could feel himself being jostled around – this time in a car.

Emily looked back, her smile wary. Then she turned to Anna. 'He's awake.'

Anna stopped the car and faced him. 'Steven, I'm very sorry to have had to sedate you, but you made things difficult for yourself. We will be back in a few hours so I suggest you stay put and don't try anything funny. I'm sorry, but I had to tie you up.'

She did not look sorry to him.

'You are a liability out in the open. We do everything it takes, to protect our way of life,' Anna declared, if a bit too passionate.

He did not care what she thought. With deep loathing, he scowled and glared.

'I'm sorry,' Emily muttered, her eyes glazed.

Any emotion was wasted on him.

'I'll never accept this,' Steven slurred, as he turned away and closed his eyes.

***

The truck made a sharp right, as it cruised into the facility. Anna lowered the window, pulled out her hand, and entered the security password into a concealed keypad on the tree bark. A tedious hum ensued, as the ground opened up to expose a hidden underground platform. Anna put the truck into gear and drove down. Darkness enveloped, as the ground sealed shut. A series of lights flicked on to reveal a room large enough to fit at least three cars.

Emily gave Steven a gentle shake to rouse him. The ropes that bound him, now gone.

With a grunt, Steven opened his eyes, looked at her and narrowed his eyes.

Emily gave a half smile, eased out of the car and stood next to her sister.

Side by side, they waited.

***

With limited choices, Steven shuffled to the door, a permanent scowl on his face. His mind whirled in confusion, as a dull headache lingered. There was so much to take in and so little explanation. He could not understand what they were doing.

It was obvious they had drugged him to stop him from escaping. Even if his own mother had not taken the shot, he knew she was in on it. She was a far cry from the only mother he'd ever known. He would give anything to have Clara back.

'So, where to now? Are you always going to drug me every time I don't do what you want?' he growled. He was surprised at the venom in his tone.

'If we have to,' Anna said, a nervous chuckle followed.

'It's not a joke,' he snapped.

'Don't bother trying to look threatening, I am much stronger than you,' Anna added, as she rolled her eyes. 'You are not the first, or the last, to be drugged. We do everything it takes to protect our family. You will learn our way of doing things – in time.'

'But I will get stronger,' he stressed, defiant.

'Yes, but not yet. Let's go.' Turning towards a set of double doors, she walked away from him. It was blatant he had no choice in the matter – he had to follow.

With a weak shrug, Emily gave him a fleeting look as she followed her sister.

Resigned, to his present fate, he moved.

A set of double doors blocked the path. Anna keyed in another password. A loud click gave them access to the lit tunnels, on the other side. After walking for about twenty minutes, they began a steep ascent. At the top of the narrow corridor, an archway engraved with the words *the gift of life* offered the last obstacle.

'Are you ready?' Anna asked, her face transformed, her smile beaming.

Steven thought she was trying too hard. 'You make it sound like something exciting,' he droned.

'It is exciting,' Anna added, full of confidence. 'Come on, Steven, your new life is waiting.'

Through the archway, Steven stared, shell-shocked. It looked like a hotel lobby.

The chairs and tables around the room were exquisite. Crafted out of wood, they must have been made by someone skilled in the art of carpentry. A drinks area to his right was surrounded with snacks ranging from sandwiches, to cakes and biscuits. Starved, Steven walked over, ignored the people sitting around the room and stuffed three biscuits in his mouth at once. He picked up a glass jug filled with a red, translucent liquid and took a huge slug. He was famished and thirsty.

Out of the corner of his eye, he sensed someone coming closer to him. Like a wild animal he sprung back, fixed against the wall. A familiar voice surprised him.

'Steven is that you. You look terrible.'

He looked up, and stared – it was Jensen.

'Come and sit down – you've been through a lot,' Jensen said. With a clenched fist he nudged his shoulder. 'I promise, it all gets easier from here – you'll see.'

Steven wanted to go with his old friend. He wanted to believe nothing had changed between them. But, a lot had happened. Nothing was the same. 'How can I trust you?'

Jensen huffed, than laughed. 'We're all in this together. I have to earn my trust right?'

'You sure do.' Steven walked alongside. The sedative had knocked the life out of him and he was still reeling from the effect. 'I need to sit down.'

'I guess you tried to escape them?' Jensen mocked.

'You too?'

Jensen laughed again.

'I'm glad I amuse you,' Steven remarked sarcastically.

Jensen sat next to him, his arm casually placed over the sofa cushion. 'Everyone does it. Instinctive.'

'They forgot to tell us about that one,' Steven sulked.

'To be honest, I did not try to escape. I wanted to come back, for personal reasons.'

'Susanna,' Steven stated, with a shrug.

Jensen blushed slightly. 'Maybe. Anyway, I just fancied a run. They did not let me get far,' he laughed. 'It's a hell of shot. It took me three days to feel normal again.'

'Something else to look forward to,' Steven sighed.

Steven noticed Emily approaching from the corner of his eye. He hoped she did not intend to help him again. She spoke to Jensen.

'Jensen, can you help Steven to settle into his new accommodation.'

'It's the least I can do. We are family after all,' Jensen bantered.

'Great, thanks,' she said.

Steven refused to look at her.

'Right, see you later,' Emily added, regret thick in her voice.

Jensen changed the subject; he was good at steering away from awkward discussions. 'So, are you ready to see your new room?'

Steven could not help wondering if Jensen knew Emily more than he let on. Ignoring the suspicion, he replied. 'Sure, so long as it has a bed where I can rest, I'll be happy.'

'Oh, you'll be happy,' Jensen remarked. The way he raised his eyebrows made Steven wonder what Jensen was up to now.

Chapter 39

Getting A Part Of Your Life Back

Steven doubted anything about his new accommodation would be exciting. The fact Jensen looked smug, and kept giving him little amused glances made him remotely curious, if a tad annoyed. On route to the usual accommodation area, they suddenly forked to the left not right, as he had grown accustomed too. After passing a few curtained entrances, they got to a room with a black door – at least his room had a door. It was a welcome relief. Jensen opened it and stepped aside. He wanted Steven to walk in first.

As he stepped in to the room, Steven was completely taken aback. All of his memorabilia from his old life was neatly placed everywhere. His old bed covers lay on the bed with his pillow. His books, CDs, DVDs, and even his old board games were stacked on a bookshelf on the far corner. A 32 inch flat screen TV sat happily on a large stand, with his Nintendo Wii Console, Xbox 360 and his old games opposite his bed. It was like walking into a different, yet, familiar version of his old room. The most important item they had included was a picture of him with his Dad. With obvious consideration, it had been placed on the beautifully carved, wooden bedside table.

'That was my favourite picture,' Steven said out loud.

'I'll leave you to it,' Jensen said, not waiting for an answer. In a split second he was gone.

Pride made him swallow the tears building up. Steven took a deep gulp to appease the gigantic lump settling in his throat. Had it not been for his incredible control of rash emotions, he would surely have burst into tears. Instead, he made his way over to the bed, sat down and picked up the frame. After studying it for a few minutes, he lay back on the bed and closed his eyes.

***

Jensen knew Steven was best left alone. Perhaps, the creature comforts would improve his mood.

Pushing the curtain aside, he walked into the room. 'Emily?'

Emily popped her head out of the side room. 'Did he like it?'

'I think so.'

Emily gave him a relieved smile, 'anything to make him feel at home.'

'Anyway, I'll keep an eye on him for you, like I promised.'

'Thanks, Jensen.'

Jensen turned around to leave.

'How are you coping with the change?' Emily asked.

'Fine, it's like nothing has really happened. My appetite is not like it used to be. I guess that's normal. I am developing an infatuation with monkey blood though.'

Emily laughed. 'If you need to talk I'll always be here for you. You are a great friend to Steven – he needs that right now.'

Jensen smiled, and turned to walk out. Glancing back, he saw signs of apprehension in her face, as she stared away from him, deep in thought. She was obviously worried. He was not surprised. He was not the only one wondering if Steven would be any different to the rest of them? Time would tell.

***

Steven had not been able to sleep. He had closed his eyes and tried, only to fail. There were too many thoughts swishing around in his head. The picture in the frame had been taken the day he obtained his A level results – it had been a great day. He missed his dad, he missed his life – in truth, he still could not get Catlin out of his mind. His collection of books beckoned, so he got up and made his way over. Sentimentally, he picked up his favourite – A Time to Kill by John Grisham. Ironic, it was his favourite. As he flicked through the pages, he wondered if it was *his* time to kill.

A distinctive smell, made his stomach churn. It was an interesting scent. He got up and tried to figure out where it came from. His eyes focused on the chest of drawers. Someone had left a bottle and a glass. Scrunching up his nose, he studied the bottle. A piece of paper was folded up under the bottle with his name on it. Curious, he opened it, and read two simple words, 'drink me.'

A reluctant smile graced his face – Alice in Wonderland, cute. With some luck, it would not shrink him.

He pulled out the cork and was instantly overcome by a scent so sweet and delectable that he drank straight from the bottle, unable to wait. The liquid gushed down his throat. Instant gratification for his thirst. He did not stop for a breath as he finished the whole bottle in one – it was an impressive display of downing a drink. As he finished, he wiped his mouth and felt an instant rush. He bounced off the floor like a gazelle and smiled. He doubted he'd want to know what was actually in the bottle. Energised, he ventured out to ascertain the time of day. The lights were still on around him, which made him assume it was daytime.

Now his thirst was appeased, food was his next priority.

With caution he retraced his steps and made his way to the main food hall. From the entrance, he was surprised to find Jensen sitting with the others at their usual table. The hall was busy which meant that it was actually food time. Impeccable timing.

Jensen got up to greet him, 'the prodigal son returns again.'

Steven glanced at Suzanna, Gideon, Kayla and a new boy that he did not know as they sat around the table.

Jensen was about to place his hand on his shoulder when he stopped himself. 'Sorry Steven, I would normally place my hand on you, but at the moment, you smell like really bad.'

The others giggled and held their noses as a joke.

Steven laughed at ease, for the first time in ages. 'I know I need to freshen up, but food was my first priority.'

'Don't let us stop you,' Susanna teased, waving him on with her arms held high.

At the food counter, he became aware of the fact that he was drawing a lot of attention. It was making him paranoid. What was disconcerting, was the fact that he did not know if they were looking at him because of his bad smell or because he had changed and was here to tell the tale. Not wanting to hang around, he took a couple of steaks and a jacket potato, and hastily smothered them in a mushroom sauce. Then he made his way back.

Immediately after sitting down, he started to wolf down the food.

'Slow down tiger, you'll get indigestion,' Jensen remarked.

Steven found this hysterical, and burst out laughing. 'That's the least of my worries,' he spluttered.

'But what other worries could you possibly have?' Susanna asked, with big eyes and a startled expression.

Steven stopped putting food in his mouth, chewed slowly and stared at her. Her innocent comment had inadvertently tipped him over the edge.

'What could be more worrying than knowing that my life can go on forever? Isn't the whole point of human existence to live, learn from our past and pass on our knowledge and understanding to the next generation? What is the point of my existence now? You have not changed. You have no idea what you are up against. Our whole existence is wrong – don't you get it?'

Jensen held up his hand, and scowled. 'Enough.'

Susanna's bottom lip started to wobble.

Steven continued, angry at the fact that no-one was told that they would feel like caged animals. 'Why do we not explain that…?'

'Stop,' Jenson interrupted again, standing up. 'Just because you don't understand your existence, does not mean you have to judge ours. Speak to one of the originals if you want to vent – don't pick on someone like Susanna. She has done you no harm, other than to try to be your friend.' Jensen placed his hand on Susanna's shoulder, and gave a gentle squeeze.

Steven finished off his mouthful, grimaced at the show of affection and got up. 'I'll go and shower.'

As he walked through the hall, he could sense the stares like prickles on the back of his neck. In a move totally out of character, he turned and shouted. 'I have changed, I am one of you. Now stop staring at me and leave me alone!'

Everyone paused, frozen by his outburst. Steven grunted and stomped off like a petulant child. A fire deep within, burned out of control.

The sound of gushing water gave Steven some much needed comfort. The texture of the rock fascinated him. Its sharp edges contrasted against its smooth shiny face. It was amazing how sharp his vision had become. His hearing also seemed magnified. The change was making everything different. It was like for the first time, he knew how to listen, to see, and to taste. Only now, could he appreciate how predators used their senses to find unsuspecting prey.

Instinct – it was definitely a powerful commodity.

With a sigh of relief, he stripped off without a further thought and launched himself into the lukewarm water.

At least he was alone.

Under the waterfall, he closed his eyes and let the pressure of the water erase any thoughts. After a few minutes, he raced towards the larger expanse and forged ahead, as his powerful muscles took the strain with ease. When he touched the cave wall, he yelled in euphoria.

Speed – the ultimate adrenaline boost.

Disappointment followed. An escape route would have made his sense of freedom complete. Unfortunately, there seemed to be no options open for an escape.

With a huge intake of air, he dived under the water to see how deep it went. After swimming for what seemed like minutes, he finally touched the bottom and looked up. He was really far down. A thought crossed his mind – he could run out of air before he got back up. The thought of drowning was a good one. It would be an easier way out of his messy existence. As he sat on the bottom, waiting, it dawned on him – he had not run out of breath. He took a gulp of water and blew it out of his nose. It was strange. He was energised not drowned. Fascinating. Somehow, he was able to swallow water, obtain the oxygen from it and release hydrogen gas – incredible, another new talent.

Another adrenaline surge led to him swimming like a dolphin underwater. In no time at all, he managed to reach the bubbling water under the waterfall. It had to be at least a couple of pool lengths away. As he flipped out to break the surface, his head met the shower of water – he felt rejuvenated. Perhaps, he was not in a hurry to return to his former life yet. There was a lot to explore. He cringed; as he remembered his outburst…it was highly embarrassing. Jensen had been right. Susanna had done nothing to incur his wrath.

Even though he could have stayed there for days, he decided to face the music and return. Once out of the water, he grabbed his clothes and started to get dressed.

A familiar voice broke the moment. 'Now that's a sight to behold.'

Steven looked up, unashamed this time. 'What do you want now, Ingrid?'

***

It amused Ingrid – he was not embarrassed to be naked in front of her anymore. 'I didn't realise you cared about what we thought. Your little outburst was out of character, to say the least.' She paused as she watched him put his clothes back on. This was her chance, it was now or never. 'You don't need to cover up. Now you are changed, maybe, you want to know what is special about us.'

'Enlighten me,' Steven asked in a dull voice, as he hoisted his trousers back on.

'We are supposed to make excellent lovers,' she whispered, walking forward to reach touching distance. Perhaps, if she played her cards right, he would change his mind. She would do anything to make him love her.

'Really? Well I'm not in the mood right now. Don't you have another victim in mind,' he added.

The way he looked at her made her falter. Regardless, he had to see what he meant to her – he had to know. She was in love with him, she was sure of it. 'Ever since I met you I have only ever wanted you. I had to wait until you changed, but now, well, let's just say…the time is right. We are meant to be together.'

Barely inches apart from his face, she saw his expression transform from anger to bewilderment.

She probed him with her eyes and continued, her voice full of emotion. 'I am in love with you Steven. From the first time we met, I felt a connection. I know you felt it too, even though you now ignore it. Give me a chance. Please, I can help you to become everything you are destined for. Together, we would make an excellent match. In time, you might even learn to love me.'

Without hesitation she lunged towards him and kissed him. At first, he did not seem to respond, but then his lips moved with hers and she felt his hands caress the back of her neck. It made her shiver involuntarily. Things were going in the right direction. He was aroused – finally. Her hands gripped his back, as she let out a low moan.

A loud bang broke the moment.

'Am I interrupting something?' Kayla asked, as she flung her shoe at Ingrid.

'Kayla!' Ingrid gasped.

'You bitch, how could you? You are my cousin. You know how much I like him, but you don't care, do you?' Kayla shouted, eyes narrowed on Ingrid. Then she turned to face Steven. 'And you, to think I was worried about you, to think that I wanted to help you. All you've ever done is reject me, and why, for her? You have to be joking. I'm out of here, you can have each other,' Kayla snapped, as she turned and fled.

Chapter 40

Temptation

Steven frowned at Ingrid, his momentary lust replaced by disgust. It was the first time he had consciously kissed her back. Fortunately, Kayla's interruption had kicked his brain into gear. His head would not ignore his heart. 'Ingrid, I'm sorry. Look, I don't want to hurt you anymore. This shouldn't have got out of hand. I don't think we are right. I was just, well, tempted.'

'Tempted is good, you have needs. I can help with that,' Ingrid teased.

It was too late for that.

'No, not now. Not ever. You'll only get hurt. I don't have, how can I say this, feelings for you. It would only ever be lust. You don't want that, trust me. As much as I don't want to care, I do. I don't want to use you.' A shag would have been nice all the same, but it wouldn't have made him feel better in the long term.

'But, in time, in time. You could learn to love me. I never expected love at first sight. I…'

Steven shook his head, so she stopped talking. In a stern tone, he repeated his intent. 'I'm sorry. Find someone else.' He picked up his shirt, put it on and started to leave.

'Steven, please…'

Nothing she said would make him go back. It *was* foolish to walk away from a blond bombshell and he did want to have sex with her. The point was that's all it would be – sex. Nothing more. He had some pride left.

Just because she threw herself at him did not mean he would take her up on the offer. Well, he would have – he had been tempted. If Kayla had not shown up, things could have got interesting.

He needed a place to think. A place where he could be alone. The only place he knew where that was possible was the farming area. It was one of only places where he could see the sky. It was already dark outside, the sky full of stars. The sight was breathtaking. The fluorescent lights in front of him made him look up. The lights came from the greenhouse. He walked along the periphery, conscious of the fact Lucy might be around. Lucy was eccentric, to say the least, yet perhaps, he sensed she was also disheartened by the supposed utopia the community had created.

Through the shady glass panel, he saw some movement, so he stopped and kept still. Lucy was singing a gentle song as she went about her business. Even at this time of night she was still working. Saying that, he doubted it was work – it was her life. The words formed a familiar melody he recognised – a Beatles track. Caught off guard by the fact she liked his choice of music, he found himself wandering to the entrance to watch.

From the distance, he could see her delicately lifting a seedling from one of the small containers and placing it into a larger pot. With care, she started to place more soil around it and lovingly pressed it down. Unaware of his attention, she continued to fetch the next seedling to repeat the process. It was entrancing to see the gentle manner in which she treated the young plant – as though it was a fragile treasure. Taking the opportunity, he looked carefully at her disguised features. Covered in dirt, with loose shapeless clothing, he found himself studying her features as though it was the first time he had set eyes on her.

He could not help wondering if he would end up like a recluse if he did not let go of his love for Caitlin?

He frowned and briefly closed his eyes, then he attempted to leave unobserved. His attempt was thwarted as he accidentally knocked over a pot by the doorway.

'I know you're there Steven, please come in?' Lucy said, her tone amused. She lifted her head and made eye contact.

Startled, he called out. 'Sorry, I didn't mean to disturb you. I just needed some space.'

'I understand what it's like to want to get away,' she said. She momentarily glanced at him, before diverting her eyes back to her seedling.

Taken aback by the set of sparkling eyes that greeted him, he waited for her next move wondering why he wanted to stay with her. Maybe it was because of his inopportune moment with Ingrid or perhaps it was just sheer loneliness. Impulsively, he blurted out, 'why do you hide out here?'

'What I do in my time is my business.' Her tone was defensive; he had caught her off guard.

He stepped forward to get closer. 'I know, but forever could be very lonely with no-one to share it.'

'How would you know anything about loneliness?' She retorted, her face flushed.

'I know enough about it. I was torn from my life, my family and everything I ever though of as real. I killed someone to live!' He was still disgusted by his actions.

'You don't know anything about pain,' she replied, her fists clenched. She left the plants and stood up.

'So what's it like then? Enlighten me,' he challenged.

Brushing her hands against her sides, she sighed. Then she walked past him to the doorway and looked up at the sky.

After a few minutes of silence, he made his way towards her. It might be for the best if he just left. 'Look I'm sorry. I'll just go.'

Lucy stepped out of his way and kept her face shielded. 'Yes, just go,' she spluttered.

Steven could not believe she was crying. He could not understand what he had done to make her cry. Even if it was not his fault, he could not leave her like that. Without thinking, he took her in his arms. As soon as he did her head leant against his chest and her arms wrapped around him, as she continued to cry for a few more minutes. Eventually, she calmed down and started to breath normally.

Steven eased back. 'Feeling better?'

Flushed, she replied. 'Yes.'

Instinctively, he wiped her tears away from her cheek with his hand.

***

Perhaps, it was their proximity or the romantic nature of Steven's gesture that sent Lucy over the edge. She had spent twenty years refusing to get close to anyone, shying away from any potential suitors. Now, she was too weak and lonely to turn away. But, more to the point, there was nothing she could do to stop. Placing her hand firmly over his, she made her intent clear and kept his hand on her face. Then she turned and kissed his hand. A moment later,

Steven leaned in and kissed her on the lips. As she kissed him back, she was astonished at his response. His need seemed to be as great as hers as they mutually explored each others mouths. Finally, they broke for air and gasped for breath. Neither could speak. The intensity of the situation was confusing. Lucy took control, held his hand and led him to her bedroom.

*

Lucy lay on her side, facing away from Steven. She listened to the rhythmic sound of his steady and deep breathing. He had managed to fall asleep immediately. She was lying awake in awe of what she had done. It was not as though she had not enjoyed it – she definitely had. The point was – what on earth had come over her? She had never slept with anyone before. The only person she had ever wanted was Ian.

Now, she had been intimate with his nephew. Something about that sounded wrong, even if they were both, strictly speaking, the same age. She also knew he was getting over someone. A man on the rebound. Not exactly a good prospect. She could not understand how she could have got herself in the situation.

Unable to fall asleep, she carefully pulled back the sheet and picked up her clothes. As she crept away, she glanced back and noticed his angelic features. There was no denying the attraction. She had always considered him to be good looking. It just seemed wrong. Surely, it was impossible that someone like him was meant for someone like her. Yet, everything happened so naturally, they had fit perfectly, like a lock and key. Logically, she knew it was not enough to just fit with someone else – there was more to it. She was realistic. Whatever had brought them together was bound to be short lived. A fling, nothing more.

***

Steven turned around in a semi conscious state and wondered where Lucy had gone. In a way, the fact she had left made it easier for him. He was not sure what to say to her. Was 'thank you' just too rude? He was not sure if he had used her, or vice versa. He just hoped they had used each other. The last thing he needed was someone that expected more. He could not give more. Either way, he did not regret what had happened. They had simply responded to their natural instincts. It was lust, nothing else – he hoped. After looking around for signs of Lucy, he dressed, and left quietly. As he got to the door, he took one of the flowers from her vase and left it on her pillow – it was a gesture.

Out in the open, he was startled by a bird swooping down in front of him. Once on the ground, it pecked at the loose soil with conviction and snapped up the juicy worm lying dangerously close to the surface. Trapping it in its beak, it flew away triumphant.

'Now it can feed its young,' Lucy exclaimed, as she came up behind Steven.

Steven replied without emotion. 'You don't think it's just looking out for itself?'

'No, not with that much determination, its natural instinct is to do anything it takes to raise its family.'

'Is that our natural instinct?' Steven asked. He wanted to know what she thought. He did not know why, but he just did.

'I guess. Although, I've never really looked after anyone other than myself. I have never been responsible for children. Not, like that bird. If she does not feed the young, they will die. Then again, I do have my babies,' she said with a smile, as she pointed at her plants. 'They are what I love to look after.'

'I have never been responsible for anyone either.' He left the sentence hanging.

The situation was getting awkward.

***

From the moment Lucy had laid eyes on Steven, she had been intrigued by him. It had been a struggle to remember he was a student, not a potential mate. Every time he had been around, she had actively avoided being close to him, sensing an uneasy vulnerability. The fact she had been so weak, when the opportunity arose, made her wince. Running her finger over her lips, as she bit one of her nails, she remembered the feel of his lips on hers. She felt her cheeks flush, and an unfamiliar discomfort came over her. Being with Steven had awoken emotions she never knew existed. She was not convinced it was him she wanted, but she recognised there was another side to her she had ignored. There were needs she had ignored.

Eyes on the ground, she ignored the silence between them, as she considered the turn of events.

Until yesterday, she had heard talk of his change. As far as everyone was concerned, it appeared nothing was untoward. Now, she knew for herself, there was nothing abnormal about him – in fact, he looked better than ever. Even though she was not interested in a relationship, she was still reeling from the effects of their close encounter. Inadvertently, she blushed again at the memory – it was nice to be surprised after all this time. For a long time, she had convinced herself that she would never make love to any man – she had convinced herself that it was not important. For the first time in her life, doubt surfaced. She had tasted the forbidden fruit, and she liked it.

***

In this situation, it would be common to leave quickly with minimum conversation – after all it was just a one night stand. However, Steven had never had a one night stand before and even though he was trying not to make things complicated, he just wasn't the kind of man that could walk away without clearing the air. With hesitation, he spoke. 'Anyway, I hope you didn't mind, I mean, are you alright about what happened?'

'Of course,' she replied with a smile. She seemed lost.

Shuffling from one foot to the next, he considered his words. This was getting unbearable.

Lucy turned, and started fiddling with one of the seedlings by the entrance. Looking up, she faced him, and added in a matter of fact voice. 'Did you want anything else?'

In a bid to be upfront and honest, he came out with what was on his mind. 'Look, it was a bit full on. I enjoyed being with you – a lot – but I'm not really looking for a commitment at the moment. I just wanted to check that you didn't want more. It's not that I'm not attracted to you, I hope you know that – I need to figure out what I'm all about, before I get involved with anyone.' He knew he was rambling, as he ran his hand through his hair.

A smile broke out of Lucy's face. 'Are you in love with someone else?'

The fact she seemed relieved, and not upset, confused Steven. He had never understood women, and now he definitely had no idea how to read her. 'Yes, I am. How did you know?'

'I've been in love before. I saw the signs.' Cocking her head to the side, she gave him an apologetic smile. 'Don't feel bad about what happened. It's been great for me to know I could still be with someone in that way after all these years. Sometimes, it's just nice to take comfort with someone who can relate to the pain. I think I'll go and check on the vegetables now,' she sighed, before continuing, almost absentmindedly. 'If you need a friend you know where I am. Whatever you are trying to sort out, I hope you work it out – don't end up like me.' Aloud she continued, as though talking to herself, 'I've always thought that it was a shame that love was not a vegetable – I'd have grown it for myself years ago.'

Steven watched Lucy walk away, confused and speechless. He had taken advantage of the situation. But now, he realised; she had been an equal partner in the event. The fact that she had read him like a book was unnerving. Was he that easy to read? She knew what they had done was not love. In a way, what he had done made him embarrassed. Had he come across as a foolish teenager? Was he so blinded by anguish that he would use someone else to replace Caitlin that easily?

The truth was he was not surprised.

He was selfish.

There was nothing he could say to himself to justify the fact he had recently killed someone to live. Even if it had not been a truly conscious decision, it had still been his action that caused the death of that old woman. In the same way, he had used Lucy. It was irrelevant if she had used him back.

Chapter 41

You Can't Change Who You Are

The promise Jensen made Emily, weighed on his mind. He did not mind keeping an eye out for Steven, but he was not going to let him hurt Susanna. She came first, she always would. Unfortunately, this meant he had failed to look out for his friend. It was tricky. Even though Steven was going through a rough time, it did not justify Steven behaving like a jerk. He snapped out of his thoughts as Susanna glanced in his direction. Every time she looked at him he felt her magnetic pull, luring him in.

Susanna gave him the smile he loved before she spoke. 'Have you seen Steven since yesterday?'

It was typical of Susanna to show concern; she was always the first to forgive.

'No.'

She pursed her lips. 'I don't want you to fall out over me.'

'Don't worry, we won't. I'll sort it out,' Jensen reassured. He picked up a slice of toast and took a bite, he needed the distraction.

'He doesn't look that stable. Is that how I'll be?'

There was fear in her eyes, he could tell. He put down the bread, sipped his orange juice and looked thoughtful. 'I don't know. It's not easy to change. There is an aggressive side that seems to surface, in some men in particular. Most women develop their own instincts, and seem to weigh up their options more carefully. That's only from what I've been told.'

'I hope I keep level headed. I don't like the thought of going crazy,' she laughed.

'I'm sure you will.' His eyes lingered on hers for a moment longer than he dared. 'I'll do my best to keep you sane.'

There was nothing he wanted more than to be close to her. He had imagined on numerous occasions what it would be like to kiss her. Ever since his change, the need to be with her was becoming unbearable – it was getting harder and harder for him to ignore the attraction.

He finished his breakfast and got up to go. 'I'll go and ask if anyone has seen him. He probably needs a friend.'

'Somehow I think you're the only one he'll talk to,' she said, all serious.

'Maybe. I'll see you later?' he asked, hopeful.

She gave a small smile, and then bit her lip. 'Later.'

Jensen hoped later would hurry the hell up.

***

Steven felt foolish as he walked back to his room. He could not understand what he had been so angry about earlier. After leaving Lucy, he was definitely more relaxed. As he rounded the corner, a figure came into view. Someone was leaning against his door.

'I'd almost given up on you. A part of me wondered if you'd figured out how to escape?' Ian chuckled aloud. He sounded relaxed and his hair fell loosely around his face, giving him a dishevelled appearance.

'No such luck,' Steven muttered. Even though Ian came across as friendly, he would never forget that Ian had been responsible for kidnapping his girlfriend Caitlin. Of course, if he had not come, things could have got ugly. Overall, Steven had reached an impasse. Even though he did not hate him, he doubted he'd ever be jubilant to see him either.

'Shame. Are you having a bad day?' Ian asked, as he folded his arms over his chest.

'I've had better ones. What do you want, Ian?'

'Look, my sister is not going to be happy if you're not. Let's talk, okay,' Ian asked.

It was clear the discussion was not optional.

'Come on in,' Steven said, as he walked past Ian and made his way into his room.

'So, I see that you got your stuff back,' Ian remarked, in an obvious attempt to be friendly.

Steven looked at his things and wondered how it was possible for his meagre items to bring out so many memories. 'So tell me, how exactly did you do it anyway? How did you erase me?'

'You really want to know?'

Steven sat down on his red reclining chair, leant back to look at the stone ceiling and paused. Turning to face Ian, he challenged. 'Try me.'

'Okay then,' Ian smirked. 'After our little get together in the woods, we managed to sedate both of you. We left you in your rooms to sleep, and of course, Eilif erased Caitlin's memory. Meanwhile, we took a trip up to your home town and packed up your room whilst your parents slept. We placed everything in containers ready for shipment to arrive at the same time as us.'

'Those were the extra things we drove to the ship.'

'Yes. Eilif then had to cast his hypnotic enchantment around to make sure that everyone who had ever known you forgot about you. Don't ask me how that works, I have no idea.'

Steven interrupted. 'But, what if someone was away – they'd still remember me wouldn't they?'

'The enchantment captures anyone with a memory of you. That's why it reached out to Southampton as well. To be foolproof, he also placed an aura over you that would prevent anyone coming near you, from recognising you.'

'Is it permanent?'

'As far as we know, it's always worked for us in the past. No-one will ever know you existed.'

'And then?'

'Eilif used his abilities to ensure you were erased from every government system with a record of your existence. The only one we kept active, until we arrived in Brazil, was your passport – you needed that one to travel. Then, we drove back to Southampton and waited for your call.'

'How did you clear my room?'

'That was fun actually,' Ian smiled, as though it was amusing. 'No-one knew who you were anyway, so we pretended to be cleaners. We had taken a copy of your key, so we used it to clear out the place. We got some strange looks from some of the students, and I think someone even registered that the Halls did not have cleaners, but Eilif erased any mention of us to be sure.'

'You had it all figured out,' Steven remarked, oozing sarcasm.

'You know the rest, so are you satisfied now?'

'You are sure that no-one will ever remember me.'

'There is no certainty in life,' Ian said seriously. 'But it's highly unlikely anyone will ever consciously remember you.'

'What does that mean?' Steven hated the fact everything was so ambiguous.

'We checked up on some of Eilif's victims over the years. You know, to see if the effects were long lasting. Only once, did we hear of a situation.' Ian paused.

Steven noted the uneasiness. 'What was the situation?'

Ian brushed it off casually. 'Nothing serious, the woman dreamt about what happened, and came up with a great story. It actually got published and became a best seller! The funny thing is it was all true.'

'What was the story?' He had nothing to lose by finding out as much as possible.

'It was about a vampire that did not kill humans. Even though Eilif did drink her blood she lived to tell the tale. Eilif hypnotised her to forget, when he saw she was still alive. He did not want to kill her. She seemed to remember his sympathy. It was a moment of weakness – it happens to us all sometimes.'

'So, not everyone kills?'

'No, not all of us kill. For a change, it is essential, so all of us will be killers at least once in our lives. Can you live with that?'

'I have no choice but to live with it,' Steven said, as he sat on his bed and stared at the picture in the frame.

'So do you choose to live, or to wallow in self pity?' The question hung unanswered, before Ian added with enthusiasm. 'I could really use someone with your skills on deck, but I need to know that you are with me, not trying to find a way to escape.'

Steven continued to avert his eyes. He knew that at the first sign of an escape, he would take it.

Ian laughed, as though he had understood the meaning of Steven's expression. 'Did you really think that we would not know that you would want to escape? This is not a prison Steven, it's your home. We are protecting you. You need to see what you are made of before we ever let you loose out there. Do you not understand that it is people's lives we are trying to protect?'

'I will never kill anyone again,' Steven stated.

'You know that for sure, do you? You want to risk going back even though you might not be able to resist the temptation. I'm sorry but we can't allow that. Hell, even I can't stop myself from killing, and I've been practising for years. What do you think makes you so special?' Ian's tone was taking on an edge of annoyance.

'I'm not like you,' Steven shouted, unable to contain his frustration. 'You don't know anything about me. I'm more human than you will ever be, so how can you be sure that I'm not lying. I repeat – I will never kill again.'

'Fine, be like that,' Ian huffed. 'You'll be confined to work in the retail shops and to taking classes until you see some sense. Maybe you can take out some of your frustration on making bread. I'll see you later.' Ian turned around and walked a few paces. Then he turned, and added with a hint of sadness. 'I'm not your enemy – someday you'll appreciate that fact.'

Steven kept quiet, got up from the chair and stopped short of slamming his fist into the stone walls. The lack of natural light made him claustrophobic. His thoughts drifted to home. He'd give anything to go back. If only, he'd enjoyed his freedom more.

A knock on the door startled him – surely Ian was not back for more. When he opened the door and he was relieved to see a friendly face.

'You alright, Steven?'

Steven gave Jensen a noncommittal smile – could he trust him? 'No, but that's pretty obvious isn't it?' Steven mumbled, dejected. After a pregnant pause, he added. 'Look I'm sorry for my outburst yesterday. I haven't had enough time to take this all in.'

'Fair enough.'

'I'm not the same as you. I have not been raised to think that what I am is normal.'

'You are one of us, Steven. That's not an option. Look, I haven't come to make things hard for you. If you want to talk, you know where I am.' As Jensen turned to go, Steven was torn. He needed a friend.

***

'Steven is angry,' Anna frowned.

'I know he is,' Emily sighed, she had heard about Steven's outburst the previous day. 'I don't know how to help him. I'm pretty sure he hates me.'

'You don't know that Emily,' Anna huffed, waving her hands in the air. 'We need to find a way to help him. I can't stand feeling your emotional trauma – you are driving me crazy.'

Emily knew Anna found the link draining. Unlike Emily, Anna always maintained a very positive outlook on life. If Emily could have wished for anything, it would have been to have their connection severed. She hated the fact that Anna always knew when something was wrong.

'What do you suggest?'

'Be a mother, that's all,' Anna replied, as she took a seat on a black leather sofa chair in the corner of the room.

'Easy for you to say, you know what it is to bring up your child. I've got a huge gap in my knowledge base,' Emily noted.

'Look I know that you didn't raise him, but you did give birth to him. You cared for him as a baby. That counts for something. He won't expect you to know him. I just think that if you don't even try to find out, then you'll never know. Will you?'

'You're right, as always,' Emily sighed. 'What can I do?'

'You know, I think I have an idea,' Anna mused. She tapped her nose and smiled, a twinkle in her eye.

It was always worrying when Anna had a plan.

Chapter 42

Relationships

Jensen tousled his hair as he sat up in bed. An image of Susanna conjured up in his mind and he smiled. Ever since his change he had realised every thought seemed more vibrant, alive. The sluggish sensation he had been plagued with prior to his change had completely vanished. For this, he was extremely grateful. What the change meant for him – he had no idea. He gave a muffled laugh as he mulled over the fact Emily wanted *him* to advise Steven. It was laughable really – he wasn't exactly an expert. He needed a confidant of his own. At least for the next year there would be support. As far as he knew there was a rigorous series of assessments designed to discover extra abilities. Not forgetting more classes designed to help them deal with misunderstandings. It would definitely help Steven. That is, *if* Steven agreed to attend.

When Jensen made his way towards the dining area a tempting aroma of eggs and tomatoes wafted through the air. Portion in hand he moved to sit at his familiar seat. It was silly to pretend he was intending to sit somewhere else, but he had to keep up appearances. With a strategic and well rehearsed manoeuvre, he eased towards the direction Susanna sat and faked surprise when she waved. Coincidentally, a spare seat happened to be next to her. He gave a half smile and a curt nod. They both knew how to give fate a helping hand.

'May I?' He asked, in an attempt to keep up the appearance of friendship.

'Jensen, good morning, course you can sit here,' Susanna replied.

Jensen felt himself waver as he focused on her sparkling emerald eyes. They never failed to entrance him.

After he sat down, Gideon shook his head. 'You know, you're not fooling anyone,' he commented, an amused grin plastered on his face.

'What do you mean Gideon?' Susanna's mother, Lina, asked.

It was typical of Gideon to pipe up when she was around. Jensen knew the question was not innocent. As if sharing his thoughts, Susanna shot a warning glance in Gideon's direction. Jensen knew if she had been close enough, she would have kicked him under the table. Jensen was not stupid. He knew he was tenuously related to Susanna. Susanna's grandmother Catherine was also Jensen's Great Aunt. Jensen and Susanna had discussed the issue, and come to the conclusion that the fact that they were seen as friends would hide the fact there was anything more to it. After the change, Susanna' parents would not be able to stop them from being together – if she chose him.

Gideon seemed to find her reaction hilarious, so he appeared to stifle a laugh by coughing loudly. 'Sorry, mum, Susanna was just making a joke with me about something else.'

Lina seemed to survey her children with curiosity. Jensen eyed her suspiciously. It would be amazing if anyone had failed to notice the amount of time Jensen spent with Susanna. Tenuous links could not stop relationships from happening. The only clean option was for Susanna to fall for a son of Morten and Arla Clausen. However, since their two boys were already partnered, and all their other children were girls it left very few options open for Susanna.

Unless, Lina was willing to wait for them to have a son, and hope that after twenty years he would choose Susanna for a mate. Jensen could not imagine Lina would expect Susanna to wait that long.

'Jensen, are you coping well with your change?' Lina asked. The question took him by surprise.

'U-up to now,' he stuttered. 'I have no idea what else is coming up.'

'You'll find out soon, I'm sure. How is Steven?' Lina asked. Again he was surprised at her concern.

'I don't want to speak for him, but I think it's fair to say that he's been better,' Jensen admitted, as he placed a large helping of eggs and toast in his mouth. If she saw he was eating, she might hold back on the questions.

'Susanna, Gideon – are you heading off to class soon?' Lina asked.

Gideon had finished his food, so he got his plate and cup to take to the clearing area and cheerfully told everyone that he's see them later.

Susanna toyed with her last mouthful of yoghurt, before placing it in her mouth and glancing across at Jensen. Finished, she had no choice but to leave.

'I'll see you around.' Her eyes looked sad, and Jensen sensed and hoped, she did not want to leave.

As Susanna left the table, Jensen drowned his juice and made to get up.

'Jensen, can I ask you something?' Lina said, as she moved to the seat next to him.

Jensen looked at Lina and noticed that Susanna had her mother's eyes. He felt uncomfortable and instantly worried about what she was going to ask. 'Sure, if there is something I can help you with.'

'Are you in love with my daughter?' She whispered.

Jensen gulped, before decided to throw caution to the wind. With confidence, he replied. 'Yes.'

Lina smiled, her eyes kind. 'Good, better to hear it straight. I like it when a man is honest. When the time comes you will have my blessing – now stop worrying, or you will make people know before they have to.'

Jensen smiled. 'Thanks, it means a lot. You won't regret it.' After stacking up his plate and cutlery, he got up and gave her a half smile. A cheery whistle escaped, as he made his way to class.

***

Emily wrung her hands together as she approached Steven's room. She would find it unbearable if he was mean to her again. Even though she acknowledged he had every reason to blame her, it did not ease the blow. She was convinced her only son hated her. She wished he could see things from her side. There had been no other option. She could not stand by and watch him die. She had to enable the change. And now, even though Jensen had tried to reassure her, she was not convinced Steven was handling things well at all. All she could do was hold on to the hope that Anna's idea would cheer him up.

She made her way down the silent corridor. It felt eerie when no-one was around. By now, everyone was either having breakfast or working. The electric lighting radiating from the cables overhead would never compensate for natural sunlight. They made the corridor glow in an unnatural way, casting a range of shadows of different shapes and sizes as the light came into contact with the rough walls of rock around.

At the entrance to Steven's room, she knocked and waited for a reply. When none came, she grabbed the handle. It was pitch black inside. The only sound being Steven's deep breathing. When her eyesight adjusted she breathed a sigh of relief – night vision was a handy side effect. The floor was littered with stuff, as though Steven had thrown everything he owned around. She hoped he had not done it in anger. He would regret it if any of his personal belongings were ruined.

It was hard for her to think anyone would intentionally make so much mess. She thrived on order. On autopilot, she started to tidy his things. She could do something to help after all – even if it was just housework. When she inadvertently rustled the books on the floor, Steven jerked up. A second later the light switch flicked on – he was obviously still on autopilot. He did not need light to see.

'Who's there?' He asked as he rubbed his eyes. Slowly, they focused on her. 'Oh, it's you,' he said, in a dry monotone voice. 'What do you want?'

Emily had the feeling she should have waited a few more days. Either way, she doubted the extra time would change the way he saw her. Her nose flared as she decided enough was enough. 'Steven, you don't need to talk to me like that. What has happened is in the past. You need to look to the future now. You can't just sleep all day and hope your existence ceases to occur. Get out of bed and come with me, I have something to cheer you up.' Emily inwardly gave a huge cheer – she had never sounded so assertive in her life. She sounded just like *her* mother.

Steven stared, his eyes wide, as if taken aback. After a painstaking minute, he cocked his head to the side and his shoulders relaxed. 'Okay, if you wait outside, I'll get ready.'

Emily waited. It was weird to hang around the corridor. Out of the corner of her eye, she saw the door edge open. She turned to face him with an enthusiastic grin. She was pulling out all the stops. 'Are you ready?'

'Can I eat something first?'

'Of course you can,' she sighed, relieved he was acting normal again.

Breakfast over, Steven asked. 'So, what do you have in store for me then?'

'Lessons.'

'In what – how to be a hermit?' he chuckled.

She frowned, unable to suppress her annoyance. 'We are not hermits.'

'You sure fooled me. I always thought that people who liked to keep to themselves were hermits. It's easier to hide in a shell than to confront the problem.'

She composed herself, adopting her new assertive tone. 'Living within a community is not what a hermit would do – we don't live in isolation.'

'Really, you believe that do you? Is everyone happy here? Answer me truthfully.'

She knew he was finding the cracks in her armour. 'People can't always stay happy. It's the choices you make that lead to isolation.'

'Like Lucy, she chose to be alone in her greenhouse.'

'Lucy, what do you know of her?'

'We have become friends,' Steven added.

Emily noticed he averted his eyes. 'Really? She used to be a very good friend of mine.'

'I know.'

'I didn't realise you knew. She used to be in love with Ian. Did you know that too?'

'Yes.'

The short answers were blunt. She could not understand how he had made friends with Lucy. Why would Lucy talk to him? Unless? The thought lingered in a place she did not want to consider. 'Things changed after I got back; we both had problems we did not want to share. It's not that easy to talk about emotions.'

'You both fell in love with men you could not be with. Then chose to lead the spinster lives,' he added, with a scowl. 'What's complicated about that? You should have been her friend. She needed you.'

'I couldn't help myself, let alone Lucy,' Emily snapped. Steven took too many liberties – he could not claim to understand the choices she made and had to live with. 'I still have free will.'

'So if you have free will, can we leave here then?'

Emily sighed and dropped her head. Game over. 'You know we

can't.'

***

In silence, Steven gritted his teeth for a second then he went back to his food. Food was not complicated. It was easy to seek the sanctuary of sustenance. The truth was impossible to overturn. He doubted he would ever be able to respect Emily. With a cursory glance, he realised the hall was nearly empty. Plate in hand, he got up and helped himself to more toast and juice. When he sat down again, he sipped, then chewed, avoiding eye contact.

'You know normal human beings take a lot for granted,' Emily noted, as she held her coffee cup in front of her. 'It's like a cup of coffee. There is excellent coffee and there's bad coffee. We tend to know the difference. So, tell me, you're not still thinking of running away are you?'

'I don't think I'd tell you if I was.'

'Fair enough, I wouldn't try any time soon if I were you. Give yourself some time to adjust.'

Steven seemed to need a change of subject. 'So where do I have to go for these lessons?'

'You'll see. Are you done now?'

'For now.'

Chapter 43

Hostile Territory

Emily made her way towards the staircase leading to the Ground floor. Steven resisted the urge to turn back; he did not want to bump into Lucy. Even though he had told Emily they were friends, he had exaggerated the truth. They had slept together, and shared a moment – that was all. However, instead of turning towards the produce area, they turned towards the livestock area. At the approach, he saw Jensen talking to a man Steven had never seen before. A few other people stood behind them. Steven vaguely recalled seeing them in the dining hall over the past few months.

The man looked like a young version of Indiana Jones; he even wore the traditional tan hat. He made his way towards Emily and gave her a beaming smile. At least she had one friend.

'Emily, it's so good to see you again. You should really visit me more often.'

'Jan, this is my son Steven.'

'Steven, nice to meet you at last. I hear your echolocation skills are superb.'

'Well, I don't know about that,' Steven replied.

'Jensen has assured me that they are excellent. We might put them to the test today. Are you staying Emily?' He asked, keen.

'Not today, Jan. Enjoy yourself Steven. I'll come by later on to see how you get on.'

'You don't have to, I might be busy,' Steven replied, noncommittally.

'I see,' she paused, her eyebrows narrowed. 'Okay, I'll keep an eye out for you.'

As she walked away, Jan glanced at him and frowned. Then he snapped. 'Right class, this is Steven. I'll give you five minutes whilst I make preparations. Now, please make him feel welcome.' Jan glanced in the direction Emily had gone, then turned on his heels and disappeared into a large dilapidated shed. Steven was left at the mercy of the group. He focused on his feet and waited. A minute later, a tall, muscular man stepped out of the group and flexed his muscles in front of Steven. His shoulder length, curly, jet black hair and olive complexion left Steven without any doubt as to his origin – he was most certainly a member of the Spanish Santos family.

His voice was heavily accented. 'We have heard a lot about you. Is it true that you speak my native tongue, Español?'

'Not that well, I understand more than I can speak,' Steven replied.

'Sure you do. Entonces, entiende esto – nadie te accepta en mi familia. Eres un problema para nosotros. Conque ten quidado y mantengate legos – vale.'

Steven knew exactly what he had said, but he chose to bluff. 'Like I say, my Spanish is not that good. You'll have to say that in English.' It was clear to Steven he was not accepted by the Santos family. They viewed him as a *problem*. From the way he advised him to keep his distance, Steven was happy to stall for time.

'That's a shame,' he remarked sarcastically, glancing at the girl and boy beside him. 'My name is Francis. I suggest that you follow our lead today. We can teach you what you need to know.'

Steven calmly stated. 'I'll follow Jensen.'

The girl standing behind Francis chuckled. She had long, straight, blond hair and must have been nearly six feet in height. 'You don't want to become an *outcast* do you?'

'Sorry, and you are?' Steven could not help himself, as he adopted his most condescending tone.

'Louisa,' she sneered. 'You know my sister Ingrid. She told me you were close.'

'Not really,' Steven answered.

Louisa giggled in a mean way, before looking at Francis and the other boy beside them. 'That's not what I heard.'

'Do you think you could at least try to make Steven feel welcome?' Jensen interrupted.

'Sure,' the other boy stepped forward, and held out his hand. He also had dark brown hair, but his complexion was fairer. 'My name is Enrique and we are cousins. My mum's name is Anna – your aunt. I think she had to sedate you,' he laughed out loud, unable to suppress his amusement.

Steven stared at the outstretched hand. Supposedly, he was trying to be friendly. He decided not to take it. 'She did, but I gather that's pretty common.'

'Yeah, she's had to take others down.' He lowered his hand. 'My uncle Ian took me down in my moment of madness,' Enrique's tone softened. 'Everyone tries to escape after the change. It's a bit of a joke for us now. You should see the lighter side of things.'

'I'll try,' Steven replied, looking towards Jensen, who shrugged his shoulders noncommittally. It was difficult to read Enrique – he was not sure if he was a friend or foe.

'Right then girls and boys, sorry to keep you waiting, make your way over here,' Jan exclaimed, as he came out of the shed and signalled for them to get closer. 'Everyone, take a bag.'

On the floor of the shed were several bags, full of what looked like food scraps. Steven had no idea what he was up against.

'Follow me,' Jan said, as he wondered towards a huge tunnel carved out of the rock which seemed to start behind the shed.

Steven waited for the others to go first – he had had enough of mingling. Jensen saw him stay back and decided to wait for him.

'Hey, are you holding on?' Jensen asked.

'Just about, so much for getting a welcome right. I don't sense that I'm very popular.'

'Give it time – they feel threatened by you. They don't like the fact you're new. It's not something anyone has ever had to get used to. We don't normally get any visitors remember.'

'I guess.'

'Anyway, Enrique wasn't so bad. Louisa and Francis like tormenting anyone they find. It's just a game to them. I'm sure once they get to know you, they'll give the tough act a rest.'

'I think I'd rather steer clear of them for now – not really my type, if you know what I mean.'

'They are not my type either, if it's any consolation.'

Steven relaxed, for the first time in a while. 'That's a relief. So where's he taking us then?'

'You'll see. He likes his field trips.'

'Interesting.'

After walking for approximately twenty minutes, a password protected wooden door barred the way. Jan entered the code and the doors opened to reveal a dense undergrowth of trees and shrubs.

The greenery was haphazardly growing, with no real structure. It was clear human interference was limited. The only sign showing disturbance, was a well trodden path, snaking through the bracken and broken bark lying on the floor straight ahead.

'Where does this lead?' Steven asked, perplexed.

'This is no-mans land, but don't get any ideas. It leads to the heart of the Amazon. It's no place to seek refuge.'

'I'll take your word for it. I'm not sure I'm up to doing a runner anyway.'

'That's good to know, I don't want to be checking up on you all the time,' Jensen said, as he raised his eyebrows. 'So, are we good now? Can I relax?'

'Yeah, I'll be okay. You don't have to babysit me anymore.'

'I didn't mean it like that.'

'I know, just a joke.' Steven wondered how he could ever expect Jensen to understand the internal dilemma he was facing. As much as he was glad to have a friend he was wary of getting too close to anyone who accepted this destiny.

The noises within the Amazon rainforest were both bewildering and frightening. Steven heard a low growl and immediately an image of a jaguar stalking its prey came to mind. He suspected that if it was hunting them it would adopt a considerably stealthier approach. This world was so alien. He had no idea what skill or lessons they would be taught.

Jan paused and turned to face the group. 'Does anyone know why we are here?'

Louisa called out in a confident tone. 'To kick some animal butt?'

'Not how I would have put it,' Jan grimaced. 'But, yes, we are on a hunting expedition. It is important for you all to appreciate that the natural balance of life in the Amazon is maintained by all the animals that live here. If we eat too much of one animal, and not enough of another, we upset the Ecosystem. Predators, as well as prey, need to be controlled. For millions of years, this balance has worked, but the introduction, or should I say, dominance of humanity, has on many occasions around the world caused havoc with natural habitats. It is not our intention as a society to add to this, so I ask that you all seriously take this into consideration. As our community grows, its needs will grow, and it is up to all of us to be mindful of what lies on our doorstep. Even you, Louisa, might want to think before you *kick butt*.'

Francis nudged Louisa in the ribs and laughed at her. She smirked back, defiant, and crossed her arms over her chest.

Jan watched the exchange and rolled his eyes. 'We have several predators in the jungle. The ones that will most satisfy our needs tend to be the larger predators, but I advise that you steer clear of the likes of the cougar or jaguar. They will break your necks easily – you are no match for them at the moment. If you find yourself up against one of these majestic creatures, you should always attempt to fight back to scare it off. If you run, it will hunt you down. Try and make loud noises, or beat large pieces of wood on the ground or trees to seem more menacing. If this does not work, the last resort is to use a weapon. But we would advocate the use of sedative darts only. We do not use guns here.'

'Has anyone ever been killed from an attack?' Jensen asked, out of curiosity.

'Amazingly, no. A few years back Ian had a narrow escape. The cat managed to catch him unawares and came up from behind. However, because our sense of hearing is superior to theirs, he heard it just before it landed and managed to get out of the way. The others, one of which was your mother, Steven, succeeded in scaring the animal away. Safety in numbers, an important lesson – it is important to always stay in a group. If you venture out on your own, then you are inviting trouble. Of course in the community we are completely protected, so you have nothing to worry about there. But, out in the open…well, I don't rate your chances.'

Jensen whispered in Steven's ear. 'Now, you see what we've been saying.'

Steven could not help wondering if the lecture was directed at him, as Jan droned on.

'After the change we all need animal blood at least once a week. The animal we tend to hunt for blood is the Capybara. The adult ones in particular can reach up to 130 centimetres in length. After a kill, we take the body back to the community to cook and eat the flesh. We also use the skins to make shoes and clothing so nothing is wasted.'

'That's good to know,' said Louisa, with a hint of sarcasm. 'I need a new pair of shoes.'

'Louisa I hope you grow up soon, otherwise I might have to exclude you from class for a while. You must respect the things around you,' Jan sternly interjected.

Louisa took the caution and said sorry.

Jan continued, after giving Louisa a warning glance. 'We can best find them near the water which is why we are heading for the river. By leaving a few of their favourite scraps lying around us, we will set the trap.' He gave his bag a shake. 'You will have to watch what I do first. Then you will all have a go. For some of you, this will be your first kill, so make sure you pay attention. I assure you that there is nothing like the taste of fresh blood.'

Even thought Steven knew he should find the taste of blood disgusting, he strangely relished the idea of it. They approached the river and waited, hidden by the undergrowth. Jan signalled for them to be quiet and stealthily made his way down to the waters edge. A group of different sized capybaras stood at the water's edge.

Jan remained hidden in the bushes behind the animal. Steven was getting curious. A spilt second later, he lunged on one of the larger animals back. Steven was mesmerised, as he saw him latch onto the animal's neck. The animal shook at first, before dropping to the ground. A few last minute shivers run over the animal's body. Even though it was obvious, it was dead. Jan stood over the animal for a few minutes, before calling out to the group. A trace of blood remained over Jan's lips. The sight made Steven lick his lips. Jan wiped his mouth with the back of his hand.

'Feel your teeth,' Jan ordered.

Steven put his finger into his mouth and run it along his upper canine teeth. They were now pointed, longer and very, very sharp. He knew they were lying about what they were all along. Without thinking, he blurted out, 'just like a vampire.'

Chapter 44

The Predator Becomes The Victim

The stare Jan gave Steven, made Steven avert his eyes. Jan did not like the fact he had referred to the *v* word.

His tone dismissive, Jan continued. 'Correction, just like a vampire bat we have the ability to alter the size of our upper canines, as you've just witnessed. Anyway, the challenge today…,' he paused, wide eyed, and rubbed his hands together.

Steven could not help being curious, even if Jan was milking it for all it was worth. He had to admit Jan's childish expression was amusing. At least he *tried* to make whatever it was they were going to do sound exciting.

'…you have to hunt your own capybara.'

Steven's shoulders slumped. The revelation did not live up to the hype.

As Jan droned on, Steven was not enthused. 'If you don't succeed you can drink from my kill, but hopefully it won't come to that. We have to stay in groups of at least three for the reasons I mentioned earlier.'

Enrique, Louisa and Francis immediately grouped together. Steven stood next to Jensen. It was a relief when Jensen did not abandon him. Two other groups formed from the remaining students. It was not a surprise that no-one seemed keen to join them.

Jan faced Jensen, shrugged and half smiled. 'Looks like I'm with you.'

After Jan had reeled off the rest of the instructions, they were ready to set off. Steven was surprised to see Jan punch a tree, but then he figured it was as good a way as any to leave a marker. They would meet back at the same spot after two hours.

When the other groups had dispersed, Steven turned to Jan and asked. 'Will no-one get lost?'

'No, we all have very good navigational skills. It's one of the perks of the change. Let's get moving.'

As they walked, Steven kept the questions up. 'So how often does everyone come out to hunt?'

Jan replied whilst maintaining a brisk pace. 'We have a rotation system. Fresh blood is better than blood brought back, so we take it in turns. The fact we need food to survive, kills two birds with one stone.' Jan made his way towards the waters edge and became serious. 'Right let's focus, quiet now.'

In silence they waited.

Steven could not help wondering if he would actually go through with it. Before long, four capybara ranging in size eased up to the water to have a drink. Jan nodded his head towards Jensen, and Jensen made his way down. Jensen strategically placed himself behind the animals and crouched, ready to pounce. Steven could not help being in awe as he witnessed Jensen leap into mid air, he was so graceful in his flight. When he landed on the victim's back he did not get a grip straight away. A second later he corrected his stance, steadied on the moving animal and then struck his debilitating blow. The animal collapsed in submission and the other capybara scattered.

Jan and Steven came out of their hiding place and made their way over to Jensen. It looked like Jensen was in a feeding frenzy, his eyes closed in concentration. Steven felt his canines extend, and for the second time in the same day, he licked his lips.

'Jensen,' Jan called out sharply. 'You must stop, and bring your kill with you.'

Jensen's eyes flickered open, yet he did not stop.

Jan waited until Jensen managed to pull away. When he did Jan shook his head as said, 'next time you stop sooner.'

Jensen's eyes were crazed. 'That was a rush,' he said, he sounded drunk. 'It was easier to pull away this time, but I still find it hard.'

'You'll get used to it. You did better this time, you should be proud of yourself,' Jan added.

Steven was impressed. It was the first time he'd heard Jan make a compliment.

Jensen hauled the animal over his back. Jan told them they would have to find a new place to strike. It would be Steven's turn next. After waiting for an hour, a family of tapir's came across the assortment of treats left on the ground.

'Tapir's are just as good as capybara. Your turn Steven,' Jan encouraged.

Steven made his way behind a bush by the bank and positioned himself behind a medium sized tapir, of about one metre in length. He tried to get ready to attack but he could not focus. Time slipped by and a few tapir's drifted off. A small, baby tapir remained behind. The other large tapir nearby was best avoided. He did not want to kill a baby, but he did not feel up to tackling a larger animal. He shook his head and tried to concentrate on doing the right thing. When that did not work, he thought of the taste from the bottle in his room. Immediately, his canines extended. He closed his eyes and let his senses take over. Ready, he opened his eyes and leapt on the animal. The time to procrastinate had passed.

As his heals dug into the side of the animal, he got a firm grip and aimed at the neck. The skin felt warm and inviting as he got close enough to bite. The texture of the fur was relatively easy to break through – it was amazing how sharp his canines had become. As he started to drink, his senses took over. He was aware of acute pain in his lower ankle and he winced, but he could not stop. As the blood gushed in, the animal collapsed. The taste was so satisfying. He was a monster. He had become a killer. When the blood started to dry up, he started to come out of his trance. Only then did he hear the shouting. It was Jensen.

'Steven, wake up.'

Steven growled as Jan pulled him off his kill. When he tried to stand, he realised what had happened as intense pain ricochet down his leg. He collapsed in agony. There so much blood – his blood. It seeped out of a deep gash on his ankle.

As the large tapir started to run towards him, nostrils flared, Jan rammed into it and hauled it over him to the other side of the river.

'Steven, are you alright?' Jensen asked.

Steven could not reply as a piercing scream escaped.

***

Jan did not have too much time to think. In a fluid motion, he hauled Steven over his shoulder. 'We must hurry,' he said, a quick glance over his shoulder told Jensen to follow. He did not have time to explain.

Jensen was obviously at a loss, but he took the hint. Jan had already noticed that Jensen was not the type to argue. It was lucky given the circumstances. The dead tapir and capybara would have to be wasted, although Jan figured they would be a welcome meal for other predators.

Jan cursed as he run. He could not believe he had been so stupid. He had forgotten to warn Steven about attacking the young. Steven had gone for the attack before he'd had a chance to react. Tapir rarely attacked, but when they did they could certainly cause a lot of damage.

Back at the meeting point, Jan saw the other three groups had returned safely. Each one of them carried a kill over their shoulders. Their expressions were of bemusement as they focused on the blood trickling out of Steven's ankle. Jan got into action. He did not have any time to lose. 'We have to get back as quickly as possible, predators will smell the blood.'

On the route home, Steven's cries became subdued until all that was left were low whimpers. When he fell silent, they run faster. Jan was glad everyone realised the severity of the situation. Boosted by the recent feeds, they forged ahead, the pace impossible. At the entrance, Jan entered the code and one after the other they made their way in. The prey dumped on the floor in a heap. Everyone was covered in sweat, animal blood and mud. They looked like a motley crew. Once the exit was secure, Jan run off. Steven was his priority; the others could find their own way back.

At the infirmary, Jan shouted for help before he lowered Steven onto one of the beds. Immediately, he was surrounded by a group of healers.

'What happened?' his friend, Doctor Johannes, asked. It was always weird to see a friend in a formal role when you weren't use to it.

One of the auxiliary staff started to cut Steven's trousers off to allow the doctor to examine the wound. Jan winced as he saw the extent of the damage. Several bite marks had twisted the ankle to an odd angle – it was definitely broken. A lot of flesh had also been torn off and was hanging loosely off the bone.

He shook his head, focused and relayed the events. 'He got attacked by a tapir whilst he was feeding – he was not completely conscious of what was happening. I think the blood he was drinking must have acted as a natural sedative so it was only when we managed to disengage him that he noticed he was being attacked.'

'How long has he been unconscious for?' a second Doctor, Else, asked, as she opened Steven's eyes and shone her small torch in them.

Jan guessed. 'Twenty minutes, maybe more.'

'We need blood fast. Get Emily now – she is the only one that can help him,' Doctor Johannes yelled.

Jan ran out of the room in the direction of the control room. Even though he knew the sound of the public address system would alarm people, he had no choice. It was only meant for emergencies and this was definitely an emergency. After a slight crackle, Jan made his announcement. 'This is an urgent request – can Emily Roberts please make her way to the infirmary immediately? I repeat – can Emily Roberts make her way to the infirmary immediately?'

***

Emily was about to address her class of young pupils, when the alarm stopped her in her tracks. As soon as Jan had finished the first sentence, she zoomed out of the room. She did not need the second reminder. As she got to the entrance, Sofia rushed past her to take her place. She barely heard her words, but she knew Sofia would take care of the class. In record time she got to the infirmary. It was clear someone was hurt and somehow, she already knew who it was.

She had been so sure that letting him out in the open would be good for him. Now, she cursed inwardly – Steven had not been ready. At the small infirmary entrance, she was met by Doctor Else Abel.

Doctor Else explained, 'Emily, your son has been hurt. He needs blood and your blood is the only one that can help.' Her tone was calm but Emily could tell things were far from normal.

'What if it does not work?' Emily asked, her heart beating fast, in overdrive.

'We'll cross that bridge when we get to it. Doctor Johannes has been getting him ready. He has lost a lot of blood and is unconscious – we need to act fast. He is still not as strong as us, as you know.'

'I know. How could I be so stupid and allow him to go out after such a short time?' Emily said aloud, as she hurried after Doctor Else.

'If it's any consolation – he was attacked by a large tapir. It could have happened to anyone.'

When Emily entered the room, Doctor Johannes immediately beckoned her over to sit down. A drip was already set up for Steven and they had got all the equipment ready for a blood transfusion. Emily sat down and they inserted a needle into her arm, the blood immediately gushed into the plastic piping making its way towards Steven. Emily gave a huge sigh. Steven's face was sickly white. After a few minutes, they stopped the blood to Steven, but they collected some more blood from Emily. Finally, the needle was removed. Emily felt drained, empty. She probably was.

'Emily you need to go to feed otherwise you will become ill, they just brought in several animals that are still fresh. It's not a request, you must go. It will save him,' Doctor Johannes insisted, then continued, his face serious. 'We will look after him. If we need more blood, you need to be at your best.'

Reluctant, Emily left the room. She could sense her emotional barriers crashing down around her. Her eyes darted around as she walked and ran both of her hands through her hair. Eyes wide, she contemplated what had happened. The injury looked serious, really serious. There was no way her blood would be enough to heal him completely. Even if miracles were possible, she doubted they stretched that far. A million questions raced through her mind. *What if Steven lost the use of his foot? How would he react? Would he accept it? Would he want to do what it took to get better? Could they convince him?*

She had to think that he would want to recover. He would be stupid not to. She had to hope he would see sense. That he would accept what he was capable of. She had not lost all of her optimism yet. She couldn't afford to.

Chapter 45

Consequences

When Emily returned, Anna was waiting.

'I came as soon as I heard. I can help too – our blood type is identical,' Anna stressed, before she gave Emily a much needed hug. 'He'll be alright, you'll see.'

Emily accepted Anna's hand as they made their way to the room where Steven lay recovering. When they got in Emily let go. It was nice to have sisterly support, but she did not want to look weak in front of Steven. She felt a weight go off her shoulders when she saw Steven was awake again, his eyes focused on the ceiling.

'Thank God you're awake,' Emily gasped, her voice betrayed her anxiety. She wanted to rush to his side but she couldn't.

'I can't feel a thing, they must have sedated me. What is going on?' Steven mumbled, turning his head for a second. His eyes seemed to glaze over.

'You were attacked by a large female tapir. You passed out,' Emily explained.

'Bloody tapir, I thought we were the hunters,' Steven exclaimed, as he shook his head from side to side.

Lying down, Steven reminded Emily of his father, Paul. It sent a shiver down her spine.

Anna spoke up, 'every animal instinctively defends and protects it's young.'

Emily wondered if one day Anna would *not* feel obliged to explain everything. Steven grumbled something barely audible, but Emily heard it. He did not think *she* had ever defended him in any way. Before either of them could retaliate, Doctor Johannes came back in.

'Welcome back,' Doctor Johannes smiled, as he approached his patient. 'We have stitched up your wounds as best as possible. Unfortunately, I don't have good news. I don't like being the bearer of bad news, but I guess…'

'Just tell me,' Steven snapped, his expression devoid of all emotion.

'You need human blood to make a full recovery,' Doctor Johannes explained.

Emily winced as she anticipated Steven's reaction.

'Then I'll stay as I am,' Steven declared, his face had a certain finality.

Doctor Johannes glanced at Emily and Anna, and nodded gently. Emily knew he wanted to talk to them alone. 'We'll let you think about it.'

'There's nothing to think about, but you go ahead and have your *chat*,' Steven said, his eyes now closed.

Once outside Doctor Johannes switched to their mixed tongue. It was wise, Steven would not understand. 'This is not a good situation. He only just changed. His body hasn't even started to adapt. Human blood *can* heal and fix the problem.'

'I will not force him to drink human blood again. Not against his own will,' Emily said. She could not do that to him again.

Doctor Johannes shook his head. 'He will have to live with the disability. The chances are that if untreated, he will never walk normally again.'

'What do you suggest?' Anna asked, her hands on her waist.

'You could bring him human blood.'

'That might be possible, but it'll take days,' Anna sighed.

'Then you need to take him,' Doctor Johannes stated, as though it was a matter of fact.

Emily suppressed a smile. She could not believe it would be that easy for Steven to leave the community? She wondered if this could be *her* chance.

'What if he escapes, after he is healed?' Anna asked.

Emily frowned, annoyed. It was typical of Anna to worry – Steven's strength would double after feeding on human blood.

'You know how to stop him, Anna,' Doctor Johannes added.

Anna shook her head, unconvinced. 'I won't have the element of surprise, he will expect it.'

'Then think of something,' Doctor Johannes stipulated. 'I have to go; you have to figure this out. Emily, he is your son – *help him*.'

Emily decided now was the time to play along. If she pretended to think he would not accept it, Steven might stand a chance. In a resigned voice, she said, 'I don't even know if he'll agree to it.'

'Make him,' Anna stated. 'If he doesn't, he'll never integrate.'

'Maybe it's for the best,' Emily said, she kept her expression forlorn. She could sense Anna was falling for it.

'Don't give up on him. The community needs to know that we look out for everyone. If he chooses not to be healed, some will question why we have done it in the past. He needs to do what we do – and now is as good a time as any to resolve the problem.'

Emily nodded, and gave an apologetic frown. 'I'll talk to him.'

'You do that. I'll go and talk to mum and dad. They'll know what to do.'

Emily dropped her head and looked at the floor as Anna strode off. Once she was sure she had gone, she grinned and narrowed her eyes. Her plan was starting to take form. If she played her cards right, she would soon find her way out whilst giving her son the freedom he wanted. With a few carefree steps she was back in the room. Steven had his eyes shut again. As she sat down, his voice startled her. He sounded so much like Paul.

'I won't do it.'

'Do what Steven?'

He shook his head. 'Whatever you're planning.'

Emily had to see her plan through. She hated not being able to include him in her idea, but it was for the best. 'You have to follow our lifestyle now.'

'No, I don't. A wonky ankle won't stop me from living.'

She definitely did not agree with him on that point. 'You might not say that in ten years time. If you don't heal it now, it might never be possible to correct.'

Steven pouted, then retaliated. 'You don't know that for sure.'

Emily knew it was time for the clincher. 'All we know is that everything we become happens on the first year after we change. An injury of this severity at this stage is unpredictable, dangerous.'

'I am not killing anyone to survive again.'

The statement hang in the air for a few minutes as neither spoke. Finally, Emily answered. 'I don't doubt that you don't want to kill. We'll find another way to fix this. I'll let you rest.' She already suspected her solution was bound to please everyone, and she knew just who to plant the idea with – her mum, Judith. Guilt was definitely a tool worth manipulating.

***

Jeff Roberts stormed into the room and paced up and down several times. It was his way of collecting his thoughts. His wife, Judith, watched him as she continued to study her book. After everything they had been through together, she had learnt to be patient. It was incredible to consider they had been married for over fifty years. She continued reading, even though she knew the words off by heart.

Finally, Jeff spoke. 'It's all going wrong.'

'We don't live in a utopia dear,' she said, her eyes raised to meet his. She put her book down and waited.

'I know that – I'm not a fool. It's just, why this? We nearly lost Emily, and now this happens to her only son. All around us, we see new life being born every day. And yet, we can't have any more. Our four children mean everything to me.'

Judith felt sorry for Jeff. She knew he loved his children, she just did not think they knew it as much as she did. 'Emily was always the hardest to figure out. Don't beat yourself up over it. I still don't know what she's thinking most of the time.' Even then, Judith realised it had been a nice change for Emily to confide in her. It was clear Emily loved her son.

Jeff sat down and rubbed his fingers through his moustache. 'Did you know Steven has to leave the community? Have you heard the talk?'

'Yes, I've heard.' Judith did not think it was a good idea to tell him that Emily told her all the details. Emily barely spoke to him; it was not worth the rub. Judith let Jeff talk uninterrupted.

'Someone has to take him. I've heard Emily wants to go, but I don't want her to go alone. The question is who can go with her. Juan won't let Anna go again. What if something else happened? What if Emily got hurt? I could never forgive myself,' Jeff rambled.

'In that case we should go?' Judith stated.

From the moment Anna had explained what had happened, the option was clear. When Emily also came to talk to her the plan was formed.

She knew he would see it her way with a bit of persuasion. 'We've lived our life many times over. Let's live a bit dangerously for a change.'

Jeff looked bemused, if taken with the idea. 'Really? You would leave here? – after all this time.'

'Our lives are too sheltered – just because we are one of the first. So what? There are many that understand our principles – if something happens to us, then so be it. Like you say she's our daughter and he is our grandson – we have to help.'

Jeff knelt down in front of her, and leant his head on her lap. As she slowly caressed his face, she could not believe time could not erode their love. They were meant to help Emily, they were meant to go back. It was redemption.

***

Emily watched Steven as he lay on the bed, fast asleep. He looked so peaceful. It felt cruel for fate to deal them both with a bad hand, but she was determined that his luck would change. He was meant for greater things – he had to be. Even if it took everything she had left, she would make sure that his life was worth living. She heard a sound by the door, and turned to see her father standing there. 'Dad, what are you doing here?'

'Just coming to check on my daughter,' he added. His eyes showed concern and his grey moustache tweaked as he gave her a smile.

'Thanks,' Emily said. She could not believe her mum had worked so fast. She could not help the nerves, yet she kept outwardly calm. Her future was at stake.

'I know I have not been the best father in the world, but I'm willing to make amends. We are going to help you.'

'Who do you mean by *we*?'

'Your mother and I. We will not let you down, and we are not going to leave you to do this with your sister or alone again. You don't know how many times we wished we'd come to get you in England all those years ago. We were too proud to admit that we wanted to help you back then – we were foolish, too concerned with keeping appearances. Now things have changed. We will help you to take Steven where he needs to go.'

Emily was stunned. Even though she hoped they would do it, she never actually allowed herself to truly believe it was possible. Her parents had never left the sanctuary of their brainchild.

'But dad, you are needed here; if anything happened to you or mum I don't know what I'd do.' Emily could not help being sceptical, they could change their minds.

'We have led very full lives, we know the risks and are happy to take them for you,' Judith said, as she eased into the room and entwined her arm with her husbands.

Emotion overcame her. Emily could sense that she was on the verge of tears – it was unbearable. She did not want to cry now, not in front of them. Taking a deep breath, she replied. 'I really appreciate it, what do you have in mind?'

It was a genuine question, even though she knew exactly what was going to happen.

***

Judith knew Catherine, Anna and Ian were suspicious. Ian in particular had that uneasy look about him. She would not allow them to sway her. She would see her plan through. With a deep breath, she began. 'Thank you for coming.'

Jeff squeezed her hand, and continued. 'Your mother and I have decided to go with Emily and Steven. Steven does not want to kill anyone so we need to enable a slow recovery. It might take a few days or a month; we have no way of knowing. We can not let anyone else put themselves in danger for something we feel is our responsibility.'

Almost immediately, Ian protested and burst out in anger. 'Are you crazy? We can't allow this. What if something happens to you? You need to be protected, not sent out in the open.'

'Exactly,' Jeff calmly continued. 'We do not need protection. What *if* something happened to us? We have lived long lives, full of unexpected twists and new discoveries. We are not afraid of death.'

'So you are inviting it then?' Catherine added, her head shaking in disbelief.

'Many of you have managed to go back to normal civilization with no ill effects. Why should it be different for us? We are curious to see how mankind has changed after all this time. We need to take Steven to recover, and he is adamant that he does not want to kill. So, we have come up with a plan. If he feeds regularly, he will recover, without having to kill anyone. There is no reason why we should be harmed.'

'What about the journey there?' Catherine continued. 'How will you protect yourselves?'

'We are not children Catherine. We will take the same route that you always take on the ship. We have money. Then, as soon as he is better, we will come back.'

'And he'll agree to this will he?' Ian growled.

'We have to trust him, or he will never allow himself to become one of us.'

Anna got up and made her way over to her mother. She gave her a hug and smiled. 'Please be careful.'

'If, and that is a big if,' Judith added. 'If we don't come back make sure that you keep the values we have cherished for our community alive. You need to stay focused and not worry about us. If the bats had not given us this remarkable immortality, we would probably be dead already.'

Ian's face turned puce. Her son always wanted to do things himself.

This time she would not let him. In a firm voice, she repeated the intent, eyes fixed on Ian. 'We will go, no matter what you think.'

With a firm shake of the head, Ian got up from the chair, turned around and left without looking back.

Catherine gave them both a hug, then glanced over her shoulder as she walked out the door, and smiled.

Anna held on tightly to her mother's hand, and made a final request. 'Promise me you'll come back safely.'

'We'll do our best,' Judith replied.

As Anna left and they were left alone, Jeff and Judith held hands. Judith nuzzled into his shoulder. It felt right to make the sacrifice. There had to be another way for Steven – if anyone could find it, they could. It was impossible to know how long it would take for Steven's injury to heal. Regardless, it was exciting to consider the stories they'd come back with. Whenever anyone else left, it was always interesting to hear what they had to say upon their return. Now, it was their turn to leave. The trip could bring them closer. She could not think of anything that could possibly go wrong.

Epilogue

A Voice From The Past

Caitlin screamed at the top of her voice, 'Steven, no.'

Perplexed, by the strength of the dream, she sat up confused. Sweat streamed down her back and head. The dream seemed so real. In it she had seen Georgina's ghost take her hand, and lead her out of her room. Ethereal, Georgina's hand held tight as it forced Caitlin to follow. When an opening arose in front of them Georgina disappeared and left Caitlin alone in the middle of the New Forest.

Faint voices whispered through the trees. As she peered through, she gasped. In the middle of the clearing stood her image holding hands with the student that had come to her door a few months earlier. She recalled his name, Steven – she remembered him shouting it when she had shut the door in his face.

The thing was – her image looked scared standing next to him.

As though he knew she was there, he turned to face her and gave a cunning smile. It revealed a set of white glinting canine teeth which leaned towards her image, headed straight at her throat.

At that point, she had woken up.

Why would that person, Steven or whatever his name was, be doing that? What on earth could it mean? She had never been into vampire stories. And what did Georgina have to do with it? She was convinced she did not know this Steven, yet something told her she should.

She stood up and paced her room. The first year at university had gone really well, other than the incident with Georgina. The reason for Georgina's death was still a mystery – she did not buy into the suicide theory. Yet, for the past few months Caitlin had felt so inexplicably sad and lonely. Something niggled at the back of her mind – a missing piece of the puzzle eluded her.

She fumbled around to find the light switch on the wall. Once on, she blinked, as her eyes adjusted, and scoured through the drawers.

It had to be somewhere. Finally, she breathed a sigh of relief, as she opened the letter she had concealed in the drawer, and read it again to try and make some sense of what it meant.

Dear Caitlin,

You might not remember me now but if someday you do, leave me a message on my Facebook page – Steven Thorn, England, D.O.B. 4th September. If I ever manage to retrieve it, I promise that I'll find you. If not, I hope you lead a happy and fulfilled life.

Always yours, Steven Thorn

Powering up her laptop, she looked at the Facebook entry for Steven Thorn again. There was no picture and the details were minimal. She thumped the table and sighed. She could not understand why he had slid the note under her room door. She did not remember anything about him and she was certainly not going to leave a message to a total stranger. The problem remained – there was no logical explanation for him featuring so vividly in her dream.

Why had the fact that he had been holding her hand, as though they were a couple, looked right to her? And more importantly, why had he leaned towards her as though he wanted to suck her blood? She could not shake the feeling she should know more.

THE END

About The Author

Vanessa Wester is bilingual in English and Spanish, since she was born and raised in Gibraltar. She obtained a degree in Accounting and Law from the University of Southampton, in England, United Kingdom. Initially, she embarked on a career in Chartered Accountancy. After less than a year, it was obvious she was not cut out to be an Accountant! A change in vocation led her to become a Secondary School Teacher of Mathematics. For the last ten years, she has been a stay at home mum and gives up a lot of her time towards voluntary organisations. Her favourite hobbies include singing, reading and swimming. She is also a qualified A.S.A. Swimming Teacher. Writing is a way to express herself and escape from everyday life. She now lives in the Isle of Wight.

Connect Online

Twitter: @vanessa_wester
www.blogger.com http://vanessawesterwriter.blogspot.co.uk/
www.thewordcloud.org
http://writing-community.writersworkshop.co.uk/members
/profile/4791/Vanessa

eBook

Order this book as an eBook via:

www.smashwords.com for Apple devices,
Nook, Kindle, Kobo and Android devices
http://www.smashwords.com/books/view/145641
OR
Amazon for Kindle devices

References

In my book I have had to research various topics. The following links on the internet helped me create my work of fiction:

http://www.southampton.ac.uk/
http://en.wikipedia.org/wiki/Los_Alamos_National_Laboratory
http://www.lonelyplanet.com/travelblogs/1139/109159/Brazil%3A+Rio+to+the+Amazon+Rainforest?destId=363150
http://www.igorilla.com/gorilla/animal/tapir_attack_in_Oklahoma_City_PartTwo.html
http://www.tapirs.org/tapirs/tapir-faq.html

Proof

Made in the USA
Charleston, SC
11 May 2012